THE WIND FROM NEW JERSEY

JOHN MICHELL

The Wind From New Jersey © John Michell 2024

ISBN: 978-1-923122-91-8 (paperback)

Published in Australia by John Michell and InHouse Publishing.
www.inhousepublishing.com.au

A catalogue record for this book is available from the National Library of Australia

PREFACE

In 2023 while researching in New York City I made a visit to the 9/11 Memorial & Museum. Of the many impressive exhibits, I was most taken by the Vesey Street Stairs. These are a set of concrete steps that originally descended from the World Trade Centre's Tobin Plaza to, unsurprisingly, Vesey Street. Many fortunate people, in the narrow sense that they survived the carnage of the day, used the stairs to escape.

On viewing the display I decided there and then that Vesey Street would feature in my next novel. I accept some might question my choice of it as the scene of Daniel Lincoln's suicide. But the book is fictitious and in my judgement naming the street, if it's to have any effect at all, is likely to do more good than harm.

I did, however, make one concession in that the building at the corner of Vesey and Church Streets, which in my mind's eye I pictured while writing, is actually 30 Vesey Street. I chose, though, to adopt 388 Vesey Street, noting that to the best of my knowledge no such address exists. A small courtesy to be sure, but whereas I named Vesey Street in honour of its eponymous stairs, I felt the use of a "live" address might be a bridge too far.

John Michell
Adelaide, Australia
Autumn 2024

DISCLAIMER

This book is a work of fiction. Comments or actions attributed to public figures, organisations or other entities are either inventions or loosely based on historical fact. In the latter case, summaries and accounts provided are not intended to be of academic quality, accuracy or balance. Otherwise, any character's resemblance in the book to any individual living or dead is purely coincidental.

The novel's inscription, John Donne's poem *No Man is an Island*, comes from the internet where it is freely available. Like Ernest Hemingway in his epigraph to *For Whom the Bell Tolls*, I have elected to reproduce it in its old English form.

By the author of:

Dublin Zoo
The Far Grass
Weather over Mendoza

No man is an Iland, intire of itselfe; every man is a peece of the Continent, a part of the maine; if a Clod bee washed away by the Sea, Europe is the lesse, as well as if a Promontorie were, as well as if a Manor of thy friends or of thine owne were; any mans death diminishes me, because I am involved in Mankinde; And therefore never send to know for whom the bell tolls; It tolls for thee.

John Donne 1572–1631

CHAPTER 1

They had the laboratory check three times before sending the report. Check again, Century House demanded, dismissing protests that Christmas 1964 was looming and all the testing facilities were about to shut down. And while we're at it, the spies added, what of the forensic pathology done when we got the remains back at the end of September, specifically the skull and bone fragments said to belong to a Caucasian English male in his thirties to forties? So chastised, the Foreign Office went belt and braces. It fudged an excuse to ask the Americans for a fresh set of fingerprints and got another lab willing to stay open to take a look. Same result, it reported. The New York City jumper was unquestionably Daniel Hubble Lincoln.

MI6's bluster turned to alarm. Don't tell anybody, it instructed the diplomats, and certainly not the bloody Americans. Let them think for now the dead man is actually named Frank Middlemiss. Those few in the deep know privately caucused. The truth was painfully obvious. The East Germans had fooled them, done them neck and crop. Daniel Lincoln, alias Frank Middlemiss, hadn't died in a hotel fire in East Berlin four months ago in August. Evidently, they lamented, his death was staged, presumably after the Ossis twigged to the fact that he was one of ours. But why the subterfuge and how come Lincoln ended up in New York? Elke Über had a hand in this, the smart ones reasoned – and they were right.

***

Peter Parnell-Brown was a tall, fair-haired man of forty-eight with a thin face and intelligent blue eyes capable of good humour. It was noon on 22 April 1964, almost two years to the day since he had been promoted to be the Deputy Director General of Britain's Secret Intelligence Service. *The Deputy*, to use MI6's cliquey parlance, was out on the floor, which is to say he had left his office on the top level of Century House in south London and come down to an agency work area, namely its East German section.

'This Daniel Lincoln fellow,' Parnell-Brown said, standing in the doorway of the section head's office, 'speaks a bit of German, doesn't he?'

The section head was intrigued. From July 1960 Daniel had been on Parnell-Brown's staff in Washington DC, up until Parnell-Brown's term as station head expired in April 1962. It surprised him that the Deputy should have to ask if Daniel spoke German.

'Yes he does, Peter,' the section head replied, playing safe. 'He's a smart lad. Very studious. Prefers his own company, mostly.'

Parnell-Brown briefly raised his eyebrows. His recollection of Daniel from his Washington days was of a young man inclined to buoyancy. Still, people change. 'And he acquired the German how?'

The section head made a show of consulting his memory. 'If I'm not mistaken,' he said, 'his family is from near Leeds. Mother's deceased from way back, but the father's going strong and still farms up there in rural Yorkshire. Being from that part of the country he went to a West Riding grammar school.'

The section head paused, this time really needing to collect his thoughts. 'Later accepted into Cambridge where he read literature and gained a first for his thesis on John Donne's poem *No Man is an Island*. But for some reason also took German as an elective. Carried on the German studies until he graduated in 1952. Spent three years working for the British High Commissioner for Germany up until our occupation ended in May 1955. Recruited by the Service in '56 on rating as a German specialist with level five language.'

The section head smiled at Parnell-Brown, pleased to have remembered his reading of Daniel's biography from back in July 1963, shortly before Daniel joined the section. But the Deputy's thoughts appeared elsewhere.

'And no problems that came to light while he was in Germany?' Parnell-Brown asked after a moment's hesitation. 'Nothing he brags about when in his cups?'

The questions made the section head cautious. If anybody would know whether Daniel had been involved in inappropriate behaviour surely it would be the Deputy? 'Problems?' he queried.

'Well, fraternising with German women, for example.'

It was common knowledge that fraternisation by occupying civilians in positions of authority was frowned upon. But the section head did have the wit to understand the Deputy's question ran deeper than this, that it went to any form of misbehaviour by Daniel while in Germany. Even so, it was another puzzling enquiry.

'No, nothing like that, of which I'm aware,' the section head replied, his brow furrowing in confusion.

Parnell-Brown noted the bemused expression. 'I was on Field Marshal Montgomery's staff when Monty administered the British zone in Germany immediately after the war,' he explained. 'That experience taught me it always pays to check when talking about the occupation years.' Parnell-Brown smiled ruefully. 'It was a time when many normally law-abiding people broke many rules.'

'Peter,' the section head said politely, but nonetheless wanting to put an end to the shadowboxing. 'Do you mind me asking what you have in mind for Dan Lincoln?'

Parnell-Brown grimaced. 'Possible job over the Wall,' he said softly, referring to the East German-built concrete barrier that since August 1961 had divided Berlin's Eastern and Western sectors. 'There's a minor aspect of it that requires someone with good language. If we did decide to use Daniel, it's vital he has no skeletons in the cupboard. Wouldn't want someone with long memories of the old days latching on to him.'

The section head nodded, searching Parnell-Brown's eyes for more on what this possible job might be perhaps involving a bit part for Daniel Lincoln. After all, East Germany was his patch.

But the Deputy's face was impassive. 'Nothing definite on Daniel as yet,' Parnell-Brown said giving nothing away other than directing a wink at the section head. It was neither an unfriendly nor meaningless gesture. Rather, it was a measured instruction telling Daniel's boss to ask no further questions. Peter Parnell-Brown, you see, had made up his mind. Daniel Lincoln it would be.

***

At the very time when Peter Parnell-Brown was speaking with Daniel Lincoln's section head, Daniel was loping along the northern Thames riverbank, weaving through the lunchtime crowd. Daniel loved to run. Indeed he needed to run, for he was in the grip of a crippling mental illness and had been for nearly a year now.

The exercise made Daniel feel stronger. It was one of two tools he used to combat the debilitating affliction he had been suffering ever since the events with Kristiina Ahnger in May 1963 when he was attached to the MI6 station in the British embassy in Washington DC. The other was a photograph in a small metal frame supported by a cardboard wing stand. It was an image of a smiling Kristiina taken in better times. These were the devices that Daniel used to hide his condition from MI6 colleagues, along with keeping his distance from people as much as possible.

The running worked best, especially if Daniel ran at lunchtime. The dopamine fed to his brain dampened his fluctuating fight or flight responses and usually left him in control for the remainder of the day. The photograph was in fact a complement to the running, a better than nothing alternative if Daniel could not get out to exercise. It helped because it stimulated his anger, which overrode his illness and calmed him. To be sure the effect was short-lived. But to examine the photograph did remind Daniel he'd been weak, gullible and incautious.

Daniel had entered the runner's trance, his long muscular legs warm now and propelling him along. Freed of the conscious effort of placing one foot ahead of the other, his thoughts turned to his personal demons, as often they did. For the umpteenth time, he reflected on the fact that he could never tell MI6 about his illness and its sapping drain on his self-confidence. It was 1964 and he worked for a spy agency with no tolerance for weaklings. Moreover, to come clean would necessitate owning up to the horrible mess with Kristiina and his shameful treatment of his then boss Ray Solter the morning after he learned he'd been duped.

Nor was there solace to be found in his family. Daniel's farming father was the guiding inspiration in his life. And Daniel craved paternal praise. He had only vague memories of a mother who died when he was young, even if her maiden name of Hubble lived on as his middle given name. But Daniel's father was a tough, old school Yorkshire countryman, a pull yourself together type of individual who as a badge of honour gave little credence to psychological disorders.

Daniel had spent three years in Washington, from July 1960 to July 1963. It was his first overseas posting since joining MI6, completing his training and spending a stint as a desk officer in headquarters to gain experience. In those days he was bullish and strong. When told in 1960 he was to be posted to Washington under cover as a junior diplomat, Daniel was excited beyond words. He had just turned thirty and wasn't bothered to ask MI6 why it was not making use of his excellent German, the reason why the spy agency tapped on his shoulder in the first place.

For his first twenty-one months in Washington, Daniel's assignment lived up to all expectations. The station head Peter Parnell-Brown was a considerate, hands-on manager only too ready to give newcomers a chance to learn their trade. But such is the nature of posting life that people come and go. In April 1962 Parnell-Brown completed his three-year term and returned to London on well-deserved promotion. A new station chief rotated in and immediately devolved day-to-day staff management to his deputy. And to Daniel's dismay, his new supervisor, Ray Solter, soon revealed a previously hidden contempt, that at age thirty-two Daniel should be the station's junior spy.

Daniel was bemused by Solter's attitude, if for no other reason than Solter was rather old himself to be the station number two. A knockabout sort of fellow who despite a good war, or perhaps because of it, drank too much, Solter was from a military background. In truth, he had made the transition into MI6 too late in his working life to come to terms with the organisation's culture. And indeed his posting to Washington was a valedictory appointment, granted by MI6 in observance of his war service on the understanding he would retire at the end of the tour.

The fact was that most in MI6 of Solter's age were senior officers. And beneath a bluff exterior masking his insecurity,

Solter's middling status troubled him to the extent that it resulted in self-loathing. In Daniel, someone unusually old to be the office novice, Solter saw a younger version of himself, someone to be disdained. Daniel rolled with the punches as best he could. But when Solter, seeking further to belittle Daniel, added responsibility for the station's filing to his list of humdrum duties, Daniel was obliged to grit his teeth especially tight. It was a stoic attitude made possible only by the fact that the crippling illness nowadays tormenting him was yet to materialise. It only surfaced in May 1963 in the aftermath of Kristiina.

'Kristiina was a trap I should have seen coming,' Daniel raged out loud as he galloped along. It was hardly a new notion popping into his head. Since the night of Tuesday 28 May 1963 he'd thought the same thing each and every day, for nearly a year now. Nearing Westminster Bridge, Daniel prepared to return to the southern side of the Thames and wend his way back to MI6 headquarters where a shower awaited him in Century House's spartan basement. *Kristiina*, Daniel thought bitterly, *the one who taught me that hope is the most dangerous thing of all.*

Ever since the debacle, Daniel could physically feel the darkness that had claimed his soul. It was a sensation made all the more pronounced when he recalled the act of unmitigated bastardry he perpetrated against Ray Solter the morning after the shocking truth about Kristiina was revealed. Only as Daniel was to discover, the ultimate cost was not Ray Solter's: it was his.

***

The lights in the harbour... bom, bom, bom... Don't shine for me... Clarice was singing into her feather duster, curling and swaying between the furniture. Three years in New York City now, she was originally from Baton Rouge, Louisiana. And she loved the sweet harmony of Country and Western. When WMCA played Don Gibson's *Sea of Heartbreak* it put wind beneath her wings.

Then as suddenly as Clarice had started, she stopped. For fully fifteen seconds she stared in disbelief, wondering if her eyes were deceiving her. Only when her heart stopped pounding did Clarice stagger unsteadily to the apartment's kitchen window. Standing on tiptoe, nerves tingling, she peered downwards straining to catch a glimpse of the sidewalk below. Unable to do so, she clasped a hand to her forehead, pausing only briefly before diving for the telephone.

'Nine-one-one,' the dispatcher answered, her voice calm and metallic. 'Which service do you require?'

'Hello, hello,' Clarice spluttered breathlessly. Her body was trembling as if she had fever.

The operator repeated the question, steady and firm as trained.

'Someone's just jumped,' Clarice shrieked. 'Glory me,' she added. 'I seen his blue-green eyes as he whizzed by. They was *wiiide* open, like he was starin' at somethin'. Oh, my God. Send someone, quick.'

'Your saying a male person has jumped off something?' came the unflustered enquiry. 'What has he jumped off?'

'He's dead. He has to be. Send someone. Please, oh, Lord.'

'What's your name, ma'am?'

A silence ensued. 'Ma'am?' the dispatcher prompted.

'Clarice,' Clarice whispered. She was close to exhaustion and her voice was beginning to fail.

'Where do you live, Clarice?'

Clarice almost scoffed in frustration, forgetting in the moment the operator could not know from where she was calling. 'I'm the housemaid at the Rickman residence,' she replied with haughty formality, 'apartment 12G, 388 Vesey Street, New York City Financial District, Lower Manhattan, on the corner with Church.'

'The incident took place at 388 Vesey Street in the Financial District,' came the deadpan response. 'Is that correct?'

'Yes, ma'am,' Clarice mumbled, her voice as flat as the mighty Mississippi back home. 'He jumped from the roof.'

'I'm sending a patrol car right away, Clarice; and paramedics too. Can you see if the man is moving?'

But the line was dead. Clarice was in shock and the last question was just too much for her.

CHAPTER 2

The head of the MI6 East German section was mystified. Just seconds earlier Peter Parnell-Brown had shut down discussion on a possible minor job in East Berlin for Daniel Lincoln, a matter first raised by the Deputy himself. But afterwards, rather than leaving as expected, Parnell-Brown had taken a seat and as if intending to chat began to reminisce about postwar Germany.

'Yes,' Parnell-Brown said reflectively, 'I was still quite young when the war ended. The rapacious black market that operated in Germany from 1945 to 1948 when I was over there on Montgomery's staff especially disturbed me.' The Deputy frowned. 'It stemmed from a plan to inject hard currency into the flattened German economy by allowing British forces to use reichsmarks for NAAFI purchases.' The NAAFI was a British civilian company that supplied food, beverages and household goods to British service personnel at home and abroad. And reichsmarks were Germany's otherwise worthless wartime currency.

'Our service personnel,' Parnell-Brown continued, 'were duly authorised to informally negotiate the exchange of sterling for reichsmarks with ordinary Germans. To ensure no British person was left out of pocket after buying NAAFI items, our people were permitted to convert any remaining reichsmarks into sterling at a rate of forty reichsmarks to the pound and repatriate those funds home.'

Parnell-Brown smiled wryly. 'But the scheme quickly degenerated into a free-for-all, with little will to police the excesses, primarily because the Americans had a similar arrangement and between them and us a lot of people were making a lot of hay.'

'Human greed knows few limits,' the section head observed, feeling like he should make a sympathetic contribution.

Parnell-Brown pouted in agreement. 'Some were worse than others,' he said. 'Have you ever heard of Ronald Kendall Hunt?'

'No, can't say I have.'

'Lucky you,' Parnell-Brown said with a dry laugh. 'He was British, someone whom I originally met in Malta during the war. He worked at the NAAFI bulk issue store in Berlin and was the worst of the worst.' Parnell-Brown sighed. 'NAAFI cross-posted Hunt from Malta to Berlin in July 1945. He would buy huge stocks of cigarettes at the NAAFI rack rate of a shilling per pack of ten and sell them to a German called Josef Sterck who had millions of reichsmarks.'

The mention of Josef Sterck enlivened the section head's interest. 'Is that the same Josef Sterck who in the late fifties was something of a rising star in the SED,' he asked, 'until he flamed out?' The SED was the East German communist party.

'The one and the same,' Parnell-Brown confirmed. 'Slippery bastard. Hunt would undercut NAAFI's reichsmark asking price by selling Sterck bulk quantities of tobacco for 150 marks per ten-pack and convert the proceeds into sterling at the permitted exchange rate. That way he was able to turn his initial investment of a shilling per pack into nearly four pounds for each ten-packet sold.'

'But he came unstuck, I take it, this Hunt?' the section head said, thinking that the Deputy's anecdote had to have a purpose to it. Peter Parnell-Brown simply didn't waste precious time gasbagging.

'The introduction of the convertible West German Deutschmark in 1948 pretty much eliminated the black market,' Parnell-Brown said, 'although not before Hunt made a killing. He was very cunning. The huge increase in sales of NAAFI cigarettes he attributed to bulk orders placed by the British electrical and mechanical engineers working at the Volkswagen plant at Wolfsburg. Hunt's wife was the personal secretary to the NAAFI operations boss in London. Under duress from Hunt she managed to convince the NAAFI management to send him the colossal number of cigarettes supposedly ordered by the people in Wolfsburg but actually being sold to Josef Sterck.'

'And who uncovered the corruption?' the section head asked dutifully, clear now that all this talk about Germany, the black market and some of its more disreputable players pointed to other on the boil than just the Deputy's enquiry about Daniel Lincoln.

Parnell-Brown squeezed his lips together before sighing briefly. 'Even allowing for the lax policing at the time, it was too much for Hunt to convert vast amounts of reichsmarks into sterling in his own name. So he enlisted Sterck's help to find a way to launder the money. They became involved with two American GIs, Neitz and Foster, who had their own scam going. Long story cut short, the villains fell out. Sterck shot and killed Neitz in Munich in November 1946 but, under political pressure, was sent back to the Soviet zone leaving Hunt holding the baby.'

Parnell-Brown smiled bleakly. 'Hunt was extradited to the US in 1950 where he was convicted of aiding and abetting in Neitz's murder. He's been in the US Federal Penitentiary at Leavenworth in Kansas ever since.'

Parnell-Brown exhaled. 'Anyway, I must go,' he said, slapping his thigh to signal he was finished. And to be sure the Deputy had nothing further to say, principally because he was not about to confide it was he who persuaded the Americans to bring charges against Ronald Hunt. Nor was he going to volunteer he had recently recommended Hunt for a key role in operation Leopard, a complex MI6–CIA joint undertaking aimed at East Germany to be implemented the coming August. Indeed, Parnell-Brown was conducting a form of due diligence, seeking to gauge if the section head had heard of Ronald Hunt or his backstory. For the less the English public knew of Hunt, the more it suited Peter Parnell-Brown. It was all to do with Hunt still being a British citizen and his envisaged part in operation Leopard entailing some risk – personal for Hunt and political for MI6.

And the Daniel Lincoln matter? Well, much as with the Ronald Hunt name, the Deputy's probing was largely a check. Only Daniel, under the alias Frank Middlemiss, was to be the lynchpin and, moreover, not operation Leopard's. In Daniel's case the delving in fact went to operation Spot, so named to reflect it was an adjunct to Leopard, an undertaking so secret that currently no one other than Parnell-Brown and the MI6 Director General knew about it – and assuredly not the CIA; not now, and not ever if MI6 had its way.

***

Seven months on and it was 30 November 1964, about ten after twelve in the afternoon. Winter had arrived early in New York City and the day was grey and frigid. Officer Patrick Doherty had spent the last four of his seven years with the NYPD based in the first precinct covering the southern end of Manhattan Island. Lucy Rodriguez was his patrol partner. Originally from Puerto Rico, she had only recently graduated from the NYPD training academy.

Lucy took the call. 'Jumper at 388 Vesey Street,' she repeated into the radio. 'Copy that. On our way.' The pair was parked just south of Battery Park. 'ETA seven minutes,' she said.

Doherty flicked on the car's siren and flashing lights and took off at speed. He glanced at Lucy and saw the excitement in her eyes. It gave Doherty a buzz to see Lucy react whenever the patrol was called to an urgent job. But he knew it wouldn't last. Six months from now and she would be just as jaded as the rest of them.

The patrol car's arrival coincided with that of a blaring ambulance carrying New York Fire Department paramedics. A shape was visible on the sidewalk around which several horrified on-lookers had gathered, all breathing clouds of steam.

Doherty alighted. 'Get some tape around the incident scene, Lucy,' he ordered from over his shoulder. 'And keep the crowd back to give the NYFD boys plenty of room to work in.'

The senior medic introduced himself to Doherty. 'Looks bad,' he said, jerking his thumb in the direction of the crumpled figure. 'Seems some guy jumped or fell from the roof, over twenty floors.'

'Let's take a look,' Doherty said grimly. The two men ducked under Lucy's police tape to be joined shortly after by a younger medic carrying an emergency medical kit.

The human form on the ground was limp like a rag doll – there would be no need for the medical kit. 'My guess,' the older medic said, 'is that every bone in his body is broken.' He and Doherty shared a glance. Both had seen it all before. Yet another life brought to a premature end on New York City's mean streets. 'We'll wait for you to do your investigation,' the senior man added. 'After that we'll take him to the morgue at New York-Presbyterian. The coroner will probably want an autopsy done.'

Doherty nodded. In his notebook he began to record the deceased was a white male not yet forty casually dressed in what appeared to be suit trousers, a business shirt with no tie, and a heavy, navy blue herringbone jacket with black leather elbow patches that Doherty reasonably, if erroneously, assumed was to protect against the cold. He rolled over the corpse until it was face down noting from the herringbone jacket's label that it was Austrian-made. In the man's hip pocket Doherty saw a billfold wallet. Withdrawing it, he extracted a US immigration department identity card.

The card declared the dead man to be Francis Carmichael Middlemiss, date of birth 25 May 1930 and a United States permanent resident since September 1963. Funny thing, though, the residential address imprinted on the card was 134 East 125th Street in Harlem. The Financial District was a well-to-do area at the southern tip of Manhattan Island and Harlem a poor, predominately black neighbourhood in Upper Manhattan. Doherty shrugged. For every question there usually was an answer – eventually.

***

Ronald Kendall Hunt, for whom MI6's Peter Parnell-Brown had so little time, was born to be a criminal. His father, George, was an on and off merchant seaman who occasionally used the fictitious surname of Kendall. Ronald had inherited from George a certain London cockney charm along with a predisposition to baldness owing to the testosterone that, like his father, fuelled a prodigious sex drive.

Born in 1919, Ronald's earliest memories of George were visiting him at London's Pentonville Prison where George was interned for swindling the widow Dunville of Sevenoaks of her substantial inheritance. For some reason Ronald thought there was something glamorous about George being in prison, something that made his father a figure to which he should aspire.

The truth was George had mistaken Mrs Dunville's loneliness for a lack of guile. Once her common sense had overcome her need for companionship, Margaret Dunville soon worked out that the money she gave to this George Kendall to invest in a South African diamond mine was solicited under false pretences. So informed, she made a hasty visit to her late husband's lawyer where she issued instructions that no prisoners were to be taken.

George might have had a glib tongue and a sexual appetite, but how he thought he could lay claim to a fifty per cent share in a diamond mine without paperwork to back it up is anybody's guess. This sort of blinkered approach to crime, daring yet breathtaking in its stupidity, was a trait that had passed on to his son, along with most other of his dubious personal characteristics. But George never became aware of this. In 1934 while banged up again, this time in Wormwood Scrubs for his part in an armed robbery on a bookmaking shop, he got embroiled in dangerous inmate politics. A shiv to the right kidney in the recreation yard did for George, leaving Ronald Hunt fatherless at age fifteen.

Thereafter, Ronald began to replicate his father's life. Ignoring his mother's pleas to get a steady job, he preferred the easy-come, easy-go existence. And when six months later his poor mother died – a cruel cancer ending her sad and troubled life – Ronald found himself with no ambition other than to be a hustler.

Come the war's outbreak in 1939, having just turned twenty, Ronald was by any definition his father's son, right down to his premature baldness. As with George, he was most at home over a pint and a fag, chatting up the birds with effortless ease, for he was one of those lucky men for whom baldness enhanced his looks and signalled sexual prowess. And in the less salubrious pubs and clubs Ronald frequented around London's East End almost anything went. From prostitution, illegal bookmaking and loan sharking to acting as clearing houses for stolen goods, the trade was booming. And Ronald gravitated to them all.

By 1940 Ronald had decided that his future lay in fencing. Not fencing of the paling type it hardly needs be said, but in buying stolen goods and on-selling them for a profit. Thanks in large measure to his innate criminal skill he managed to avoid running seriously afoul of the police, while a well-developed sense of self-preservation protected him in his business dealings such that he seldom cheated those on either side of the transaction, at least to the extent where retribution might be sought.

The war, however, was starting to be a headache. Goods available to be fenced had sharply reduced in volume and there were simply fewer people around either doing the thieving or wanting to buy. Conscription, though, was Ronald's biggest concern. By the autumn of 1940 it had been compulsory for a year now for someone of his age, twenty-one, to register for military service. But Ronald had ignored the government edict, often obliging him to move from place to place in order to avoid arrest for failing to comply.

And although the bulk of Ronald's associates asked no questions, there were some who queried why he was not in uniform. His response was to say he was a baker, since bakers were a reserved occupation, albeit the exemption applied to bakers much older than Ronald. For this reason, Ronald knew his excuse for remaining a civilian was far from watertight and that his luck could not last forever. Then, however, Lady Fortune had the good grace to smile on him, and her name was Janice.

CHAPTER 3

Janice Bolitho came into Ronald Hunt's life at the Carlton Club in Aldwych Street in central London one evening in November 1940. Ronald had ventured to the West End on the back of a tip-off that hot ration books were for sale. He was less comfortable in upmarket places, mainly because as a rule the clientele did not warm to his larrikin demeanour. But with trade slow, and Ronald increasingly desperate for business, he was prepared to give it a go.

At the same time, however, Ronald held reservations about venturing into the West End nightlife as a civilian, knowing most of the club's male customers would be in uniform and that his baker's cover would take him only so far. Indeed had he known the Carlton Club was without a bar, where he could settle in with a drink and a gasper, he would likely have not gone there at all. But picturing himself beforehand in that familiar pose gave Ronald faith in his ability to talk his way out of trouble should the issue of his conscription dodging blow up before he could sound out the barman on the rumoured commercial opportunity.

The Carlton Club's exterior was totally blacked out owing to the fact that since September the Germans had been bombing London on a nightly basis. But the subdued lighting inside the club was a pleasant contrast to its grim street appearance. The only visible concession to the war was the illuminated sign pointing to the bomb shelter in the building's basement.

Ronald's eyes took a moment to adjust. To his consternation he found the club offered patrons the use only of tables. Ronald surveyed the scene, feeling exposed. Finally he spied a small table on the floor's fringe, its seclusion enhanced by the fact that it received very little of the club's dim illumination. Ronald made a hurried beeline in that direction, glancing furtively about as he took a seat.

Soon, however, a sizeable contingent of men in RAF uniforms took up position nearby at a larger, better-lit table. They were accompanied by a small bevy of females. Some of the men were clearly the worse for drink and a couple began to hiss derisively at Ronald until hushed by their women. Ronald lit a cigarette and tried to act unconcerned, wishing the waiter would appear so he could order a calming drink and perhaps drop a hint he was interested in any business that might be going on.

But the club's wait staff were busily engaged with arriving guests starting to occupy the bigger tables in the middle of the room. Without alcohol to steady his nerves, Ronald began to fray, fearing it was only a matter of time before the RAF men at the next table physically confronted him. Ronald looked anxiously about, his gaze fixing on a table of four young women in the centre of the floor. He noted with interest that while three of the females were chatting animatedly, the fourth woman was smiling awkwardly, her tension clear to see. Ronald appraised the outlier. She was not much more than twenty in his estimation, neither a plain girl nor a raving beauty. Somewhere in between, but frumpish comparative to her companions in the sense that her dark hair was not as stylishly cut and nor was her face as meticulously made up.

The club's small orchestra sprang into life, goading Ronald into action. He walked across the floor towards the women just as the charmed luck to which he had become accustomed arrived in the nick of time. Three burly soldiers had descended on the targets as he was in transit, leaving Ronald to reach the table with timing sufficiently precise to resolve the problem bedevilling the three cheerfully excited girls asked to dance by the soldiers – namely what to do with their dour companion, the young woman who seemed so ill at ease in the club environment.

If not a meeting of minds, then it was certainly one of mutual need. Ronald needed the protection of the dance floor and the unsmiling girl saving from her embarrassment. With a fleeting grimace that might have passed for gratitude, she accepted Ronald's offer to dance.

'What's your name, then?' Ronald asked once they'd shuffled a couple of steps and merged into the milling throng. He was comfortable enough now to slap on the cockney charm, while simultaneously deploying the smile that always melted female hearts, down in the East End at least.

'Janice.'

'Janice. Nice, that. Lovely. And what do you do, Janice, if you don't mind me asking? That is provided you're not a general or *summit* secret like that in your spare time.'

Janice briefly sniggered. Ronald winked at her, pleased to have put a modest dent in her reserve. But it was not with an eye to another notch on his belt that Ronald felt compelled to regale Janice with the full force of his cheeky personality. Rather, it was the rat cunning inherited from his father telling him that – someway, somehow – Janice could be the solution to his pesky problem with conscription. With that, Ronald began to roll out the charm arsenal, starting as always with another roguish smile.

'I'm with the NAAFI,' Janice said in answer to Ronald's question, her apparent reluctance to admit this telling Ronald Janice was a nut that would take some cracking.

'NAAFI?'

'No ambition and fuck-all interest,' Janice said, this time with discernible bitterness.

Ronald was genuinely bewildered. That this prim young woman should swear so robustly was surprise enough, but the venom in her voice was even more astounding. 'What do you mean?' he asked in sincere enquiry.

'The NAAFI stands for the Navy, Army and Air Force Institutes,' Janice said, before briefly describing the role it played in supporting British service personnel. Ronald's raised eyebrows encouraged her to continue. 'But because it's civilian,' Janice went on, 'ill-informed people think it's a lark. Some of the comments you get are really hurtful. Those people just don't want to understand what an important role NAAFI plays in keeping up war morale. The demand for our services is phenomenal and we can barely find enough people to meet the growing need.'

Ronald briefly looked into the distance over Janice's shoulder, struggling to believe his good fortune. He now understood what his intuition was trying to tell him. Janice, Ronald realised, was his salvation, principally because they were both peas in the civilian pod.

'You may not believe this, Janice,' Ronald said, pressing home his advantage, 'but I'm also a civilian, a baker which is a reserved occupation. I can't tell you how much it also hurts me to put up with the rubbish that thoughtless people throw at you. Even tonight, after baking for fourteen days straight, I had some RAF geezers heckle me.' Ronald felt Janice move her lower torso such that it came into light contact with his, whereas previously she had kept it chastely at a distance. It had been hard work but things were now starting to fall into place.

Back at the table Janice's three friends and their newfound soldier companions were waiting when Janice and Ronald joined them. Rapid introductions were made, after which glasses of beer and tumblers of Pimms and lemonade appeared. The soldiers settled in to concentrate on their bubbly female friends. Ronald was grateful for their inattention. He was in spitting distance of closing the deal and being able to concentrate on Janice without interruption made this task much easier. Chit-chat was Ronald's strong suit and soon, aided by a second serve of Pimms, the last of Janice's reserve had melted away; laughing and smiling she was now enjoying herself. For Ronald, it was time to pounce.

'You and I are fellow travellers,' Ronald passionately declared, whispering into Janice's ear. It was a clever line rewarded by a squeeze of his hand under the table, an act of affection Janice would live to regret and one forever linking Ronald Hunt to Daniel Lincoln even though the two men would never meet.

***

Many years after Ronald Hunt's fateful encounter with Janice in the Carlton Club in London, Daniel Lincoln had a similarly seminal experience – a meeting in March 1963 in Washington DC with a Finnish woman called Kristiina Ahnger. Kristiina hailed originally from Helsinki, home to Finland's largest Jewish population of which, undisclosed to Daniel, she was one. And also unbeknown to Daniel, until the dreadful reveal two months later in May, Kristiina was in the employ of Mossad, the Israeli national intelligence agency.

Including Daniel, there were six officers in the MI6 station in the British embassy in Washington DC. After Peter Parnell-Brown's departure the office had become highly stratified, the station head barely deigning to speak to his staff and the deputy Ray Solter left to dole out work as he saw fit. As the office novice at the bottom of the pecking order Daniel was given the station's most mundane tasks.

Kristiina worked at the World Bank headquarters in Washington DC. The World Bank was an international organisation affiliated with the United Nations from where loans and grants to poor countries around the globe were dispensed. The Bank employed any number of non-Americans. Wanting to do good works, Kristiina had successfully applied for a position in 1960. Mossad had come to her in 1962 upon noticing her devotion to her faith. An appeal to her sense of duty followed, with Kristiina duly agreeing to keep an eye out for World Bank personnel appearing to be hostile to Israel.

Meanwhile in the MI6 Washington station, the new broom in force, Ray Solter had recently allocated Daniel the mind-numbingly boring job of monitoring Washington's so-called international financial institutions, prime among which was the World Bank. He was to combine this with his current responsibilities, including of course doing the station's filing. Daniel didn't object. He was at the time strong and determined and focused on coping with all Solter might throw at him; eyes firmly fixed on the end of his posting when he could escape with an unblemished copybook.

So it was that the paths of Daniel and Kristiina were destined to cross. But when they did intersect it was no random accident. As Daniel was painfully to learn, Kristiina had found him. It was all to do with the new Israeli nuclear reactor at Dimona. When Israel failed to commit to an international inspection regime, the Americans feared the Middle East would be catastrophically destabilised. They began to demand private access for US experts in order to verify Israel's watery guarantees that the Dimona facility was to be used only for peaceful purposes. Naturally enough, the Israelis demurred and soon the issue had become an irritant in US–Israel affairs.

The start of 1963 marked eight months since Ray Solter had become Daniel's supervisor. By now, despite his best intentions, Daniel was jaded and demotivated. Still, Solter demanded he press on. 'Things just don't fall into your lap, you know lad,' the ex-warrant officer would say. 'You've got to work at it.'

The fourteenth day of March 1963 was a Thursday and Daniel was attending yet another briefing in the World Bank auditorium. He was daydreaming when suddenly he felt the presence of a person in the seat next to him. It was a blond woman who seemed to be around his age. She met his gaze and smiled. 'I've seen you here before,' she said, whispering in a Nordic lilt that Daniel found enticing. 'Are you an economist?'

'No,' Daniel replied with a soft laugh. 'Just a humble second secretary at the British embassy working on economic affairs.'

'Oh,' the woman said, but with a twinkle in her eye inviting further conversation.

'Are you also with an embassy?'

'I'm Kristiina Ahnger from Finland,' the blond woman replied. 'I'm a strategic risk analyst here at the Bank.' Her eyes lit up as if an idea had just popped into her head. 'Why don't we have lunch?'

Daniel would later reflect on Kristiina's offer, telling himself that her pointed invitation should have been a sign. The truth was that by March 1963 Daniel was beginning to wonder if he would ever marry. Indeed when leaving for Washington in the summer of 1960, his farmer father had given him a copy of Ernest Hemingway's *For Whom the Bell Tolls*. The book had been chosen for its lead-in quotation, its epigraph featuring the subject of Daniel's university dissertation, the English poet John Donne's *No Man is an Island*. But his father had also long admired Donne's seventeenth century work for its tribute to family, and Daniel understood the gift underlined his widowed parent's heartfelt desire for grandchildren. Now nearly three years on, with still no likely marriage candidate in sight, the thought of disappointing his father was beginning to gnaw at Daniel.

Moreover, Daniel was disillusioned and not terribly focused on being a careful spy. Members of the Washington diplomatic community frequently met over lunch as a means for expanding their contact lists. And, frankly, he welcomed the unexpected chance to break the tedium. But for all his incaution and justification, any self-criticism was unwarranted. Kristiina in fact had delivered her lunch invitation in her assertively clipped northern European accent. It was a natural directness that would have fooled spies more experienced than Daniel.

Kristiina was relieved to see Daniel's shy smile and the nod of his head, not that she showed it. Mossad understood that the Americans shared all nature of intelligence with the British, including on Israel's nuclear ambition. And with an expert American delegation scheduled to visit Tel Aviv sometime next May to settle the inspection question once and for all, Kristiina had been tasked to befriend the young man first spotted at World Bank events. It was Daniel's attentive mingling that led the Mossad watchers to judge he was MI6. Discreet enquiries next revealed he was a heterosexual man of sober habits who at the advanced age of thirty-three – by 1963 standards – was still single. Daniel self-selected. Kristiina's job was to eke out of him all he knew about the US bottom line on Israel's nuclear reactor that the American delegation would take to Tel Aviv.

Kristiina had asked her Mossad handler only one question. 'What if he wants our relationship to become sexual?'

'We will discuss that if and when it arises, my dear,' replied the small woman of advanced years in the white blouse and black cardigan, putting the issue on the back burner for now. The two in fact were sitting at a table in an apartment in Chevy Chase in Maryland, a dwelling that doubled as a Mossad safe house.

CHAPTER 4

Daniel Lincoln was getting angry with himself. He was too old, for God's sake, to be nervous about having lunch with Kristiina Ahnger, the Finnish national whom he'd met at last week's World Bank briefing. But the voice in his head was chipping away, reminding him he had always struggled to find girlfriends. True, he'd had dalliances, especially in the early 1950s when stationed in Bonn, with British women also working for the British High Commissioner for Germany. These, though, had quickly run out of steam, in part because his patch was Berlin and he was often away.

After that Daniel joined MI6 and was told never to speak about his work, which left him rather light on for social conversation considering the few women he did meet did not share his passion for poetry. Still Kristiina seemed interested – much as he tried to counter this positivity with the thought that for her the lunch was just another work chore.

Whatever, it was lunchtime on Tuesday 19 March 1963 and Daniel was standing in front of the Jefferson Hotel on 16th Street in the District of Columbia. It was at the Jefferson Grill where he had booked a table. Pacing up and down while waiting outside the restaurant, it took Daniel's breath away to see the tall, blond Kristiina shimmy around the corner from M Street and make for the hotel. He walked towards her, sauntering in an effort to appear relaxed.

'Am I late?' Kristiina said on seeing Daniel, a smile lighting up her face.

'No, no, not at all,' Daniel stammered, extending his right hand. But rather than engaging in a simple handshake, Kristiina drew Daniel to her, puckering her lips into a pout for him to kiss. Kristiina to be sure was new to recruitment and moving too fast. Nonetheless, her overreach did send a shudder of excitement through Daniel.

It is at this point that Daniel comes in for some justifiable criticism. The sad fact was that women found little animal magnetism in him, and he knew this. Moreover, it was supposedly a business lunch – World Bank risk analyst meeting British diplomat to discuss global affairs. Yet Daniel chose to ignore Kristiina's mistake, asking himself at the time why he should have to place limits on his romantic ambition. Well, one apt reply might be because his intelligence training had drummed into him the difference between *distinct* as opposed to *maybe* warning signals.

The luncheon spanned two hours. Conversation ranged widely across backgrounds; future plans; and personal interests, including for a brief time Daniel holding forth on his literary studies and the thesis he wrote on John Donne's *No Man is an Island*. Eventually, it was time to go. Home telephone numbers were exchanged, followed by a warm hug occasioning a brush of lips, and an agreement to have dinner the coming Saturday night.

***

Later on, after the damage was done, Daniel would lie awake at night and wonder about his dereliction of duty. It was reprehensible, he would rail, to have allowed himself to be beguiled by Kristiina, simply because he was not honest enough to admit his fingers were crossed that finally she might be the one. 'Hope,' he would bitterly conclude, 'is the most dangerous thing of all.'

***

'He's very pleasant, actually,' Kristiina told Mrs Ruby the evening of the Jefferson Grill lunch. *Ruby* was a truncation of Rubenstein, a means for building rapport between the Finnish agent and her Mossad controller. 'And he's already quite keen on me, after just one outing.'

Mrs Ruby grimaced. 'That is undeniably good news,' she said. 'It also indicates, however, he will make a sexual advance sooner or later.' Mrs Ruby was seventy if a day – a diminutive, long-time Mossad warrior. It was now time to address the issue she had deflected when Kristiina first raised it. 'How do you feel about that?' she asked, pulling her favoured black cardigan tight as if to signal sleeping with Daniel held no appeal to her.

Kristiina stood at the window of the Mossad safe house. 'I've known men,' she said softly. 'But I do like to have an emotional and intellectual connection with a man before I sleep with him.'

Mrs Ruby did not respond immediately. 'Sit down, child,' she said after a time. She waited for Kristiina to comply before continuing. 'Nobody will think the less of you for doing your duty to your creed. Quite the contrary. Please understand that.'

Kristiina stared at the older woman. 'So you want me to sleep with him?' she asked softly.

'Yes, but not this Saturday night.' Mrs Ruby sighed. 'Men can be such pigs. If you let him have his way too easily he will think you a slut. No. You should allow him increased liberties over the next few outings. Then early in April finally give in to his advances.' Mrs Ruby smiled. 'If you make him work for it he will respect you and want to continue the relationship.'

'And what happens if I don't enjoy sex with him?'

Mrs Ruby smiled again. 'Oh, but you must, my dear. We women have been faking orgasms since time immemorial. Done properly it will fool most men into thinking they are lions, especially someone actively in search of a female companion like your Mr Lincoln. After that you will have him in the palm of your hand and he will be prepared to do almost anything for you.' Mrs Ruby was a wily old bird.

***

Ronald Hunt and his new consort Janice were seated on a bench in Battersea Park. It had been three months since they first met at the Carlton Club in central London. Although it was not yet the end of February 1941, hints of a promising spring were in the air.

'Like I told you,' Janice repeated animatedly – Battersea Park's lush greenness always eased her natural inclination to restraint – 'NAAFI is a not-for-profit organisation. Remember that and don't go asking too many questions about your salary.'

'Got it,' Ronald interrupted, taking care not to sound impatient. 'I'll tell your boss, this Jim Warren fellow, that I want to do more for the war effort than just be a baker. That is, I'd rather help the services directly instead of working in a reserved occupation.' Ronald shook his head. It all sounded like a bunch of old cobblers to him. But he accepted that Janice knew best.

Janice kissed him on the cheek and immediately rubbed off the trace of lipstick. 'Good boy,' she said. 'I've worked hard to get you this interview and don't want you cocking up the bleeding thing.'

Ronald smiled warmly at Janice. Their relationship had only recently turned intimate. Janice, as Ronald found, most enjoyed being affectionate in a non-sexual way. Her family operated a plot in rural Uxbridge. When Janice was fourteen Miss Fellows, her spinster schoolmistress, had warned the girls that sex was a necessary evil not to be enjoyed but rather endured. Its purpose was to attract and hold a man so that women might marry and have children. The lessons learned in adolescence were deeply buried in the otherwise earthy Janice: now a twenty-one-year-old adult, recreational intercourse was not something she actively sought.

Ronald, conversely, was the polar opposite to Janice in his attitude to sex, and just about everything else. So he pressed the case and Janice finally relented, pragmatically accepting he was a man with uncontrollable urges needing to be satisfied. Only nearly a year later did Janice find the unintended consequence of her preconditioning not to enjoy sex was the engendering in her of a subliminal anxiety of being left on her own, something that in due course would manifest as a pathological fear of rejection.

Ronald had been content in the relationship from the outset. For a while he continued the pretence of being a baker. But no sooner had he bedded Janice for the first time, in her tiny flat in Streatham one Saturday afternoon, than he announced he was giving up the trade. NAAFI intrigued him and that was where he wanted to work. On this pretext Ronald moved in with Janice the very next day, pleased finally to be free of the need to keep moving from place to place to avoid someone reporting him for failing to register for conscription.

Before long Ronald was luxuriating in Janice waiting on him hand and foot. But as she had repeatedly told him, NAAFI was desperately short of people to meet the soaring demand for its services. Rather too soon for Ronald's liking, Janice had arranged an interview for him with NAAFI's operations manager Jim Warren, at the Imperial Court building in London's Kennington where Janice worked as Warren's personal assistant.

Ronald was aware that if posted overseas with NAAFI he'd automatically be enlisted in the Royal Army Service Corps. But even though being in uniform had its advantages, he wasn't at all keen on going any place where there was fighting. Indeed, Janice had already made mention of NAAFI employees overseas being killed. Still NAAFI was a much preferable alternative to conscription into the regular army, particularly if he could arrange to be sent somewhere free of conflict. For as Ronald had worked out, if sent abroad by NAAFI there were bound to be opportunities for a little creativity.

Two weeks later, Ronald reported to the NAAFI canteen at RAF Kenley on London's southern outskirts. He had negotiated his interview with ease – its somewhat perfunctory nature underlining NAAFI's pressing need to fill vacancies. Ronald was well pleased. The conscription conundrum was thankfully behind him and although he didn't love Janice it suited to have her on his arm – for now. And when, on his very first day at Kenley, a pimply boy from a family living on the base offered to pay a few pennies over the NAAFI asking price for a packet of cigarettes, Ronald was more convinced than ever he was working for an organisation offering scope to make serious money.

***

On Saturday evening 6 April 1963, Kristiina and Daniel had their fifth date. They were in a French restaurant in the Rosslyn neighbourhood of Arlington county on the Virginia side of the Potomac River separating northern Virginia from Washington DC.

In the preceding weeks Kristiina had done exactly as Mrs Ruby instructed and allowed Daniel certain liberties. Her apartment block was a red-brick monolith on the corner of Van Ness Street and Wisconsin Avenue in the District of Columbia. The building's size and sheer number of residents were not to Kristiina's liking, but it was a convenient location that obviated the need to buy a car.

Visitor parking, however, ranged from limited to impossible. For this reason, what recent canoodling not done spontaneously in Daniel's car had mostly taken place at his apartment in McLean, Virginia. Either way, after the usually brief interludes Daniel would drop Kristiina at her apartment block in a touch-and-go exercise necessitated by the dearth of parking. The time, though, was fast approaching when full sexual relations would have to commence.

In April 1963 the mood in the US was one of optimism. The January 1961 swearing in of the young and charismatic president John F. Kennedy had galvanised the American people. It was President Kennedy that Kristiina and Daniel began to discuss as they ate their meal, a relaxed mood already cloaking the candlelit table in the restaurant's front bay window. Daniel was promptly into full stride and expanding with eloquence on Kennedy's impact on US and global affairs. His formidable intellect, fully on display for the first time, substantially impressed Kristiina. Soon the atmospherics between the pair were as convivial as they ever had been.

'You are a man of letters,' Kristiina said, re-charging their wine glasses. 'What is your favourite Kennedy quote?' By now she was no longer an agent cultivating her source but rather a young woman enjoying an evening out; and Kennedy was renowned for peppering his speeches with inspiring phrases.

'From his inauguration in '61,' Daniel replied in an instant, hitting the jackpot without the faintest idea he had done so. He mimicked Kennedy's dulcet Bostonian tones. 'Ask not what your country can do for you, ask what you can do for your country.'

They both roared with laughter, Daniel because of the merriment of his play-acting and Kristiina because Daniel's selection of that particular Kennedy quote had touched a chord. She was doing for her fellow Jews in Israel exactly what Kennedy had exhorted the American people to do two years earlier. Tonight, she would sleep with Daniel – but in her own bed.

CHAPTER 5

Almost exactly a year to the day after Kristiina Ahnger made her *tonight's the night* decision in the French restaurant in Rosslyn, Virginia, Daniel's former Washington station head Peter Parnell-Brown was also in a restaurant, at London's Claridge's Hotel. It was 23 April 1964 and the now MI6 Deputy Director General was waiting for a man by the name of Michael Anjelico. A brusque, forty-five-year-old Italian-American, Anjelico happened to be the head of the CIA's East German and Soviet Satellites Division.

Parnell-Brown nursed a whisky as he waited, recalling his conversation earlier in the day with the MI6 Director General – or the DG as the service head Sir Roger Holbrook was known.

'I think you should encourage the Americans to get cracking on this, Peter,' Sir Roger had said. 'I want it all wrapped up before I retire at the end of January next year. Your coming up with a suitable fellow to act as the decoy – to run interference as some might say – was both timely and sound. Now that the Americans have given their blessing, there's no good reason for further delay.' The DG took a deep breath. 'Yes, when you see Anjelico tonight give him a decent push along. Tell him to piss or get off the pot.' The DG laughed. 'These CIA fellows like that sort of talk.'

Michael Anjelico swaggered into the Claridge's dining room, confidence personified. He headed in Parnell-Brown's direction, right hand outstretched. 'Peter,' he boomed.

Parnell-Brown winced. He had chosen a discreet table but now the whole dining room was watching. 'Mike,' Parnell-Brown said, standing and taking a couple of paces in Anjelico's direction. The two shook hands. 'How was the flight?'

'Great. Those Pan Am 707s are quite a machine. Non-stop flight from New York to here in dear old Blighty.'

'Really?' Parnell-Brown said, as if he was interested.

'Yep. You know, I take it, that they renamed the airport in New York *JFK* after Kennedy got himself topped last November?'

Parnell-Brown winced again. It was President Kennedy's assassination in Dallas in November 1963 that had led to operation Leopard, the matter they were about to discuss. Yet here was Anjelico shouting Kennedy's name at the top of his voice.

'Can I get you a drink?' Parnell-Brown said in polite substitute for telling the CIA man to tone it down.

'Dry martini would be nice,' Anjelico said, smiling and looking around.

The drink arrived. Anjelico raised his glass in a toast. 'Ich bin ein Berliner,' he said softly, his conspiratorial wink indicating the business part of the evening was about to get underway.

'Konrad Voite,' Angelico began, recapping for their mutual benefit, 'born 1905, meaning he will turn sixty next year. He's the sole economic liberal in the SED politburo and highly respected in the party for his willingness to criticise the East German leadership when it deserves it.'

'Which is most days of the week,' Parnell-Brown muttered.

'You bet,' Angelico replied. 'And all credit to Voite. It takes balls to speak up over there.' Parnell-Brown grimaced in agreement. 'We can have confidence,' Anjelico continued, 'that discrediting Ulbricht and Honecker on the floor of the party conference on 28 August will pave the way for Voite to come through on the rail.' Walter Ulbricht and Erich Honecker were the current number one and two in the East German government.

Parnell-Brown was the MI6 station head in Washington when he first met Anjelico. In those days Anjelico was a CIA up-and-comer, and his subsequent rise through the ranks had been rapid. From the outset Parnell-Brown had decided he wouldn't trust him any further than he could kick him. And by April 1964 nothing had convinced Parnell-Brown to change his mind, not even after the DG made him Anjelico's direct counterpart, the MI6 point man on the Anglo–American undertaking dubbed operation Leopard.

***

Sir Roger Holbrook and his CIA counterpart had hatched operation Leopard in the aftermath of President Kennedy's assassination. In the preceding years there had been much discontent in MI6 and the CIA over Kennedy's failure to threaten a punitive response when the Soviet-sponsored, East German-built Berlin Wall went up in August 1961. People understood the President feared that an aggressive posture could spiral out of control and lead to a nuclear conflict. But that was cold comfort for the spies on either side of the Atlantic, principally because the Wall curtailed their running of espionage networks in East Germany. To be sure West Germans and foreigners bearing hard currency could obtain visas to visit East Berlin with relative ease. But for spy controllers to connect with and equip agents under the eye of the vigilant East German state security service, the Stasi, was another thing altogether.

With Kennedy's death the political dynamic changed. MI6 and the CIA began to consider fresh approaches. In truth the Americans were much keener than the British. Indeed, Kennedy's inaction when the Wall went up had positively rankled with some in the CIA. It came as a surprise, therefore, when at the end of January 1964 Sir Roger Holbrook had suddenly proposed a plan to mark, he said, the one-year point before his retirement. The concept became known as operation Leopard, so-called as to conjure a mental image of a surgical strike against the East German leadership. It was shrouded in extreme secrecy, with both sides agreeing to restrict indoctrination to as few people as possible.

Operation Leopard's objective was to place a moderate at the head of the East German government, and Konrad Voite was the chosen candidate. It was based on the belief that Voite would relax the current blanket ban on East Germans visiting the West. Only with this doff of its cap to its citizens' human rights could East Germany hope to gain the Western assistance necessary to develop into a functioning economy free of Soviet reliance. And for MI6 and the CIA, of course, freer movement from East to West would facilitate the resumption of agent running in East Germany.

Sir Roger Holbrook, however, had neglected to inform the CIA that his proposal ultimately concerned the woman who currently headed the secretariat to the all-powerful East German communist party. Her name was Fräulein Elke Über. She had once been on MI6's books but became inactive when the Berlin Wall went up. Now, however, as a full stop to his career, Sir Roger wanted to reactivate Elke, on specific terms. That's why he had conceived operation Spot, the undertaking's name reflecting the DG's intention that Spot be executed as a secret British add-on to the two-hander operation Leopard.

Meanwhile in the dining room at Claridge's Hotel in April 1964, the CIA's Michael Anjelico wiped his lips with his table napkin. 'And this expendable, Peter,' the American queried, 'that you personally identified to be the Leopard decoy, the guy who's going to arrange for Konrad Voite to have a free run at the SED conference agenda. What's his name again?'

The thought flashed through Peter Parnell-Brown's mind to snap at Anjelico, primarily because the American was well aware of the decoy's name. After all, not only had the CIA recently endorsed the proposal to conscript the man but the individual in question was also presently in the US federal prison in Leavenworth, Kansas, and had been there since 1950. In the end, though, Parnell-Brown opted to be diplomatic. 'Ronald Hunt,' he replied evenly, as if the question warranted a respectful response. 'Ronald Kendall Hunt.'

***

Peter Parnell-Brown's sparing Michael Anjelico the sharp edge of his tongue had everything to do with operation Spot. Better to keep relations on an even keel, the MI6 Deputy had judged, because the CIA would surely go ballistic were it ever to learn of Sir Roger's secret plan. The thought took Parnell-Brown back to a frigid Sunday afternoon the preceding February. He and the DG had just arrived at a decrepit country house to the north of London, in the home county of Hertfordshire.

'It was mid-week one night in June 1959,' Henry Grahame said. A large man who had gone to seed, Grahame was morbidly obese. He sported equally unkempt long white hair with a matching beard. Grahame was just two years retired from MI6.

'Fopsy Phillips and I had gone over to the Konzerthaus in East Berlin,' Grahame continued. 'Fopsy was the station head,' he explained for Parnell-Brown's benefit. 'We were working out of the British Army set-up in JHQ Rheindahlan in those days. Fopsy and the missus would often go to the East to attend the opera and the like.' He smiled. 'So did I from time to time. Official reason being that many Russian lads from the Soviet military HQ in Berlin-Karlhorst were usually there.' Grahame sighed, making no effort to disguise the homosexuality he had never declared to MI6. 'Lovely little backsides some of those peasant boys.'

Sir Roger Holbrook suddenly snorted, seemingly in irritation, causing Parnell-Brown to wonder if Grahame's overtness was unsettling him. 'Cut out the waffle, Henry, please, if you don't mind. All I want is for Peter here to hear how you came across Elke Über and managed to recruit her.'

Grahame smiled again, clearly finding enjoyment in the DG's discomfort. 'Fopsy had taken me along that night only because the good lady was suddenly indisposed.' Grahame giggled. 'Old Freddie didn't much like having me on the strength. Of course, I had never made my preferences clear. But he always treated me like a milksop who liked boys.' The trace of bitterness hung in the air as Sir Roger glared, urging Grahame to get on with it.

Having got in a dig at his former boss, Grahame heeded the instruction. 'It was the interval,' he said briskly, like a horse upping from a walk to a trot. 'We were out having a drink, looking for any Sov we might chat up. We cornered a captain from the Sixth Motor Rifle Brigade standing on his own. He was an unsophisticated bunyip who became distinctly uneasy on learning we were British. He panicked a little, I think, and turned to a group of Ossis standing nearby. "Secretariat work," he snapped in German before stalking off.'

Grahame glanced at the blank faces of the two men opposite. 'East Germans, Ossis,' he explained unnecessarily. 'A youngish woman came over. Mid to late thirties, dark and sultry, very attractive, and as cheerful as you like.' Grahame pouted. 'Even so, I found it fascinating she bothered to respond at all seeing as the Russian had addressed her so curtly.'

'Yes, yes, thank you, Henry,' Sir Roger said wearily. 'So, the Russian referred the pair of you to the woman and she obliged.'

Grahame shrugged and gave a theatrical sniff. He thought it had been a point worth making. His pique passed and he pressed on. 'It turns out that the East German woman spoke excellent English. She introduced herself as Elke Über and explained she was Bavarian by birth but for some years now had been based in Berlin where currently she headed the East German communist party secretariat, otherwise known as the SED secretariat. We were impressed – quite the big fish and, moreover, it clarified the Russian's *Secretariat work* remark.

'"Is there a problem?" Elke the Bavarian good-looker says, telling us that for a time after the war she worked in an administrative role for the Soviets occupying the German state of Thuringia. "Their bark is usually worse than their bite," she said with a laugh.'

Grahame stroked his long beard while thinking. 'Fopsy was an awful spy,' he said matter-of-factly, 'no tact or brains. Instead of first indulging in a spot of foreplay, he asked her straight up if she'd like to have a chat when next over in the West. It was pre-Wall, remember, and East Berliners could visit West Berlin at will.'

'Yes, yes,' the DG said irritably, 'we all know that in 1959 the West Berlin subway was still operating into East Berlin. Shake a leg, will you?'

Grahame grimaced for the second time in a minute, seemingly of the opinion he had received another unnecessary rebuke. 'Elke didn't miss a beat,' he continued, now with defiant haughtiness. 'She simply said it would be inappropriate for someone heading the SED secretariat to be seen spending too much time in the West. But if Fopsy could come back with some nice silk underwear unable to be sourced in the East, she'd be happy to have a cup of tea with us.'

Grahame suddenly chortled. 'Fopsy didn't quite know what to say,' he said, breaking into laughter so genuine that it caused him to double over. 'The nervous way in which he was tweaking his moustache,' Grahame added, his eyes twinkling mischievously, 'gave me the distinct impression that Mrs Phillips wore underwear more given over to foundation than getting Fopsy to man up.' He laughed again, this time irreverently. 'Not that I was much use, me being more interested in boxer shorts.'

'So Elke eventually got on board?' Parnell-Brown piped up, causing the DG to swivel his head in surprise, leaving the Deputy unsure whether Sir Roger was irked because he had interrupted Grahame or if the DG had forgotten he was in the room.

Grahame blew his nose noisily. 'We got to talking music, Eisler and Strauss to be precise,' he said in answer to Parnell-Brown's question. 'Fopsy didn't know an oboe from his elbow. But I did.' Grahame rubbed his chin, appearing to reflect fondly on the time. 'Elke and I were soon chatting away like old friends.' He turned the palms of his hands upwards signalling he was approaching the end of his story. 'I didn't miss the opening. Arranged to see her again. Mutual love of music plus a few Western luxury items thrown in from time to time, undies included. I put it to her six weeks later and she jumped in the bag.' He inclined his head reflectively – an old man remembering a rare triumph from a chequered past. 'Pure gold she was.'

And in observing Henry Grahame's moment of reminiscence, it suddenly dawned on Peter Parnell-Brown why the DG had dragged him out on a cold Sunday. Sir Roger wanted his operation Leopard point man to hear first-hand from Henry Grahame the ease with which an influential SED official like Elke Über had been recruited on the back of two MI6 incompetents making a pitch in front of a battalion of East Berlin opera-goers. All of which could mean only one thing: that Elke Über was a double, a Stasi plant. Yet, Parnell-Brown thought, wasn't her reactivation the whole point of operation Spot, the DG's secret add-on to operation Leopard?

CHAPTER 6

Back in the French restaurant in Rosslyn, Virginia on Saturday night 6 April 1963 Daniel Lincoln called for the bill. Dinner was over, but now he faced a dilemma well known to young men with amorous intent, namely how to make an advance sound like a perfectly reasonable suggestion.

'Would you like to come back to my place?' Daniel said, striving to present as the epitome of innocence. 'We could watch Saturday Night at the Movies on NBC.' He looked hopefully at Kristiina. 'They often televise in colour these days,' he added lamely.

Fortunately for Daniel in view of his inept sell, Kristiina had already made her decision. But it was not to his place that she wanted to go. 'You've already come in to the District to collect me earlier tonight,' Kristiina said. 'It seems a lot of running around to go back to your place only to have to later return to DC to drop me off.'

Daniel felt the all too familiar pang of his accustomed so near, yet so far rejection. But Kristiina spoke again before he could start feeling sorry for himself. 'Why don't you come back to my place and I'll make you a cup of hot chocolate?'

'What about the parking?' Daniel said, immediately regretting the obstacle he had placed in front of Kristiina's offer.

'We'll go back via Wisconsin Avenue,' Kristiina said. 'The first park we spot within walking distance of my place we'll take it.'

41

Daniel's senses tingled. Had Kristiina declared her hand? 'Good idea,' he said levelly, uncertain if he was talking about the hot chocolate or the proposed parking arrangement. But he was not about to shoot himself in the foot again by dreaming up good reasons why not. Daniel smiled and dropped a handful of notes on top of the folder the waiter had left on the table. 'Let's go,' he said brightly.

***

'He's totally infatuated,' Kristiina said. 'Completely. Now the relationship has turned sexual, all his training has gone out the window.' She giggled in girlish embarrassment. After all, it was May 1963 and thought to be bad form for females to discuss their sex lives – even in private conversations with their Mossad controllers. Around six weeks earlier, in her apartment on that auspicious night of 6 April, Kristiina had first slept with Daniel.

Mrs Ruby nodded soberly. 'It has been confirmed,' she said, 'that talks with American nuclear experts will be held in Tel Aviv on Wednesday 29 May, eight days from now. I am under some pressure to provide an insight into the negotiating stance the US delegation will take on the all-important matter of inspecting the Dimona nuclear reactor.' Mrs Ruby wrapped her black cardigan tightly around her, as was her habit, causing Kristiina briefly to wonder if her mentor owned any other garment.

'At an appropriate time,' Mrs Ruby continued, 'you must tell this British fellow that your superiors at the World Bank have reprimanded you for tardy performance. Confide in him and make him feel sorry for you; hint, but without suggestion of recrimination, it is your preoccupation with him that has caused your work standard to decline.'

'What would you define as an appropriate time?' Kristiina asked earnestly, wanting to fully understand her instructions.

Mrs Ruby sighed as if Kristiina had missed a fundamental point. 'Post coitus,' she said abruptly, 'immediately after enjoying rapturous pleasure at the hands of your skilled lover.' Mrs Ruby laughed briefly. 'Like all men, he will be thinking he is Lothario at this time. He will not have it in him to deny you.' Kristiina stared at the tiny woman so prudish yet seemingly so assured in the science of sexual manipulation.

'Taking advantage of his deluded state,' Mrs Ruby said, 'you should seek his advice on what to do. You've already told him you are a strategic risk analyst. Confide that you are currently involved in confidential planning for a large loan to Egypt. But stress that your superiors are reluctant to approve a loan while there is strategic uncertainty in the region.' Mrs Ruby smiled. 'And the cause of this strategic uncertainty?' she asked rhetorically. 'Why, of course, it is the Dimona nuclear reactor in Israel.'

With that, Mrs Ruby looked keenly at Kristiina, preparing her for the key instruction. 'Ask Mr Lincoln if just this once he could help restore your standing with your supervisors by advising what he knows about US intentions vis-à-vis the plant. Are the Americans confident they can browbeat the Israelis into accepting their demand for inspections or will they, for example, try to buy cooperation with increased military assistance?'

Daniel, of course, was the MI6 Washington station novice resented by his supervisor Ray Solter for reminding Solter of his own inadequacies. And although Mossad knew nothing of the MI6 station's internal politics, Daniel's situation was in fact a boon for it: among his many uninspiring responsibilities was the requirement to do the station's filing.

***

On Thursday night 23 May 1963, a little over forty-eight hours since last meeting her Mossad controller, Kristiina was in her apartment with Daniel. Earlier she had prepared him a traditional meal of Finnish herrings and pickled vegetables. By now the relationship was past solidified and Daniel beyond bliss, and impervious to cues.

The couple had intended to watch television but inevitably ended up in the bedroom. Kristiina wrapped herself around Daniel, marvelling that now for the third time in a row she had experienced a frisson of excitement. But for all that the task set by Mrs Ruby hovered over Kristiina like a dark cloud. And the more she thought about it, the more burdened she became. Then suddenly, like a collapsing dam wall, Kristiina began to weep, overwhelmed by the weight of her conflicting emotions.

'What is it, darling?' the startled Daniel asked.

The tenderness in Daniel's voice tugged at Kristiina's heartstrings. But there was no way on God's earth she could tell him the truth. Absent alternatives, she resorted to her cover story. 'I'm having some trouble at the office,' she said. 'My boss is a very driven fellow who thinks I've been shirking.' Kristiina gave a bitter laugh. 'And sadly,' she said with regret, 'he's right. The fact is I've been swept off my feet since meeting you and not giving my job enough attention. I'm worried that my contract may not be renewed. In which case I will never work in this field again.' Kristiina kissed Daniel's neck. 'I'm not blaming you, Daniel,' she said gently, 'please believe that. But it seems my personal gain has come at a professional cost.'

'Kristiina,' Daniel croaked. He was devastated by the revelation.

Kristiina was too far in to back out. 'Strictly between us,' she said, 'we're currently designing a loan package for Egypt, a substantial loan package. But there's a lot of tension among people at the Bank who worry about possible instability in the Middle East because of uncertainty over Israel's intentions.' She looked up at Daniel, her eyes wide-open in appeal. 'Israel is developing a nuclear reactor at a place called Dimona,' she said, whispering to convey secrecy. 'Some in the Bank are concerned it could be used for the production of nuclear weapons.' Kristiina laughed humourlessly. 'We could hardly hand a billion dollars to Egypt only for a nuclear conflict to break out in the region.'

'And what's this mean for you?' Daniel asked anxiously.

Prompted by Daniel's concern, Kristiina made her pitch. 'As an analyst in the Bank's Strategic Risk Section,' she said, 'senior staff are looking to me for answers. But the honest truth is that much of what I do is guesswork. If just this once I could lay my hands on some factual information clarifying the situation, particularly on private US thinking, I'm sure it would rescue my professional reputation.' Kristiina exhaled forcefully. 'But if that's to happen, it must be by next Tuesday at the latest because the final decision will be made at a loan committee meeting the next morning, Wednesday 29 May.'

Kristiina held her breath. To be sure she could now look Mrs Ruby in the eye and tell her she had done her best. But equally her pleading had sounded awfully lame to her ears, and she worried that Daniel would wake to her intention. It was an unnecessary concern.

The besotted Daniel hugged Kristiina to him. His racing mind, prepared to believe anything she told him, turned to the filing responsibility foisted on him by Ray Solter. Daniel seldom read any of the documents he handled but, by virtue of his task, did have unrestricted access to the station's most sensitive material. And he also knew the combination to the safe in the station's secure vault where secret reports shared by the CIA were stored. 'I'll see what I can find out,' Daniel said, adopting the alpha male protector role. 'Nobody is going to besmirch your standing while I'm around.'

Kristiina kissed Daniel deeply. She did so in a combination of relief and genuine affection for him. 'My hero,' she breathed, sliding her hand down to Daniel's groin. And with that any second thoughts Daniel might have had evaporated in an instant.

***

Ronald Hunt was growing restless, and concerned. Restless because for over six months now he had dutifully trekked from his place of residence, Janice's small flat in Streatham, to RAF Kenley where he worked at the base's NAAFI canteen. He had soon found the routine both boring and depressing – but for the time being it was unavoidable. Still, Ronald had plans, although in the long run they did not involve Janice. Herein, indirectly, was the cause of his concern. It was now September 1941 and, rather than things improving, the bloody war was sinking deeper into the mire. More and more service personnel were being deployed overseas, with a commensurate increase in demand for NAAFI services.

Worse, the NAAFI management was about to ask all male employees who were single or married without children to serve overseas – in places where people were shooting at each other. The policy was not yet official. But Janice had typed the minutes of the management meeting. From what she had said it was only a matter of time before all single men and those without children got the tap on the shoulder, he included. That is unless he put Janice up the spout and got married, the thought of which made Ronald even unhappier; neither fatherhood nor marriage to Janice had ever featured in his calculations.

The British Crown colony of Malta was vital to the Allied war effort, not least because of its proximity to North Africa. Since June 1940 the British defenders of Malta had withstood every attempt by German-led Axis forces to seize the island.

The number of NAAFI canteens on Malta had more than doubled in line with the rapid build up of UK military personnel. And now reports of NAAFI canteens being damaged by bombing were appearing in London's newspapers. This was highly concerning for Ronald, chiefly because Janice had said it was in Malta where the NAAFI bosses identified that staffing levels were most in need of bolstering.

Later on that same night Janice took a bath, as without fail she did every Sunday, Tuesday and Friday. Ronald was sitting at the flat's small dining table, thinking. Janice could be irritating but he liked to have sex with her immediately after she bathed, when she smelled sweet and fresh. But Janice was also a woman blessed with a predictable menstrual cycle gifting her the capacity for natural contraception – mostly involving her insistence on abstinence. This grated on Ronald. But he was still hiding under Janice's protective wing and really had no option other than to comply.

Ronald sucked unhappily on his cigarette. He was grumpy because sex with Janice was currently off-limits and, disturbingly, he now had the threat of deployment to Malta hanging over his head. Suddenly, the thought that Janice was presently at her most fertile convinced him it was time to act. Ronald stubbed out his cigarette and walked into the bathroom, intent on asserting himself no matter what Janice had to say about it.

'Ronald,' Janice exclaimed in surprise. She was relaxing in the bath reading a magazine and Ronald's entry into the tiny room had caught her unawares.

'How's the water then, pet?' Ronald asked, propping on the side of the bath. Janice giggled, half in alarm and half in contrived good humour. Ronald placed his hand under the water, reaching for the arch where Janice's legs met her body, whereupon he began to caress her.

'Not tonight, love,' Janice said as genially as she could. 'Remember, we can't afford the pitter-patter of little feet.'

Janice watched dumbfounded as Ronald removed his clothes. Only when he made to climb into the bath did she snap out of her fog. 'Ronald,' Janice said sternly. 'I said no.'

'A man has got the right to shag his missus whenever he wants,' Ronald declared, lowering himself into the water.

'We ain't married, need I remind you?'

'Damn right we're not. And unless you open up that little cunnie of yours in the next ten seconds, I might need to go somewhere else for my nooky.'

Janice scoffed; her dander was up. 'And where would that be?'

'You've got no idea the looks that some of them pretty RAF girls out at Kenley give me,' Ronald retorted.

Ronald was his father's son and quite prepared to resort to emotional blackmail if it meant getting his own way. But his threat to take up with another woman, of course, was an empty one. It surprised him, therefore, to see Janice's resolve seep away, understanding in that instant how the spectre of him leaving had psychologically intimidated her. Indeed after lying latent for years since the misguided sex education of her youth, Janice had experienced for the first time a compelling fear of rejection. New rules governing the relationship were now in force.

Ronald seized the moment, fondling Janice's breast and drawing her towards him. He kissed her roughly on the mouth. 'Come on, baby,' Ronald said. 'Let's not argue. Give it to me, now.'

'Only if you promise to pull out,' Janice whispered meekly.

'Sure, darling,' Ronald said carelessly, turning Janice around until her back was to him.

Janice waited patiently as Ronald rhythmically thrust at her, ignoring the discomfort that came with kneeling on the floor of the bath. Ronald tensed as his climax neared, the time when during sex in borderline moments in Janice's cycle he usually disentangled. But this time he did not and instead discharged into her, panting heavily.

Ronald sat back in the bath, cradling Janice in his arms. He knew he had far exceeded some boundaries in forcing himself on her. But he was also well aware of the leverage he now held. 'I love you, Janny,' he whispered, shushing the softly weeping Janice and stroking her hair.

Janice took no comfort from Ronald's words. But the power balance had dramatically shifted, shockingly so, and she was no longer capable of being the feisty young woman she was just a few minutes ago. 'I love you too, Ronald,' she said stiffly.

A month later, coincident with the issue in October 1941 of a NAAFI internal memorandum seeking expressions of interest from single male employees and those married without children to serve overseas, Janice returned home one night wearing a long face. 'I missed my last period,' she told Ronald. 'And now Doctor Cobble has confirmed I'm pregnant.'

CHAPTER 7

On 30 November 1964 the man carrying a US immigration card in the name of Frank Middlemiss lay dead on the cold as charity sidewalk in New York City's Financial District, paramedics at his side. NYPD officers Patrick Doherty and Lucy Rodriguez looked on. 'I guess the next thing is to interview all the building occupants,' Lucy said, citing the procedure taught at the NYPD training academy. But her streetwise partner knew better than to waste time and energy trying to talk to every resident.

'Looks like the guy in 18E at the back end of the hallway,' the building superintendent said, once Doherty had ferreted him out, taken him down to the sidewalk and lifted the plastic sheet covering the shattered body. 'Frank Middlemiss is his name.'

The super had turned visibly grey. 'You wanna throw-up or something?' Doherty said. 'Take deep breaths if you do.'

The super breathed as recommended. 'Kept to himself and caused no trouble,' he said when he was steady. 'He was English. I took him up a letter just this morning in fact, postmarked West Berlin of all places.'

'How long has he been a resident?' Doherty said, inclining his head in the direction of the 388 Vesey Street building.

'Not long,' the super replied. 'Less than three months, I'd say. Nothing unusual in that; lots of people come and go from here.'

Doherty nodded. 'Let's take a look at his apartment,' he said.

The superintendent led Doherty and Lucy to the elevator, after which he opened the door on the eighteenth floor with his master key and stood aside to allow them to enter. The apartment was a sparsely furnished, three-room studio bed-sitter. Rinsed breakfast dishes were stacked in a rack on the sink and in the bedroom a double bed was untidily made up.

Doherty flicked open a wardrobe to find a small amount of clothing on hangers. All the garments bore English labels, unlike the Austrian-made blue herringbone jacket worn by the dead man. Two drawerless nightstands were positioned on either side of the bedhead with a book, Ernest Hemingway's *For Whom the Bell Tolls*, on the stand closest to the door. A three-drawer pine chest positioned against the wall at the foot of the bed seemed only to add to the room's austerity.

Doherty picked up the book and leafed through it. 'I've heard of this Hemingway guy,' he said to Lucy. 'Committed suicide a couple of years back.' Hemingway in fact had died by his own hand over three years earlier. But Doherty's mind was on other things. He turned to the chest of drawers. The top drawer contained four pairs each of socks and underwear. The second drawer was empty. Doherty opened the bottom drawer, whereupon he emitted a soft whistle. 'Hey, Lucy,' he called. 'Take a look at this.'

Lucy watched as Doherty removed four items and laid them on the bed. One was a small picture frame containing a photograph of a pretty blond woman of early thirties appearance. There were also a British passport in the name of Frank Middlemiss and a sum of US dollars, 270 of them according to Lucy's count. Finally, the two officers pored over the letter the super had brought to the apartment that morning. A lone newspaper clipping was inside. Neither Doherty nor Lucy could read the German text beneath a large photograph of a couple smiling vacantly. But the names of the female holding a posy of flowers, confetti visible in her hair, and an older-looking male were discernible: Elke Über and Josef Sterck.

'Looks like these two just got married,' Lucy said. 'But they don't seem awful happy about it.'

***

Back outside in the freezing cold the ambulance containing the lifeless body of Frank Middlemiss slowly drove off. Life in Vesey Street, Lower Manhattan had returned to normal. Now only Doherty and Lucy were at the scene, stomping their feet to keep warm while awaiting the dispatcher's response.

'NYPD six, seven; NYPD six, seven,' a nasal female voice crackled from the radio inside the patrol vehicle. Doherty reached through the window for the handset and acknowledged the dispatcher's call. 'US Immigration advises,' the woman began immediately, 'that the permanent resident card found on the victim is registered to Francis Carmichael Middlemiss, date of birth 25 May 1930, Leeds, United Kingdom. On 31 August 1962 Middlemiss married Rigoberta Dolores Garcia, an American citizen.'

The dispatcher cleared her throat, forewarning Doherty something important was to follow. 'The wife's formerly from Mexico,' the dispatcher said of Rigoberta Dolores Garcia. 'The vic was granted United States permanent residence in February 1963, six months after his marriage. Reported home address at the time of receiving PR was 134 East 125th Street in Harlem. A condition of PR is that for the first five years of residency changes of address must be notified. None are recorded.'

'Ten-four,' Doherty replied, inviting the dispatcher to proceed.

'Apartment 18E, 388 Vesey Street in the Financial District,' the woman continued, her voice now monotone as she read from notes, 'was purchased on 22 October 1962 by a company out of El Paso, Texas called Alamo Holdings. The sole director of

52

Alamo Holdings is Miguel Rodolfo Jimenez. He is the registered owner of the apartment but has no known connection with the deceased. Alamo Holdings has a listed address in Biggs Field, El Paso.' The dispatcher paused momentarily. 'For an English guy,' she said, adlibbing, 'it's passing strange that he has a Mexican connection to both his PR and place of residence.'

You bet it is, Doherty thought as he signed off. He turned to Lucy who had been listening. 'This has got a whiff to it they can smell out in Queens,' Doherty said. 'And as the NYPD ain't likely to send us on a trip to Texas, Lucy, I guess that leaves us with the Harlem address to check out.'

***

Rigoberta Dolores Garcia was startled to find two uniformed NYPD officers knocking on her door. Doherty and Lucy had just driven to the north of Manhattan, travelling crosstown east from Vesey Street onto Madison Avenue and following it all the way up through Midtown, the Upper East Side and beyond Central Park before eventually reaching Harlem. It was quicker to make the enquiry themselves than have the NYPD in Harlem do it. The woman standing before the officers was short and stout and of an indeterminate age, the by-product of an adult life of near perennial pregnancy and unending menial work.

'I ain't never laid eyes on him,' she told Doherty and Lucy bluntly when they asked about Frank Middlemiss.

Doherty sensibly let Lucy take the lead. 'US immigration says that Middlemiss married you in August 1962,' she said gently.

The sound of children squabbling from inside the apartment reached the doorway. Rigoberta stepped back into the hallway, motioning for the officers to follow. 'Fidel, Oralia, you two be quiet,' she yelled before turning back to Lucy. 'Miss,' she said softly, 'a few months back, three, four maybe I don't remember exactly, but recent-like, some Hispanic guy came here and offered me money to sign forms.' Rigoberta shrugged. 'It was either sign or have my throat cut. I got kids to feed. So I took the money.'

'You done this sort of thing before?' Lucy asked.

Rigoberta wiped tears from her eyes. 'These are heavy guys, Miss. Mean fuckers. I say anything, I'm dead.'

Doherty and Lucy left it there. Others would attend to the immigration fraud. Next stop for the NYPD pair was the morgue at New York-Presbyterian Hospital, where they obtained a set of Frank Middlemiss's fingerprints. Immigration identity cards could be forged with relative ease but not so fingerprints. That's why, on leaving the hospital, the officers made their way back up to Midtown, to the British Consulate. In a plush office overlooking Fifth Avenue, they requested a British official to initiate urgent enquiries back home to confirm the deceased person's identity.

***

The two men were seated at a small conference table in the secure room attached to the MI6 Director General's office. It was mid-morning Friday 24 April 1964, two days since Peter Parnell-Brown had discussed Daniel Lincoln with MI6's East German section head and taken soundings on his awareness of Ronald Hunt's name. It was also the day after Parnell-Brown had dined with the CIA's Michael Anjelico at Claridge's Hotel, and today's first item of business was to brief Sir Roger Holbrook on this meeting.

'Anjelico,' Parnell-Brown began formally, 'has endorsed operation Leopard's stated objective to install Konrad Voite as East German prime minister. The CIA agrees this will be achieved by discrediting the current East German leadership of Walter Ulbricht and Erich Honecker at the SED plenary conference on 28 August next.'

Parnell-Brown smiled briefly at the DG. 'Anjelico also confirmed,' he added, 'the CIA will release Ronald Hunt from Leavenworth a week before the conference and fly him direct to West Berlin. Anjelico will accompany and personally oversee Hunt's departure for East Berlin on 24 August where he is to renew acquaintances with Josef Sterck.' Parnell-Brown pulled a face. 'A piece of work, that fellow,' he said with uncharacteristic vehemence.

The DG chuckled, aware of the Deputy's contempt for the German. 'I share your disdain for Sterck, Peter,' he said. 'But he was Hunt's primary collaborator when Hunt was in Berlin with NAAFI after the war and playing the black market for all it was worth.'

'Too true,' Parnell-Brown said, nodding grimly. 'Leopard,' he continued, 'envisages Hunt blackmailing Sterck into making public allegations against Ulbricht and Honecker. Hunt will give Sterck supporting documents. The operation's key judgement is that Klaus Borkh will overreact to Sterck's outburst thereby diverting Borkh's attention from safeguarding the conference agenda.'

Klaus Borkh was originally from Pomerania and currently the head of the so-called office of the council of ministers, the body responsible for the reputational integrity of the East German leadership. In other words, he was Ulbricht and Honecker's minder-in-chief. Borkh had been parachuted into the job the preceding year, in May 1963, leaving most Western analysts scratching their heads as to why a mid-thirties, ex-Stasi thug originally from East Germany's outer reaches should have been promoted so rapidly. Most considered him lacking in experience and temperament, and it was this MI6 and the CIA intended to exploit.

The DG knew operation Leopard back to front. After all, he was the architect of the plan – the *whole* plan. 'The documents Hunt gives Sterck will be genuine,' Sir Roger chimed in softly, 'hotel receipts showing that when in Czechoslovakia in December last year Ulbricht and Honecker charged a tourist trip to their official expenses. This is sure to rankle with the masses who rarely get an opportunity to holiday, if you don't count stringing up a tent to the back of a Trabant for a few days once a year.'

Parnell-Brown smiled at the DG, doing so with a slight shake of his head. 'I really must congratulate you, Roger, on your ingenuity. It's a brilliant smokescreen. The East German political elite understands how it works. A little off the top here and there must be roundly condemned in public, but privately they all accept it's par for the course. Borkh knows this and will not fear blowback at the party conference. Rather, he'll be fully occupied with planting stories to discredit Josef Sterck and assuage public disquiet over Ulbricht and Honecker's liberty. Provided the Americans can get the authenticated Swiss banking records to Konrad Voite in good time, he can add an item to the conference agenda free of Borkh's vetting.'

'Well, it wasn't my idea alone,' the DG said modestly, embarrassed by the Deputy's praise. 'I mean you helpfully suggested Ronald Hunt when the search for a suitable decoy bogged down and we faced losing momentum. And the CIA Director also had input. It was his idea to have an Agency Cuban asset join a tour group scheduled to visit East Berlin in August and, when he arrives there, post the Swiss documents to Voite's office.'

Sir Roger rubbed his chin. It was a nervous reaction because, like Parnell-Brown, he had reservations about the delivery method. 'The CIA assures me the Stasi does not monitor mail posted to senior party members from within East Germany, only that which comes in from outside.'

'And what about the Cuban?' Parnell-Brown asked. 'Even if we accept the Stasi will not be monitoring the mail, will they be watching the postman?'

The DG rubbed his forehead. 'The courier's name is Paian Diaz. He is a lowly official in the Cuban set-up.' Sir Roger paused and shrugged. 'The CIA is adamant that the Stasi regards East Germany's Cuban allies as compliant dummies not requiring surveillance.'

'Good God,' Parnell-Brown muttered.

With that, the two men sat in pensive silence. Sir Roger's deep intake of breath broke the quiet. 'Which brings us to Daniel Lincoln,' he said.

CHAPTER 8

In Washington DC in May 1963 Daniel Lincoln was at a crossroads. A lover's thrall had muddled his mind and neutered his common sense. The Finnish woman whom he loved and obsessed over needed his protection. And by hook or by crook he was going to provide it, by the night of Tuesday 28 May at the latest ahead of a Wednesday morning decision on the World Bank loan to Egypt.

Kristiina Ahnger, conversely, had no such clarity of purpose. She was distressed she should have to trick Daniel into revealing what he knew about the US bottom line on inspecting Israel's nuclear facility at Dimona. At the same time her Mossad handler Mrs Ruby was constantly reinforcing her duty to the Jewish people. 'Your Mr Lincoln can likely answer a question bearing directly on Israel's very existence,' Mrs Ruby said. Moments earlier Kristiina had reported Daniel's previous night's pledge to help her. 'Be confident that any damage he may incur will be in the name of our survival.'

Mrs Ruby waited for Kristiina to leave the Mossad safe house before picking up the telephone. 'She's teetering,' she said dourly into the mouthpiece, 'but I judge still sufficiently committed to see it through. I reiterated that we must have something within four days, before next Wednesday.' Mrs Ruby's nominated deadline was Wednesday 29 May 1963, when a US delegation would be in Tel Aviv for talks to definitively settle the inspection question.

***

First thing the following Monday, staff at the MI6 station in the British embassy in Washington DC gathered for their usual start-of-week meeting. After which Daniel returned to his office where he girded his loins for the task before him. His diary was empty and it would arouse no suspicion were he to spend time filing in the station's secure vault. He had little choice but to act now – Kristiina needed something by tomorrow night. Daniel waited patiently until station others had drawn their files until finally, after a seeming eternity, he was in the vault with the door closed behind him.

Daniel was anxious and sweating but thoughts of Kristiina steeled him. Soon the cabinet holding the sensitive CIA reports was open. Documents were filed alphabetically under country names. Turning to those under *I* he quickly sifted through the papers, finding to his disappointment nothing on the Israeli nuclear reactor.

Shoulders tensing, Daniel moved to the lower shelf and the CIA reports that an MI6 courier would pack on Wednesday afternoon and on Thursday morning ferry to London in a diplomatic pouch. It was of great relief to discover several documents banded together under a cover sheet bearing the words *Dimona Reactor*. The first report Daniel perused was dry and technical. But the second caught his eye, not because its summary page provided a truncated recitation of why the US needed to conduct inspections, but rather because of a sub-heading further down reading: *Heinrich Keller*.

Heinrich Keller was a Nazi rocket scientist detained by the Israelis in Uruguay in 1962, when Keller was visiting from nearby Argentina to where he absconded after the war under the name Harry Kellaway. Keller's story also concerned a forged American passport used by Mossad to get him to Israel and, curiously, the moon.

Suffice to say the false passport led the Americans to discover in early 1963 that Keller was in Israeli custody. Lunar considerations, on the other hand, involved the delegation scheduled to hold talks in Tel Aviv on Wednesday 29 May. The delegation, in fact, had recently been ordered to adopt a top secret, last resort negotiating position under which the US would drop demands for inspections of the Dimona plant in return for Israel handing over Heinrich Keller.

And the reason for this extraordinary about-face? Well, in September 1962 President Kennedy made public America's ambition to put a man on the moon. 'We choose to go to the moon,' was his rallying call. Left unsaid, however, was Kennedy's imperative for the US to get there before the Soviets, such that by May 1963 the White House had come to place a very high value on Heinrich Keller's missile re-entry expertise.

Inside the MI6 vault in the British embassy in Washington DC, Daniel Lincoln had no time to fully absorb the detail of the secret Heinrich Keller exchange proposal. But the little he did read made him sure the document would be of assistance to Kristiina. Daniel crossed the Rubicon. Today was Monday 27 May 1963. He would secrete the document on his person and read it closely that night ahead of letting Kristiina read it on Tuesday night. Early on Wednesday morning he would return the report to the filing cabinet in good time for the courier to pack it on Wednesday afternoon in the diplomatic pouch destined for London. It was a calculation that would haunt Daniel until the day he died – eighteen months later after plummeting off the apartment building at 388 Vesey Street in the New York City Financial District.

That night Daniel was steadfast. It was a very serious matter to remove sensitive intelligence material from the MI6 station and an even more serious offence to share it with unauthorised persons. But Daniel had committed. He returned to the Keller story, taking in its every nuance. Elated and relieved in equal measure, Daniel let the CIA report fall into his lap, placing his hands behind his head and closing his eyes. 'This is precisely what Kristiina needs to know,' he whispered, tingling. Daniel in truth was not focused solely on saving Kristiina's job: he had also been growing increasingly nervous at the prospect of her leaving Washington. But revealing the document's contents to Kristiina tomorrow night would neatly kill those two birds with the one stone.

***

Eleven months later in April 1964 neither Sir Roger Holbrook nor his Deputy Peter Parnell-Brown had any inkling of Daniel Lincoln's betrayal. On the contrary, seated in the DG's secure room, they were about to discuss the role intended for him in Sir Roger's secret operation Spot.

'If operation Leopard goes to plan,' Parnell-Brown said, 'it will prepare the ground for Spot given Konrad Voite can be expected to reform East German border policy early on in his tenure. The relaxation will have limits initially, of course. But exit permits will be granted for senior officials like Elke Über.'

The DG briefly gazed into the distance. 'And you're confident that Daniel Lincoln can pass her my letter the day before the party conference?'

Parnell-Brown considered the DG's question, for he held some private concerns on the matter. 'Daniel will have no role in Leopard nor know anything of it,' he said levelly, 'making Spot as straightforward as these things can be. We'll give him a passport and papers depicting him as a British salesman from a firm in Cardiff.' Sir Roger nodded and Parnell-Brown ploughed on. 'As one Frank Middlemiss he will lodge a visa application with KfA in time for his arrival in East Berlin a couple of days before the SED conference.'

KfA Ltd was officially a private East German company based in London. But in reality it was East Germany's de facto embassy.

'Good,' Sir Roger said. 'Just recap his sequence of events on the ground, if you wouldn't mind.'

'On 26 August, two days before the SED conference, he's in East Berlin to meet the trade ministry, having arrived in West Berlin the night before. On conference day minus one, 27 August, he concludes his trade talks, which will be as inconclusive as ever. That afternoon he wanders around before reaching the Weidendammer Bridge where he will set the signal on the first ornamental lamp post at the bridge's eastern end. All this happens before 6 pm. He repairs to his accommodation, the Frund Hotel adjacent to the bridge. Just after six he takes another stroll – nice summer's night and all that. He arrives at the front of the Tränenpalast pavilion by 6:30 pm. The ID is by means of a folded copy of the *Berliner Zeitung* newspaper he's to hold in his right hand. If nothing by 7 pm he aborts. The next day he comes home, just another empty-handed businessman unable to penetrate the East German bureaucracy.'

'How's he to set the signal without the Stasi spotting him?' the DG interjected, his eyes bright and intense. After all, operation Spot was Sir Roger's last big enterprise before he retired.

'The Stasi team trailing him will be nothing out of the ordinary, just the standard plodders they allocate to monitoring Western businessmen. So long as he doesn't talk to anybody, they will keep their distance. Daniel will lean against the lamp post while gazing at the river. We think that from behind the screen of his body he can fasten the padlock to the post's latticework without being seen.'

Parnell-Brown smiled. It was the habit of East Berlin lovers to attach padlocks to the Weidendammer Bridge. 'The padlock will be a security lock on his suitcase. It's specially coated with soft metal so that in his hotel room the night before he can scratch the meeting request on it. As you know, *Karl loves Ilsa* will direct Elke to the Tränenpalast pavilion.' Parnell-Brown laughed dryly. 'It's unlikely the border guards will notice the missing padlock on departure. But if queried he'll say it was stolen from his hotel room, which will ring true given most Ossi hotel staff like to pilfer from foreigners.'

Parnell-Brown hesitated, collecting himself. He was about to seek clarification on the issues that were niggling at him. Not that he lacked the gumption. But, out of respect for Sir Roger, he was treading lightly. 'Roger,' he said finally, 'how does Elke know about the meeting request signal? The Tränenpalast pavilion wasn't built until 1962, yet she's been inactive since the Wall went up in '61. And then there's the matter of how can we be sure that she'll be checking for the signal?'

Parnell-Brown waited for the DG to respond. But Sir Roger stared straight ahead. Parnell-Brown took a deep breath. He had asked the questions and now thought it prudent to explain. 'I raise these matters,' he said deferentially, 'only because my understanding is you took me to see Henry Grahame last February to make me aware that Elke Über is a double agent. That is, you intended I should draw this conclusion on hearing how Fopsy Phillips and Henry Grahame wandered over to the Konzerthaus in East Berlin and in front of all and sundry laid the groundwork for her recruitment.'

Parnell-Brown studied the DG, finding his face inscrutable. But the fire in Sir Roger's eyes sent a chill down his spine. Suddenly Parnell-Brown was unnerved, wondering where the conversation was headed. 'And if Elke Über *is* a double,' Parnell-Brown said cautiously, 'where does this leave Daniel Lincoln?'

The DG again peered into the distance before finally opening his suit coat, extracting two crumpled pages and smoothing them with the flat of his hand. 'You should read these,' he said, sliding the pages across the table. They were handwritten, in English. Glancing at the bottom of the second page, Parnell-Brown was staggered to see the words: *Yours sincerely, Fräulein Elke Über.*

'It's a letter mailed from Copenhagen in January this year,' the DG said. 'To my home address in Chiswick,' he added with a restrained laugh, 'and not to my Service flat where these days I'm imprisoned most of the time. You will see that Elke herself proposed the padlock signal on the Weidendammer Bridge. She also stipulated the newspaper recognition signal at the Tränenpalast pavilion and that the meeting window close at 7 pm.' The DG nodded in affirmation. 'She knows we can't have people hanging around a meet point all night.' Sir Roger breathed in deeply through his nose, his chest deflating as he exhaled. 'Having set out these arrangements,' he summarised, 'we can be confident she'll be checking for the meeting request signal every single day.'

Peter Parnell-Brown scanned Elke's letter as if seeking to confirm the meeting details were in there as the DG had said. 'In case you're wondering,' Sir Roger interrupted, 'she has an apartment on Unter den Linden and has long made a habit of crossing the Weidendammer Bridge shortly after six each evening when walking home. That way she's sticking to an established routine.'

Parnell-Brown looked up and the DG smiled again. 'Daniel's Stasi watchers will not be keen on mixing it with a lot of upset East Berliners at the Tränenpalast pavilion. They're conspicuous to East Germans and will stay back rather than risk a knife between the ribs. That way Elke can safely accept the letter.'

The DG was right. The Tränenpalast pavilion was not called the Palace of Tears for nothing. It was a building attached to Friedrichstrasse station and housed an official East German border crossing. With many German families arbitrarily separated by the Berlin Wall, the area in front of the Tränenpalast pavilion was regularly chock full of resentfully emotional East Germans farewelling family members returning to the West.

Parnell-Brown returned to reading Elke's letter, his brow furrowing in concentration. 'She's given up on East Germany because it is too beholden to the Soviets and doomed to fail,' he said, paraphrasing. 'And her offer is if we get her out she'll unload everything she knows in return for relocation to Sandymount in Dublin under a false identity.'

Parnell-Brown read on. Suddenly he started, scarcely able to believe his eyes. 'And we're to buy her a bloody house on the Sandymount Strand?' he said indignantly. Since becoming the MI6 Deputy Parnell-Brown had come to appreciate the true beauty of responsible budgeting.

'Yes,' the DG said simply.

Parnell-Brown shook his head in a briefly vigorous movement. 'Why the Sandymount Strand, for God's sake?' he barked, forgetting his manners in the moment. 'Doesn't she realise how expensive the real estate is over there?'

CHAPTER 9

In November 1941 Ronald Hunt married Janice Bolitho, his visibly pregnant girlfriend, in a Registry office on London's Curzon Street. Besides the bride and groom, others present were a marriage celebrant and two Registry officials, the latter duo acting as witnesses as required under the law. Janice had hoped to invite her mother and father from rural Uxbridge but Ronald quickly put the kybosh on this.

'Suppose we do have them come along,' Ronald said when Janice first raised the matter. 'Imagine the commotion when they see you're in the family way. They don't even know about me, much less that we're living together in your flat.'

'Well, I have told them in letters that I have a friend called Ronald who works with me at the NAAFI,' Janice said defensively.

Ronald snorted. 'Knowing you, I doubt they would think we've so much as held hands. They'd roll over and die if they found out that for months now we've been playing mummies and daddies.'

As usual these days Janice was powerless to deny Ronald's wishes. 'I suppose you're right,' she said with a sigh. 'But afterwards you have to take me to Fortnum and Masons for afternoon tea.'

Ronald smiled, as he always did when Janice backed down. 'Consider it done, darling,' he said. 'We'll have a Devonshire Tea with all the works.'

The child, a girl they called Carmel, was born on 17 June 1942. Ronald was to smother her to death three months later. Other than the cold-blooded snuffing out of the defenceless infant's life, the event was notable for Ronald's crossover from larrikin lawlessness to full-blown criminality, a position from where he never retreated.

Carmel had been a sickly baby from the moment Janice brought her home to the flat in Streatham. It was probably colic. Whatever, Carmel's non-stop crying began to wear on Ronald. He was fed up with the war, the rationing and its many other hardships. He also begrudged that he still needed Janice's help to implement his future plans, this despite the power he now wielded over her. And above all he was resentful of the introduction into his life of a demanding, six-pound bundle of noise that denied him both sleep and sex.

With that Ronald's narcissism bloomed, coming to a catastrophic head one Sunday in late September 1942. Janice had gone to Uxbridge for a long overdue visit to her parents. Ronald was hungover and sleep-deprived, the latter the result of Carmel waking just three hours after he had gone to bed. The night before Ronald had drunk a pint of illegally distilled hooch, diluting it with lemonade over the course of his lengthy drinking session. Janice's parents, of course, knew nothing of Carmel's existence. This left Janice unable to take the child with her, and with that fate's black hand was unleashed to do its devastating worst.

Ronald briefly felt numb when the unthinkable occurred. But he quickly realised he had tracks to cover. In a state of contrived panic, he raced to the adjoining flat and pounded on the door. 'My little baby,' he screamed, real tears born of criminal need flowing down his cheeks. 'She's not breathing.'

The police came eventually, followed later by a doctor. A young uniformed officer took Ronald's statement while the doctor examined the blue-faced child. At another time suspicions might have been aroused. But Ronald's show of grief was convincing. And by September 1942 Britain had been fighting for its very life for three wearisome years. For those in the beleaguered emergency services it was a time when tragedy had heaped upon tragedy, dulling the senses of emotionally exhausted people.

Janice did not arrive home until after the ambulance, an olive-coloured military vehicle with giant red crosses on both sides of its rear canopy, had taken away Carmel's lifeless body. Her first thought was to think it strange that a man of the cloth, deathly pale with a sombre look on his face, should be loitering on the first floor landing outside the door to her flat. Confusion soon turned into a gut-wrenching premonition of terror. For long after the residents of the apartment block would speak in shocked awe when recalling her screams. 'Like a werewolf at night deep in the woods,' some would later agree.

Thereafter Janice seldom spoke. As best as Ronald could ascertain when interrogating her pained and empty eyes, she had accepted the overburdened doctor's finding of cot death, if not the cruel injustice of it. A life of sorts went on, Janice cooking and cleaning for Ronald, and occasionally submitting to his sexual advances – accompanied, until he gave up, by the promise they would make a new Carmel.

After a month of grieving for the loss of her daughter, Janice returned to her job with NAAFI. She did so on the advice of a well-meaning lady from a local church group who thought the workplace interaction might be good for her. But Janice was irreparably crushed, illustrated by her speaking only when she must and then in monosyllabic whispers.

Two months on from Carmel's death, in November 1942, Allied Forces invaded French North Africa. This was a pivotal moment turning the tide of war in favour of the Allies.

The invasion also effectively ended the siege of Malta, where for over two years the Mediterranean island had been subject to constant German bombardment. With that, Malta became a crucial cog in the North African campaign, a staging area for the Allied forces taking the fight to the retreating Germans. The upshot was that by early 1943 Malta was free of conflict and full to overflowing with British service personnel requiring NAAFI services.

Ronald had been closely watching developments in Malta. He was also keen to get away from Janice's maudlin presence. Yet Ronald calculated he should not be in a rush to sever ties with her. The solution was soon obvious. He would not divorce Janice. Instead, he would continue to make use of her influence in NAAFI but go to Malta where he could live as a single man. And in Malta, where a welter of NAAFI business was taking place, he could start to look for opportunities to make some serious money. So off to Malta Ronald went, with a little help from Janice. Whereas Janice once feared being left on her own, she now craved solitude. She wanted Ronald gone and had been happy to stick his request for overseas transfer under the right nose.

***

Inside Sir Roger Holbrook's secure room the tension was mounting now that the DG had shown Peter Parnell-Brown Elke Über's letter containing her offer to defect. It was Friday 24 April 1964 and Parnell-Brown had just expressed dismay at Elke's asking price, namely that MI6 buy her a home on the Sandymount Strand in Dublin. Sir Roger smiled at the Deputy. He valued Parnell-Brown and was quite prepared to treat his outburst for what it was – confusion rather than insubordination.

'In the summer of 1938,' the DG explained, 'Elke and her family took a vacation in Dublin. She has particularly fond memories of visiting the Sandymount Strand and evidently that's where she wants to settle.'

'How do you know this background, Roger?' Parnell-Brown asked warily. 'There's no mention of it in the letter.'

The DG sighed. 'A few weeks after Elke got on board in 1959, I reviewed the recruitment. It was clear, as you say, that she'd come across too readily. I was in your current job in those days and took my concerns to Sir Norman. But Norman had been badly burned by the Suez catastrophe.' The DG smiled sadly. 'When I tried to tell him that Elke was a Stasi plant, he wouldn't listen, simply because he needed some runs on the board. "Already told the Foreign Secretary it's a triumph," he said.'

'What then?'

'It was all a bit tricky politically. But eventually I took myself to Berlin. It was early 1961 and pre-Wall. Elke was in West Berlin for a station debrief. I waited for her at her hotel, explained who I was and took her for a stroll in the Tiergarten. It was during this private chat she told me about her love of the Sandymount Strand.'

Parnell-Brown frowned. 'So tell me, Sir Roger,' he said softly. 'What did you say to Elke Über?'

The DG pursed his lips. 'I told her she was blown at a senior level in MI6, even if not with lesser lights like Henry Grahame. But for now I wasn't going to burn her. Told her to think hard about this, especially the Stasi reaction should it learn she had been tumbled. I suggested she consider coming over and gave her my private postal address in case she wanted to make contact.'

'And she said?'

'She just laughed,' the DG said. '"I warned them that some in MI6 would see through my double game," was all she said. We left it there. Frankly, I was quite taken by her intelligence. It convinced me she was worth persevering with.'

'OK,' Parnell-Brown said. 'Where to from here?'

The DG smiled wryly. 'I've made Elke's reactivation my last hurrah,' he said. 'Fortunately, the minister likes the idea of an agent at the heart of the East German communist party; he's a relative innocent in such things.' The DG pouted. 'But clearly I can't agree to her coming out immediately – ministers and others are expecting her to be in place for some time. The letter Daniel Lincoln is to carry, therefore, will ask her to stay on for a minimum of three years, after which her wish to defect will be granted in full, house on the Sandymount Strand, etcetera. I will place that promise on file in order to bind my successor to it.'

Parnell-Brown raised his eyebrows. 'It's a long game, Peter,' Sir Roger continued. 'As for feeding information back to us, she's smart enough to understand that we're behind it as and when Konrad Voite becomes the East German leader. When the border rules are relaxed, she'll start to visit West Berlin from time to time.' The DG smiled fondly as if talking about his grandchildren. 'Once she judges it's safe, she'll make contact with us.'

With that, the DG clenched his hands on the table in front of him, telling Parnell-Brown they had reached the nub of the matter. 'But drip-feeding us bits and pieces,' Sir Roger said softly, 'is just a side game designed to satisfy our domestic audience. The main prize she will deliver, albeit in three years from now, is a first-hand readout on whether Konrad Voite is willing and able to stay the reformist course.'

The DG looked hard at Parnell-Brown. 'Understand, Peter, this stands to be real gold, not the piffle that Henry Grahame boasts about. The West must know for certain if Voite is skilled and strong enough to resist pressure from Moscow to return to the old ways. And I don't mean just on border rules. That's nothing in the great scheme of things. The ultimate question is whether Konrad Voite has the will and capability to sow the seeds of German reunification.'

'Reunification?' Parnell-Brown echoed, as if he'd never heard of the word.

'That's the pinnacle, clear guidance on whether the West should go for broke and commit vast resources in seeking to raise a reunified Germany from Hitler's ashes.' The DG smiled at Parnell-Brown, his eyes gleaming. 'Pray that the answer is yes, Peter. Because, if we're ever going to avoid a nuclear World War, Germany must become a bulwark against Soviet expansionism. Unfortunately, it will take time for the signs to emerge. About three years I calculate. And until Voite's want and capacity to achieve reunification are evident, or not, you must be the guardian of the secret in my absence. Remember that. The West risks obliteration if word leaks of Elke's criticality to our survival.'

Sir Roger Holbrook was a wily old bird, not unlike Mrs Ruby, the venerable Mossad officer who a year earlier had overseen Kristiina Ahnger's seduction of Daniel Lincoln. Not once did he mention to Peter Parnell-Brown the strategic advantage Elke Über's assessment of Konrad Voite would gift the British over the Americans. Herein lay the DG's private reason for creating operation Spot, something so revered that he sheltered it from all minds bar his own: his quest to reverse the trans-Atlantic power dynamic.

CHAPTER 10

On the night of Tuesday 28 May 1963 Daniel Lincoln drove from his apartment in McLean, Virginia to Kristiina Ahnger's residence on Van Ness Street in Washington DC. He carried in the inside pocket of his suit jacket the CIA report revealing the secret US negotiating position on the Israeli nuclear reactor at Dimona. Daniel had been wrestling with how best to inform Kristiina of its contents, but after weighing alternatives finally elected to stick to his original plan. He would allow Kristiina to read the document so as to be confident of its authenticity. After which he would invite her to note down its main point, namely that the US would be prepared to cease demands to inspect the Dimona reactor provided the Nazi rocket scientist Heinrich Keller was quietly handed over, in order to be put to work on President Kennedy's program to put a man on the moon.

Parking around Kristiina's apartment was the usual nightmare. As such, Daniel was obliged to walk some distance from where he left his car until he reached her building. Along the way, he had a brief moment of doubt. The thought that Kristiina's World Bank superiors would want to know the source of her information began to niggle at him.

Daniel considered possible options. Perhaps Kristiina could say a senior American contact she promised not to name had told her there were soon to be US–Israel talks to address the

Dimona inspection impasse? And the more Daniel thought about this approach, the more he liked it. Dimona was vital to the Israelis; their negotiators would be resolute. Faced with this determination, and the pressure to get to the moon before the Soviets, chances were the US delegation would resort to its bottom line. Yet that alone would not remove doubts about the reactor's use. The Israelis, Daniel came to see, could accept the American offer only subject to the US publicly expressing confidence that the reactor was solely for peaceful purposes.

Now Daniel was excited. This meant Kristiina could recommend delaying a decision on the Egyptian loan until it was clear what, if anything, the Tel Aviv meeting revealed. And when a communiqué was issued at the conclusion of the talks, her counsel would be seen as tactically brilliant. Buoyed, Daniel took the elevator up to Kristiina's apartment ready to coach her on the stance she should take.

'What's the matter, darling?' Daniel was confused. He had expected Kristiina to shower him with affection on answering the door. But instead she stood awkwardly on the threshold as if debating whether to let him in, a distant look in her eyes.

'Sorry,' Kristiina said, her back to Daniel as she walked down the apartment's short hallway. 'I've had a difficult day, everyone shouting and arguing. I've got a terrible headache.' She took a seat in an armchair and with a weary sweep of her hand gestured for Daniel to sit on the sofa.

Daniel did as bid, removing the CIA report from his jacket in the one motion. He smiled at Kristiina. 'This might cheer you up,' he said with a wink, holding up the document.

'What is it?' Kristiina asked with a distinct lack of enthusiasm.

Daniel was miffed at Kristiina's lukewarm response. 'I would get into a lot of trouble if my embassy knew I had removed this from the office,' he said sternly. 'I've only done it for you.'

Kristiina smiled but the effort involved in creasing her face was all too obvious. 'Can I see it, please?' she said.

Daniel hesitated. Kristiina's strange behaviour had made him unsure if letting her read the report was now the right way to go. The thought made his nerves tingle. 'It's Top Secret – UK/US Eyes Only,' he said. 'It might be best if I just told you the salient point.'

'The salient point?' Kristiina echoed in an unsteady whisper.

Daniel was taken aback. The slur in Kristiina's voice made him wonder if she was drugged. 'Have you taken medicine for your headache or something?' he queried, fervently hoping that Kristiina would give him the answer he wanted to hear. Meanwhile the alarm bells in his head began to jangle, louder by the second.

Kristiina stared at Daniel before suddenly starting to cry, tears flooding her face. 'They gave me a sedative,' she sobbed. 'Daniel, I'm so, so sorry. It had to be done. Duty. I didn't want to hurt you.'

For a moment Daniel was too stunned to think. Then the penny dropped. 'Oh Jesus,' he moaned as reality swept over him, much like the fog that would roll in to envelop his beloved West Yorkshire moors. Daniel had no idea who was responsible for the sting; all he knew was he had to get out of the apartment, and now.

But no sooner had Daniel stuffed the report back in his suit coat and started for the exit than Kristiina's bedroom door opened. Two large men dressed in black descended on him at speed, sticking a cloth in his mouth, a blindfold over his eyes and forcing him back down on the sofa whereupon his assailants sat on either side gripping his arms. Next, Daniel felt a hand inside his jacket and a female voice speaking in a language he didn't understand that in fact was Hebrew. The voice spoke twice.

Once in an authoritative manner as if issuing instructions and once in a soothing lilt that resulted in the fading of Kristiina's crying.

Ten minutes of silence ensued broken only by the sound of paper rustling as someone read the report. Thereafter, Daniel heard repeated clicking noises followed by a terse utterance that led to the removal of his gag and eye mask. Daniel blinked to find a small woman of advanced years standing before him. She wore a black cardigan over a white blouse. Behind her, Kristiina was curled up in a foetal position in her armchair.

'Mr Lincoln,' the older woman said, holding out the CIA report, inviting him to take it back, 'thank you for providing this very valuable document. I have now photographed it and you may return it to wherever you found it, as I expect was your intention.'

'Who are you?' Daniel whispered.

The older woman opened her mouth only for a voice behind her to speak before she could. 'She's Mossad. They're Israeli spies.' It was Kristiina.

Mrs Ruby snorted in annoyance and snapped at one of the men beside Daniel. 'I got in over my head, Daniel,' Kristiina screeched before the man could scramble to her side. 'It was something bigger than both of us. I had duty to do. Please believe that.' The bedroom door slammed and Daniel never saw Kristiina Ahnger again.

***

The snow fell relentlessly in New York City on the first day of December 1964. NYPD officers Patrick Doherty and Lucy Rodriguez were sensibly indoors, considering next steps. Only the day before they had attended the British Consulate on Fifth Avenue and provided it with a set of fingerprints belonging to the man who jumped off the roof of the building at 388 Vesey Street in the Financial District. Both officers agreed that pending positive identification they should concentrate on the German newspaper clipping mailed from West Berlin and the framed photograph of the pretty blond woman seemingly in her early thirties, both of which had been found in the bottom of a drawer in Frank Middlemiss's spartan apartment.

The newspaper clipping, according to an officer in the first precinct who spoke German, was East German. It consisted of a short article dominated by a large photograph. 'It's a report,' the German-speaking officer said, 'of a marriage on 3 October this year between a man called Josef Sterck and a woman called Elke Über. Seems he's a communist party elder and she's a party official. The last sentence says they're soon to move to Guben where this Sterck guy is to open a branch of the Ministry of Cultural Harmony.' The officer laughed. 'Guben's in the boondocks on the border with Poland,' he said. 'Ain't an awful lot out there so far as I know.'

Doherty and Lucy looked at one another. Middlemiss's passport showed he had entered East Berlin on 26 August but departed on 6 September, well before the wedding. After which he made his way to Mexico City arriving on 7 September before continuing on to New York the same day. Clearly there had been an unrecorded stop somewhere between East Berlin and Mexico City on the night of 6 September. But that could wait for now while they examined the framed photograph of the young woman.

Lucy probed at the picture frame with a nail file. Soon the hard cardboard backing had been removed. She extracted the image taking care not to crease it. The inside of the frame gave no hint as to its place of purchase. Turning to the image, the pretty blond girl was backdropped by a wide expanse of fresh water, presumably a river. But the shot's angle was too narrow to identify where. Daniel Lincoln in fact had taken it at Harpers Ferry in West Virginia, at the point of confluence of the Potomac and Shenandoah rivers. Its subject, of course, was his Finnish lover Kristiina Ahnger. Daniel and Kristiina had visited there one weekend in April 1963, just over a month before Daniel discovered she was a Mossad agent.

'Looks like somewhere scenic,' Lucy said. 'Possibly a tourist place.' She turned over the image to inspect its plain back. Suddenly Lucy stiffened. 'There's something here,' she exclaimed, 'a stamp in the bottom left corner. Hand me that magnifying glass.' Lucy squinted at the small blue marking. 'It says: Abells dispensary, McLean VA. There's also a four-digit number. From what I can make out it's six, three dash eight, seven.'

'Right,' Doherty said, picking up the telephone and dialling zero. 'Meredith,' he said to the station switchboard operator, 'can you connect me to Abells dispensary in McLean, Virginia? Yes, I'll wait. Thank you.' He passed the handset to Lucy. 'You're more patient than me,' he said with a smile.

In 1963 photographs had to be developed, most conveniently at drug stores. It transpires that Daniel had dropped his roll of film into a drug store close to his McLean apartment on the Saturday following his and Kristiina's visit to Harpers Ferry. The shop in question had the habit of imprinting a business code on the back of each photograph in every batch developed.

The telephone call came through. A firm male voice filled the earpiece. 'This is the store manager speaking,' the man said crisply. 'How may I be of assistance?'

'Good day, sir,' Lucy said. 'I am officer Lucy Rodriguez from the NYPD first precinct in New York City. We have recently come into possession of a photograph that your store appears to have developed.'

'Yes?' the manager said, less formal now.

'We are particularly interested in the four-digit code stamped on the back of the picture,' Lucy said, 'six, three dash eight, seven. Can you tell me the purpose of the code?'

'It's a customer reference number,' the man replied. 'The six, three digits indicate the image was developed in 1963.' He paused and Lucy could sense his hesitancy. 'But I'm not sure I can give you the details on the eight, seven part because that will identify the customer.' The man paused again. 'I'd need the customer's say-so to do that.'

Lucy took a deep breath, prompting Doherty to wink at her. 'Sir,' Lucy said, 'I wouldn't be bothering you unless the matter was urgent. If you want reassurance you're quite welcome to ring the station here at Ericsson Place in the City and ask for me. Alternatively, I could have McLean district officers come to your store.' She let her voice trail off.

The store manager exhaled. He didn't want to be making expensive long distance telephone calls and nor did he need police officers trampling through his shop and scaring off customers. 'Let me see what I can find out,' he said.

Doherty and Lucy waited patiently while the manager set about searching for paperwork. 'The film from which the photograph was developed,' the store boss said when back on the line, reading from his records, 'was lodged by a Daniel Lincoln, 1601 Anderson Road, McLean, apartment 26307.' The man's voice brightened. 'I remember Mr Lincoln, actually,' he said. 'He was English, a diplomat attached to the British embassy in DC. His term finished last year I recall and he went home. We haven't seen him since.'

Lucy scribbled down the details as the man spoke. Then, as much for Doherty's benefit as anything, she read them back to the manager, hanging up once she had his confirmation.

Silence ensued as Lucy and Doherty absorbed the information gleaned. Doherty spoke first. 'It's possible,' he said slowly, defying his gut instinct, 'that this Daniel Lincoln diplomat guy gave the photograph to his countryman, Frank Middlemiss.'

Lucy read his mind. 'But it's also possible the British are playing games and that Daniel Lincoln and Frank Middlemiss are the one and the same person.'

Doherty smiled. 'That's what my quarterback's knee is telling me,' he said wryly. 'And don't forget this East German newspaper article that appears to have driven Frank Middlemiss to suicide.'

'So, what now?' Lucy asked.

'I think we wait,' Doherty said, 'and see if the British Consulate can provide positive identification.' He grimaced. 'I'm betting this matter needs federal attention. But before we go off half-cocked and elevate it to Division, let's wait for the British.'

***

And that's how it began. When the British Consul General, the consulate's ranking diplomat no less, rang just before Christmas 1964 to advise in convoluted diplomatic mumbo jumbo that he was in receipt of no evidence to indicate the Vesey Street jumper *wasn't* Frank Middlemiss, Patrick Doherty knew he had hit on something. The United States, of course, less avidly celebrates Christmas than the United Kingdom. So, when Doherty elevated the matter to Division later that day, it did not languish on a desk for days on end waiting for people to return from holidays.

Soon the US State Department, counterpart to the British Foreign Office, was in the loop. Yes, a British diplomat called Daniel Hubble Lincoln had served in Washington from July 1960 to July1963. But in view of the advice coming out of the NYPD – to the effect there was a possibility of Frank Middlemiss and Daniel Lincoln being the same person – State had the good sense to consult the CIA before rushing off to query the Foreign Office.

CHAPTER 11

At 2 pm on Tuesday 28 April 1964, a woman from the office of the MI6 Deputy Director General came to Daniel Lincoln's desk in MI6's East German section. Her arrival surprised Daniel because it was rare for the Deputy's staff to come to an operational area when a telephone call would usually suffice. 'Could you come with me, please,' the woman said politely but with sufficient firmness to tell Daniel this was an instruction and not a request.

Only an hour earlier Daniel had returned to his work unit on the third floor of Century House on Westminster Bridge Road in London. He was feeling as positive as he was likely to be for the day. His thirty-minute run along the Thames, followed by a refreshing shower and a healthy lunch had temporarily pacified his illness. Now, however, the woman's authoritative summons had alarmed him and caused his anxiety to flare.

'Is there something wrong?' he said, immediately cursing himself for asking the question when he should have acted unconcerned. But thoughts of Kristiina and his appalling treatment of Ray Solter were never far from Daniel's mind. He lived in constant fear of being called to account and of the summary dismissal and prison time that would follow.

The woman did not answer immediately. Rather she set off at pace, Daniel hastening behind her. Only on reaching the elevator did she respond. 'Mr Parnell-Brown wants to see you,' she said stiffly. 'That's all I know.'

***

'Young Daniel,' Peter Parnell-Brown said, giving Daniel the fatherly treatment. 'Come in and take a pew.'

Daniel could scarcely believe his luck. The Deputy wouldn't be treating him like a long lost son if something serious were afoot, like treason for example. Daniel smiled, less anxious now, and took up occupancy in one of Parnell-Brown's visitor chairs.

'So you've been back, what nine months now?' Parnell-Brown said. 'You were well settled in by the time I left. How did you find the rest of the posting?'

Daniel's good feeling evaporated. Parnell-Brown was right to say nine months had elapsed since his return from Washington. But that was the problem. Senior people like the Deputy did not summon juniors just to chat about posting experiences – something was in the air. 'It was excellent,' Daniel said, giving the pat answer. 'The whole US experience was amazing.'

'Yes,' Parnell-Brown said, still radiating warmth. 'Shame about that unfortunate matter with Ray Solter shortly before you came home,' he added with a shake of his head. 'But that's water under the bridge.'

Daniel understood that Parnell-Brown's mention of his Washington supervisor was benign. Nonetheless it caused his stomach to churn, primarily because it took him back to Wednesday 29 May 1963, the day after he learned that Kristiina Ahnger was a Mossad plant, a trap he'd fallen into like a lovesick fool.

***

Kristiina's handler Mrs Ruby, of course, had allowed Daniel to leave Kristiina's apartment after photographing the *Top Secret* CIA report he carried on him. This reflected Mossad's calculation that Daniel would return the illegally removed document without others in the MI6 station knowing, in which case the US delegation soon to embark on talks in Tel Aviv would be none the wiser.

Mossad's judgement was sound. But it was a closer run thing than the Israelis realised. Daniel did eventually decide to restore the report to its rightful place before the MI6 courier arrived later in the day to pack it in the diplomatic bag bound for London. He did, though, only after wrestling endlessly with his conscience. Indeed, the sun was well up before Daniel reached his swaying conclusion, that he must return the report to spare his father the humiliation of his criminal stupidity.

On Wednesday morning Daniel arrived for work at the usual starting time. Well beforehand he had tried to tell himself he could deal with a sleepless night. But in his heart Daniel knew he was in no shape to go in and put the report back in its secure cabinet before station others got there. An early start would entail an explanation of his out of the ordinary behaviour to the on duty station security guard, and with this Daniel could not cope. So instead he wore a smart suit, hoping this would replenish the confidence eroded by the torment of Kristiina's distress and thoughts of his ruinous gullibility.

Daniel hung his jacket containing the CIA report in his office, after which he went to the vault to collect his in-tray where security regulations dictated it be stored for the night. Daniel was anxious to return the CIA document as soon as possible, to have the issue behind him. But first he had to wait until all in the MI6 complement had retrieved their trays from the vault.

Lingering in his office, itching to pounce and barely able to sit still, Daniel suddenly heard a distinctive male voice that caused his blood to run cold. His head nearly exploded as his pulse pounded and sweat flooded his armpits. Daniel in fact was experiencing for the first time the mental illness incubated overnight by his trauma and its assault on his fight or flight protective responses. Indeed, so strange and unprecedented was the sensation that he briefly wondered if he was having a heart attack. But he was not – to Daniel's mortification he had just heard the voice of the MI6 courier.

The courier had arrived from London the night before with a consignment of inward bags he subsequently transported into the MI6 station and lodged in the vault. His usual practice was to have the morning off to compensate for his late night finish. Around lunchtime the courier would come into the MI6 station to collate and pack the papers he was to take back to London the next morning.

'Yeah,' the courier said from the station's common area. 'I've been invited to lunch at the naval college at Annapolis. I'll pack the bags this morning so I can get over to Maryland by noon.'

Daniel moaned inwardly. The courier, he remembered, was a former Royal Navy petty officer.

'No problem,' Ray Solter's voice answered. 'By now the others should have what they need from the vault. I'll get my stuff right away, then it's all yours.'

'I'll come down with you and get started,' the courier said. And with those few innocent words the ex-RN man effectively destroyed Ray Solter's life. That is, the courier had just denied Solter the chance to later point out that, were he in possession of the missing document, he would have returned it while alone in the vault.

By now Daniel was frozen rigid with fear. Once the courier had opened the vault's internal safes, it was off-limits to station staff until his diplomatic bags were sealed. Even more concerning was the fact that he would count the number of CIA reports to be taken to MI6 headquarters, to ensure the total corresponded with the log recording each document as it came in from Langley.

In that instant it permeated Daniel's nervous fug that, right now, Solter would be in the vault collecting his papers. Shaking violently, he placed the CIA report inside a manila folder. Locking his door, as security practice required, Daniel strode down the short corridor to Solter's office feeling like he was dreaming.

As deputy station head, Solter enjoyed a greater degree of privacy than the lower ranks. But on reaching the office Daniel's heart sank. The door was closed, seemingly locked. He had been clinging to the hope of Solter leaving his door ajar in his haste to greet a fellow ex-serviceman also working in a sea of civilians. Nearly turning heel as his stimulus disintegrated, Daniel was saved by his desperation forcing him to test the door handle.

Solter, it transpires, had done exactly as Daniel's frazzled instincts speculated. He had closed but not locked his office door upon hearing the courier arrive and, when diverted, dashed straight to the vault. Heart pounding, Daniel stepped into the office, closing the door behind him. He had just seconds at his disposal. Looking wildly about, his eyes fixed on the rectangular leather mat on Solter's desk inserted in which was a sheet of blotting paper. MI6 security rules stipulated a clear-desk policy. And by clear, it meant clear. At night, therefore, Solter stored the leather mat in a cupboard.

But Solter was also a creature of habit. Each morning, after collecting the keys to his office from the security guard, he would take the blotter from the cupboard and place it on his desk. There followed a trip to the vault to pick up his work papers. It was a routine born of years of military service and one for which Daniel now thanked his lucky stars. In the blink of an eye, the CIA report was out of the manila folder and slipped under the blotting pad. Then Daniel fled, first to the toilet where he hid in a stall until his legs stopped shaking, after which he washed his face and returned to his office. Thirty minutes later all hell broke loose.

'There's a CIA TS missing, folks,' the MI6 courier bellowed from the station floor. 'I'm declaring a Code Blue.' TS was an abbreviation of the *Top Secret* security classification and a Code Blue was the authority invested in the courier to direct all station staff to lock their offices and wait in the common area until the missing document was located. After which, the courier briefed the station head before beginning to search individual offices.

Ray Solter, of course, expressed complete bewilderment when the missing CIA report was found under his blotting pad. But to use the station head's mashed metaphor, when the music stopped Solter was left holding the baby. Nor did the station head much enjoy his obligation to report the security breach to the MI6 Deputy Director General, who just happened to be his predecessor and professional rival, Peter Parnell-Brown. With that, Solter was thrown under the bus. Yes, the station head told the security mandarins charged with investigating, Solter deserved to be recognised for his war service. But his best days were behind him and, frankly, the fact that he drank too much made him something of a liability, as evidenced by his admission not to have locked his office door while collecting items from the vault.

So Ray Solter was crucified. The popular theory was the Soviets had set a trap into which the bibulous Solter stumbled only to be caught out by the courier's early arrival preventing him from returning the CIA report recently shared with his handler. But in the face of Solter's vigorous denials and the absence of evidence no charges could be preferred. And informing the CIA of a possible leak without proof would unleash so many hares as to place the prospect beyond contemplation. A solution was hatched, one that culminated in Solter being quietly marched out the door, with no pension, no nothing bar the bitter knowledge he had been done over.

***

The fire lit by Daniel Lincoln in framing Ray Solter had many unforeseen consequences, not least that it ultimately came to play a central part in Daniel's death. But the chain reaction Daniel triggered did cast one bright light on an otherwise bleak landscape in that some eighteen months later it led to the rapprochement.

The CIA's Michael Anjelico, of course, was too senior to attend routine meetings with State Department officials. But beneath a brash exterior he had a keen mind. On learning on the first working day of 1965 that State wanted to discuss an odd affair in New York that might or might not involve a British diplomat called Daniel Lincoln, Anjelico was prompted to check. And when he found that Daniel Lincoln was an MI6 officer, he was energised.

At no point did Anjelico suspect a link between Daniel Lincoln and operation Leopard. Rather, his ever so ironic aim was to put Peter Parnell-Brown on the spot, to hit back at the MI6 Deputy's choice words late the previous August when they last spoke. To that end, Anjelico knew there had to be history to an MI6 officer apparently jumping to his death under an assumed name. So he went on a fishing expedition. Funny how it works because, from the chill aftermath of operation Leopard, Anjelico's initiative would produce a long overdue truce between the intelligence services – an armistice that came to be known as the rapprochement.

The head of the MI6 station was called in on Tuesday 5 January 1965 – the station chief's first day back from Christmas vacation. At Anjelico's behest, a CIA officer floated some nonsense about the Mayor's office in Washington DC complaining of unpaid parking tickets issued to a diplomatic vehicle then registered to Daniel Lincoln. 'We thought it best,' the CIA man said, 'to raise this on the quiet as Lincoln is one of yours and was possibly out working when the tickets were written.' The CIA officer smiled. 'State's getting a lot of heat from the Mayor who needs every penny he can lay his hands on.'

The station head was flummoxed and a little annoyed to be bothered with an essentially run-of-the-mill administrative issue. 'Can't you just get State to turn off the Mayor?' he said tersely.

The CIA officer feigned indignation. 'Yeah, sure,' he said sarcastically. 'The Mayor would be thrilled to bits with that idea. The British lining up with the Soviets not to pay their parking fines.'

Soviet diplomats reputedly owed the District of Columbia millions of dollars for parking infringements, which they dodged by claiming diplomatic immunity. The station head sighed in exasperation. 'How much is it?' he said.

'Five dollars,' the CIA man replied straight-faced.

The message finally permeated. Later that day in London Peter Parnell-Brown came to Sir Roger Holbrook. Sir Roger was due to finish at the end of the month. 'The CIA has a scent, I'm afraid,' Parnell-Brown said. 'They just called in Justin on the pretext of Daniel Lincoln owing five dollars in parking fines.'

The DG suddenly looked frail. 'The CIA may still not know of operation Spot,' he mused, 'but it's suspicious enough of Daniel Lincoln to shake the tree.' Sir Roger slumped wearily in his chair. 'Contact Anjelico, Peter, and sue for peace. It's time to come clean.'

CHAPTER 12

March 1943 and Ronald Hunt was in Malta, and in uniform as was the norm for NAAFI personnel posted abroad. His wife Janice, prepared to do anything to see him gone from her flat, of course, had arranged his transfer. By now Ronald was free of the flashbacks reminding him he had murdered their infant daughter. Indeed, he was quite pleased to have gotten away with a crime of that magnitude and now keenly on the lookout for opportunities to make money.

A month went by and Ronald had already dabbled in two affairs aided by his ready prattle and excess testosterone. On the money side of things, life was not as productive. Ronald's vision was too grand to bother with petty theft, and in any event there was little scope for pinching the odd packet of fags or slipping his hand into the cash drawer. NAAFI regulations obliged its outlets to operate locked till systems. This meant monies taken were kept under lock and key until the end of each trading day when receipts were reconciled against stock listed as sold.

Ronald worked at the main NAAFI warehouse at the Barriera Wharf in Malta's capital, Valletta. His focus initially was on alcohol and cigarettes as these were the items most in demand by service personnel. But the NAAFI principals were not silly and, much to Ronald's frustration, special care was taken to safeguard these stocks. Fed up, he was beginning to think about asking for a shift to a new NAAFI job when an article in the *Times of*

Malta caught his eye. The puff piece was intended to be a morale booster, its theme being how the devastating food shortages of the siege years of 1941 and 1942 were now a thing of the past. But the article did mention that some minor rationing would be continued, including of household commodities such as toothpaste.

Ronald's fertile criminal mind sprang into action. He knew there would be Maltese people willing to collaborate. After all, the Maltese black market had boomed during the siege years. And unlike alcohol and cigarettes, toothpaste stores were not as closely guarded. Ronald set about examining the NAAFI warehouse security procedures. The building was locked at night and a small team of Maltese working under the supervision of a NAAFI security officer patrolled the complex. Ronald's plan firmed up. Once he found a suitable accomplice to on-sell the stolen goods, he would either bribe or coerce one of the Maltese security staff to look the other way while pallets of toothpaste were loaded onto a truck, at a time when the NAAFI supervisor was taking his tea break.

The MI6 station in Malta at the time was small, consisting of a head of station and one support operative. In recent years, the station had busied itself trying to insert agents into German-occupied North Africa, with mostly disastrous results it must be said. In January 1943, a new support operative arrived. He was a twenty-seven-year-old Oxford graduate fresh out of MI6 training school called Peter Parnell-Brown. The focus of the MI6 office was no longer south to North Africa but north to Sicily where an Allied invasion was planned to take place later in the year.

The ambition of the MI6 pair in Malta was to smuggle saboteurs into the area around Pozzallo on Sicily's southern coast. Pozzallo was less than 150 kilometres from Malta, close enough for an unlit vessel sailing at night to deposit infiltrators and return home before dawn. But such a vessel would need to be piloted by someone familiar with the southern Sicilian landscape and the stretch of Mediterranean between it and Malta. Otherwise boats risked becoming lost and still at sea when daylight came. This, indirectly, was how Peter Parnell-Brown came to recruit Ronald Hunt.

It was all to do with a Maltese man called Charlie Borg. Borg was an out and out crook. Before the war, while still a teenager, he had been involved in smuggling Italian goods into Malta. Later during the siege years he moved seamlessly into black marketeering where he avoided sanction for his illegal activities through a combination of cunning and ruthlessness. He was the sort of person the MI6 station was seeking, a resourceful criminal who knew Malta and its surrounding ocean like the back of his hand.

In February 1943 Parnell-Brown made his initial trawl of Valletta's waterfront bars, a practice he kept up for the next three weeks. But Oxford graduates did not blend in easily in the seedy environment and Parnell-Brown's enquiries were generally met with suspicious silence. Ronald Hunt, in contrast, was right at home on the Maltese fringe when three months later he followed in Parnell-Brown's footsteps – looking for the same type of person but for a vastly different reason. Always happy to share a drink or offer a cigarette, Ronald spoke the language of graft. And when he confided to a third party that he was in the market for a spot of business, it led him to Charlie Borg.

By late May 1943 there was tension in the MI6 office in Malta. The station's several efforts to land saboteurs in Sicily had amounted to nothing. Now a sniffy telegram had arrived from London headquarters conveying disappointment at the lack of progress. The cable exhorted the station to try again, this time to find the means for inserting a pathfinder into Sicily, a British soldier equipped with a radio with which to guide the Allied forces imminently to invade the island. Parnell-Brown and his boss conferred. The station head would consult the military command on its choice of serviceman to be the pathfinder, while Parnell-Brown was again to venture to the Valletta seafront with the aim of finding a suitable transport contractor.

***

Ronald Hunt and Charlie Borg were drinking in the Ionian Inn when Peter Parnell-Brown entered the bar. Ronald and Borg were well advanced in their planning to steal two pallets of toothpaste, some 2,000 tubes, from the NAAFI warehouse at the Barriera Wharf. Borg knew virtually every Maltese in Valletta and had identified one of the warehouse security staff to bribe. Now only the split of the proceeds had to be agreed.

The Ionian Inn was a small establishment and the entry of the tall man dressed in casual trousers and a roll neck sweater caused the patrons to turn their heads. Borg summoned an underling and a whispered conversation in Maltese ensued.

'Another Englishman,' Borg said, looking suspiciously at Ronald. 'He was around here three months ago also claiming he had business to discuss. Now he's back.'

Ronald was nonplussed and anxious to assure Borg he knew nothing about the man. 'Never seen him in my life,' he said. 'On my mother's grave,' he added cynically.

The two Englishmen briefly locked eyes across the small room. Ronald was also in civilian attire, but this did not disguise that he was not Maltese. Both simultaneously averted their gaze.

'Find out who he is,' Borg directed.

'Me?' Ronald queried in alarm. 'What if he's a military copper in mufti?'

'Do it.'

Ronald knew he had no choice. He wouldn't put it past Borg to cut his throat if the Maltese thought he was being double-crossed. Ronald stood awkwardly, wondering if he should pretend to be an American before realising he could not sustain the accent.

'Rare to see anybody but locals in this watering hole,' Ronald said, sidling up to Parnell-Brown. 'Bob Johnson,' he added unconvincingly, extending his hand. 'Airframe fitter, number 126 Squadron. Spitfires.' Ronald had learned to speak the airman's jargon while working in the NAAFI canteen at RAF Kenley in London.

'Harry Cramer,' Parnell-Brown replied with a spy's smoothness, smiling but not with his eyes. 'Dental technician attached to Army Command, Malta.'

'Can I get you a drink?' Ronald said for want of something better to say.

'Let me buy you one,' Parnell-Brown replied holding his nearly full glass aloft. 'I'm still working on this one.'

The two men stared at one another each unsure what to say. And when Parnell-Brown did think of a topic, he tried to speak just as Ronald did the same. An effusion of *No, no after you* and *No, no please you go ahead* was followed by more uncomfortable silence. It was eventually too much for Ronald.

'Mate, what the fucking hell are you doing here?' he snapped once his patience had failed him. 'You're making the locals nervous.'

'And you're not?' Parnell-Brown retorted. He had taken an instant dislike to his shifty, prematurely bald countryman.

'Listen, I got mates here. But you're some sort of dental something, or so you say. You stick out like a set of dog's balls.'

The men again stared at one another, but with all semblance of politeness now gone. Charlie Borg joining them broke the impasse. 'What's going on?' Borg asked, his voice a threatening low growl.

Parnell-Brown by this time had reached the all too obvious conclusion that Ronald – or Bob Johnson, as he knew him – was up to no good with the powerful Maltese. He decided to pitch there and then, before matters deteriorated further. 'I need someone to run an errand for me,' Parnell-Brown said. 'On the QT.'

'What kind of errand?' Borg asked.

'Is there somewhere where we can speak privately?' Parnell-Brown said, his instincts telling him that in Borg he was on to something.

Borg glanced at Ronald. 'Come with me,' the Maltese said, setting off immediately through a side door leading to a deserted alleyway.

'OK, shoot,' Borg said once the three were standing in the darkened back half of the lane.

Parnell-Brown took a deep breath. 'I have a need to drop someone on-shore near Pozzallo.'

'Where the fuck's that?' Ronald squawked.

Parnell-Brown continued as if Ronald had not spoken. 'And I need someone reliable to take him there. Someone with a boat who knows the waters and can get up to Sicily and back in the dark.'

Borg had summed it up faster and far better than Ronald. 'So, you're some sort of spy?' he said, beading Parnell-Brown.

'I work for the British government, that's all I'm able to say.'

'Don't listen to him,' Ronald interjected. 'He's a copper who wants to know our plans.'

Years later Parnell-Brown would reflect on that moment when Charlie Borg made the decision to believe him. He had been lucky, Parnell-Brown decided. He could have quite easily ended up dead.

'How much?' Borg said.

'One thousand American,' Parnell-Brown replied. 'Two hundred down and eight hundred on successful completion.'

'Fifteen hundred American,' Borg countered. 'A thousand down, five hundred on completion. And you don't deal with me but through my friend here,' Borg added, gesturing at Ronald. He laughed coarsely. 'Two English homosexuals sucking each other's cocks. Business as usual, nobody would suspect a thing.'

Parnell-Brown hesitated. He would have preferred to consult the station head on Borg's counter-offer; money did not grow on trees. But Parnell-Brown also judged that the Maltese was the man he was seeking and didn't want to lose him. 'Both aspects should be manageable,' he said evenly. He would worry later about convincing his boss of the merits of Borg's proposal.

It was the first of many sound judgements Peter Parnell-Brown would make over the whiles following, an early sign of the enduring quality that twenty-one years later convinced the MI6 Director General Sir Roger Holbrook to make him the MI6 lead on operation Leopard. It was also why Sir Roger bestowed the ultimate accolade on Parnell-Brown, by making him privy to Leopard's secret add-on – the DG's operation Spot.

CHAPTER 13

Daniel Lincoln suppressed a shudder. It was 28 April 1964 and he had just relived the shame of Ray Solter, prompted by Peter Parnell-Brown's conversational mention of his former Washington supervisor. To be sure Parnell-Brown was engaging in nothing more than banter as a preliminary to explaining why he had called Daniel to his office. But not quite a year on from the incident and Daniel was still tormented by it. Solter had certainly been no friend of his. But Daniel's farmer father had taught him never to lower himself to the level of those with less than exemplary standards. And now all Daniel could do was think of his father's emphasis on principle and integrity and how it would break his heart were he to learn his only son had cravenly disregarded the values instilled in him in boyhood.

'…East Berlin?' It was the only part of Peter Parnell-Brown's question that Daniel had heard.

Daniel willed himself to concentrate. 'East Berlin?' he echoed with a croak.

'Yes,' Parnell-Brown replied, frowning slightly at Daniel's inattention before letting it go. 'Just for two days and a bit. You know your way around Berlin, the Weidendammer Bridge and down to Friedrichstrasse station, that sort of thing.'

'Oh, yes,' Daniel said. He felt less buried now the discussion had moved to safer ground, to after the war and his many visits to Berlin on behalf of the British High Commissioner for Germany. 'I spent a lot of time in that part of the city.'

'Good, good,' Parnell-Brown said. 'But clearly you can't go over East as an MI6 officer,' he added jovially. 'They'll think you've been sent to poison the water supply.'

Daniel tittered politely at the Deputy's joke. 'So, who am I to go as?' he asked.

Parnell-Brown was suddenly all business, as if he'd tired of the good fellowship. He leant forward to speak. 'We want you to go to East Berlin as a postman,' he said softly, not directly answering Daniel's question. 'There's an important letter we want you to deliver, shortly after you set the signal for its intended recipient.'

With that, the Deputy removed a form from a drawer in his desk. It was a legal document indoctrinating Daniel into operation Spot. 'Read and sign this,' Parnell-Brown instructed Daniel. 'Then we'll get down to brass tacks.'

Parnell-Brown watched Daniel as he read, reflecting on the time they spent together in Washington, when Parnell-Brown was the MI6 head of station and Daniel the office junior. During this time Parnell-Brown had become aware Daniel knew Berlin and spoke fluent German. But it was also pre-Kristiina Ahnger and the Deputy could not know his memory of Daniel was outdated, that Daniel was no longer a rock-solid young man ideally suited to deliver the DG's letter to Elke Über.

For all that, Parnell-Brown was no fool and a supremely skilled intelligence officer generally able to read people. Daniel, though, hid his current-day affliction with an addict's skill, petrified of his father coming to know of his catastrophic failing and suffering all that went with it. So far as Peter Parnell-Brown was concerned, he was offering the young MI6 officer sitting opposite an exciting opportunity to win his spying spurs, to exercise his excellent language skills and couple this with advantageous geographic knowledge. Parnell-Brown smiled inwardly, thinking of his own experiences as a young officer.

The thought took him back to 1943 in Malta at a time when, like Daniel, he was about to be thrust into the heart of a secret operation.

***

The three men stood in the half-light of the laneway outside the Ionian Inn in Valletta. Charlie Borg, the Maltese criminal roughneck, spoke first. 'So, when am I supposed to take this night trip to Sicily and back?' He was referring to Peter Parnell-Brown's undeclared plan to insert a pathfinder into Sicily in aid of the planned Allied invasion later in 1943.

'I'll give you forty-eight hours warning,' Parnell-Brown replied. 'Or at least tell him,' he added, mindful of Borg's wish to avoid suspicious face-to-face meetings and jerking a thumb in Ronald Hunt's direction, 'so he can tell you. You'll have one other with you, someone to be landed near Pozzallo.'

Ronald made a scoffing sound. He would have liked to be more emphatic but feared Borg might take it the wrong way. 'I don't like this, Charlie,' he said, 'not one little bit. This character, whoever he is, has admitted he works for the British government.' Ronald looked pleadingly at Borg. 'Can't we just stick to our plans and not complicate things?'

Charlie Borg rubbed his chin, the action briefly raising Ronald's hope he was reconsidering. But, as ever, Charlie was a step ahead of the game. He looked at Parnell-Brown. 'There's one other condition,' he said quietly.

'What's that?' Parnell-Brown enquired calmly, disguising the fact that his nerves were tingling.

'My *friend* and I,' Borg said, his emphasis on the word unsettling Ronald, 'have a little business we are shortly to conduct. It would be helpful, Mr British government man, if you could ensure it went smoothly.'

Parnell-Brown realised he was at another crossroads, that Borg was talking about a substantial criminal undertaking. This was tricky, but yet again not something on which he could go away and consult. Borg was the sort of man who liked immediate answers.

'Depends on what it is,' Parnell-Brown replied, seeking to gain an insight into the planned enterprise. 'I mean if you're wanting to murder someone, I'm not your man. Ditto in spades if what you're concocting is going to impede our war effort.'

'Toothpaste,' Borg said, rather too candidly for Ronald's liking.

'What?' Parnell-Brown said, genuinely stumped.

'We're going to pinch 2,000 tubes of toothpaste from the NAAFI warehouse and sell them on the black market,' Borg explained, his frankness adding to Ronald's consternation.

'That's an awful lot of toothpaste,' Parnell-Brown replied, dissembling to buy himself time to think.

'It's not really that much,' Ronald broke in, misreading Parnell-Brown and thinking his remark amounted to concern over the size of the intended theft. 'Only a couple of pallets.'

'I want you to arrange for us to have a free run at the merchandise and for there to be no investigation afterwards,' Borg said, ignoring Ronald.

Peter Parnell-Brown did a quick mental calculation. A pathfinder agent in Pozzallo stood to significantly reduce the number of casualties when the Allies landed on Sicily. And this at a cost to NAAFI of a couple of thousand tubes of toothpaste? *No contest*, he thought.

'All right,' he said soberly. 'Count me in.' Then without warning, Parnell-Brown shot out an arm and grabbed Borg by the throat. 'If you so much as think about fucking me over, you devious bastard,' he said, spitting out the words in a staccato stream, 'I'll have the devil himself come crashing down on you. Understand that.'

Charlie Borg's feathers were rarely ruffled. But as the Maltese rubbed his neck, it occurred to him this tall and toffy Englishman was graced with a touch of steel that was best left undisturbed.

Ten nights later, on Friday 4 June 1943, in the company of two others, Parnell-Brown watched from a distance as an unlit lorry made its way to the NAAFI warehouse's perimeter gate. A figure alighted carrying bolt-cutters. With the padlock cut, the lorry passed through the open gate and pulled up at a large brick shed.

In the preceding days, the MI6 station head had reluctantly approved the plan, once Parnell-Brown pointed out how pleased MI6 headquarters would be to hear of the station unearthing someone capable of securely transporting a pathfinder to Sicily. Next came the colonel in charge of the British military police contingent in Malta. Like the MI6 station head, he baulked at first. But when the question of expected Allied losses in the invasion of Sicily came up, the colonel soon saw the merit of the MI6 proposal. There followed a judgement NAAFI should not be briefed, to avoid possible whispers that something beyond common theft had occurred. Charlie Borg, it was decided, would be left free to bribe one of the Maltese warehouse security detail as originally planned.

'I hope this is worth it, sir,' the military police colonel said from the unmarked car's back seat, addressing the MI6 station head in the front passenger seat.

'It's a war matter, Anthony,' the station head replied evenly, casting a quick sideways glance at Parnell-Brown. 'An important war matter.' He paused to change the subject. 'You're sure the Maltese police won't want to get involved?'

'The Commissioner of Police is a reliable chap,' the colonel said. 'From the little I could tell him, he agreed that his people should lie doggo. As it is, the local force has enough on its plate with all the unexploded ordnance and suchlike around the place.'

***

Daniel Lincoln's preparation for operation Spot was well advanced. On completing a range of training courses in June 1964, he had travelled to Cardiff and called on the W.H. Jenkins clothing factory. The young Mr Jenkins as he was known – for his grandfather had established the firm – showed Daniel around, introducing him to the underwear, cotton shirts and other cheap clothing manufactured at the plant. After which the proprietor gave Daniel a sales brochure cataloguing the items Jenkins produced, followed by Daniel signing a receipt that Mr Jenkins would later mail to a post office box in order to be reimbursed for his consultative services. The visit ended in the privacy of Mr Jenkins's office where Daniel was given twenty business cards, a letter introducing him as the Jenkins representative Frank Middlemiss, and a packet of Marlboro cigarettes.

Daniel had enjoyed his time in Cardiff. Being away from the office, he found, helped with his debilitating illness. There was also a pleasing sense of doing real fieldwork, albeit absent any element of risk. The danger would come later, when in East Berlin. On the train back to London this thought bedevilled Daniel, something he wrestled with all night long in his Camden Town flat. But he knew he had no option but to accept the task on offer. To decline so career enhancing an opportunity would inevitably lead those on the top floor of Century House to ask why.

Mid-morning the next day, Daniel submitted his passport, visa application and letter of introduction, all bearing the name Frank Middlemiss, to the office of KfA Limited in Belgrave Square, East Germany's de facto embassy. And that was that. All Daniel could now do was wait for departure day.

***

'The order for the consignment of denim is ready for pick up,' Mr Jenkins said. It was Friday 14 August 1964 and he was calling the London number Daniel had provided.

'Thank you,' replied the young woman seated outside the MI6 Deputy Director General's office. She had answered the telephone with the words: *Beryl, despatch room*. It was the one and only time the instrument on her desk had been used since its installation two months ago. 'Our driver will drop around shortly to collect it.'

Peter Parnell-Brown raised his head. 'KfA has mailed back the Frank Middlemiss passport with a visa in it,' said the young woman who had knocked. Her real name was Sandra. 'I told the Cardiff end in code it will be picked up as scheduled on 25 August.'

'Good,' Parnell-Brown said. 'And his flight to West Berlin and all the other arrangements?'

'Also confirmed,' Sandra said with brisk efficiency. 'After training to Cardiff on the morning of 25 August and picking up his passport, he'll fly direct to West Berlin. Overnights there before going East next morning, 26 August. Checks into the Frund Hotel – chosen because it's close to the Weidendammer Bridge and its loo has its own little room. Has a scheduled meeting that afternoon with Ministry of Foreign Trade officials. Returns to the ministry on Thursday afternoon, 27 August, for more punishment before giving up – standard fare for most foreign sales representatives touting wares in East Germany. At twenty to six on 27 August – although earlier's fine – sets the *Karl loves Ilsa* padlock signal on the bridge. Returns to the hotel to freshen up, and have a dicky knee if he likes. Shortly after six proceeds to Friedrichstrasse station, as if taking a pre-dinner stroll.'

Sandra gulped before continuing – successive rapid-fire sentences had robbed her of breath. 'Buys a copy of *Berliner Zeitung* at the kiosk and at 6:30 pm sharp goes to the Tränenpalast pavilion. Mingles with the folks out the front saying goodbye to each other while holding the newspaper folded in his right hand so she can recognise him. Ten minutes after making the drop, or at 7 pm when the delivery window closes, he leaves the pavilion forecourt and goes to the Am Zwinger cafeteria in Brecht-Platz to eat dinner. Next morning 28 August, delivery or no delivery, extracts to West Berlin around nineish, prior to the SED plenary conference getting underway and hopefully a leadership spill occurring not long after.'

Parnell-Brown smiled his thanks, all the while thinking that his formidable personal assistant was the sort of person who could make the trains run on time. 'Excellent,' he said. 'Could you ask Daniel to come and see me this afternoon, please Sandra?'

CHAPTER 14

The Allied invasion of Sicily was launched on 9 July 1943. Two days earlier, in the dead of night, Charlie Borg had set off in his little wooden boat with a passenger dressed in the clothes of a Sicilian peasant. The man in fact was a British Special Forces combat signaller. At close to 2 am on 8 July, Borg watched his human cargo wade ashore at a secluded cove on Sicily's southern coast carting a portable radio set. Three hours later Borg was back at the Valletta harbor. He apparently did not hear the man in leather-soled shoes who crept forward from his hiding place to shoot him in the back of the head with a silenced pistol, just as Borg jumped onto the wharf to tie up.

Peter Parnell-Brown was shocked on first learning that MI6 headquarters wanted Borg dead as soon as possible after dropping the pathfinder in Sicily. But it was true that many Maltese citizens had Italian heritage and the invasion of Sicily was too important for anything to be left to chance. Indeed, in November 1942 a Maltese artist by the name of Carmelo Borg Pisani was hanged for treason. To what extent the Borg part of the hung traitor's unhyphenated surname influenced the MI6 decision, Parnell-Brown did not know. Not in dispute, however, was that unlike the Ronald Hunts of this world, Borg knew exactly where he dropped his passenger and, moreover, how the man had gone ashore equipped with a radio transmitter. Whatever, Charlie Borg's elimination was a toughening-up event for the young MI6 man, one that hardened him for his stellar espionage career to come.

Ronald Hunt was a shuddering mess. News of Charlie Borg's shooting death had just reached him, causing him to bolt for the latrine where he vomited up his fear in several violent heaves. Ronald knew that Borg's execution related to the Sicily trip and the *one other* he took with him. Was this character pretending to be Harry Cramer going to knock him next?

As thoughts of Borg's death slowly receded, the venal side of Ronald took over. 'And what about the toothpaste?' he mused, shaking his head. Borg had hidden the pallets somewhere unknown to Ronald. So far, he lamented, he'd received only two payments – a measly total of 150 Maltese pounds. He was due more, much more. But the truth of it was that now Charlie was dead his cronies would seize the stolen goods and flog them off, meaning he was unlikely to see any further cash.

Ronald cleaned up before returning to the NAAFI receiving area. A consignment of Corn Flakes, a British breakfast staple since the 1930s, had earlier arrived and Ronald had been slacking off rather than help unpack it. 'Must have eaten something dodgy,' he said to his colleagues who had seen him throw down his newspaper and rush off. 'Right attack of the trots, it was.'

'Methinks the badger was upset by the prospect of doing some work,' an unsympathetic colleague stage whispered. The derisory nickname bestowed on Ronald was a play on the phrase *bald as a badger*. It was ironic, therefore, that baldness should suit Ronald, enhancing his good looks as it had his father, George. And like George, it also accounted for the sexual virility that women passing in the night regularly sensed in Ronald. But these were facts too complex to throw back at detractors in the course of a rapid-fire exchange of insults.

'What's it with you, faceache?' Ronald barked. He knew his co-workers thought he was a malingerer and that some even suspected his involvement in the toothpaste break-in a few weeks back. Not that either factor particularly bothered Ronald, in the case of the latter mainly because there was no evidence to support the perception. Or so Ronald thought.

'Hunt,' a male voice called, causing the laughter in the shed to subside. It was the warehouse manager, a NAAFI lieutenant. He was standing at the building's distant side entrance his shape silhouetted by the sunlight behind him.

'Yes, sir.'

'Front office counter, quickish-like. Someone to see you.'

'Probably Mr Churchill with me medal,' Ronald joked, winking in the direction of his colleagues before slouching off, affecting nonchalance as he always did, but anxious nonetheless as to what the summons was about.

Hands in pockets, Ronald insolently sauntered into the warehouse's entrance foyer, only to jump in fright. Waiting for him was the tall man he had first met at the Ionian Inn on the Valletta waterfront, the one who called himself Harry Cramer. The last time Ronald had seen him was late one night near the bomb-damaged Church of the Flight into Egypt. He had gone there to meet the so-called Cramer and receive Borg's down payment of 1,000 US dollars along with the instruction that Borg was to sail at eleven on the night of 7 July. The passenger Borg was to carry would meet him alongside at that time.

'Let's take a walk around the yard,' Peter Parnell-Brown said.

The pair had gone no more than fifty yards before the rattled Ronald began gabbling. 'I dunno what your game is, mate, but you ain't gonna be doing me in the neck.' Ronald stopped walking for a second, unsure if he should clarify he meant Cramer killing him rather than exposing his part in the toothpaste theft. He eventually decided it was best to treat the robbery and the possibility of being murdered with the same seriousness. 'You turn me in for the toothpaste job and I'd be stiff to get more than a year in Corradino,' Ronald said, referring to Malta's main prison. 'But if you do,' he ranted, 'I'll squeal like a stuck pig about you topping Charlie Borg.'

Peter Parnell-Brown had not pulled the trigger on Charlie Borg. And although he knew it was going to happen, he had no idea of the shooter's identity. He assumed it was someone from the military, possibly an assassin mobilised at MI6's behest. But now he was calm and dispassionate as he confronted Ronald, like the seasoned operative that virtually overnight he had become.

'Are you quite finished,' Parnell-Brown said softly, 'you contemptible piece of criminal garbage?' He noted with grim satisfaction Ronald's blanch at the threat in his voice. Ronald nodded meekly, his boldness gone. 'I could have you thrown in the slammer with a snap of my fingers,' Parnell-Brown continued, 'and nothing you could say or do would ever touch me. Never lose sight of that fact.'

Ronald stared straight ahead. He somehow knew this pretend Harry Cramer fellow was telling the truth and was now too scared to look at him. 'What do you want?' he whispered to the air.

'You're to keep working with NAAFI by day, but at night you're going to work for me,' Parnell-Brown said. With that, he grabbed Ronald by the shirt under his chin and pushed him roughly against a wall, leaning in until his face was barely six inches from the terrified Ronald. 'You're one lucky bastard,' Parnell-Brown hissed. 'It would give me great pleasure to bury you. But the fact that you're right at home among the crims in this town compels me not to.'

'What?' Ronald gasped.

'You're to be my snout. I want you out there in those places around the waterfront where I can't blend in, with your ear to the ground. Your job is to warn me of anybody or anything that, however remotely, might be damaging to the war effort, particularly any person who might conceivably be an Axis spy.' Parnell-Brown squashed Ronald more forcefully against the wall. 'Got it?'

Ronald managed to nod.

'We'll meet once a week for debriefings. The first contact will be seven days from now at the church where I gave you Charlie Borg's advance payment. Ten pm precisely, on the dot.'

'Understood,' Ronald puffed, causing Parnell-Brown to relax his grip and fling Ronald away as if discarding something soiled.

'Hunt,' Parnell-Brown called to Ronald's departing back. 'From now on if I ever hear of you so much as pinching a toothpick from NAAFI, I will personally rip out your voice box.' It was a promise Peter Parnell-Brown would keep, figuratively speaking, three short years later – in Berlin.

***

On Saturday 2 May 1964, three months before the scheduled launch of operation Leopard, the CIA point man Michael Anjelico was in New York City, at a Midtown apartment on the corner of East 55th Street and First Avenue. He was gazing out of the window at the East River a block away when the CIA Director entered the room.

'Thanks for coming up on a weekend, Michael,' the Director said. 'How was London?' Nine days earlier Anjelico had dined with his Leopard counterpart, MI6's Peter Parnell-Brown, at Claridge's Hotel in London's up-market Mayfair.

'No problem and wet and gloomy,' Anjelico replied, smiling at his boss and admiring his perceived wit at responding to the greeting and answering the question in the one breath.

But the Director was in no mood for lame humour. He'd just had a tedious secret meeting with a South African intelligence fellow whose going on about the merits of apartheid soon wore thin. The meeting had been scheduled on a weekend in New York because of concerns that alert media would learn of it were it held during the working week at the CIA's Langley headquarters outside Washington DC.

'What do you think?'

Anjelico considered the Director's question, aware that his boss was asking if he thought MI6 could be trusted, and amused by the CIA head's inborn suspicion of the British even though he was third generation American. The hereditary ties extending back to Tralee in County Kerry were never far from the surface.

'Parnell-Brown,' Anjelico said, 'does not give much away. But there's no doubt in my mind that MI6 is heavily invested in the plan to install Konrad Voite as prime minister of East Germany.' Anjelico paused. 'Although I'd qualify this by saying I'm suspicious of the fact that last January, with no prior notice, your opposite number should have come forward with the plan for Leopard.'

It was an astute observation by Anjelico: he had no inkling that January 1964 was when Sir Roger Holbrook received Elke Über's letter offering to defect. But the CIA Director was impatient. 'You're speaking in riddles, Michael,' he said tersely. 'Explain yourself.'

'Well, there's no question that both services want a relaxation of the East German border regime, so we might recommence running agents in the East. But let's face it MI6 did nothing but cry in its beer when Kennedy refused to push back against the Wall at the time of its construction. Conversely, we in the Agency went before Congressional hearings and bared our soul.'

Anjelico rubbed his chin. 'It's the Brits' sudden enthusiasm for correcting Kennedy's error that I find strange, when until last January there was none. And later on, when we were casting around for a suitable Leopard decoy, it was Parnell-Brown who rushed in to nominate Ronald Hunt all because years ago in Berlin he had witnessed Hunt's criminal association with Josef Sterck.' Anjelico grimaced. 'And suitable decoy or not, Hunt's still a British citizen. I'm curious why the Brits seem fine with that.'

'Fuck them,' the Director roared, his exclamation causing Anjelico to start. 'They love being opaque. They think it makes them clever. The English have never got over the loss of Empire, you know. It sticks in their craw that ever since the war, we've been the big dog on the Western block.' Had Sir Roger Holbrook been in the room he could not have put it better.

Having let his sentiment get the better of him, the Director calmed. 'But let's not waste time trying to psychoanalyse the British, Michael,' he said with a smile, 'or we'll both end up in Bellevue.' Bellevue was a large New York City mental hospital. The Director poured himself a small whisky, airily inviting Anjelico to do the same. 'Ronald Hunt,' the Director said, choosing a fresh subject, 'first came to light as Peter Parnell-Brown's Joe, correct?'

A convoy of fire tenders wailed its way up First Avenue, although neither man in the apartment saw fit to remark on the hubbub. It was just New York City in perpetual motion. 'Yeah, he did,' Anjelico replied over the din, swirling the whisky in his glass. 'For about twenty months.' He smiled briefly. 'Peter made a big impact when in Malta, particularly by managing to land a pathfinder in Sicily ahead of the invasion. In March 1945 he was seconded to Montgomery's personal staff in readiness for Germany's surrender and the occupation to come. He left Malta the same month.'

'I take it then that Parnell-Brown's successor took over running Ronald Hunt?' the Director said.

Anjelico smiled wryly. 'The successor never got the chance. MI6 had turned a blind eye to a break-in at a NAAFI warehouse by Hunt and an accomplice involving the theft of a substantial quantity of toothpaste.' Anjelico shook his head in mock bewilderment. 'And it was hell-bent on avoiding embarrassing questions on the subject. For that reason MI6 ensured no charges were brought against Hunt. When Hunt's two-year term in Malta expired, not long after Parnell-Brown left, NAAFI was still clueless about his part in the toothpaste heist and his association with MI6.' Anjelico sniggered. 'Yet MI6 remained unwilling to refer Hunt to the police. So finally it wrote to NAAFI to advise in confidence that MI6 considered Hunt should not remain in NAAFI's employ.'

'Peter Parnell-Brown told you this?'

'Yeah,' Anjelico replied. 'But later, fourteen years later in fact, when he arrived over here to head up the MI6 station.' This time Anjelico laughed heartily. 'Like I say, Peter was usually very circumspect. But there was no hiding his frustration when telling me that after Hunt finished in Malta, NAAFI sent him direct to Germany where his black market activities became the stuff of legend.'

'How come NAAFI didn't act on the MI6 advice to sack Hunt?' the Director asked.

Michael Anjelico suddenly sobered. 'I never found out from Peter, actually. He just clammed up. But I subsequently heard whispers that Hunt's wife, who worked for a senior guy in the NAAFI head office, managed to pull a rabbit out of the hat to get him off.'

'And did Hunt and Parnell-Brown's paths cross in Germany?'

Anjelico laughed. 'You bet; big time, eventually. Peter was attached to Montgomery's headquarters in Bad Oeynhausen and Hunt based at the NAAFI bulk store in Berlin, cities that were nearly 250 miles apart. But they did meet again in Munich in late 1946, when Peter put in train the process that later saw Hunt convicted and imprisoned here in the States.'

CHAPTER 15

Janice Hunt had not seen her husband at law for two years. Ronald had written to Janice once a month for the first three months of his Malta posting. But he'd never received a reply and by June 1943 was so enjoying life as a single man that he ceased the practice. The reason Ronald wrote at all, albeit briefly, reflected his deep reluctance to divorce Janice. After all, she had indispensible clout as the personal assistant to the NAAFI operations manager in London.

In the period after Ronald's murder of the couple's three-month-old daughter, Janice had found a form of equilibrium. Of course were she aware her husband had smothered the child, in all probability she would have reached no plateau whatsoever. But the doctor's cot death verdict did bring Janice some solace; at least she knew how Carmel died – or so she thought – if not the why. So, in time, Janice began to function in a manner of speaking. This primarily entailed burying herself in her work. Outside of NAAFI, however, she spent most of her time alone in her darkened flat, feeling nothing but a clawing emptiness inside. And Ronald? Well, it was as if he were dead to her.

Given this, the arrival of a letter from Ronald in May 1945 advising he was shortly to return to England where he planned to take up residence in Janice's Streatham flat was a most unpleasant surprise. The thought of again living with Ronald under the same roof made Janice feel physically ill. It was not so much her very real disdain for him that caused her distress. Rather, it was Janice's dread of Ronald's presence, of the fact of someone being around to intrude on the quiet space of her home, that which she so badly needed for her sanity.

For once, however, fate dealt Janice a stroke of luck. On Tuesday 8 May 1945, the same day that Ronald's letter arrived, Germany unconditionally surrendered. NAAFI had been preparing for this, knowing that a huge British force would take up occupation of some part of Germany, stoking a related demand for NAAFI services. But that was only part of it. Janice's real good fortune was to open her boss's mail three days later and come across a letter from MI6 painting Ronald in a less than glowing light and urging NAAFI to dismiss him. For fully a minute Janice was dumbstruck by what she read. But then it dawned on her that were Ronald sacked by NAAFI, he would spend even more time in her flat lolling about under her feet and compromising her sacred personal space. With that, Janice rammed a blank piece of paper into her typewriter and began to tap furiously at the keys.

Jim Warren, Janice's boss, looked up. It was nearly 4:30 pm on Friday 11 May 1945 and he was keen to get away. His plan was to take a quick pint at the Coxbridge Arms to celebrate Hitler's defeat before getting home to his wife in Islington.

'Excuse me, sir,' Janice said. 'If you could sign these letters before you go, I'll get them in the mail tonight. It will leave us a free run at things on Monday morning.'

Warren frowned in irritation. But he wasn't about to berate Janice, his trusted and valued assistant. Added to which he was also fond of the withdrawn young woman, for whom he had developed a fatherly soft spot in the aftermath of the terrible business with her daughter. 'All right, but quickly please. I do need to leave soon.' Permission granted, Janice placed a buff folder marked *correspondence pack* on the desk.

Warren opened the binder at speed, making a great show of being in a hurry. With barely a glance at the text in the body of the letters within, he scrawled his name in the signature block of each of the six items. Only when he got to the last document in the pack did he pause, his wish to leave briefly dimmed by the fact that he was looking not at a letter but rather an internal transfer order.

'What's this?' Warren asked, holding up the form.

'Ronald's terribly keen on it,' Janice said softly, aided in her quest to tug at Warren's heartstrings in appearing to be nervously vulnerable by the fact that she was.

'But… but, you haven't seen your husband for two years. I mean I know we need as many people on the ground as soon as possible. But don't you and he want to spend some time together?'

'We discussed this,' Janice said. 'In our letters,' she added as Warren's face became even more puzzled. 'Now that the war's over, he can come back to London when on leave, meaning we would still have a family life. We think we can make the arrangement work.'

Warren wasn't sure what to say, and he certainly didn't want to stray into matters of intimacy. 'Well, if that's what the two of you want,' he said. Then with a flourish he signed the order directing that Ronald Hunt be cross-posted direct from Malta to Germany.

Janice walked from the office tightly clutching the correspondence folder, her heart pounding. Only once Warren had rushed from the office did she dare separate the MI6 letter from the others. Dating it by hand, she read once more through the text she had drafted, nodding in grim satisfaction.

The correspondence thanked MI6 for its advice while indicating that NAAFI would treat the Ronald Hunt matter with extreme seriousness, alacrity and utmost discretion. A process would be immediately instituted to review Hunt's conduct in

Malta ahead of the anticipated termination of his services. Please accept the assurances of my highest consideration, yours sincerely, Jim Warren, Operations Manager. Janice could write such letters in her sleep, something hinting at decisive action while promising nothing. She hoped this would satisfy MI6 sufficient to avoid further communication on the matter.

And indeed it did. Janice did not know that the people in MI6 to whom the letter ostensibly from Jim Warren was directed were somewhat vague as to the background to the recommendation for Ronald Hunt's dismissal, such was the nature of MI6's compartmentalisation. And with Peter Parnell-Brown, who had initiated the process to write to NAAFI, now in Germany with Field Marshal Montgomery's occupation force they were unlikely to get much the wiser.

**

Meanwhile on Saturday 2 May 1964, in the apartment on the corner of First Avenue and East 55th Street in New York City, the CIA Director had poured himself and Michael Anjelico another whisky. 'I have to go soon,' the Director said. 'I have a dinner engagement tonight at the Brookhaven Laboratory on Long Island. Professor Harry Kellaway from the NASA space program is the guest speaker.'

The CIA head glanced at Anjelico, a hint of embarrassment in his eyes. Both men knew Kellaway's real name was Heinrich Keller, the Nazi scientist bartered to the Americans by Israel in May 1963 in return for the US abandoning demands to inspect Israel's nuclear reactor at Dimona. Of course neither the Director nor Michael Anjelico was aware of Daniel Lincoln's self-defeating contribution to the negotiated settlement. The Director hastened to continue, anxious to change the subject. 'So how precisely did Ronald Hunt end up Stateside?' he said.

'Well,' Anjelico said, clearing his throat, 'there's a lot to it. But the potted version is that Hunt had accrued millions of reichsmarks playing the German black market. He couldn't launder all of them through the British repatriation scheme and needed to find conspirators to assist him. This led him to a couple of GIs called Neitz and Foster. Neitz was based in Munich and Foster in London and they were running their own reichsmark laundering scam. To cut to the chase, Neitz started washing reichsmarks for Ronald Hunt but after a while withheld some of the proceeds. In November 1946 Neitz was murdered in Munich by Hunt's collaborator, Josef Sterck.'

'The current East German communist party elder,' the Director interjected wryly, 'and soon to be star player in operation Leopard.'

'Correct,' Anjelico said, smiling broadly. 'Foster turned state witness and gave evidence of Neitz's involvement with Hunt. By this stage Sterck was hiding out in the Soviet occupation zone, and naturally the Sovs refused to hand him over. Hunt, though, was in reach of American justice. After the Brits agreed to his extradition to the US in 1950, he was found guilty of aiding and abetting in the murder of Neitz. He's been in Leavenworth ever since.'

The CIA Director shook his head. 'And we're letting him out to be the operation Leopard decoy?' he asked bemusedly.

'New era coming, Chief,' Anjelico replied with a sigh. 'Since last year a left wing guy called Harold Wilson has been leader of the Labour opposition in Britain. All reports indicate he's likely to win the general election this coming October.' It was Anjelico's turn to shake his head. 'Activists are already lobbying to have Hunt released should that be the case. Bleeding hearts who say the sixty-six-year sentence Hunt received was manifestly excessive because the US was upset it couldn't get its hands on Josef Sterck. So, when Peter Parnell-Brown came up with Hunt's name to be the decoy, it suited us to release him, to avoid a future political rift with the likely new British government.'

'But as you say,' the Director observed dryly, 'Hunt is still a British citizen. MI6 could get into big trouble for placing him at risk when in the eyes of a leftist government his release from prison is the overdue correction of a long outstanding wrong.'

Anjelico nodded in agreement. 'My point exactly,' he said. 'It might all come to nothing – Leopard has Hunt getting in and out of East Berlin on the same day, 24 August. Even so, it's hard to escape the impression that MI6 is up to something.'

***

Ronald Hunt was puzzled to say the least when called into the NAAFI headquarters in Malta and advised he'd been cross-posted to recently defeated Germany, effective 5 July 1945. He was half-expecting the summons would be to announce his dismissal courtesy of this Harry Cramer who until recently had controlled his life. Peter Parnell-Brown, of course, had left Malta two months earlier.

Once he had recovered from the shock news of his posting, a deeply embedded instinct told Ronald that Janice's fingerprints were all over this fortuitous development. That night he got rollickingly drunk, feeling like a deadweight had been lifted from his shoulders. Most obvious to Ronald was that Janice didn't want him back in the flat. But this did not faze him in the slightest. Janice's arranging his cross-posting, despite resenting his refusal to grant her a divorce, clearly indicated she did not suspect he had killed Carmel, that and the fact she had never gone to the police.

Moreover going to Germany, Ronald believed, would get him off the hook with the mysterious crowd for which this Harry Cramer worked. At long last his freedom had been restored. No longer would he have to spend his nights skulking around seedy bars on the Valletta waterfront looking for Axis spies or sympathisers and, like a patsy stool pigeon, reporting back to Cramer, something that offended Ronald's skewed value system and occasionally made him worry if he might be in danger.

But the thing that pleased Ronald most was the realisation he would no longer have to tread the straight and narrow path demanded by Cramer. Ronald's greed asserted. Having miraculously risen from the ashes smelling of roses just like his old man used to, once in Germany he would make the big coin that he'd joined NAAFI for in the first place.

Ronald arrived in Germany as scheduled in July 1945, in one of the early NAAFI contingents to reach the devastated country. After a period spent in a British staging area at Brunswick in western Germany, he was sent to the NAAFI bulk issue store in the Berlin suburb of Spandau. This suited Ronald nicely. The Spandau depot was the receiving point for consolidated consignments sent from England. It was from Spandau where the NAAFI mobile and fixed canteens to be established in Germany would source and later replenish supplies to be sold to British service personnel.

***

Josef Sterck had negotiated the war and the rise of the Nazis in the years before through a combination of good luck, zero principles and a touch of rat cunning. He came from the central German state of Thuringia where in the pre-war years the Nazis gained an early foothold. This led to the eventual purging of any anti-fascist public office holder, the Thuringian police force being a prime example.

Sterck was not an ideologue – money was his deity. But he was an opportunist who could sniff the wind. In 1930, at the age of twenty-eight, he threw his lot in with the Nazis. Shortly after, he joined the state police force. Posted to Erfurt, Thuringia's largest city, he stayed there for eight years, availing himself of each and every opportunity for corruption his police work presented.

Kristallnacht on 9–10 November 1938 was a turning point for Sterck. As Nazi thugs engaged in widespread looting of Jewish property in Erfurt, Sterck was content to look the other way while patrolling the streets. But it was the follow-up decree from Berlin, which prohibited Jews from owning or operating businesses, that shaped his future. Introducing sham appropriation powers, the Nazis were intent on seizing and on-selling all Jewish businesses, a process known as Aryanisation. So-called regional economic offices were set up across Germany to facilitate the theft, in Thuringia's case in the then capital, Weimar.

It was in Weimar where Josef Sterck made a fortune. His first step was to lobby political decision-makers to be made the official in charge of the Thuringian regional office. He did so upon reading a newspaper report that the costs of establishing and operating the regional offices were to be covered from the proceeds of the sale of usurped Jewish businesses, citing a notional ten per cent overhead. But Sterck's instincts told him that nobody in Berlin would be too concerned if a little more was shaved off the top and ended up in his pocket. And Sterck's ultimately successful quest to head the Thuringian office had one other important perk. It classified him as a *deserving National Socialist*, allowing him to dodge military service.

As a previously corrupt policeman, Josef Sterck had learned never to sign documents that one day might come back to bite. By the time of his appointment to head the Thuringia regional office the habit was ingrained. From the outset, therefore, Sterck directed underlings to sign letters informing Jewish Germans property was to be Aryanised. It was an arrangement destined to stand Josef Sterck in good stead because it meant there was virtually no documented evidence of his Nazi crimes. And in the immediate postwar period, the thought of Nazi hunters in hot pursuit made Sterck very grateful for this. Even so, the absence of substantiating proof did not later deter political rivals from circulating rumours of a Nazi past.

Back in 1938, with Jewish businesses by the score undergoing Aryanisation, Sterck made so much money in the next seven years that he thought it prudent not to keep the bulk of it in a bank for fear of people learning just how much he was raking off. To this end, he built a small concrete room in the basement of his Weimar house and secured it with a heavy padlock.

When Germany surrendered in May 1945 over three million reichsmarks were hidden in the crypt. But Sterck had a problem in that Germany was decimated and his reichsmarks worthless. Then one day by chance he discovered that the American and British governments had introduced exchange schemes permitting respective service personnel to convert reichsmarks into perfectly negotiable home currencies. Overnight, Sterck's hopes were raised that his vast stash of Nazi script might not be as valueless as he feared.

In July 1945, however, occupation arrangements were revised. The Soviets took control of Thuringia from the Americans. This was both a boon and a headache for Josef Sterck. On one hand, the Soviets were not especially concerned with economic crimes against German Jews or who had perpetrated the larceny on behalf of the Nazis. But problematically for Sterck nor did the Soviets allow for the conversion of reichsmarks into hard currency.

Sterck became not unlike millions of other Germans – exhausted, hungry and bewildered that it should have all gone so wrong – differentiated from his countrymen only by the once more worthless three million reichsmarks on which he was sitting. But all this was to change when Sterck stumbled across a young woman hailing from Coburg in neighbouring Bavaria. Her name was Fräulein Elke Über.

CHAPTER 16

Cardiff on 25 August 1964 was balmy and bright. Daniel Lincoln alighted at Queen Street station before noon and set off with a spring in his step. He was heading for the Jenkins clothing factory where he was to pick up his passport in the name of Frank Middlemiss. Daniel strolled, changing his suitcase from hand to hand as he went. During one such shift he felt the security padlock on his case brush against his leg. With that, his happy mood evaporated. It was on the padlock that later in East Berlin Daniel would scratch the *Karl loves Ilsa* calling card to Elke Über. He was to do so on the night of 26 August while sitting on the enclosed toilet in his tiny East Berlin hotel room, when in the bog, as Peter Parnell-Brown put it, where even the Stasi respected a person's right to privacy.

Daniel ploughed on towards his destination, slouching where before his shoulders had been squared and chest extended. Nervously touching inside his suit coat to feel the DG's letter to Elke, which before crossing into East Berlin he would secrete in the false bottom of the bag containing his shaving kit, Daniel began to contemplate returning to London and confessing. As usual, he envisaged explaining the Kristiina Ahnger debacle to MI6 and how it had left him emotionally unsuitable for clandestine work, and how in the process this would unburden him of the guilt over his framing of Ray Solter. But the moment passed, as all such thoughts of confession did, not least because

Daniel knew that revealing everything would involve spending time in prison, which apart from ruining him would also kill his beloved father.

***

Daniel was not the only one thinking of East Berlin on that same 25 August day. So was a man called Paian Diaz, who for the past two years had been in the pay of the American Central Intelligence Agency. Diaz, of course, was a low-level Cuban bureaucrat. But his government appointment did make him a trusted Cuban citizen. With that came the right to travel abroad, permitting Diaz to book passage on a Cuban group tour intending to visit East Berlin.

Three days earlier, on 22 August, a CIA officer posing as a Mexican businessman had visited Havana to connect with Diaz. Of the few Western hemisphere countries maintaining diplomatic ties with Cuba, Mexico had by far the most cordial relationship. As such, CIA agents based in Mexico City were running Diaz, taking advantage of the air links between the Mexican capital and Havana.

The CIA operative handed Diaz six pages of authenticated Swiss bank records containing evidence of fraud against the East German state by its political leaders, Walter Ulbricht and Erich Honecker. Diaz's riding instructions were to mail the bank records to Konrad Voite's office on 25 August, the day after his tour group arrived in East Berlin. Sir Roger Holbrook, the MI6 Director General and prime architect of operation Leopard, had been assured by the CIA that the Stasi took its Cuban comrades so much for granted as not to bother to monitor them. Even so, Sir Roger and his Deputy Peter Parnell-Brown held reservations about the wisdom of the delivery method – a keen insight as it transpires.

Diaz's tour party left Havana as scheduled on 24 August on a Cubana charter operating an ancient Soviet Ilyushin turboprop aircraft. They had crossed the North Atlantic and landed safely in newly independent Mauritania. Unbeknown to the passengers, however, the last two hundred kilometres had been completed with red lights flashing in the cockpit and alarms suppressed. On the ground at Nouakchott airport, technicians familiar with old Ilyushins were few and far between. Diaz was stuck. His itinerary envisaged an arrival in East Berlin in the evening of 24 August, where the next day he would post the Swiss banking records to Konrad Voite. But the hours ticked away, with still no sign of his plane being fixed. By noon on 25 August Diaz accepted the likelihood of posting his documents in East Berlin on time was precisely zero.

The timing of Diaz's mailing was critical to operation Leopard. Key was that the day after the scheduled dispatch Josef Sterck, subjected to pressure by Ronald Hunt, was publicly to accuse Walter Ulbricht and Erich Honecker of corruption, acting on receipts supplied by Ronald. Provided Diaz did as operation Leopard stipulated and mailed the Swiss banking records on 25 August, Konrad Voite would receive them on 27 August, the day after Sterck's outburst.

There was some clever science behind this timeline jointly developed by MI6 and the CIA. To be sure the receipts taken to East Berlin by Ronald Hunt for Josef Sterck were genuine. But unlike the documents carried by Paian Diaz they were not explosive. Rather, Ronald's receipts reflected only minor corruption of the type engaged in by most of the SED executive. Sterck's speaking out, using the receipts as justification, would nonetheless plant the thorny issue of corruption in the minds of delegates just two days before the SED plenary conference on 28 August.

The British and Americans judged this would have two important impacts. It would have Konrad Voite thinking about corruption when, lo and behold, the material posted by Paian Diaz turned up on 27 August. And second, Sterck's allegations on 26 August would distract Klaus Borkh, Ulbricht and Honecker's minder. So the operation Leopard theory ran, the gullible Borkh would embark on a wild goose chase aimed at Josef Sterck. This would grant the reformist Voite otherwise denied leeway to add an item to the SED conference agenda guaranteed to politically kneecap Ulbricht and Honecker and pave the way for his installation as East German prime minister.

***

For his part, Ronald Hunt was not only thinking of East Berlin on 25 August 1964, he was actually there. How this came to be was a long story. Suffice to say, it started with Josef Sterck meeting Elke Über in October 1945 in Soviet-occupied Weimar.

Elke and Sterck were seated in Elke's candlelit office in the neo-Gothic Weimar city hall. The building, like the rest of the state of Thuringia, had no electric power. Two days earlier Sterck had been served a curt note instructing him to attend the meeting.

'I am a member of the organising committee of the housing secretariat of the occupying Soviet command,' Elke began. 'Your house has been selected for requisition.'

Sterck stared at the young woman he could barely make out, shocked by her words. Elke had been in the job less than a month. She was originally from Bayreuth in Bavaria where Hitler's Nazis had murdered her parents, both communists, in 1939 when Elke was just seventeen. After that Elke fled to Coburg, also in Bavaria, as her mother and father had told her to do in the event of their arrest. Elke had spent the war in Coburg sheltered by a non-communist family, the matriarch of which was once her mother's schoolmate.

Now twenty-three, with the memory of her parents' dream burning inside her, Elke was anxious to further the socialist cause in their honour. With the Americans formally in occupation of Bavaria, the Soviet takeover of Thuringia had been Elke's cue to move from Coburg to Weimar. The Soviet command in Thuringia was cautious at first but warmed to Elke upon her producing an introductory letter written by her father the night before his arrest. The late Professor Hans Über was a well-known and valued comrade. Once convinced of Elke's communist pedigree, the Soviets came around, aided by the fact that they were in urgent need of trusted German speakers to assist in key areas such as housing requisition.

'Why my house?' Josef Sterck finally managed to blurt. 'Yes, I was an official of the Nazi economic office in Thuringia. But I only joined the party as a safety measure. To do otherwise would have made me a marked man. I was not a Nazi supporter.'

Elke laughed. Sterck's house had been chosen only because it was undamaged by bombing and centrally located in Weimar. The rooting out of former Nazis and establishing who did what was still to come. But instead of allaying Sterck's fears, an instinct caused Elke to hesitate. 'What was your role in the economic office?' she asked.

Sterck did a quick mental calculation. 'I was its head,' he said softly. His preference was to lie. But on thinking it through, he soon grasped it would be unwise to try to hide his Nazi position, not when the Soviets would inevitably learn of it. 'We were responsible for the sale of Jewish property, businesses here in Thuringia initially and later housing and personal valuables.' With that, Sterck sunk back in his chair fervently hoping that the olive-skinned woman opposite him with the deep black eyes and raven hair was not Jewish.

It was now Elke's turn to think. Gaining the appointment as the head of the economic office, she calculated, would have required a certain amount of political nous. And once in the job, the scope for corruption would have been huge. 'What did you do with the money you syphoned off?' she asked, her mind racing ahead.

Sterck was at the point of no return. 'To be perfectly honest,' he said with a resigned smile, unsure if what he was about to say would be his saviour or his death sentence, 'I've got three million reichsmarks hidden in the basement of my house.'

Elke stared briefly at the ceiling. 'I am young and female,' she said finally. 'If I am to have any sort of career in this chauvinist world, I will need a male political champion to push my name forward.' And with that, Josef Sterck gained the distinct impression he was now somehow in Elke Über's employ.

***

The Potsdam Conference at which the victorious Allies had pledged jointly to govern Germany until the country could be reconstituted was only two months concluded when Elke and Sterck conversed in the gloom of the Weimar city hall. But already the Soviets were squabbling with their partners. Elke had seen the writing on the wall – sooner or later, the Soviets would go their own way. Eventually, she judged, there would be some form of socialist government in Soviet-occupied Germany, and it was this administration in which she planned to be senior.

'What do you propose to do with the reichsmarks?' Elke asked.

Sterck liked the sound of the question, especially that it had been couched in the future tense. 'Well,' he said, 'Germany is currently destroyed and the currency worthless. I suppose I will have to wait until our conquerors have re-built the place and the money has regained its value.'

Elke scoffed. 'It will take years for Germany to recover,' she said, 'with every likelihood that a new German currency will be adopted in the process.' She looked keenly at Sterck. 'You must immediately convert your ill-gotten gains into the current German currency, by which I mean cigarettes, Western cigarettes.'

'And how do you suggest I do that?'

'You will be aware that American and British service personnel are currently entitled to convert reichsmarks into home currencies for repatriation. But this will not last forever. You must find a British or American serviceman with access to bulk quantities of cigarettes. With cigarettes you can buy inflation-proof items – jewellery, furs and the like – that starving people will be prepared to trade. Later on you will sell these at my direction, once a new and negotiable German script is introduced.' Elke did not volunteer that she had already earmarked the anticipated funds for advancing Sterck's political career, and by extension her own.

Sterck bridled before restraining himself. 'But madam,' he said evenly, 'leaving aside that I am the owner of the reichsmarks, you are telling me to find a way to purchase the cigarettes, the alternative currency as you term it, and after that buy valuables for later re-sale at your direction. Surely, as I am doing all the work and taking all the risks, I deserve a commission, say one-third of the profits?'

'You have exactly ten seconds to withdraw your objection,' Elke spat, 'before I call the guard detachment.'

Even in the gloom, Elke's hard face told Sterck he had crossed a dangerous line. 'I withdraw,' he said with humiliating haste.

'And one other thing,' Elke said.

'Yes,' Sterck said meekly.

'At a time of my choosing you will join a political movement I shall nominate, whereupon you will use your undoubted skills to gain high office.' Elke smiled. She was rather pleased to have come across Josef Sterck. 'And once in a position of authority you will appoint me to a senior governing post.'

Sterck swallowed nervously, squeezing his lips to produce a tight smile. 'As you wish, madam.'

***

A month later Josef Sterck discovered Ronald Hunt. The two were like lonely lovers trailing their coats. Yet they existed in different orbits: Ronald was working with NAAFI in Berlin; and the former Nazi Sterck living nearly 300 kilometres away in the Thuringian capital, Weimar. There was one significant commonality, however. Sterck needed access to large quantities of Western cigarettes, and Ronald was just the man to supply them.

At first, Sterck judged the Americans would be his best bet. In early November 1945 he took himself to the Thuringian exclave of Ostheim in northern Bavaria. Located there was an American Post Exchange shop, a PX so-called catering to US military personnel. American soldiers by now were enthusiastic exploiters of the German black market. Soon Sterck had the ear of a captain from Minnesota he'd buttonholed on the street. But when the man's promise of a large consignment of cigarettes turned out to be four cartons of *Lucky Strike*, Sterck realised his task was not going to be as straightforward as hoped.

Still, Sterck's interaction with the American was not entirely fruitless. It had been observed by one of the thousands of women across Germany now forced into prostitution. She made an approach, offering to give Sterck the name of her sister in Berlin in exchange for one of his *Lucky Strike* cartons. 'Sophie will be doing as I am to survive and feed her family,' the woman said resignedly. 'But there are many more Allied soldiers in Berlin. This will make it easier to find someone to assist you.'

Sophie Lange was just another impoverished, beaten-down Berliner whom life could no longer surprise. She did briefly wonder, however, how the man from Thuringia called Brenner who arrived at her all but destroyed basement apartment in Charlottenburg had managed to get all the way to the British Zone in Berlin. But the thought passed, once Sterck offered her a carton of cigarettes, sparing him the need to finesse the fact that his travel to Berlin in a Soviet military lorry had been coordinated by Elke Über.

For her part, Sophie was pleased that the mid-forties man with the darting eyes did not want sex. For a fee she readily agreed to help him. The first step was simple. The British equivalent of the American PX, she advised, was called the NAAFI. And it so happened that a NAAFI bulk store was located in nearby Spandau. 'Many girls around here deal with British soldiers,' she said. 'I will ask about to see if any have customers from the NAAFI shop.'

The former Hitler Youth headquarters in Berlin was now in Soviet hands and had been converted into a semi-functioning hotel. In 1945 it was one of the few accommodation options in the Soviet zone. It was to here that Josef Sterck repaired after speaking to Sophie Lange, to the room Elke Über had reserved for him. Daily thereafter, Sterck made the long trek to Charlottenburg to enquire on progress. On the third day, Sophie had some encouraging news.

CHAPTER 17

British army rules circa 1945 prohibited fraternisation with German women. But the edict was largely ignored, none more so than by the likes of Ronald Hunt. The German people were destitute and a handful of English cigarettes bought just about anything. Sophie Lange, the prostitute employed by Josef Sterck, had recently been alerted to the prematurely bald NAAFI soldier who frequently partook of the services offered by the small army of street workers in the Berlin suburb of Spandau. Now Sophie had spied the man near the remains of the S-Bahn station and was about to engage him.

'Hello, Tommy,' Sophie lisped in broken English. She had sidled up to Ronald as he walked briskly down the street. 'You want come my place?'

Ronald laughed. He had sowed his oats and was heading home. 'Not right now, darling,' he said in his best cockney, 'I've had my fill for tonight. Got to catch me ride.'

'Come tomorrow night. This time,' Sophie said on Sterck's behalf. 'German gentleman want see you. Much, much money.'

Ronald stopped and stared. The mere mention of money was enough to cause him to salivate. He glanced at his watch, looking furtively about him. Tapping the dial he showed it to Sophie. 'Eight o'clock it is then. I'll wait five minutes.' With that, he strode off.

Sterck and Ronald had first circled one another like a pair of wary street dogs. The German was shorter and older with continually darting eyes, whereas Ronald was baldly louche with uneven teeth. But each knew there was business to be conducted. Soon enough, thanks to Sterck's intelligible if heavily accented English, they began to communicate.

'Two hundred marks for a ten-packet of Player's Mediums,' Ronald offered from inside Sophie's bombed-out apartment, once the two men had sought more privacy to discuss the detail of Sterck's wish to buy vast quantities of British cigarettes. Two hundred reichsmarks at the forty to one exchange rate would convert to five pounds. Ronald was excited at the prospect of this excellent return, especially when considering he could buy Player's at NAAFI for one shilling per ten-pack. But as Ronald soon discovered, the word *vast* can mean different things to different people.

'What?' Ronald gasped. For some reason – perhaps it was Sterck's uninspiring physical appearance – he had assumed the German was talking about a much smaller investment. 'Three million marks, for fuck's sake,' he blurted in shock. 'How am I supposed to find that many packets of fags?'

'We will stagger the purchases in manageable lots,' Sterck replied. 'And the cost per packet will be one hundred marks,' he countered, before finally agreeing to a price of 150 reichsmarks.

That night Ronald did not sleep well. Behind his unimposing exterior Josef Sterck was a shrewd businessman. He knew greed better than most and in Ronald had identified a kindred spirit. And once Sterck mentioned that the favourable black market conditions would not last forever, Ronald's avarice got the better of him.

But now in his bed at the NAAFI barracks in Spandau, Ronald was suffering buyer's remorse. The main cause of his anxiety was his guarantee to deliver Sterck 5,000 ten-packets of Player's Medium cigarettes each month for the next four months.

But equally Ronald craved a solution. After all, if he could pull it off he stood to make 75,000 pounds on an outlay of just 1,000 pounds to buy 20,000 ten-packets, there being twenty shillings to the pound. This was the big money of which he long had dreamt. Suddenly Ronald cursed for not thinking of the answer earlier: he would lean on Janice.

***

Eight days later and Ronald was back in England on a week's leave, having sold his superiors a story with his usual consummate ease that his wife was ill. 'Plumbing,' he said, his cunning invention designed to ward off questions on so delicate a female matter.

Janice's heart sank on returning home from work that night to find Ronald lounging insolently against the door of her Streatham flat. Ronald opened his arms wide. 'Ain't ya gonna give yer old man a hug, Janny?' he said.

Janice stood before Ronald, a forlorn figure, her chin resting on her chest. 'What do you want?' she said quietly without looking up.

'We need to talk, doll,' he said.

'Say what you've got to say and leave, please,' Janice said once they were standing in her sitting room.

Ronald laughed, amused at Janice's distress. He slapped her backside. 'Thought you might like to give me old John Thomas here a little nibble before that,' he said, twisting the emotional knife.

'You disgust me,' Janice said, looking up through pained eyes.

Ronald sniffed and looked around. 'I gather from my cross-posting that you've still got the ear of the great Jim Warren,' he began flippantly, only seamlessly to turn serious. 'I've a need to sell 20,000 packets of fags over the next four months in four lots of 5,000 a month,' Ronald spat. 'I want you to arrange this for me.'

'Me?' Janice gasped involuntarily. 'How?'

'You get your boss to tell whoever is in charge of sending supplies to Germany that for the next four months, starting this month, there's to be an additional 5,000 packets of Player's Mediums directed to the Spandau bulk store.'

Janice did not respond, biting her lip instead.

'You'd best find a way, Janice,' Ronald hissed, his voice low and menacing. 'Otherwise, I'll have to come home. Imagine that, me here all day, every day, sniffing around your little cunnie.'

Janice's shocked face told Ronald he'd hit a raw nerve. 'Tell 'em the extra gaspers are for the British engineers currently starting up the old Hun Volkswagen plant at Wolfsburg. Say the engineers want to build up a store of fags for use over Christmas and into the New Year.' Ronald paused. 'Now get me your post office savings book.'

Janice looked up, startled. 'Why?' she whispered.

'Just get the fucking thing, will you?'

The book showed a balance of eighty-three pounds. 'Ain't much of a ferret, are you?' Ronald scoffed. He was broke and seeking seed funding, 250 pounds to buy the first tranche of 5,000 ten-packets, after which the scheme would become self-funding. Ronald also needed a bank account in England for wire transferring sterling converted from reichsmarks. He was hoping Janice's post office account would resolve both issues.

But as ever when it came to criminal matters, Ronald was quick on his feet. 'Tomorrow,' he instructed Janice, 'you will withdraw eighty quid. I'll be back here tomorrow night to collect it.' He had decided to split the November tranche of cigarettes into two, buying what he could with Janice's eighty pounds. The sale proceeds, he judged, would allow for the purchase of the outstanding in December, to be added to the 5,000 ten-packets due that month.

Janice's anger finally asserted. 'You black-hearted beast,' she screamed, fearless now. 'You'll not be getting a penny out of me.'

The back of Ronald's right hand hit Janice flush on the cheek causing her to fall on to the sofa, the red welt stinging her face. In a flash Ronald was on top of her, pushing up her skirt and ripping at her underwear. She could smell his stale brandy breath.

'Listen to me, you stupid fucking cow,' Ronald panted. 'I wasn't joking when I said if I couldn't get the fags I need, I would have to come home. Unless you want me back here and rough shagging you every night, you'd better take note.'

Ronald stood and watched the softly weeping Janice restore her clothing. 'Shut up your snivelling and get me a pencil and paper,' he demanded. 'I need to write down the number of your savings account. Over the next few months I'll be depositing money into it from Berlin. I'll write to you via the NAAFI mail system and advise the payment schedule when I know it.' Ronald took a threatening step forward. 'And don't get any smart ideas, you morbid slag. I'll tell you exactly how much lolly is coming back and will expect every penny to be there.' Ronald abruptly turned heel. 'I'll be back tomorrow night for the eighty nicker,' he said from the doorway. 'After that, provided you're a good girl, you'll only see me once more – when I'm back here to pick up all my earnings.'

***

Paian Diaz, the Cuban government official doubling as a CIA document courier, was tired, hungry and increasingly anxious by the time he landed at Schönefeld airport in East Berlin late on the night of 26 August 1964. Stranded at Nouakchott in Mauritania while awaiting technicians from Havana to fix his tour group's broken aircraft, he was woefully behind schedule. The papers secreted in the lining of his suitcase should have been mailed to Konrad Voite's office thirty-six hours earlier. And the rapacious East German customs officials had not helped, going to great lengths to search the visiting party's luggage for anything to confiscate – mainly bottles of Cuban rum, but for some lucky inspectors a sprinkling of hard-won US dollars brought along for the trip.

It was close to 2 am on 27 August when the jaded Cuban tourists reached their foul hostel near Alexanderplatz. Most were exhausted and fell straight into bed. Paian Diaz did likewise, but unlike his soon comatose roommates he only slumbered. The thing most bothering Diaz was the CIA's strict instruction to mail the documents he carried to Konrad Voite's office by no later than noon on 25 August.

Diaz was unaware the papers were Swiss banking records or that they would reveal the East German political leadership's systemic and sustained corruption. Nor did he know that on 26 August Josef Sterck was publicly to release information showing minor fraud on the part of Walter Ulbricht and Erich Honecker, even if Sterck was to avow it as something far more serious. Operation Leopard had established this timeline in the expectation of the East German postal service delivering Paian Diaz's incriminating proof to Konrad Voite's office on 27 August.

But although Diaz was unaware of the nature of the CIA exercise in which he was entangled, he knew his role was important. Self-evidently, the CIA would not have sent him across the Atlantic to East Berlin without good reason. Diaz cursed that the breakdown of the old Ilyushin in Mauritania had delayed his arrival by two days, and most of all he cursed the invidious situation in which this placed him. For a time he considered flushing the documents down the toilet and forgetting about them. He further warmed to the idea when the thought entered his head that were the papers to block the system, they gave no indication of a connection to him. But this rush of blood soon turned to a chill shudder, once he visualised the CIA's reaction to him unilaterally abandoning his mission.

Finally, Diaz settled on the only viable course of action open to him. He was supposed to have posted his cache by noon on 25 August so it would reach its intended recipient on 27 August. And, of course, on the front of the envelope containing the banking records hidden in Diaz's luggage was the postal address to where the documents were to be sent, right down to the room number.

The destination for the papers was in fact the former Nazi Reichsbank building on Kurstrasse, nowadays SED headquarters. A concrete and stone edifice located on the western side of the River Spree, Konrad Voite had a permanent office there, in a suite on the third floor. It was to here that Paian Diaz decided to make his way later on 27 August, after breakfast. His key judgement was that in hand delivering his secret cargo to Voite's office, the currently off-track CIA operation would be back on course. There was, however, one major problem in that the address Diaz sought to commit to memory was written in German.

CHAPTER 18

Unlike the CIA's Cuban courier Paian Diaz, MI6's Daniel Lincoln had reached Berlin on schedule. And also unlike Diaz, Daniel had landed in West as opposed to East Berlin. He did so on 25 August 1964 posing as the salesman Frank Middlemiss. That night Daniel prepared for his visit to East Berlin. His main concern was to ensure the DG's letter to Elke Über was safely stowed in the false bottom of his shaving kit bag. Next he wrapped the framed photograph of Kristiina Ahnger in a shirt and buried it deep in his suitcase before placing his father's gift on top of his other packed clothes – Hemingway's book *For Whom the Bell Tolls*, John Donne's poem inscribed inside. The book was there for his reading pleasure, the photograph Daniel's hoped-for safeguard against a runaway panic attack turning into disaster.

And finally Daniel checked the small padlock securing his suitcase. It was on the padlock the following night in East Berlin he would scratch the *Karl loves Ilsa* message before attaching it to the Weidendammer Bridge late afternoon on 27 August. Daniel, of course, was unaware that Ronald Hunt had crossed into East Berlin on 24 August. Indeed, he knew nothing of operation Leopard, let alone its decoy, and how, starting with Ronald Hunt, everything was about to turn to dust.

***

Ronald Hunt had arrived in West Berlin on 22 August 1964 on a special CIA flight. For the past fourteen years he'd been a prisoner at the US Federal Penitentiary at Leavenworth, Kansas, serving a sixty-six-year sentence for aiding and abetting in the murder of Master Sergeant Horace Neitz in Munich in November 1946. For a time after his arrest, Ronald had been detained at HMP Dartmoor in the UK while his legal representatives argued the British government should refuse his extradition to the United States.

But in 1950, after Janice Hunt admitted to a number of irregularities in her work at the NAAFI head office and waived her right not to testify against her husband, details became clearer. It was soon apparent to the British government that removing Ronald to the US neatly avoided the need for otherwise embarrassing disclosures about his manipulation of the black market in occupied Germany.

Years in prison had not dulled Ronald Hunt's appetite for a deal. As such on Monday 3 August 1964 when two stern men in dark suits arrived and announced themselves as representatives of the US government, Ronald was intrigued to hear what they had to say. No introductions were made. The oldest of the pair, the officer in charge, was in fact Michael Anjelico, the CIA officer with carriage for operation Leopard and counterpart to MI6's Peter Parnell-Brown.

'Berlin? East Berlin? Are you guys kidding?' Ronald said, his diction reflecting his Americanisation over the past fourteen years of incarceration. 'You want me to make a day trip to East Berlin on 24 August and look up Josef Sterck?'

'More than that, Ronald,' Anjelico said, deadpan, 'we want you to give him some documents he's to reveal to the East German public on a day you will nominate, information that will damage the East German communist party leadership.'

Anjelico and his companion looked at one another, waiting for Ronald to absorb this instruction. Finally, Anjelico nodded briefly to the younger man. 'On the twenty-eighth of this month,' the junior CIA officer began, 'an East German communist party plenary conference will be held. In the days before, the state television service, DFF, will televise what passes for a series of debates on its main news program, a production called *Aktuelle Kamera*.' Ronald continued to stare, his brow increasingly furrowed.

'Our people in West Berlin regularly monitor East German television,' Anjelico broke in. 'DFF started advertising these debates three months ago. We want Josef Sterck to participate in the 26 August discussion – it's scheduled for lunchtime so that all the factory workers can watch it live. During the course of the program he will reveal the documents you are to give him.'

Ronald's mind was whirling. 'And how do I find Sterck?' he asked aggressively.

'I was about to explain that,' Anjelico said sharply, putting Ronald in his place. 'In the days before the conference, party members from across East Germany will gather at the SED headquarters in the old Reichsbank building on Kurstrasse. First thing on 24 August you go to Checkpoint Charlie, buy a one-day visa to enter East Berlin, and proceed immediately to Kurstrasse where you will find Sterck. That night you will return to West Berlin via the same border crossing. Simple.'

Several questions surfaced in Ronald's mind. But, as ever, self-interest was top of his list. 'So, what's in it for me?' he said.

'Unconditional release, other than your deportation to the United Kingdom,' Anjelico replied. 'The mechanism to be employed is that immediately after we bring you back here from Berlin, the US government will announce it has bowed to long-standing demands and recently reviewed your case.' Anjelico smiled tightly. 'The public findings of this supposed review will be that although the fourteen years you have spent in prison is not unjust, the sixty-six-year sentence was excessive. As a result you are to be released forthwith. But it will also be confirmed that the panel found the US government incurs no legal liability for the time you served.'

'If, however, you decline to assist us,' Anjelico's younger colleague broke in, 'or deliberately fail to execute your task in East Berlin, we will continue to ignore the unwashed handful in the UK that, for want of something better to do, pesters our London embassy on your behalf. In which case you'll die in prison. Be clear on that.'

Ronald was. But now the parameters for his release were established other things were occupying his thoughts. 'Assuming I find Sterck at the SED head office,' Ronald said after a ponderous pause, 'how am I to convince him on your say-so to publicly release information on 26 August? I'm sure it won't surprise you to know that the leadership's chief minder, currently a guy called Klaus Borkh, tightly controls what comes out of the East German media.' Ronald laughed on seeing the young CIA officer raise an eyebrow. '*Time Magazine*,' he explained, adopting a faux American accent. 'Ain't too many copies of *Playboy* to be found in here.'

The junior officer allowed himself a brief smile before resuming. 'In case you missed it while you've been inside, Josef Sterck made a bit of a name for himself in the years after his retreat into the Soviet bosom upon leaving you to answer for the murder of Horace Neitz. That is, things opened up politically for him after East Germany's creation in 1949. The landscape was very fluid at that time and skilled political operatives thin on the ground. Sterck got himself onto several important SED committees and in the latter part of the 1950s seemed certain to win a seat on the SED executive. But then rumours of a Nazi past started to circulate – nothing definite but enough to stymie his ambition. Publicising the information you feed him offers Sterck a chance for revenge.'

Suddenly Ronald was exasperated, fed up with all the hedging and double-speak. 'How the fuck is Sterck supposed to arrange a television appearance on 26 August?' he asked. 'And while I'm at it, there's also the small matter of whether he'd want to criticise the party leadership in public, revenge or no revenge.'

'Sterck's a political animal,' Anjelico interjected. 'He will have contacts in the *Aktuelle Kamera* production team. All the SED politicians do. And the program's always on the lookout for talent, particularly for live broadcasts ordered by the party bigwigs that many in the SED avoid for fear of making mistakes unable to be edited out. Sterck giving notice on 24 August that he wants to appear live on 26 August will be sufficient time.' Anjelico beaded Ronald. 'As for the risk factor facing Sterck, that's where you come into it.'

'What? I'm supposed to remind him that some party snitch once white-anted his political career and this convinces him to put his balls on the chopping block?'

'No,' Anjelico replied with deliberate blandness. 'But you will tell him we've found his daughter, the one he fathered to the communist woman in Thuringia in 1939, at a time when he was supposedly a committed Nazi dedicated to ridding Germany of the scourge of socialism.'

***

Janice Hunt's disdain for her husband Ronald was undoubtedly profound. But it paled into insignificance when she considered the disastrous impact on her life were he to return to live in her flat, as Ronald had threatened to do if unable to lay his hands on the large amount of cigarettes he needed. In an ideal world, Janice thought, she would go to her NAAFI boss Mr Warren, explain her mistake in marrying Ronald and her part in his Berlin cross-posting. Mr Warren would not be happy but he would forgive her.

Ever since the death of her daughter over three years ago, though, Janice had lived in a hermetically sealed world. Her work was her therapy, a preoccupying vacuum in which she immersed undistracted by thoughts of family holidays, milestones and the other of motherhood's simple pleasures denied to her. In between, she would retreat to the still dark of her flat where, bathed in the memory of Carmel, she would lurk until re-entering the world. This was an apple cart Janice did not want to upset.

It was November 1945, a week since Ronald's intimidation of Janice during his leave in London, and Mr Warren was puzzled. 'The chairman wants me to send an extra 5,000 ten-packets of Player's Mediums to Berlin in each of the next four months,' he said, looking up at Janice. 'It's supposed to cater for the British engineering personnel working at the Volkswagen plant at Wolfsburg. They want stocks of cigarettes for Christmas and into the New Year when more engineers arrive. Truly bizarre.'

Janice smiled, but her heart was pounding. She had forged the signature of the NAAFI chairman Sir Lancelot Royle on the typed letter Mr Warren had just read, containing as it did Ronald's suggested words. 'Sir Lancelot was a sprinter at the Paris Olympics in 1924,' she replied, as if that explained everything.

The truth was Mr Warren had become over-reliant on Janice – such was her unstinting devotion to her work. For that reason, even though he didn't understand it, he took her cryptic observation to be justification for the directive, when in fact the nervous Janice was attempting to draw the long bow that anybody who made it to the Olympics must know what they're doing.

'Well, if that's what the chair wants, I suppose,' Mr Warren said after puzzling some more. He had reached the mistaken conclusion that Janice's reference to Sir Lancelot's participation in the 1924 Olympics was meant to reflect the chairman's emphasis on the importance of good staff morale. After all, he had been a member of the silver medal-winning 4 x 100 metre relay team.

In the interim, as Janice's manipulation of Jim Warren played out, Ronald was back at his NAAFI job in Berlin armed with the eighty pounds extorted from Janice and the number of her post office savings account. He was waiting for Janice to deliver on his demands, as he knew she would. It came, therefore, as no surprise to Ronald when ten days later her endeavours bore fruit.

'Those bloody cretins in London,' the NAAFI corporal fumed. The man was responsible for the receipt of incoming supplies at the Spandau bulk issue store. Standing in the warehouse administration office doorway, he had just opened the NAAFI mail pouch from London to learn he was to be sent an additional 20,000 ten-packets of Player's Medium cigarettes over the next four months, with the first consignment of 5,000 packets already on its way.

Ronald smiled inwardly. It amused him to think of Janice's fear and how his hold over her outweighed her hatred of him. 'What's the problem, corp?' he said.

The corporal let loose. 'Where the fuck am I going to put these fags?' he raged. 'We're up to here with stuff coming out of our arse.'

'We'll sort it, mate,' Ronald replied, in deliberate disregard of the corporal's rank, all the while thinking that his superior's anxiety augured well for his plan to convince the corporal of the solution to the storage problem.

***

Later, in January 1965, when the temperature had cooled a little, MI6's Peter Parnell-Brown and the CIA's Michael Anjelico agreed to hold talks. It was a dialogue triggered by Daniel Lincoln's death, one that eventually culminated in the rapprochement. When they did get together, initially in Langley, there was general agreement that operation Leopard first started to wobble on Monday 24 August 1964, at a time when Leopard envisaged both Paian Diaz and Ronald Hunt arriving in East Berlin. But although Ronald was there as scheduled, having bought a day visa at Checkpoint Charlie as directed, Diaz was stranded in Mauritania.

As for operation Spot, Parnell-Brown was reluctant to mention Daniel Lincoln and risk raising Anjelico's ever-ready hackles. Spot for the record was actually on track on 24 August, although at a very early stage, which is to say the only development of note had been the issue of a visa to Daniel Lincoln alias Frank Middlemiss by the East German KfA office in London. But for now, Parnell-Brown calculated, talking through the Spot calamity could wait. So he played it safe and stuck with operation Leopard.

A second round of talks following much the same format took place in early February 1965, this time hosted by MI6 at its London headquarters. The CIA's Michael Anjelico had just poured himself a cup of coffee. He sighed. 'Paian Diaz should have arrived in East Berlin on 24 August, that was the plan.'

'Yes,' Peter Parnell-Brown confirmed. 'On the same day that Ronald Hunt confronted Josef Sterck.'

Anjelico briefly glared, thinking Parnell-Brown was bragging that his nomination as operation Leopard's decoy had done his bit, whereas the CIA's Cuban courier had fallen short. But on recalling Parnell-Brown's distress at Hunt's conduct subsequent to meeting Josef Sterck he thought the better of it and softened.

'Correct,' Anjelico said, 'the same day.' He took a sip of coffee, screwing up his face in distaste. 'But as we know Diaz's aircraft from Havana broke down in West Africa and he didn't get there until late on 26 August, thirty-six hours after he should have posted the papers to Konrad Voite.' Anjelico gave a bitter laugh. 'So the stupid bastard decided to make up for lost time. Only he fucked up and took the banking records to the wrong place.'

CHAPTER 19

Paian Diaz stood on the far side of Schumannstrasse intimidated by the sight of the SED administrative office and without inkling that he should have gone to the old Reichsbank building on Kurstrasse. The mistake stemmed from Diaz telling his Spanish-speaking East German tour guide that his practice was always to inspect party buildings when in any Soviet bloc country. But Diaz could not properly pronounce the German-language address he had tried to commit to memory. In the end the busy guide made the decision for him, thinking that as an administrator Diaz would want to visit the SED administrative centre located on the eastern side of the River Spree and not its political headquarters on the opposite side of the river a few kilometres from the tour group's hostel.

So, with the documents he was meant to have posted to Konrad Voite's office two days earlier tucked down the back of his shirt – obscured by his singlet and anchored inside his underpants – Diaz made the long trek up Friedrichstrasse, over the Weidendammer Bridge spanning the River Spree until, as per the guide's directions, he turned left two blocks later and wended his way to Schumannstrasse.

The tourist guide in fact had been nervous about letting Diaz go off on his own. Not that the guide's in-built prejudice made him think for a second that a dumb Cuban might be an agent of foreign intelligence. Rather, it was because of the outbreak of pandemonium the previous day, 26 August 1964, when an SED hack called Josef Sterck appeared on the *Aktuelle Kamera* television program.

The event had been screened live at lunchtime so that ahead of the party conference on 28 August workers across the country could watch a political debate during their meal break. But without warning, thirty minutes into what was threatening to be a predictably dull show, Sterck had extracted some documents from his suit coat.

Suddenly the watching audience was galvanised, by the documents and the fact that Sterck appeared somewhat drunk. The papers, Sterck slurred, were receipts showing that last December the East German political leaders Walter Ulbricht and Erich Honecker had charged a day tour to their official expenses, while supposedly in Brno to attend a Warsaw Pact summit meeting.

'Ordinary East German workers,' Sterck thundered, developing an alcohol-powered head of steam, 'dedicated to building our socialist nation can barely afford the cost of food let alone charge the state for exotic holidays.' Disbelieving television staff snapped from their torpor and scurried on set. One ripped at the microphone on Sterck's suit lapel, tearing the cheap material. 'Our leadership is corrupt while millions of workers suffer,' Sterck managed in one last gasp before he was dragged away.

It was the instruction subsequently issued by the head of the office of the council of ministers Klaus Borkh that had unnerved Diaz's guide. The terse directive reminded state travel bureau officials interacting with foreigners, of which the guide was one, of their responsibility to speak highly of East Germany's leaders at all times. This was a warning to be heeded. Borkh had been an unusual choice to head the unit responsible for Ulbricht and Honecker's reputational integrity. And he was not one to be trifled with: since his surprise appointment to the job in May 1963 the former Stasi officer from Pomerania had shown himself to be, if not especially smart, then certainly unrestrainedly vicious.

***

Paian Diaz was unaware of Josef Sterck's previous day televised outburst. But he felt the tension in the air when he walked through the front door of the SED administrative centre, which only added to his own considerable anxiety. And it was hot, and Paian was a natural sweater. A surly teenage girl staffed the booth immediately inside the building, while the usually languid East German People's Police providing security – the *Volkspolizei*, VoPos so-called – were stiffly alert, all thanks to Josef Sterck.

The sight of a never-before-seen-in-the-flesh foreigner petrified the girl inside the cubicle, particularly as he resembled a human sprinkler. All the while the increasingly attentive VoPos looked on. The girl reluctantly opened a perspex flap and asked Paian Diaz what he wanted, hiding her insecurity behind aggression. Diaz, of course, could not understand her. But out of the back of his shirt he did produce a sweat-stained envelope, following which, from his stream of otherwise incomprehensible Spanish, the girl and the curious VoPos detected a name: *Konrad Voite*.

A hurried discussion ensued between the East German actors. There was ready agreement that now was not a good time to be opening any SED politburo member's correspondence, even if the envelope containing it was soaked in sweat and strangely delivered. Nor was there much interest in the complicated exercise of directing the dripping man to the old Reichsbank building. At the bidding of a VoPo the girl tried an internal telephone number, which wouldn't connect. Urged on, she tried another, which rang out. With that the sullen girl sunk back in her chair, arms folded. She'd given up.

One of the more enterprising VoPos walked around the desk and perused a much-fingered internal telephone directory. 'Fuck it,' he said, commencing to dial while the scowling girl rolled her eyes. Throwing caution to the wind, he had just called the office of the head of the SED secretariat. A female voice answered. The man's eyes widened on realising he was actually talking to the secretariat head, Fräulein Elke Über, and not her assistant. The overawed VoPo tried to explain the situation, stammering away in halting sentences.

At the other end of the line, Elke raised her eyes to the ceiling, holding the handset against her chest as the man continued to blabber. Taking a deep breath she restored the receiver to her ear. 'Bring him up here,' she snapped before hanging up.

Paian Diaz sat sipping a glass of water, wondering if he would ever see Havana's waterfront again, his beloved Malecón. The woman who took his envelope had understood him when he said *Kuba* in his best German. She had also examined his personal papers: the form identifying him as a member of a tour group; the name and address of the group's hostel; and its tour program included in which was the departure time of the contingent's charter flight on 6 September, ten days from now. More to the point, he thought, she had smiled kindly when telling him to wait in Spanish. *Esperar*, she said, calling him *Señor Diaz*, and never before had Paian Diaz so enjoyed hearing his mother tongue. But that was over an hour ago and Paian's anxiety was again on the rise.

Elke Über could hardly believe her eyes. Her first instinct was to find someone who could speak Spanish to interrogate the Cuban who had arrived out of the blue with six pages of damning Swiss bank statements. But as Elke thought it through, she came to appreciate that the arrival of the documents politically crucifying Walter Ulbricht and Erich Honecker had not occurred in a vacuum. Ever methodical, and resisting the urge to write down anything, she began to piece things together in her head.

***

At 9 am on 24 August 1964, three days before Elke Über took possession of the Swiss banking records, Ronald Hunt, in his capacity as the operation Leopard decoy, had arrived at the SED headquarters in the old Reichsbank building. A young man in a Volkspolizei uniform immediately intercepted him. The VoPo spoke curtly prompting Ronald to extract a note written in German from his coat: *Mein Name ist Ronald Hunt. Ich habe einen Termin bei Josef Sterck.*

The young policeman eyed Ronald suspiciously before shrugging. His seniors had told him never to mess with party heavyweights and Josef Sterck was a party elder. 'Four... one... seven,' the VoPo said, spelling out Sterck's office number in laboured English as if speaking to a dull child.

'*Danke*,' Ronald replied when pointed to a set of stairs, jittery now that his reunion with Josef Sterck was imminent. He began to scale the steps, thinking that the last time he had seen Sterck was in November 1946 in Munich, when Sterck shot dead the American serviceman Horace Neitz, just five minutes walk from the US Army building. American military police had quickly arrested Sterck. But the German was one of those characters who seemed always able to wriggle out of trouble. And, Ronald thought, the murder of Neitz was no exception.

***

The East German communist party, the SED, was formed in April 1946 from the remnants of several fragmented German communist movements. Its head, Friedrich Reinhold, had spent the war exiled in Russia and was high on the shortlist to lead the German state the Soviets would eventually stand up in their occupation zone. So when the Soviets suggested in November 1946 that Josef Sterck's shooting of Horace Neitz was a good opportunity to burnish his credentials in a battle with the Americans, Reinhold did not quibble.

Unbeknown to all bar Josef Sterck, however, here was irony at its richest. Before the war, while heading the Weimar economic office, Sterck had exploited and impregnated the wife of Reinhold's deceased younger brother. Exiled in Moscow, Reinhold believed that both brother and wife had perished; and naturally Sterck had stayed quiet about the widowed sister-in-law, aided by the fact that shortly before the war he'd sent her abroad never to return. None the wiser, therefore, the leader-in-waiting proceeded to agitate for Sterck's release, ratcheting up the rhetoric at every turn.

After three intense weeks, the Americans decided that Sterck wasn't worth the candle. Moreover, a forensic audit of documents found in Master Sergeant Neitz's office now revealed the English NAAFI soldier detained at the scene of the shooting, Ronald Hunt, had laundered black market reichsmarks through a scheme cooked up by Neitz and a US accomplice in London, Private First Class Thomas Foster. Foster was currently assisting FBI agents with their enquiries.

**

Upstairs in the old Reichsbank building Ronald inspected Josef Sterck from across the German's desk. To Ronald's eyes Sterck had aged considerably since last seeing him in November 1946. Indeed, Sterck was now sixty-two. Time, Ronald judged, had not been kind to the German. Not only was Sterck heavier with snow-white hair, his jowly drinker's face was also unattractively spotted and pallid. Only the darting eyes remained as Ronald remembered them.

'So, what do you want?' Sterck asked. He too had been appraising Ronald, intrigued that his one-time accomplice should have reappeared after so lengthy an interval.

The question caused a wave of bitterness to crash over Ronald. 'What do I want?' he asked indignantly. 'Mate, you left me hanging by my thumbs.' Josef Sterck needed no reminding that his murder of Master Sergeant Horace Neitz was behind Ronald's accusation.

'It had to be done,' Sterck replied. 'Otherwise, he would have destroyed me.'

'Me, me, me,' Ronald retorted, further irritated by Sterck's response and oblivious to his own self-absorption. 'I never saw a penny of the money we made, unlike you. And then there's the small matter of the more than three years I spent in the general prison population in Dartmoor straight after you shot the Yank, dodging all sorts of threatening lunatics. Let me tell you, mate, it was scary. I had to request to go into iso. All the while Foster squealed like a stuck pig. Not to mention my lovely ex-wife who wouldn't stop singing at the top of her voice.' Ronald sneered, his narcissism asserting on finding brief consolation in the thought he had gotten away with murdering the child he fathered to Janice. 'And she ends up with a good behavior bond. Fuck me.'

'I heard you were extradited to the US,' Sterck said.

'Worried about me, was you? Keeping a fatherly eye out for me, perhaps?'

Sterck took a deep breath. 'No, no, not at all,' he said candidly. 'But in the mid to late fifties I did make some progress up the party ladder. People began to try to curry favour. Someone showed me an English newspaper featuring an article on protests in London over the sentence the Americans gave you.'

'Sixty-six fucking years,' Ronald exploded. 'That's what the Yanks gave me, on top of the three years I did in Dartmoor. In case you don't know, sixty-six years is a life sentence, all thanks to you.'

Sterck shrugged. He and Ronald were playing on his ground; he saw no need for false empathy. But Sterck's curiosity was real. 'So, why are you here? Why aren't you still in Leavenworth?' Sterck's cunning fed his intuition. 'It's something to do with the party conference on Friday, isn't it?'

Ronald sobered at Sterck's mention of the conference and the thought that his continued freedom relied on convincing the German to do as the Americans wanted. He took the receipts from his pocket, those showing that the East German leaders Walter Ulbricht and Erich Honecker had charged their tour of Bouzov Castle in Czechoslovakia to the East German taxpayer.

'Today's Monday, the twenty-fourth,' Ronald began slowly, consulting his memory. 'On Wednesday, we want you to go on the *Aktuelle Kamera* television program. Contact the producers today and say you want to appear on the Wednesday lunchtime program to be televised live.'

Sterck stared at Ronald in stunned amazement. 'We?' he echoed. 'Who's we? And how come *we're* so well informed about what's showing when on East German television?'

Ronald didn't answer but instead passed Sterck the receipts, sitting back to wait while the older man perused them. Seconds stretched to seem like hours. The sound of heavy boots on the concrete floor in the outside corridor broke the silence. Ronald flinched. Had Sterck pressed a button hidden under the lip of his desk to summon the guards? But as the clip of the bootsteps receded so too did Ronald's anxiety. He looked at Sterck whose brow was knotted, seemingly in a mixture of concentration and puzzlement.

'Frankly, I don't understand,' Sterck said finally, placing the papers on the desk. 'What's the point you're trying to make in giving me these receipts?'

'They're evidence of corruption,' Ronald said.

Sterck stared at Ronald before bursting out laughing. 'Corruption? That's a bit rich coming from you.' Sterck shook his head. 'Dear comrade, let me tell you that unless I'm missing something, these receipts are not evidence of corruption. At worst, they're evidence of administrative expediency.'

'Well, to the average East German factory worker who can't afford to wipe his clacker they'll be evidence of corruption. That's why we want you to go on the Wednesday lunchtime live program, when all the workers made to watch will be enjoying their grub.'

Sterck's eyes bulged. 'Are you and whoever's instructing you insane?' he bellowed. 'I would face serious repercussions were I to make any allegation, specious or otherwise, against Ulbricht and Honecker. Give me one good reason why I'd even consider this.'

Ronald paused. Here was the crunch point. 'I'm working on American instructions,' he said. 'I'm doing so because they'll let me out of the pen permanently if you do as they want.'

'Which Americans?' Sterck asked belligerently.

Ronald ignored him. 'They have your daughter,' he said simply. 'The one you fathered to the German communist woman.'

CHAPTER 20

The first batch of 5,000 packets of Player's Mediums arrived at the NAAFI bulk issue store in Spandau on Wednesday 21 November 1945. After much huffing, puffing and cursing, the corporal in charge managed to squeeze the several wrapped pallets into an area at the back of the warehouse. Shortly after Ronald made a visit to Sophie Lange, the German woman forced into prostitution who had connected him with Josef Sterck. Ronald had arrived at her Charlottenburg apartment bearing an envelope and a tin of plum jam.

Thereafter, Sophie walked all the way to the former Hitler Youth headquarters, now hotel, in Berlin's Soviet zone where she handed the Russian guard at the entrance the envelope addressed to Herr Brenner. Thirty-six hours later, as per the prearranged procedure, a Soviet military motorcycle courier delivered the correspondence to Fräulein Elke Über at the Weimar city hall in the state of Thuringia. With that, Josef Sterck was summoned.

'The first tranche of cigarettes has arrived in Spandau,' Elke told Sterck. 'You are to go to Berlin, contact this Ronald Hunt at the NAAFI bulk store and arrange to buy them as soon as possible. I have organised transport for Sunday night. I expect you to return here by no later than the middle of the week.' Elke was a skilled operator. By now she had the Russian officer in charge of logistics eating out of her hand, making the arrangement of air transport to and from Berlin and accommodation there a piece of cake.

There followed a rare thing in that Josef Sterck chose to trust Ronald Hunt. 'The fags cost me a shilling a packet, right?' Ronald said. It was Monday evening and he and Sterck were inside the bombed-out shell passing as Sophie Lange's apartment, this time Sophie earning a pair of silk stockings for her trouble.

'And 5,000 shillings comes to 250 quid, right?' Ronald said. 'But I've had a few expenses at home,' he added after a calculated pause, only for the dubious look on Sterck's face to convince him he was wasting his time. 'Mate, I've only got eighty quid,' Ronald admitted, coming clean, 'which buys me 1,600 ten-packets.' He took a deep breath. 'At 150 reichsmarks per pack that sets you back 240,000 reichsmarks. What do you say to us doing it that way and catching up the missing 3,400 packs next month?'

Josef Sterck considered Ronald's proposal. His pockets were stuffed with reichsmarks, all 750,000 he needed to buy the full tranche of 5,000 packets. To do as Ronald suggested would involve returning to Weimar with fewer packets than expected. This perturbed him, not least because he feared that Elke Über might think he was trying to swindle her. But Sterck also thought about the still substantial pile of reichsmarks on which he was sitting and how the favourable black market conditions could dissipate before he disposed of every last one of them. So he decided that, provided Ronald could adequately explain how he was going to justify the purchase of all four tranches of cigarettes, 20,000 packets, he would take a chance on him.

'The warehousing corporal,' Ronald said, 'is pissing his pants about the fags taking up space earmarked for other items.' Ronald smiled. 'So, I'm going to do him a favour and help him sell them.'

Sterck's raised eyebrows invited Ronald to continue. 'Last June,' Ronald said, 'our electrical and mechanical engineers took over the Volkswagen plant at Wolfsburg. They're about to start building cars for the British military, hundreds of the bloody things so they can employ some of your lot.'

'And?'

'I'll tell the corp I've got a mate over there who's willing to arrange a whip around to buy 5,000 ten-packets for each of the next four months. It'll be a stock of fags for the boys in Wolfsburg to have on hand over Christmas and into the New Year when other engineers arrive.' Ronald laughed. 'He's such a nervous Nellie, the corp,' he said. 'He'll be dead keen and won't ask questions.'

Sterck liked what he heard. Wolfsburg, home to the Volkswagen plant, was located in the British zone some 230 kilometres west of Berlin. The city was close enough to make it seem conceivable for quantities of cigarettes to be sent there from Spandau, but far enough away to avoid harmful accidental scrutiny.

At this point a bond of sorts was forged between Ronald Hunt and Josef Sterck. It manifested in Sterck's offer to make the full payment of 750,000 reichsmarks, yet take possession only of 1,600 of the 5,000-packet tranche. But Sterck wasn't the type to throw all caution to the wind; and he knew better than most the value of incriminating evidence. Sterck's offer, therefore, was conditional on Ronald signing an IOU committing him, as promised, to make up the 3,400-packet shortfall in December and deliver a total of 8,400 packets that month. A canny move by Sterck as it transpires.

That night, while enjoying a celebratory pint, Ronald's upbeat mood suddenly vanished. It was the realisation he could not safely repatriate all 750,000 reichsmarks received from Josef Sterck, much less transfer that same amount over each of the next three months. Ronald was crestfallen not to have thought of this earlier. Sure the authorities were content to let British personnel repatriate a couple of hundred quid here and there, aware these were black market funds. But the leniency of the British paymaster's office had its limits. It was a moment of reflection that would eventually lead Ronald to the American soldier called Master Sergeant Horace Neitz.

***

In the years before Hitler's ascension to power, the German state of Thuringia had been something of a communist stronghold, to the extent that the communists briefly partnered in a governing coalition during the 1920s. But by 1933 the Nazis had wrested political control of all Germany from all others. Communism was outlawed and purges began forcing many socialists to flee for their lives. Two Berlin-based communists, brothers called Reinhold, were among this number. The elder, Friedrich, was senior in the party and a future leader in the eyes of some. He fled to Moscow, while the younger sibling Joachim took his pregnant wife Hannah to Thuringia, trusting that despite the Nazi political dominance, people in the state would generally tolerate known communists.

Joachim and Hannah set up home in Weimar, where Joachim found work in a factory. The couple's son was born and for a short time Joachim kept his nose clean. But the siren call of socialist politics was irresistible. In 1936 Joachim was arrested for trying to organise a labour strike to protest against Nazi excesses. Hannah never saw him again. And in 1937 when the Nazis seized the Reinhold family home, Hannah aged twenty-seven and her four-year-old son were evicted.

Desperate and scared, Hannah reverted to her maiden name of Krumbach. But work was difficult to find and shelter expensive. Soon her paltry savings were exhausted. It was while begging for food in a well-to-do area of Weimar, all the while hushing her hungry child to be quiet, that Hannah encountered an elderly Jewish couple to whom she introduced herself. A conversation ensued. The old folk explained how their housemaid had resigned, no longer willing to work for a Jewish employer. They offered Hannah the job, indicating that the position came with staff accommodation, a small cottage in the garden at the rear of the main house.

Thereafter, Hannah's life turned for the better. But outside the bubble of her secluded existence in the Weimar suburbs, things were getting ugly. Jews and communists were now public enemies numbers one and two in Germany. People were leaving the country in droves. Hannah was grateful that her employers were too obstinate to be driven out by Nazi thugs. But just when it seemed things couldn't get worse, Kristallnacht occurred and the Nazis systematically began to seize Jewish property.

In March 1939, just six months before the war commenced, Hannah Krumbach's employers received advice that their home was to be appropriated. The old couple showed amazing pluck and dug in their toes. 'The Bierhoff couple are refusing to budge,' a subordinate reported to the head of the Weimar-based Thuringia regional economic office, one Josef Sterck. 'And they say if they're evicted their maid, a non-Jewish German woman with a six-year-old son who live in the servants' quarters, will be homeless.'

Sterck scowled. 'What sort of self-respecting German woman would work for a pair of Jews?' he asked rhetorically. The subordinate shrugged, the man's uncaring attitude angering Sterck. 'Don't just stand there, you dolt,' he roared at the young man. 'Go and get this slut who chooses to demean herself and bring her to me. I want to have a word.'

Josef Sterck had never married. Not that he was disinterested in women but his obsessive drive to make money was a far greater priority. He had known women, though — mainly prostitutes unable to resist an overbearing policeman. It was this experience that caused Sterck to recognise his sexual appetite was stimulated only when he held significant leverage over a woman. The sight of Hannah Krumbach, therefore, blonde, demure and scared stiff forcefully aroused Sterck. The simple fact was that he held the power of life and death over her. Tingling, almost coy, he eyed Hannah across his desk. He knew he had to have her, and soon. Aryanisation of the Bierhoff home could wait for now.

'Give me one good reason,' Sterck said, going through the motions even though his mind was made up, 'why I should not acquire the Bierhoff property.'

'They're old people who have been good Germans,' Hannah whispered. 'And they're decent people who treat my son and me like family.'

'Where's your husband?' Sterck asked, suddenly concerned he hadn't thought of this earlier.

Hannah's fear vanished. 'Dead,' she snapped. 'Murdered by the regime you serve.'

Sterck pursed his lips and tapped the silver letter opener held in his left hand against the fore and index fingers of his right. 'I could kill you just like that, you know,' he said. Hannah glared, still defiant. 'And your son too,' he added, raising his eyebrows.

The mention of her only child crushed Hannah's resolve. She hunched, the effect of which was to make it seem like she was in physical pain. 'What do you want?' she whispered. 'I'll do anything you require but don't hurt my son. Please.'

'That's more like it,' Sterck said coldly. 'I want you to tell me your life story, including your husband's background. After that, I will instruct you on how we shall proceed from here.'

Hannah nodded. Cowed, distraught and intuitively knowing what was to come, she was at the end of her tether. The thought of Sterck laying his hands on her made her wish she were dead. And from one perspective she was. In late 1938 news to the effect that the Nazis had executed Joachim, his wife and son filtered through to Friedrich Reinhold in Moscow. As the story had passed from hand to hand facts were lost in translation, whereby the eviction of Hannah and her son from the family home came to be misrepresented as their murder along with Joachim. With news of unending Nazi horrors reaching Moscow, to Friedrich the advice of all three deaths had a grim ring of truth.

Hannah Krumbach fell pregnant to Josef Sterck in June 1939, three months after her coercion began. Up until that time people with means could leave Germany with relative ease. But with certain war looming, bordering countries were no longer accepting German immigrants in numbers, not wanting to antagonise Hitler. Sterck had a decision to make. The woman whom he was forcing into once a week sex was both a Jew-lover and the sister-in-law of a senior German communist. He cursed that he should feel so sexually attracted to her. There was only one thing for it; after the next assignation she had to go, before her baby bulge was too obvious. Then she'd be out of sight and out of mind.

Sterck opened the bottom drawer of his desk. The pair had just re-clothed. 'Here, take this,' he told Hannah, handing her an even one thousand French francs. 'You and your son have twenty-four hours to leave Germany. If not I will have the Gestapo arrest you.' Hannah stared. The thought of taking money from Sterck revolted her. Nor did she stop to consider that the last thing Sterck needed was the Gestapo asking him questions about his relationship with a communist woman. But Hannah's preoccupation was her son. She knew his future hinged on leaving Germany.

'The French are no longer accepting refugees,' Sterck continued. 'But show the border guards the money and tell them you intend to travel to the United States. Provided you buy the ticket the authorities will let you go. If not, they'll return you and your son back here to Germany.'

Afterwards Sterck would occasionally think of facilitating the escape of the pregnant Hannah and her son to the United States shortly before the outbreak of the war. For a time he viewed it as an act of generosity, ignoring the fact that his overriding imperative was to protect his Nazi credentials. But as the years passed Sterck thought less and less about the matter to the extent of forgetting about it – save for a brief revival in November 1946 when the unwitting Friedrich Reinhold plucked him from the hands of the Americans.

And there the Hannah episode rested, ancient history never revisited. That is until one day in August 1964, when Ronald Hunt unexpectedly arrived in East Berlin and told Josef Sterck the CIA was in contact with the daughter Sterck had never seen.

CHAPTER 21

It all started in June 1959, of course, when by chance Elke Über attended the opera at the Konzerthaus in Berlin's Gendarmenmarkt Square on the same night as MI6's Fopsy Phillips and Henry Grahame. By then Elke had been the head of the SED secretariat for a good nine months, something that greatly impressed the inept MI6 pair when they discovered this during a clumsy recruitment attempt at the interval. The next day the Stasi decided to run a double game and instructed Elke to get on board. She signed with Henry Grahame six weeks later. Now on 27 August 1964 Elke smiled, recalling the high farce of it all. Her reflection on that time five years ago, no question, had everything to do with the batch of incriminating Swiss banking records meant for Konrad Voite that the Cuban Paian Diaz had delivered to her office earlier in the day.

The Diaz development, Elke was sure, linked back to her sham recruitment. It had come as no great surprise in January 1961 when a charming fellow called Roger Holbrook, the current MI6 Director General, waylaid her in West Berlin. Holbrook told her point-blank he knew she was a double agent. 'You're blown, Fräulein Über,' he had said with a twinkle in his eye. But rather than alerting the Stasi to her uncovering, Holbrook proposed she defect, offering her the postal address of his private London residence should she wish to make contact.

At the time, Elke still held hopes of East Germany becoming the bastion of socialist equality of which her parents had once dreamed for pre-war Germany. But it was soon obvious the country was doomed, too beholden to the Soviets, as reflected in the dreadful Wall built at the Kremlin's direction in August 1961 that to this day still divided Berlin. Finally it got too much. In January 1964 she wrote to Roger Holbrook offering to defect subject to certain conditions, arranging for her letter to be posted from Copenhagen by a friend, an unquestioning female Yugoslav diplomat who was going home via the Danish capital.

Alone in her office, the door securely locked, Elke thought of the conditions attached to her defection offer, those which traced back to Dublin in 1938. It was in front of the Martello Tower on the Sandymount Strand – one of a series of small, circular forts built to repel Napoleon – that Dougal briefly held her in his arms. Afterwards they gazed at the Irish Sea before ambling back to the hotel suite hand in hand. There the young ones waited for Elke's parents to return from their play at the Abbey theatre, infused with affection and stiff as boards with sexual tension. It was on the floor, cushioned by the deep pile carpet, that Elke lost her virginity.

And Dougal? Well, Elke had first met him in March 1938 when her father, a registrar at the Bayreuth teaching hospital in Bavaria, brought the twenty-two-year-old medical student from Yorkshire home for dinner. Dougal quickly became a family favourite, joining the Übers later in the year on summer vacation in Dublin. But after coupling with Elke, while both were beset with need, Dougal immediately fled to Liverpool, leaving a note for her parents claiming an urgent family illness.

Elke never saw Dougal again. She knew this would be the case the instant he started to cry, when in the afterglow panting and naked they were lying on the hotel room floor. 'You're only sixteen,' Dougal had wept into her ear, 'and lawfully still a child. Yet I am lawfully an adult. I will be branded as a paedophile and visit disgrace upon everyone dear to me, you most of all, my darling.'

The sight of Dougal's anguish, his blue-green eyes wounded and swollen, thereafter ate at Elke. It was a loss permanently embedded by the Nazi murder of her parents a year later. That's why Elke had made MI6 buying her a home on the Sandymount Strand a condition of her defection, once it was clear that East Germany could never live up to her parents' socialist ideal, leaving only an aching emptiness and a deep desire to live her days immersed in the memory of Dougal.

For now, however, Elke willed her introspection to be over. There was much to piece together and not much time. Josef Sterck's previous day's drunken denunciation of the party leadership on live television, she now realised, was not a random event. And with that, it occurred to Elke the key thing was the distinction between Sterck's ho-hum evidence of corruption and the dynamite sitting on the desk in front of her.

An image of Konrad Voite flashed before Elke's eyes. In the 1920s the quietly spoken fifty-nine-year-old professor from Dresden had gained a doctorate from Oxford University in which he extolled the virtues of Adam Smith's free market economic theory. For that sin, Elke mused, the hardline comrades, among them Walter Ulbricht and Erich Honecker, had never forgiven Voite, despite him later spending four years in Buchenwald concentration camp for his activist defence of socialist labour values.

Voite, nonetheless, had been a minister in the East German government since 1955. His much-needed intellectual grunt, however, was always exercised behind closed doors, which explained his universally derided portfolio of Minister for Cultural Harmony, whatever that meant. But there was no way the leadership duopoly of Ulbricht and Honecker was going to grant him formal power.

Elke nodded. She was beginning to understand. 'That is unless Ulbricht and Honecker are pushed out at tomorrow's party conference,' she said, speaking softly to herself. 'In which case Voite's talent would be on display to party members, the economically literate of whom quietly fret about East Germany's unhealthy reliance on Soviet Russia, taking him who knows where.' Elke smiled. She might never know why a Cuban armed with Swiss banking records for Konrad Voite was chosen to bring them to East Berlin. But it was clear that elements, almost certainly Western intelligence elements, were seeking to orchestrate a leadership coup at the party conference.

Elke had reached a decision point, namely what to do with the Swiss documents now that she was clear on their purpose. She considered her options. Three came to mind: one was to destroy the papers and pretend they never existed; the second was to take them to Voite's office at the old Reichsbank building as presumably the Western instigators had intended; and the third was to use them for her own advantage. The first choice was out of the question. The records were extremely valuable and not something to be discarded lightly. Should she, then, just give the material to Voite and sit back and wait for the fireworks? But did that not amount to putting her head in the sand much as if she destroyed the papers?

Turning to the third option, Elke gazed pensively through the window. How, she wondered, could she make best use of the records? 'At another time,' Elke muttered to the glass pane, 'I would have gone to Voite and said, "Here, you can have these if you promise to make me a minister in your government."' But with socialist East Germany in a slow death spiral, she had made her defection offer to Sir Roger Holbrook. And with that momentous step a chapter in Elke's life had forever closed. Relocation to the Sandymount Strand was her future and to this she was committed, Konrad Voite as East German prime minister or not.

Suddenly, Elke stood stock-still, gripped by the thought that Josef Sterck's televised carry-on and the Swiss papers meant for Voite were wholly connected. The threads swirled until they coalesced in a sudden rush of clarity. 'Tonight,' Elke whispered in shocked awe, 'tonight, on the eve of the party conference, the padlock signal will be set on the Weidendammer Bridge.'

***

Daniel Lincoln was initially oblivious to Josef Sterck's 26 August histrionics on the *Aktuelle Kamera* television program. To be sure he had crossed into East Berlin that morning as planned, two hours before the program aired live at lunchtime. But in his guise as the salesman Frank Middlemiss he had gone directly to the Frund Hotel adjacent to the Weidendammer Bridge on the eastern side of the River Spree. When told it would be an hour before he could check in, Daniel decided to take a stroll, needing to walk for his own benefit but also needing to convince the Stasi surveillance people he was someone who liked to fill in time exploring. Crossing to the western side of the river, he made his way along the bank before eventually returning to the Weidendammer Bridge. Traversing the bridge to his nearby hotel, Daniel warily inspected the lamp post on which the next afternoon he was to attach the padlock etched with the words *Karl loves Ilsa*.

Daniel, of course, spoke excellent German. When told his room was still unavailable, he grandly informed the hotel clerk of his important meeting with state trade officials at 3 pm; and no, he said in response to the clerk's attempt at amelioration, he would not care to leave his suitcase with the hotel until the room was ready. The clerk found this amusing, thinking how wise it was of Herr Middlemiss to be alert to theft in hotels like his catering to foreigners. Daniel did not disabuse the man of the notion, nor obviously did he confide that his worry was a thief might discover Sir Roger Holbrook's letter to Elke Über secreted in the false base of his shaving bag. So Daniel sat in the hotel's bleak and silent lobby unaware that operation Leopard even existed, much less how Josef Sterck had just played his part in it.

Once finally in his room Daniel unpacked, placing Hemingway's *For Whom the Bell Tolls* on his bedside table while taking care to put the all-important padlock into the small netting compartment inside his suitcase. He would need to retrieve it with a swift grasp that night. Kristiina Ahnger's photograph he kept in his case, in reserve for use as needed. Now readied, Daniel ordered a pot of coffee, which arrived cold but miraculously within minutes. Turning on the built-in radio in the bedside table, he sat at the room's small writing desk and began to eat the sandwich he'd carried with him from West Berlin. Shortly after, Daniel was startled to hear a female announcer interrupt the staid classical music. He knew enough of Eastern bloc methodology to know that disrupting the state radio broadcast heralded something important.

'It is of great regret to advise,' the woman began, her voice formal and sombre, 'that a respected party elder, Herr Josef Sterck, experienced a severe medical incident earlier today while speaking at a televised public forum.' As the woman shuffled her papers, Daniel felt a wave of relief wash over him. He knew nothing of Josef Sterck who had come to prominence only after he left Germany. The announcement, Daniel imagined, was simply to report that an old party duffer had suffered a heart attack or something equally as deadly.

But when the woman resumed speaking, Daniel's blood turned to ice. 'A British citizen, one Ronald Kendall Hunt, has been detained and charged with inciting comrade Sterck to disseminate false and defamatory material in breach of state media laws. It has been since ascertained that the Britisher Hunt is illegally present in sovereign East Germany. The *Volkspolizei* is investigating and further charges against the British enemy of the state are expected to be laid shortly.'

Daniel's hands began to shake, causing drops of coffee to spill onto the table, forcing him to grip the cup in two hands to set it down. He raced quickly into the toilet cubicle, keen to avoid the Stasi cameras and knowing from past experience that once his trembling started it could become uncontrollable. Daniel did not know either Ronald Hunt or Josef Sterck. But the announcement was not simply a case of the East Germans crowing about an allegedly meddling Englishman they'd picked up. Words like *Britisher* and *enemy of the state* were political and meant to convey a message.

Sucking in deep breaths, Daniel tried to tell himself the incident had no bearing on operation Spot. Thankfully for Daniel, as it may well have pushed him over the edge, he was unaware of the symbiotic relationship between Ronald Hunt's activities and his own undertaking. Even so, for the East Germans to be taunting the UK government about a detained British citizen was much too close to home.

The monitoring staff at Field Station Berlin, the joint US–UK listening post in the British zone in West Germany, were quick to forward the text of the East German radio announcement to their respective headquarters in London and Washington. In the Foreign Office in London there was much conferencing and debate when news of a British citizen detained in East Berlin filtered through, in the midst of which the diplomats still found time to moan that nobody in the American system had bothered to advise them of the release of the supposedly incarcerated Ronald Hunt.

***

Ronald Hunt had been meant to get in and out of East Berlin on the same day, 24 August 1964. When he didn't reappear, the CIA's Michael Anjelico in West Berlin had telephoned Peter Parnell-Brown in London. He made the call to Parnell-Brown's home on an open line in the early hours of 25 August, some thirty-six hours before Daniel Lincoln heard the East Berlin radio broadcast.

'We waited until midnight local time,' Anjelico said, 'when the day visa expired. We figured that he and the target might have kissed and made up and been out drinking, whoring, or both, meaning he wouldn't get back until late.'

'Are you sure he even went over?' Parnell-Brown asked archly. 'I mean getting him there was your responsibility under the agreed division of labour.'

Anjelico was tired and frustrated. But for once in his life he bit his tongue. 'I personally watched him buy the visa at Charlie and disappear up Friedrichstrasse,' he said curtly.

The mention of Friedrichstrasse made Parnell-Brown's heart skip. The thoroughfare began in West Berlin and ran through Checkpoint Charlie into East Berlin, continuing over Unter den Linden, on which was Elke Über's apartment, before reaching Friedrichstrasse station where on 27 August in front of the Tränenpalast pavilion Daniel Lincoln was to pass Elke the DG's letter. Further up Friedrichstrasse, one block to the right at the eastern end of the Weidendammer Bridge spanning the River Spree was the Frund Hotel where Daniel would stay when he crossed into East Berlin one day and eight hours from now. And a kilometre or so further up Friedrichstrasse, this time a couple of blocks off to the left, was the SED administrative centre on Schumannstrasse where Elke worked. But of course Michael Anjelico had no knowledge of operation Spot and

Peter Parnell-Brown was keen to avoid the impression he was harbouring secrets.

'Sorry,' Parnell-Brown said. 'It's the bloody stress. Bad news always seems worse in the early morning. I suppose all we can do is wait and hope he turns up.'

'Agreed,' Anjelico said. 'Although he's illegal now and they'll delight in cutting off his balls just for that.'

'Too true, Michael,' Parnell-Brown said, 'too true.' The Englishman sighed. 'Let's talk tomorrow. Things might be clearer by then.'

'Roger that,' Anjelico said, ringing off abruptly in the time-honoured American way. He knew Parnell-Brown was saying they should wait until lunchtime on 26 August to see if Josef Sterck made his intervention on television.

CHAPTER 22

Times were better for Ronald Hunt back in January 1946, although far from perfect. His cigarette-selling scheme was going well, so far, having managed in December under cover of supposed Christmas expenses to convince the British Army paymaster's office to convert enough reichsmarks into sterling cash to facilitate the purchase of 8,400 ten-packets. Now Josef Sterck had taken these off his hands – the 3,400 packs Ronald owed Sterck for November plus the December tranche of 5,000 packets.

But Sterck's payment had left Ronald in possession of near enough to a million and a half reichsmarks, with another million and a half to come when the January and February transactions were done. Ronald pondered his dilemma, namely how best to convert three million reichsmarks into pounds when the only avenue of exchange of which he was aware was the limited offering available to British service personnel.

Would it be possible to bribe a paymaster clerk? he wondered before accepting he had fully exhausted any goodwill to be found in the paymaster's office. What then? At this point it dawned on Ronald there was just one other person with as much to lose as him, and that was Josef Sterck. When his partner in crime returned to Berlin at the end of January to pick up that month's 5,000-packet purchase, Ronald would enlist his support.

'I can see your problem,' Sterck said two weeks later. The two men were seated inside Sophie Lange's crumbling apartment, a catering-size can of pineapple on the bench behind them.

'Yes,' Ronald said, reiterating his predicament. 'It's all very well to have these marks, three million of the bloody things by the time we're finished. But mate it's a case of water, water and not a drop to drink if I can't convert them to pounds.'

Sterck silently cursed. Once all the cigarettes had been bought with his reichsmarks, the issue of conversion to sterling was not his problem. But if this bumbling British fellow got caught trying to repatriate a colossal sum of reichsmarks, that spelled trouble. People in Britain would be sure to enquire how in the first place Josef Sterck had accumulated enough marks to buy 20,000 packets of cigarettes. And for Sterck this raised the terrifying spectre of Nazi hunters investigating his seven years in charge of the Weimar economic office.

An image of Elke Über flashed into Sterck's mind. Elke had little formal power in the Soviet set-up. But with the help of some of the more smitten Soviets, she had become an adept problem solver. Things like where to buy valuables with British cigarettes and safely store them, Elke had all the answers. Sterck exhaled. If anyone could help it would be Elke. 'Leave it with me,' Sterck told Ronald. 'There's someone back in Thuringia I will consult who may be able to assist.'

'We're three-quarters done,' Josef Sterck told Elke. They were in her dimly lit office just days on from Sterck speaking with Ronald in Berlin. 'The purchase of fifteen thousand packets of cigarettes is now complete.' With that, Sterck proceeded to explain the difficulties Ronald faced in converting reichsmarks into British pounds.

'Any delay in purchasing the last tranche of cigarettes must be avoided,' Elke said. 'Cigarettes will not be Germany's de facto currency indefinitely. Even now I'm hearing rumours that the British and Americans are considering the introduction of a new, gold-backed German currency.' She smiled grimly. 'And when that happens, there will be no more people like the Troosts willing to part with family heirlooms for a few packets of British tobacco.'

The Troosts were an elderly couple hailing from Sangerhausen in central Germany. How Elke Über found them, Josef Sterck had no idea. But the couple had turned up recently in Weimar carrying a case full of jewellery, items they were anxious to exchange for cigarettes. The valuables – diamond-encrusted rings, silver pendants and gold bands – were now secure in the safe Elke had persuaded the Russians to install in her office. The precious goods would reap a tidy sum when German script was again worth something.

'Yes, precisely, Fräulein Über,' Sterck replied. He gave a sly smile. 'But once all four tranches are bought,' he added, 'we wouldn't want Hunt letting on that the reichsmarks used to buy the cigarettes came from *us*.' Sterck's smiled again to underline his deliberate avoidance of the word *me*.

'I agree it would be unwise to leave Hunt high and dry,' Elke said, ignoring Sterck and continuing before he could try again. 'There is, though, one possible solution. It involves a person who deals in very large amounts of reichsmarks.'

'What did you have in mind?' Sterck asked apprehensively; you never knew with Elke.

Elke did not answer directly. 'I will need you to make the arrangements,' she said.

Why me? Sterck thought, sick of doing all the legwork but not game to be openly hostile. 'I am of course at your service, Fräulein Über,' he fawned.

'As you know,' Elke said, taking no notice of Sterck's attempted ingratiation, 'I am originally from Bavaria. My Soviet colleagues, those enterprising comrades who like to try and win favour with me, keep me informed of developments there. It has been brought to my attention that an American Master Sergeant in Munich, who is in charge of catering for US occupation forces in Bavaria, repatriates a large sum of pounds sterling to England each month for the purchase of British foodstuffs and other goods.' Elke smiled. 'The US Congress, apparently, has directed US forces in Bavaria to make sterling purchases as a bolster for British industry. American soldiers stationed in Bavaria can buy these items with reichsmarks, and so the cycle goes.'

'I see,' Sterck said, when in fact he had no idea how Ronald Hunt's reichsmarks might make their way into the American purchasing chain.

'The Master Sergeant,' Elke went on, 'a man called Horace Neitz, also dispatches a monthly purchasing invoice through official army channels to a Private Thomas Foster in the US victualling unit in London.' Elke paused, as if debating whether to go on. 'I mention this,' she said finally, 'because my Soviet friends have learned that the official invoice inflates the listed price of the British goods. Yet it is this authority that Sergeant Neitz uses to convert reichsmarks to sterling through the British paymaster's office.'

Elke pursed her lips. 'And more recently,' she added gravely, 'it has been further discovered that the actual purchasing in London is done in accordance with a second invoice, one which Sergeant Neitz sends to Private Foster as personal mail through the US armed forces postal service. This second invoice reflects the true price of the goods. The inescapable conclusion is that Neitz and Foster are hiving off the difference between the two purchasing invoices.'

Josef Sterck stared briefly at Elke Über. Two purchasing invoices, for the same goods but for contrasting prices, surely pointed to Neitz and Foster running a scam. 'You're telling me to go to Munich and blackmail this Neitz?' Sterck asked cautiously.

'I see no need for such crassness,' Elke replied. 'My preference is to keep things on a business footing, which involves reaching agreed terms. Provided everyone sticks to the deal struck nobody gets upset.' She smiled at Sterck's doubtful face. 'You will go to Berlin in the coming days to apprise Mr Hunt of arrangements,' she added. 'After which you will proceed directly to Munich in time to be there by Wednesday 13 February. The business proposition you will put to Neitz is that, for a fee of ten per cent of the proceeds, Ronald Hunt's reichsmarks, all three million of them, are to be converted to pounds through Neitz's purchasing activities.'

Elke took a pencil and began to scrawl figures on a pad. 'Three million reichsmarks at the forty to one rate equates to 75,000 British pounds, meaning Neitz will earn a commission of 7,500 pounds. He is to direct his accomplice in London, Foster, to deposit the remaining 67,500 pounds into an English account of Hunt's choosing.'

Elke watched as Sterck absorbed her instructions. Only when satisfied did she speak. 'Arrangements like this will always work perfectly,' Elke said, her voice ice cold, 'until such time as one of the parties gets greedy. I would ask that you keep this in mind.'

***

The CIA's Michael Anjelico and MI6's Peter Parnell-Brown spoke three times during the day on Wednesday 26 August 1964. Anjelico was still in West Berlin and Parnell-Brown in London. Unlike Anjelico's call very early on 25 August, advising that Ronald Hunt had not returned from East Berlin, this time they were on a secure line.

The first contact occurred around 7 am in London, shortly after a bleary-eyed Parnell-Brown arrived at MI6 headquarters. 'More bad news, Peter,' Anjelico said. Parnell-Brown grimaced.

The abrasive Anjelico rarely paid him the courtesy of using his Christian name. It foreshadowed advice of a CIA cock-up.

'Just got a report from Havana indicating that the charter flight taking our courier to East Berlin went US en route.' Parnell-Brown understood that in this instance *US* meant *unserviceable*. 'Yeah, cashed its chips in some place in West Africa where they stopped to refuel.'

'But it's OK now?' Parnell-Brown said. The pause that followed told him he was being optimistic. He pictured Anjelico's contorted body language as the American prepared to wriggle out from underneath.

'Well, not quite, actually. Seems the locals couldn't fix it. As ever, the Cuban comrades were slow to react and only now have sent technicians to repair it. It's supposed to leave Nouakchott today.'

'We told you we had doubts about the reliability of the courier arrangement, Michael,' Parnell-Brown said, his voice ice-cold with fury. 'If Konrad Voite doesn't get the Swiss banking records, operation Leopard is dead in the water.'

'Force majeure, my friend,' Anjelico said, 'force majeure.' He'd had his fill of eating humble pie.

'For God's sake,' Parnell-Brown spat, more exasperated by Anjelico's flippancy than the operational foul up. 'Fallback plans are the antidote to force majeure. It's basic spying tradecraft.'

'Speak later,' Anjelico said brightly before hanging up.

The second and third calls came in quick succession, but in the early afternoon. 'Fuckin' A,' Anjelico exclaimed the moment Parnell-Brown came on the line, 'Sterck's gone and done it. He was just on East German television and shit-canned Ulbricht and Honecker like it was old home week. We watched it live here. Sterck seemed wasted to me. Must have had what you Limeys call a stiffener before he went on. But boy oh boy, did he get the job done.'

'And Ronald Hunt?' Parnell-Brown asked, still pessimistic about the prospects for operation Leopard and determined not to share in Anjelico's elation.

'Nothing heard,' Anjelico said. 'But buy the man a cigar because somehow he convinced Sterck to do it.'

Twenty minutes later Anjelico called again. 'We now have confirmation that the Ossi bad guys have picked up Hunt. State radio has just broadcast a bulletin reporting his arrest. No great surprise, I guess. But for some reason he stayed on and now he's in deep shit.' Neither Anjelico nor Parnell-Brown knew that Daniel Lincoln had heard the same radio broadcast while eating lunch in his room at the Frund Hotel in East Berlin, much less of its effect on Daniel.

'We'll deny all knowledge and from here on leave it up to the Foreign Office,' Parnell-Brown said, deadpan. 'As far as you, me and Uncle Tom Cobley are concerned, Ronald Hunt's just another UK consular case.' This had been the MI6 plan all along – in anticipation of the Labour Party winning government in next October's election, Sir Roger Holbrook had decreed that if things went bad Hunt was to be depicted as a deniable consular case.

CHAPTER 23

Two days before his arrest on 26 August 1964, Ronald Hunt was in Josef Sterck's office in the old Reichsbank building. He had earlier informed Sterck of his deal with the Americans to be released from prison. Now, in aid of securing that outcome, Ronald had just dropped a bombshell.

'My daughter?' Sterck said in a shocked whisper. 'You're saying the Americans have found a daughter I didn't know I had?'

Ronald laughed at Sterck's bewilderment. 'So I'm told. The German bird you put up the spout just before the war, the one you sent to the US, ended up settling in Hackensack, New Jersey. A few months after getting there she had your kid. A girl called Lilli.'

Ronald paused, wanting to be sure he made his points in the order specified by the CIA people in West Berlin. It was only yesterday, 23 August, that they had kept him in a room until he could recite his lines by heart. But just one day on and the tutoring seemed like an eternity ago.

'The mother died last year,' Ronald said. 'But long before she went to America she'd kept a diary, from 1936 after her husband died.' Ronald smiled at the stunned Sterck. 'Several references in there, I understand, to you shagging her on your office floor in Thuringia before the war, when you was batting for the Nazis.'

Sterck stared but said nothing, prompting Ronald to press on. 'Anyway, while she was alive the mother kept the diary a secret from her children. Lilli's elder brother has his own family and lives in LA where he's essentially out of the picture. But Lilli stayed on in Hackensack. The mother gave Lilli the diary on her deathbed. Lilli's now twenty-five and took it to the New York Times and requested it to do a number on you. The Americans I'm tied up with learned about this from the newspaper. They convinced both the *Times* and Lilli to hold off until I could have a chat with you.'

Sterck momentarily rallied, aided by a thought that had just entered his head. 'There's no way they can prove I'm the girl's father,' he said. 'I deny it,' he added vehemently.

'Well, me old mate,' Ronald replied gleefully, 'remember those three weeks in November 1946 when the Yanks had you after you shot Horace Neitz? Remember them fingerprinting you and taking a blood sample?' Sterck stared, mouth agape. 'That's right,' Ronald exclaimed as if Sterck had guessed the answer to a complex question. 'The blood sample proves paternity.'

Sterck placed his face in his hands, timidly looking through his fingers like a child playing a game. 'What now?' he whispered.

'My friends assume you know that Lilli's mother was the sister-in-law of Friedrich Reinhold. Otherwise, why would you have helped her get to the US when it would have been easier to kill her.' Both propositions were statements not questions.

'Reinhold's dead,' Sterck replied flatly. 'He died in 1960.'

'Correct,' Ronald said. 'But he was the primary mentor of this Walter Ulbricht who now runs the show over here. Real old muckers they were.' Ronald struggled to control his laughter. 'I can't imagine Walter will be too pleased to hear that, against her will, you were balling Freddy Reinhold's sister-in-law. They tell me Friedrich was right peeved over his younger brother's death. If it's now revealed you were a Nazi who took advantage of the widow, I reckon Walter would go quite spare.' Ronald shook his head. 'Phew,' he said. 'That's serious shit, man.'

Sterck glared. Ronald's gloating, in its mix of English and American vernacular, had strengthened his resolve. 'I take it,' Sterck said finally, 'you're working for the CIA?' Sterck frowned, his suspicion confirmed by Ronald's lack of denial. 'But it defeats me why the CIA thinks that sending you here with this feeble evidence of corruption for me to splash on television is going to change anything.' Sterck smiled. It was now his turn to act superior. 'Although what I do know, Ronald, is that you and I want the same thing.'

'And what's that?' Ronald asked, disconcerted to be suddenly no longer in control.

'We both need me to appear on the *Aktuelle Kamera* program on Wednesday lunchtime and expose this so-called corruption – me because it will save my life and you because it will make you a free man.' Sterck paused. 'So, let's say I do it.'

'OK.'

'Ulbricht and Honecker will be upset. But as a party elder, they'll need to be circumspect in how they handle me.' Sterck smiled. 'And in this regard, I'll make it easy for them by playing on the fact that they think I'm a spent political force. I'll simply tell them I've given up on politics and decided to retire. I'll say the disappointment of knowing my career has come to an end made me bitter and led me to go on television to fire one last broadside. And lastly I'll explain how I was aware I was raising a nothing issue but nonetheless angry enough to try and make a silk purse out of a sow's ear.' Sterck briefly reflected, inclining his head to one side. 'They'll probably make me sign a letter of apology admitting to my disgrace,' he said, 'one they write, which they'll release to the state media. After that I'll be banished somewhere remote where I'll be expected to live in lonely exile.'

Ronald shrugged. 'At least you would still be alive. As you say, if you refuse to appear on television and the New York Times publishes the mother's diary, Ulbricht will have you shot.'

'That, sadly, is true,' Sterck said, sighing, while all the while his devious mind whirled. Sterck rubbed his chin, as if in thought. 'But placating Ulbricht and Honecker is only half the deal. And I do have serious reservations about the other part.'

'Like what?' Ronald said.

'Like how do I know if the CIA will uphold its end of the bargain? That is, after I appear on *Aktuelle Kamera* what's to stop it from giving Lilli the green light to go ahead with the New York Times?' Sterck held up a hand as Ronald tried to speak. 'And please, don't insult my intelligence by trying to tell me they're gentlemen who can be relied on to keep their word.'

Ronald stared vacantly. The way the earnest Americans briefed him had caused him to overlook the possibility the CIA might not honour its promise. 'Nobody said anything to me,' he mumbled, 'to suggest they weren't on the up and up.'

Sterck shook his head. 'So,' he said, 'now you finally see that if the Americans renege I will be killed anyway.'

Ronald ran a hand over his sparse scalp before brightening. 'Perhaps I could go back to the Western sector right now and return tomorrow with a letter of guarantee?'

'Horse shit,' Sterck spat in terse dismissal of Ronald's grasp at straws. 'Show me your passport,' he ordered in an abrupt change of tack. Startled, Ronald reached into his jacket and extracted the blue, hard-covered booklet that MI6's Peter Parnell-Brown had quietly obtained on behalf of the CIA.

'British,' Sterck noted with evident satisfaction. 'Did you know that East Germany is anxious to establish diplomatic relations with your country?' Ronald shook his head. 'Yes,' Sterck continued conversationally, 'the more countries that formally recognise our little republic, the more legitimacy we have on the world stage. There's already an East German company in London called KfA that acts as our embassy. The British accepting its presence and the role it plays is a sure sign the UK will recognise us one day.'

'So what?' Ronald retorted. He had no interest in international relations and thought Sterck was off on a tangent.

'Show me your visa,' Sterck instructed. Ronald shrugged and flicked to the stamped page as directed. 'A one-day visa,' Sterck noted, 'meaning you are due back tonight.'

'That's the plan.'

'I think you should stay. If you're willing to do so, I'm prepared to accept the CIA will not go back on its word. It's a gesture of good faith by you on behalf of the Americans.'

'Balls to that,' Ronald said indignantly. 'I'd be arrested for having an expired visa.' Ronald's open hand snaked to his mouth and his eyes widened. 'And when you tell them I gave you the receipts, they'll blame me for encouraging you to go on the box.' Ronald exhaled forcefully. 'Fucking hell,' he gasped.

Sterck was suddenly angry. 'Listen to me, you stupid man. If you want me to appear on television, so that you might be released from prison, I need an assurance. Yes, you will be detained. But with East Germany and the UK currently warming to one another, you're not going to be harmed. You'll get a lecture, a slap-on-the-wrist fine and be let go.'

Sterck sneered at Ronald. 'And do you really think your visit here today will have gone unnoticed?' Ronald recoiled at the thought of the German-language note he showed to the VoPo downstairs. 'It's no secret we did business together immediately after the war,' Sterck continued, now the voice of reason. 'You're a convicted criminal. Fact. You'll say you bought the receipts from a fellow in a pub in London and decided to come here and sell them to me. That's how criminals work.'

Ronald did not know what to think. The whole thing had seemed like a sweet number when the Americans first proposed it. He cursed that no one had bothered to go through all the possible pitfalls. 'And where would I stay if I waited here until you went on television?' he asked for want of something better to say.

Sterck hid his elation. 'I've got a spare room in my apartment,' he said. 'We could have a couple of drinks and talk about old times.'

Ronald nodded numbly. Sterck, he rationalised, knew international politics, and under no circumstances could he let his chance to be released fall through, not now that he was forty-five and had again tasted freedom.

Josef Sterck had grown craftier with age. And as the saying goes, he had just played Ronald like a fiddle. All along Sterck had known the CIA would keep its word. Failure to do so would greatly restrict the Agency's ability to reach accommodation with others, simply because were he betrayed enough parties would know to ensure word got around.

So why then did Josef Sterck want Ronald to remain in East Berlin? Well, when the chips were down during the interrogation sure to follow his television appearance, Sterck planned to say he laid a trap. He would tell the Stasi, Klaus Borkh and others he had delayed the English intelligence officer in East Berlin so that he could be detained and later swapped for an East German agent held in the West. In the meantime, the gullible Hunt would stick to the script he had outlined, banking on his British passport to protect him.

***

Daniel Lincoln had recovered a little from the shock of the East German state radio bulletin reporting the arrest of a British citizen called Ronald Hunt and the man's apparent connection to an SED elder by the name of Josef Sterck. Reading between the lines, it seemed to Daniel that Sterck had gone temporarily insane on a television program. Taking a deep breath, he left his hotel room toilet where he had been sheltering from the Stasi cameras hidden behind the plaster cornices in his room's bed and bathrooms.

Outside and once more in full view, Daniel washed his hands in the bathroom sink before re-seating at the small writing desk to finish his lunch. 'Bloody hell,' he said out loud, trying to convince the Stasi watchers a bout of diarrhoea was responsible for his rush to the toilet. The radio's classical music program had resumed and all was back to normal. Daniel's nerves calmed some more. *About twenty-seven hours,* he thought, *until I'm to clip the Karl loves Ilsa padlock on the Weidendammer Bridge.*

Daniel arrived smack on 3 pm for his appointment with the East German trade ministry. The reception counter was coldly curt when telling him to wait in the foyer. After nearly an hour a young official approached. 'We are very busy today, Mr Middlemiss,' he said in tortured English. 'Can you come back tomorrow at the same time?'

The young man showed no surprise when Daniel responded in fluent German. 'My employers, Jenkins and Sons of Cardiff in Wales,' Daniel said, speaking with deliberate formality, 'are seeking mutually beneficial commercial relationships with East German companies. Today's appointment with the ministry to discuss this matter was arranged some months ago through the KfA office in London. It is substantially disappointing for it to be cancelled.'

'I understand, sir,' the man replied in his fractured English. 'But you British are not very popular at the moment.'

The words caused Daniel's stomach to churn. He had sought to treat his chill welcome as just the East German way. But now he knew it was hostility. Daniel felt his pulse begin to race, begging his creator to spare him a panic attack. Fortunately, the official had nothing further to say. With a quasi-military click of his heels the man pirouetted and walked away.

'Three tomorrow it is, then,' Daniel called to the official's back, trying to sound like an ever-hopeful salesman. Outside the building Daniel gratefully sucked in the fresh air, welcoming its steadying influence on his quivering knees. He had no appetite for the grim confines of his hotel room and decided to stroll. With that, Daniel elected to walk all the way to the border checkpoint at the Brandenburg Gate, to take a look at the Berlin Wall demarcating East and West Berlin visible from behind the giant monument.

Daniel headed off, conscious that a trailing Stasi team would be on his back. He considered the tasks awaiting him as he went. 'Mind the cameras in the hotel room,' Peter Parnell-Brown had repeatedly warned. 'They have people review the tapes looking for the slightest hint of suspect behaviour.'

Daniel grimaced, remembering his practice sessions in London when they actually put cameras on him. He knew the process by heart. After eating in the hotel's austere dining room that night, he would withdraw to his room, lie on the bed and pretend to read, a business as usual pretext to which he was to devote two hours.

Then it gets tricky, Daniel thought. He was thinking of the need to extract the padlock from his suitcase in the darkened wardrobe and take it into the toilet. There in the lavatory free of the Stasi cameras, he would scratch *Karl loves Ilsa* on the padlock before hiding it behind the cistern for the night. The next morning, while doing his ablutions, he would briefly visit the toilet holding his shaving bag. The letter to Elke Über hidden in the bag's false bottom would be concealed with the padlock behind the cistern until such time as he was fully dressed and could again go to the toilet where he would secrete both items within his clothing.

Detailed planning to be sure. But fate had other ideas.

CHAPTER 24

Elke Über had arranged it of course. How she managed to enlist Soviet support to set up his meeting with Horace Neitz escaped Josef Sterck. Nonetheless, a message had been passed to the American Master Sergeant to the effect that after work on Wednesday 13 February 1946 he was to wait in Marienplatz in the Munich Old Town where a man called Rolf would contact him. The square in fact was just five minutes walk from Neitz's office in the US Army building. When Neitz objected he was simply advised to comply or his secret dealings with a certain Private Foster in London would be brought to the attention of the US authorities.

Two days earlier, on 11 February, Sterck had arrived in Berlin and proceeded to Spandau where he stood across from the NAAFI bulk store, at the place where he and Ronald Hunt earlier agreed he should wait if a meeting was needed. That night Sterck informed Ronald of the plan to repatriate reichsmarks through the corrupt Americans. Unable to resist the urge to brag, Sterck boasted he was the architect of the scheme, big-noting some more by inviting Ronald – *should anything arise to discuss* – to make contact through the man with the old lorry whom he engaged to drive his cigarette purchases from Berlin to Weimar.

Ronald was grateful and nodded enthusiastically when told by Sterck that the lead American launderer would soon pay him a visit. Ronald was to give the man a million and a half reichsmarks and an English account number into which derived sterling could be deposited. At the start of March Ronald was to hand the American the other million and a half reichsmarks he would by then have in his possession.

Janice, of course, had been forewarned to expect deposits into her post office savings account, and Ronald was confident she would remain tight-lipped. He had also advised Janice he would send her the payment schedule and amounts involved once known. This was Ronald's means of ensuring that things went smoothly, an otherwise sensible safeguard destined spectacularly to backfire.

***

Horace Neitz stood in Munich's Marienplatz looking around nervously. Josef Sterck, as Rolf, was waiting at the edge of the square. On noting Neitz's tension, he had approached the American with caution. An inauspicious start ensued. As ever, the rapid movement of Sterck's dark eyes radiated deceit. And, moreover, Neitz took badly to Sterck's clipped speech and the stridency this conveyed. From Neitz's perspective, America had just won a winner-takes-all war; he was not about to take orders from some jumped-up Kraut.

For his part, Sterck had not set out to upset Horace Neitz, heeding Elke Über's edict to keep things on a business footing. But in the face of Neitz's animosity he did become more assertive when telling the American to get up to Berlin in the next few days and look up a private Ronald Hunt at the NAAFI bulk store in Spandau.

Neitz bristled some more, causing Sterck to repeat the threat that had brought the Master Sergeant to Marienplatz in the first place – his dealings with Private Foster in London. 'It could be years,' Neitz said slyly, 'before I can convert this Hunt guy's war marks. There are limits to how much I can wash each month.'

Sterck, though, sensed he had the upper hand. 'No,' he said, angry that Neitz should attempt to wriggle off the hook, 'as soon as you have them you are to convert them. The other reichsmarks you would usually launder will have to wait.'

A poisonous silence followed until broken by Neitz. 'What if I roll over and take my medicine?' he said threateningly. 'I could tell the MPs all about you and your Mr Hunt.' Neitz snarled. 'Maybe we should just forget we've had this conversation.'

'Listen to me, you fool American,' Sterck spat, his fury overriding his usual timidity. 'You will do exactly as I say or *we* will kill you. And don't think I will be held responsible. I have influential friends in this city who will protect me.' Sterck was boasting, carried away by the fact that Elke had convinced the Soviets to send a messenger to Munich to arrange his rendezvous with Neitz. Nonetheless, Sterck's at the time baseless claim to be safe from justice should Neitz be killed proved to be entirely prophetic.

Neitz's nerve failed him. At the end of the day, the big man from Wyoming was a bully, and now his bluff had been called. Neitz also suffered from American self-sufficiency, the peculiar insecurity that afflicts some from the US when in places abroad where lifestyles and languages differ to those at home. The combined effect of both factors was to make him think that Sterck was not lying about being backed by powerful interests. 'OK, OK,' Neitz said finally, accepting he could not walk away. 'I'll do as you say. Ten per cent commission, right?'

Sterck smiled, slowly shaking his head. His anger had wrested control from Elke's wise instruction to stick to the deal agreed. Sterck lit the fuse to the powder keg. 'Owing to your bad manners, the offer of a commission is withdrawn. You will do exactly as I ask for no fee. If you fail to do so, you will be killed, simple as that.'

***

The light was beginning to fade on the night of 26 August 1964 when Daniel Lincoln returned to the Frund Hotel. After visiting the Brandenburg Gate when his meeting with the trade ministry was cancelled he had meandered some more, taking in the sights of Berlin as he remembered them from a decade ago. But with those few hours soaked up it was now time for business.

The hotel dining room was deserted save for a group of three men sitting on the far side of the room, southern Swiss Daniel guessed by their easy switch from German to Italian and back again. The unsmiling waiter recommended the *buletten*, the fabled delicacy native to Berlin. Daniel knew of the dish and was happy to concur only to be served two greasy meat patties swimming in fat and a dollop of over-boiled potato. Fortunately, though, Daniel wasn't hungry, his stomach on the prowl.

Back in his room, Daniel laid on the bed too tense even to read the John Donne *No Man is an Island* epigraph inside Hemingway's novel. Instead he slowly flicked from one page to the next, all the while thinking of his cherished father and resisting the urge to look at his watch. After a seeming eternity the night sky outside was fully darkened. With only his dull reading lamp illuminated the room was swathed in a dreary half-light. Daniel stretched, feeling his abdominal muscles twitch as tension took hold.

The pressure mounted and Daniel started to wilt. The more he wished he'd owned up to MI6 about Kristiina, doing over Ray Solter and his resulting illness, the more overwhelmed he became. Finally, he tipped. Just wanting to get the padlock hidden and be done with it, Daniel failed to turn on the room's main light as Peter Parnell-Brown had directed. Rather he went straight to the pitch-black wardrobe and thrust his hand into the netting pouch of his suitcase. Nothing. He felt again, desperately searching for the padlock. Still nothing. Daniel tried a third time, perspiration now weeping from his armpits and running down his rib cage. Nothing.

Palpably deflated, Daniel fell back on the bed, temporarily immune to any possible consequences from doing so. He knew what had happened. A hotel staff member had been in the room that afternoon when he was out. Nothing of obvious value had been taken because presumably that would create problems. So the employee had stolen the padlock, judging that a Western guest would tolerate so modest a theft.

Long into the night, Daniel lay flat on his back in bed, staring into the dark. He wondered what best to do. The logical thing, he told himself, would be to cut and run, get out of East Berlin before the Stasi could go over the tape capturing his odd behaviour. Field agents who had been tumbled did this all the time.

But then Daniel fretted. To abort because of a missing padlock, something that agents made of sterner stuff would overcome with ease, would be to heap failure upon failure, another debacle just a year after falling into the Mossad trap in Washington. He pictured his father's grim visage and the inevitable admonition to toughen up.

Why that mental image made Daniel think of disregarding Peter Parnell-Brown's instruction to act normally and turn on the room light he did not know. But he did know infrared technology was years off and that in weak light the Stasi reviewers relied more on speech than vision. And, Daniel recalled, he had not spoken but rather flopped on the end of his bed outside of the arc of the reading lamp. There must be a good chance, he thought, they'll have no clear vision or drastically unusual sound to go on.

Tenuously fortified, Daniel considered buying a padlock. But unlike London, he soon realised, East Berlin had no

F.W. Woolworth store on every street corner. In any event the local model would not be coated in a soft alloy like his missing padlock, specially prepared so that he might scratch the *Karl loves Ilsa* message on it.

So Daniel did a stocktake of his assets. He decided he had three. One was time: he didn't need to be back at the trade ministry until 3 pm; second, the Stasi had already noted his propensity to wander about, giving him relative freedom of movement; and third, he had a general description of Elke Über and knew where she worked. Somehow, he would intercept her the next morning and tell her to meet him at 6:30 pm in front of the Tränenpalast pavilion at Friedrichstrasse station, the so-called Palace of Tears. Then he slept.

The morning light beaming through the room's cheap window curtains woke Daniel early. He doubted he'd had more than three hours sleep. But the plan developed during the night had steeled him some. By 9 am he was on the move, the letter to Elke Über now snug in the inner pocket of his suit jacket, having removed it from his shaving bag in the lavatory earlier that morning. He wore business attire but an open-neck shirt as a concession to make the Stasi think he was embarking on a walk to kill time.

***

After an hour of seeming to wander Daniel reached the SED administrative centre, Elke's workplace. The bizarre events of the day before – when an SED elder went ratty on television, and the related arrest of an English citizen – had resulted in a beefing up of security. The whole precinct was swarming with VoPos.

Daniel stood opposite the Schumannstrasse building, pretending to admire its brutalist Nazi architecture while leaning against a railing. But the heavy police presence was unnerving him and he wasn't feeling half as confident as he had been ten minutes ago. In any event he was not about to walk into the SED office and ask for Elke, not with Stasi watchers on his tail. As it transpires, the unmonitored Cuban Paian Diaz would arrive just two hours later and do exactly what Daniel could not, march into the building, albeit he was in the wrong place, and ask for Konrad Voite.

Meanwhile as Daniel loitered, he spotted a young VoPo walking towards him. Daniel's heart began to race. The officer was a pimply boy, no more than eighteen if a day, a country lad fresh to the *Volkspolizei* and bored with standing around with nothing to do. Daniel sighed inwardly. No matter how casually any Westerner might dress, it was impossible to replicate the average East German male's deeply ingrained disregard for personal appearance. He would have to explain himself to the young VoPo.

'Good morning,' Daniel called in German to the approaching man, trying not to make his smile too cheesy. 'It's a lovely day.'

The boy adjusted his loose-fitting tie, tugging at his cheap collar. 'You are a Westerner who speaks German?' he asked.

Daniel didn't reply directly. 'Frank Middlemiss from England,' he said genially. 'I'm here for business meetings with the trade office.' The boy nodded disinterestedly. 'Yes,' Daniel said, pressing on regardless, 'my next appointment is not until this afternoon.' He smiled. 'So, I'm out seeing the sights.'

'Passport,' the boy spat, obeying his training.

Daniel watched the young man listlessly examine each page. 'How is it you speak German?' the VoPo said finally.

'I studied it in England and lived here in the 1950s,' Daniel said, choosing not to use the words *war* or *occupation*.

But the boy was too young to be bothered by the war, Germany's humiliating defeat and its subsequent occupation.

He shrugged again, returning Daniel his passport whereupon he stared vacantly into the distance.

'Would you care for one?' Daniel offered, producing the packet of Marlboro cigarettes that his putative employer, A.H. Jenkins and Son of Cardiff, had given him even though he did not smoke.

'No self-respecting British salesman,' the young Mr Jenkins had said, 'goes to East Germany without some American ciggies to grease the wheels.'

The boy removed two tobacco tubes from the pack, making a feeble attempt to disguise this as accidental. 'That's fine,' Daniel said, playing along, 'keep the second for later.'

The lad slipped a cigarette inside his tunic pocket and lit the other. He inhaled deeply before joining Daniel leaning against the railing. 'Do you like German girls?' he asked conversationally.

Daniel briefly wondered if the VoPo was trying to pimp his sister, cousin or something, but then decided sex was the only thing that interested the young man. Whatever, there was only one viable answer. 'Oh yes,' Daniel said, 'especially on this side of the Wall.'

With that the two lapsed into silence, lolling against the railing while the policeman smoked contentedly. They watched as two people – a man and a woman both in business attire – turned into Schumannstrasse and began walking towards them. The man was speaking earnestly to the female. Daniel studied the woman. She was beautiful by any definition – tall, raven-haired and of olive complexion. And although Daniel assessed her to be only a little older than him, at forty-two she was in fact eight years his senior.

The woman seemed to sense Daniel's gaze. Her dark eyes suddenly locked with his, upon which she smiled briefly before looking away. Daniel was mesmerised, continuing to watch the woman up until the time she entered the SED office.

The young policeman could not have failed to see Daniel's reaction. 'You like her?' he said, his grin revealing a mouth full of broken teeth.

'Not bad,' Daniel admitted, jolted from his trance by the question and somewhat embarrassed. 'You know her?'

'The Bavarian beauty,' the boy replied. 'That's what we *Volkspolizei* call her.'

'The Bavarian beauty,' Daniel exclaimed, astonished. In his fascination he had not matched the woman to any of Peter Parnell-Brown's pre-departure briefings.

'She's a big wheel in the party,' the boy said, interpreting Daniel's repetition as an enquiry. He frowned, as if he ought not speak flippantly in front of foreigners. 'Fräulein Elke Über is her name,' he said before walking away.

CHAPTER 25

Ronald Hunt was in the NAAFI bulk store's loading dock helping uncrate some pallets. 'A big Yank out the front to see you, Ronald,' little Billy Smithers said. American soldiers rarely visited the NAAFI store. But by February 1946 movement across the American and UK occupation zones in Berlin was commonplace, leading to frequent interactions between service personnel. So even little Billy, who was an inquisitive soul, didn't think the American's arrival odd. Josef Sterck had told Ronald to expect Horace Neitz in the week commencing 18 February. The weekend before Ronald had stuffed an even million and a half reichsmarks inside the lining of the greatcoat he wore when out in Berlin's chill winter.

Ronald walked Neitz a block up the street until they were out of sight of the warehouse. The American was sour but kept it civil. 'Neitz,' he said by way of introduction. 'You got the one and a half to give me?' Where reichsmarks were concerned, Master Sergeant Neitz dealt only in units of millions.

Ronald looked furtively around. It was a rogue's reflex. Satisfied all was clear, his hand darted into his greatcoat; once, twice and finally a third time until the three bundles each of 500,000 reichsmarks were handed to Neitz. 'Come back at the start of March,' Ronald said. 'I'll give you the other million and a half then.'

Ronald saw Neitz only twice again. Once was in Berlin in early March as planned, when Neitz vociferously cursed the man he knew as Rolf. Still, Neitz was in a better frame of mind than he had been in February. 'Your three million marks,' he told Ronald, 'will be converted at the forty reichsmarks to the pound exchange rate by the end of October and return you a total of 75,000 pounds.'

October was the end date, Neitz explained, because his scheme's reichsmark laundering component was only one-tenth of the face value of the inflated purchasing invoice, the larger portion directed to actual purchases. This produced a profit of around 10,000 pounds per month. His colleague in London would deposit 10,000 pound payments into Ronald's nominated post office account commencing at the end of March with a seventh disbursement in September. A final payment in October of 5,000 pounds would round out the transaction.

The last time Ronald saw Neitz was on 19 November 1946, in Munich. Ronald had gone there at Josef Sterck's behest after first writing to Neitz and claiming he was acting independent of the German intermediary, Rolf. Ronald's letter also noted missing September and October payments, of 10,000 and 5,000 pounds respectively, a sum total of 15,000 pounds. All the same, Ronald wrote, he thought it wrong that Rolf should deny Neitz the ten per cent commission he initially promised. Ronald proposed they meet to negotiate an agreed service fee to be deducted from the shortfall with the balance to be deposited in his account.

***

Ronald, of course, had written to Janice after his March meeting with Neitz to advise when payments were to commence. She was to check for the money's safe arrival and be alert to any irregularities. But as the influx of funds began and Janice's balance soared, the questioning looks of the counter staff unsettled her to the point where she avoided going to the post office to the extent possible. It was not until early November 1946 that Janice discovered no deposits had been made in September and October. Her terse letter to Ronald arrived in Berlin a week later.

To say that Ronald was alarmed to learn of two months of missing payments would be to put it mildly. His response was to turn to Josef Sterck. After all, Sterck claimed to have devised the Neitz repatriation scheme and had provided a contact if there was anything to discuss. Well, now there is, Ronald thought. *There's a big problem with the American* he scribbled on the note he later gave to the man whose old lorry shuffled between the occupation zones.

So, Sterck came to Berlin. He really had no choice. All the British cigarettes had been exchanged for precious items and his political career would be ready to launch once the valuables stored in Elke Über's safe back in Thuringia were sold for convertible currency. Right now, the last thing Sterck needed was for Horace Neitz to cause him problems.

Sterck was furious that Neitz should have acted up. He directed Ronald to write to the American and propose a meeting to discuss the discrepancy. 'Keep it nice,' Sterck said, 'lull him into a false sense of security. I'll arrange for muscle to intimidate him into making the missing payments.' Whether Neitz bought the ruse or was having second thoughts about withholding money was never clear. Whatever, the American agreed to meet Ronald in the same place where previously he met Sterck – Munich's Marienplatz adjacent to his place of work.

Unbeknown to Ronald, however, Sterck had decided to kill Neitz, chiefly because he was petrified that the loose cannon American might do something erratic, or malicious, and bring down the wrath of Nazi hunters on him. But with Neitz dead, Sterck judged, the reichsmarks laundered over the past eight months could not be traced back to him. Except by Ronald Hunt, that is.

Sterck, though, reasoned that were Ronald reminded of the IOU he signed in November 1945 he would keep quiet when questioned by the Americans and admit to no part in Neitz's scheme. In which case, seeing as Ronald was not privy to the plan to murder Neitz, he would have nothing to answer for. Meanwhile, Sterck calculated, he would bolt for the Soviet zone after executing Neitz where he would be safe from the fallout. But it didn't quite pan out as Sterck envisaged, thanks mainly to Peter Parnell-Brown.

It was, therefore, to Ronald's great surprise shortly after meeting Neitz that Josef Sterck should appear and not his promised muscle. Ronald was even more astounded when Sterck strode directly to Neitz, withdrew a pistol from his coat and fired three rapid shots into the American's upper torso before dropping his weapon and racing off.

The six US servicemen walking through Marienplatz at this time were young and fit. Two grabbed the dazed Ronald, while the others scampered after the fleeing Sterck. Ronald barely noticed the US military police arrive. But he was transfixed by the sight of Sterck being dragged back to the scene of the crime. 'I have the IOU,' Sterck hissed at Ronald. 'Shut your mouth and you will be freed. If you don't, I'll give it to the British authorities and you'll be blamed for the shooting and spend the rest of your life in prison.'

So Ronald zipped it, claiming only a drinking relationship with Neitz, while silently clinging to hopes of keeping the black money already in Janice's account and praying that Neitz had not kept records mentioning his name. And for three long weeks Ronald stuck to his guns.

'I don't suppose that by any chance *Rolf* is Josef Sterck?' The cultured English voice coming from outside his cell was familiar to Ronald. Even so, he jumped in fright when through the bars he saw the man from Malta he knew as Harry Cramer.

Peter Parnell-Brown was down from British military HQ in Bad Oeynhausen on news of a British serviceman's arrest.

'The Americans have let Sterck go,' Parnell-Brown said softly, 'thanks mostly to you. The German communists in the Soviet zone demanded him back. Sure there were others who reacted on hearing the shots. But your silence has denied the Americans the right to resist the communists on the grounds they have an eye-witness.' Parnell-Brown looked at Ronald, his face dark with contempt. 'Sterck played you for a sucker. And now he's backed by the Soviets and untouchable, even by those wondering where he got the accumulation of reichsmarks to buy your cigarettes. That leaves you all alone in the frame to answer for Neitz's death.'

'I'm innocent,' Ronald blustered in panic, 'a bystander.'

'You're a congenital liar, Hunt,' Parnell-Brown retorted. 'And I've now convinced the Americans that seeing as your letter proves you lured Horace Neitz to the place where he was killed, you should be charged with aiding and abetting in his murder. Pending extradition to the US, you'll be held in an English prison while your currency fraud is investigated.' Parnell-Brown paused and beaded Ronald. 'I warned you in Malta I would come down on you like a ton of bricks if you ever again stole from NAAFI. Well, here I am.'

The look on Ronald Hunt's face when he knew the game was up had stayed with Peter Parnell-Brown ever since. It was why Parnell-Brown thought of Ronald eighteen years later when operation Leopard's search for a suitable decoy bogged down. To the MI6 Deputy, he was the perfect fit, a past associate of Josef Sterck and totally expendable, British citizen notwithstanding.

***

The day that Daniel Lincoln first saw Elke Über outside the SED administrative centre, 27 August 1964, she and her male companion were in fact returning from Stasi headquarters. They had just attended a confidential briefing for select senior officials on the previous day's arrest of the suspected English spy Ronald Hunt and his association with the disgraced party elder, Josef Sterck.

The man with Elke was Klaus Borkh. Both were senior administrators, one level below the political elite; she the head of the SED secretariat and Borkh chief minder to the East German leaders Walter Ulbricht and Erich Honecker. Borkh, though, was less experienced and beset with professional jealousy. He watched Elke's every move in the hope of one day surpassing her in East Germany's informal bureaucratic pecking order.

Elke's glance at Daniel Lincoln stemmed from her sighting a Western man and a VoPo up ahead leaning against a railing. But her fleeting smile that followed owed everything to Daniel's origin. Like Elke's lifelong proclivity, Dougal, Daniel came from the West Riding of Yorkshire. Daniel, of course, knew nothing of Dougal. But at thirty-four, thanks to his running, he was sufficiently kempt to remind Elke of Dougal from 1938, when Dougal was twenty-two. It was this resemblance she had initially noticed. And as Elke neared Daniel her attention switched to his bluish-green eyes, the unique Celtic feature that legend apportions to the peoples of the ancient Kingdom of Elmet. Daniel, as fate would have it, had identical eyes to Dougal.

Elke's disappearing into the SED office made Daniel anxious to leave. It was clear he could not safely intercept her here. Encountering a VoPo who was young and green had been fortunate. But there were plenty of others around who might not be as placid. Daniel's pulse began to race. After all, the DG's letter to Elke was in the inside pocket of his jacket. Daniel felt clamminess tingle over his body, the warning sign his nerve was about to fail. 'Take it slowly,' he said fighting the urge to run.

'Breathe, breathe, the stage is set.' The stage to which Daniel was referring was the Weidendammer Bridge, where later that day he would brush by Fräulein Elke Über and whisper an instruction in her delightful ear.

***

Josef Sterck quickly became something of a headache for the East German communists after his return to the Soviet zone in December 1946. But with the SED head Friedrich Reinhold having made him a poster boy, the party power brokers could hardly ignore him. Yet rumours persisted of Sterck having a Nazi past in Thuringia. But with little to no hard evidence to support the rumblings, an idea surfaced to have him join the party and be made an organiser with the Free German Trade Union Federation. After consulting Elke Über, Sterck agreed. It was, as Elke told him, the first step on the road to his appointment to the SED Executive.

For her part, Elke had anticipated the introduction of a German-wide convertible currency. But the Soviets and other occupying powers were soon at loggerheads over currency reform. The West decided to act alone. On 20 June 1948 the convertible Deutschmark became West Germany's currency. The Soviets responded with a blockade of West Berlin, and in the process the holdings bought with Josef Sterck's cigarettes came to be worth a fortune.

The Soviet blockade designed to starve West Berlin into submission lasted from 24 June 1948 until 12 May 1949. Suddenly, West Berliners were without all but the essential foodstuffs airlifted in by the Western powers. Hoarding began to take place whereby West Berliners, understandably anxious about the future, actively sought valuables sure to hold their worth until things were better.

Josef Sterck, of course, was unable to visit Berlin's Western sector where he would face immediate arrest. Once again, he turned to his chief problem solver, Elke Über. But for once Sterck was able to propose the solution. 'Provided you are not selling items likely to undermine the blockade,' he told Elke, 'I see no reason why you cannot go to West Berlin and sell our precious goods.' Sterck grimaced. 'And the sooner the better,' he added, 'in case the political situation sours even further and results in a ban on movement between East and West.'

Elke thought about this. She had grown to detest Sterck but for now theirs was a relationship of mutual need. 'I think you should offer me a job,' Elke said, 'not here in Thuringia but in Berlin, as your local government liaison officer.' Elke was referring to Berlin's local administration at the time, comprising city councillors drawn from both the East and West of the city. It was not an arrangement destined to survive Berlin's political stresses. But the management condominium currently in place suited her needs perfectly.

In all, Elke Über made twelve visits to West Berlin in her guise as the humble assistant to the SED union organiser, Josef Sterck. The timing was exquisite. With Elke's insights telling her that the Soviets could not sustain the blockade, less well-versed West Berliners were nervously happy to pay a premium for the goods on offer. Indeed, people would often come to Elke, keen to part with Westmarks for a value-retaining diamond ring or bracelet. By February 1949, three months before the Soviets admitted defeat and lifted the Berlin blockade, every precious item in Elke and Sterck's possession had been sold.

CHAPTER 26

Elke Über had thought it through, at least to the extent of understanding that the Swiss banking records the Cuban tourist Paian Diaz intended to give to Konrad Voite foreshadowed a meeting with an MI6 agent later in the day. Tonight as she crossed the Weidendammer Bridge, the message request signal would be set directing her to the Tränenpalast pavilion at Friedrichstrasse station, just as she had proposed in her letter to Sir Roger Holbrook.

Guided by this conclusion, Elke decided to wait until the events of the evening of 27 August 1964 had unfolded. After hearing what MI6 had to say, she would make a final decision on how best to deal with the banking records. With that, she called Diaz to her office. Pointing to the name Konrad Voite written on the envelope, then her chest and finally jabbing her finger to the outside world, she sought to communicate she would take the documents to Voite. After two attempts Diaz understood. He gulped nervously as it dawned he was in the wrong place but cheered on thinking that, nonetheless, his delivery task was complete and on schedule. Thereafter, Elke set him loose. Not until Diaz returned to Havana on 6 September, ten days later, did the CIA get to debrief him. By then it was too late.

***

Josef Sterck moved permanently to East Berlin in May 1949 coincident with the official birth of the state of East Germany. Elke Über was already there, supposedly working as his local government research assistant but in reality positioned so that she might visit West Berlin to sell valuables. Soon after Sterck's arrival the pair commenced working out of a coveted corner suite in the old Reichsbank building, the view from which offered a pleasing panorama of the Kupfergraben canal.

The office accommodation was way above Sterck's pay grade as a union organiser. But with he and Elke flush with Westmarks, Sterck had secured it with a bribe of the building manager. It was a sign of things to come – in austere East Berlin it was rare to find office-holders not prepared to bend for the right price. Indeed, Sterck had recently lobbied a coterie of select union officials over his wish to be appointed as the head of a sectional directorate. And now palms had been greased guaranteeing the promotion.

From behind the scenes, of course, Elke Über had been pulling the strings. And nor had she been content to let the career grass grow under her feet. At Sterck's urging, party officials had recently promoted Elke from her research assistant role to a middle-ranking position with the SED secretariat, the party's peak administrative body. Elke's smouldering dark eyes, lush black hair and olive skin were much admired by the men around her, including those in the SED politburo. At age twenty-seven, Elke Über was on her way.

Thereafter, the advancement gathered pace. By the autumn of 1958 Sterck was an under-Commissioner and swimming in the pool from which the next politburo vacancy would be filled. And in the past few days the head of the SED secretariat had been fired. Nobody knew quite why, but just last week the politburo's Minister for Administration had been seen at a resort on East Germany's Baltic Sea coast in the company of *Herr Westmarks*, as Josef Sterck was disparagingly known.

'What do you see in that grubby little fellow?' the minister asked. It was Friday 31 October 1958 and he had invited Elke Über to his office for a glass of brandy to celebrate her appointment as the head of the SED secretariat, a rare coup for a woman.

'My parents were murdered by the Nazis before the war,' Elke said simply. 'I was sheltered by a family in Coburg and after the war moved to Thuringia where I found work in Weimar requisitioning properties for use by Soviet comrades.'

'And Sterck?' the minister pressed.

Elke shrugged. 'He had a house in Weimar I considered appropriating. But it proved unsuitable. He offered to assist me in my work. I was very young at the time. He became a sort of father figure.'

'An incestuous father figure?' the minister asked with a wink.

Elke took it in her stride. 'Heavens no,' she said laughing. 'He's twenty years older than me.' She smiled brightly at the minister. 'I have continued to work for him simply because he has been helpful at times.' Elke paused, now unsmiling. 'Much as he has been for you, comrade minister, if my information is correct.'

The attempted seduction was over. The minister swallowed his brandy with a single gulp and extended his hand. 'Thank you for coming up, Fräulein Über,' he said formally. 'You will be taking charge of the secretariat at a time when shortly it will relocate to the old Nazi administrative centre on Schumannstrasse. I wish you all the best and look forward to working with you.'

Elke stood at the doorway. 'He wants your job, you know,' she said matter-of-factly.

The minister stared, realising just how badly he had underestimated this young woman. 'What?' he gasped.

Elke continued as if the man had not spoken. 'It may interest you to know that Josef Sterck was once a willing and enthusiastic Nazi. If you don't believe me contact the Soviet high command and ask it to research the appointment of the head of the regional economic office in Weimar in 1938. We all know that communists were among those who suffered and had property stolen. I'm sure you would agree the Nazi hierarchy was unlikely to give responsibility for such important work to anybody.'

With her words left hanging, Elke turned heel, leaving the office door ajar. She smiled. She was now in her own position of power and no longer needed Josef Sterck. The time had arrived to cut him adrift. Suddenly, tears welled in Elke's eyes. 'Dougal,' she whispered, talking to the English medical student from Yorkshire who had deflowered her in Dublin in 1938 when she was sweet sixteen. 'I hope you are proud of me.'

***

Josef Sterck was feeling ill. It was the late afternoon of 26 August 1964 and the effect of the copious quantity of brandy he drank that morning had worn off, the Dutch courage he needed to go on the *Aktuelle Kamera* television program and accuse Walter Ulbricht and Erich Honecker of corruption. He'd now been three hours locked in a room in an East German police station.

The door crashing open startled Sterck. It was none other than Klaus Borkh, the leadership's chief minder. 'Well, well,' Sterck said, trying to crack hardy, 'if it isn't Walter and Erich's little helper.'

Borkh gave a light chuckle, as though he thought Sterck's insult was funny. He set down the folder he carried before unhurriedly removing his suit jacket and hanging it on the back of a chair. There followed two quick strides across the room and the back of Borkh's clenched right fist swinging at furious speed through the air. The blow caught Sterck flush on the nose. 'Listen to me, you piece of shit,' Borkh said, his face all but touching Sterck's. 'Don't think just because you're an SED elder you're going to get away with today's antics. If I have my way you'll hang for this.'

'The Englishman Hunt is a spy,' Sterck blurted, abandoning all attempts at bravado. 'I set a trap for him. It involved going on television and saying those stupid things. If I hadn't done as he wanted, he would have scurried back to West Berlin once I made it clear I wasn't prepared to make such outrageous claims.' Sterck looked pleadingly at Borkh. 'We both know what I said is nonsense, Klaus. The idea was to keep this Hunt fellow here so that he could be detained and traded for one of our agents held by the West.'

'The Stasi is currently speaking with your English friend,' Borkh replied. 'They will provide me and some others with a briefing tomorrow morning. After that I will decide your fate. Until then, you will be placed under house arrest at a guarded hotel.'

Ronald Hunt had watched Josef Sterck's television performance from Sterck's apartment where he spent the nights of 24 and 25 August drinking and reminiscing with the now convivial German. Ronald, of course, had no German language of which to speak. But when Sterck was literally thrown off the television stage, Ronald's first reaction was to congratulate himself for staying in East Berlin, believing it had convinced Sterck to carry out the CIA's instruction.

Hot on the heels of that thought, however, was Ronald's realisation he needed to get back to the Western sector before he was embroiled in the political fallout. He had won the right to live as a free man and was now going to enjoy it. Not for a second did Ronald consider his invalid visa. After all, Sterck had assured him that improving East German–UK relations guaranteed his overstay of two days was no big deal. It came as quite a shock to Ronald, therefore, to be detained on the East Berlin side of Checkpoint Charlie. And when the big black limousine came to take him away, that shock became gut-wrenching fear.

***

'Why don't we leave them be,' Elke Über said, 'until we have clarity on this Josef Sterck matter?' It was the morning of 27 August and Elke was one of four persons invited to Stasi headquarters to receive a confidential briefing on the bizarre events of the preceding day. 'What I mean is,' she explained, 'we don't need to be in any hurry to engage with the British about the Western agent, this Ronald Hunt. And Sterck can wait until he rots if necessary.'

Klaus Borkh audibly hissed, much like a ruptured air hose. 'Well, it was you from behind the scenes that paved the way for Sterck's rise in the party,' he retorted. 'It's you that has ultimately caused this problem.' The other two in the briefing party sat motionless, neither daring to move a face muscle. They were advisers, one from Walter Ulbricht's office and the other from Erich Honecker's. Too junior in this company to offer independent views, they were watching to see how the verbal battle between Elke and Borkh played out before committing one way or the other.

'I understand you're under pressure, Klaus,' Elke said, her voice calm and sincere. 'And, likewise, I appreciate that since your promotion last year this is probably your most onerous challenge. Leaving that aside, however, does not your present position also owe a debt to patronage?' Elke smiled, looking hard into Borkh's eyes. 'As a woman I was forced to take career help where I could find it. For a brief span of time Josef Sterck offered this and in return I gave him what support I could. But that compact has long run its course.'

Borkh bristled. He had assumed, or rather hoped, Elke was referring to his father-in-law and the open secret that was his marriage of convenience. But Elke's steely glare now had him worried she might know about the Polish general, the man twice his age who after a dark and stormy night in Warsaw in February 1963 promised to have a word with Honecker. Erich Honecker, the number two in the East German political leadership, was responsible for key security appointments, including that of leadership reputation protection. Borkh eyed Elke thinking he could not risk a confrontation with her, not when it might lead to the escape of the skeleton in his closet. He would have to live to fight another day.

The advisers sniffed the wind. 'I tend to agree with Fräulein Über,' one said while the other nodded sagely. 'This is a very fishy business and with the party conference tomorrow I think we should keep both the Britisher and comrade Sterck on ice.'

The Stasi briefer looked at Borkh. 'Let it be so,' Borkh said, smiling and level as if wedded to no particular outcome.

Elke watched as the Stasi briefer noted the file. She was in fact unaware of Klaus Borkh's dalliance in Warsaw. But equally she knew that Borkh could not have made the leap from middle-ranking Stasi officer to head of the office of the council of ministers without more support than his father-in-law could provide. This pointed to a bigger and better source of patronage on which he had been able to rely. It was to this unknown quantity Elke had alluded. And now, she grimly noted, Borkh's capitulation had confirmed the existence of a secret benefactor. Even so, Borkh would have resented being outmanoeuvred by a woman only he was too calculating to show it.

The thought that Borkh would be seeking revenge placed Elke on high alert, particularly after he chivalrously opened the door for her as they left, his cold eyes burning. 'I have some business at the SED administrative office, Fräulein Über,' Borkh said lightly as they exited Stasi headquarters. 'Perhaps we should return there together and compare notes. It's always useful to have an informal chat with esteemed comrades whenever the opportunity arises.'

CHAPTER 27

Klaus Borkh did all the talking as he and Elke Über sped below ground on the U-Bahn heading for Elke's place of work on Schumannstrasse. Borkh's intimidatory tactic in retaliation for Elke's besting him at the earlier Stasi briefing was to expand at length on the West's wish to spread propaganda damaging to the party leadership. In this he pointedly cited Josef Sterck egged on by Ronald Hunt, needling Elke and reminding that politically he would try to paint her past career support for Sterck as responsible for Sterck's conduct.

Elke had the rare ability to listen and think at the same time. She knew Borkh would be out to recover lost face and took careful note of his every utterance, while also pondering the instincts that had prompted her at the Stasi briefing to argue for a wait and see approach to Sterck and Hunt. Why she did this Elke could not precisely identify. But two hours later, when the Cuban Paian Diaz arrived bearing Swiss banking records damning Walter Ulbricht and Erich Honecker, she knew her trusted antenna had been right – clearly a Western play of some sort was on.

That said, not until after Elke sent Paian Diaz back to his tour group did she really grasp how razor sharp her instincts had been. Minutes beforehand, Elke had determined an MI6 agent would set the meeting request signal on the Weidendammer Bridge later that afternoon. But only in the lull following Diaz's departure, did she suddenly comprehend that the Westerner with

Dougal's eyes, the man whom she sighted when earlier she and Klaus Borkh were walking to her office from the underground, was the MI6 contact she was about to meet. There would be no need for newspaper recognition signals.

That same afternoon of 27 August 1964, as Elke was piecing events together, Klaus Borkh's thoughts were fulminating. He had always hated Elke because of her superior bureaucratic standing, but now the hatred was personal. Exacting revenge against Elke for humiliating him at the Stasi briefing, however, would take both caution and cunning, not least because the signs were she knew about the matter that, if aired, was guaranteed to destroy him.

Borkh's paranoid mind clicked into gear. His starting point had to be to assume that Elke knew about his strategic coming together with the Polish general and work back from there. What he needed, he concluded, was a counterpoise in the form of dirt on Elke, something he could leverage to neutralise her knowledge. Borkh picked up the telephone. 'Albert,' he said, 'could you drop in to see me in the next hour? Good, thank you. It's quite urgent.' Borkh had just called a Stasi officer, a former colleague.

Borkh's contact, Albert, was senior in the Stasi's foreign intelligence directorate, a full colonel no less. He was also one of the few people whom Borkh implicitly trusted, principally because Albert was, or had been, a serial misappropriater. Borkh had investigated certain financial discrepancies when Albert worked for the Stasi's domestic service. That was four years ago, after which Borkh arranged Albert's transfer to the Stasi foreign intelligence directorate while mopping up the mess and muddying the audit trail, save for a couple of documents he kept for insurance. He did so because he foresaw that talented people like Albert who might later be of personal use were of no value if in prison.

Ever since Albert had found the informal work doled out by Klaus Borkh, or rather more likely the associated under the table payments, quelled his kleptomania just enough to keep him out of trouble. Yet despite this flaw, Albert was a competent intelligence officer. Gradually he rose through the foreign intelligence ranks. But Albert also knew his blackmailer would eventually ask for a very large favour, particularly once, inexplicably, Borkh was made the head of the office of the council of ministers. And now, with Elke Über's wounding belittling at the Stasi meeting, the day had arrived for Klaus Borkh to exercise his cruel power.

'Starting this evening,' Borkh instructed Albert, 'I want you to wait outside the SED administrative centre and follow the secretariat head when she leaves work.'

'Fräulein Über?' Albert said, unable to hide his surprise.

'The one and the same,' Borkh said. 'I am not yet able to offer a reason why. But until further notice you are to trail her and report back to me on any unaccountable behaviour, however minor.' Borkh sighed theatrically. 'You can call me here in my office until 10 pm most nights. Our subject of interest is not so conscientious. She leaves her office at 6 pm every evening come hell or high water.' Klaus Borkh, of course, was not about to explain that Albert's real brief was to find something to counter Elke's current advantage, the stranglehold Borkh perceived she held over him.

***

It was into this maelstrom of Klaus Borkh's visceral hatred of Elke Über that Daniel Lincoln would stumble in the early evening of 27 August 1964. After sighting Elke that morning at the SED administrative office and beginning to worry about a VoPo discovering the DG's letter, things had calmed for Daniel. He had wandered for a time before returning to the Frund Hotel.

The glance he took at Kristiina Ahnger's photograph once in his room further steadied him. He now felt up to the task before him, picturing being back in London and describing the theft of his padlock and how, through a combination of resolve and resourcefulness, he had still managed to pass Elke the DG's letter at the Tränenpalast pavilion. Why, Daniel thought, if I can pull this off it might remove the Kristiina monkey from my back once and for all.

Soothed for the moment, Daniel ate a lunch of sorts in the hotel restaurant before leaving for the trade ministry and his re-scheduled appointment. An interview did ensue, but shambolically, with the two participating East German officials exhibiting signs of life and accepting the tendered A.H. Jenkins sales brochure only when Daniel – or Frank Middlemiss as he was going by – offered them a Marlboro cigarette.

At 5 pm Daniel bought a beer in a spartan café about thirty minutes walk from the Weidendammer Bridge, conscious of the tension building. His mind flashed back to Peter Parnell-Brown's pre-departure briefing. 'After leaving her Schumannstrasse office around 6 pm,' Parnell-Brown said, 'it'll take her fifteen to twenty minutes to walk to the bridge.' Parnell-Brown had smiled broadly. 'Provided the padlock's attached no later than six you should be fine. But best to do it earlier if you can.'

Daniel grimaced, remembering how simple the Deputy made it appear. If only he knew the truth. Daniel took a deep breath, trying to dampen his rising apprehension. He forced himself to consider timing, estimating he could spend up to thirty minutes on the Weidendammer Bridge watching the passing river traffic without arousing the suspicion of his Stasi tail. So long as he was on the bridge by 5:50 pm, he would be there when Elke walked by.

Daniel sipped at his beer for exactly twenty minutes before leaving the café. Thereafter time seemed to slow until it felt like it was standing still. Indeed, as Daniel was soon to learn, the frequent glances at his watch were the anomaly first noticed by his Stasi watchers. Not that Daniel was unaware of the risks of constantly checking the time. But by that point the chemicals racing to his brain and distorting his senses were in the ascendancy.

Klaus Borkh's agent Albert had been trailing Elke Über from in front. He came across the three-man Stasi surveillance team monitoring Daniel about ninety seconds before Elke approached. 'The British businessman we're watching has started to behave strangely,' the team leader said when quizzed by Albert. 'We were about to go and interdict him.'

Albert immediately sensed a connection between Elke and the fidgety Englishman. 'Just hold off for a minute or two,' he instructed the Stasi team.

At that instant Elke Über walked by, taking no notice of the group of four men conversing on the sidewalk. She stepped onto the Weidendammer Bridge looking closely at the base of the first lamp post. On sighting no *Karl loves Ilsa* padlock she hid her surprise and continued to walk. Suddenly, in breach of all her instincts, she stopped dead and did a double take. To her astonishment, the man with Dougal's eyes whom she had seen earlier in the day was standing in the middle of the bridge, an idiotic smile on his face.

Elke recovered quickly and resumed walking, averting her gaze. The man fell in beside her. 'Someone stole the padlock,' he blurted. Elke kept walking and the man skipped like a child to keep up. 'Go to the Tränenpalast pavilion at Friedrichstrasse station,' Daniel Lincoln said, unaware that with all the subtlety of a street jester he had just engaged Elke in full view of four Stasi officers. 'Wait outside in the crowd and I'll join you shortly.'

In the normal course of events Daniel's bumbling would have caused Elke to opt for safety. But the Englishman's eyes fascinated her, drawing her like a moth to a flame. And, crucially, Elke did not know about Albert's role in proceedings, which had she would likely have led to a different outcome. But absent this knowledge Elke instead calculated the Stasi on the Dougal lookalike's tail would be low-ranking foot soldiers she could stare down if push came to shove. So, Elke chose to do as Daniel had requested.

'We'll break into two teams of two,' Albert said. 'You two stick with the Englishman. You come with me to follow the woman.'

Fifteen minutes later Albert observed Elke Über reach the Tränenpalast pavilion where she merged into the throng of people, many of whom were hugging and crying. Several minutes passed before a somewhat dishevelled Daniel Lincoln walked straight past Albert, his wild eyes searching the human mass in front of the Palace of Tears as if looking for a familiar face.

***

'I'm calling from a public callbox on Unter den Linden,' Klaus Borkh's operative Albert said, 'from where I have visual of Fräulein Über's apartment. She reached the apartment six minutes ago at 7:22 pm and is currently inside.'

'Good,' Borkh said softly as he wrote down the time of Elke's return home on what was becoming a fateful night of 27 August 1964. 'Anything further to report?' he added, now more attentive.

'Quite a lot actually but of course we're on an open line.'

'Just give it to me,' Borkh spat.

'As you wish,' Albert said evenly. He was a professional. 'At twenty after six this evening an English businessman, supposedly, made brief verbal contact with comrade Über on the Weidendammer Bridge. After which she proceeded to the Tränenpalast pavilion, arriving there at six thirty-six.'

'Did you follow her into the crowd?' Borkh broke in anxiously. 'To see who she was meeting.'

Albert exhaled silently. 'At six forty-three,' he said, ignoring the interruption, 'from my position on the edge of the crowd, I observed the same English businessman arrive and also make for the front of the pavilion. He and Fräulein Über were hidden in the crowd for seventeen minutes. My strong opinion is this was meant to be a clandestine meeting. I base this on the belief that those who arranged the contact did so knowing the gathering in front of the Tränenpalast pavilion is not a place where East German secret policemen are welcome. I would also add for the sake of completeness that seventeen minutes is a very long clandestine meeting.'

'Yes, yes,' Borkh said eagerly.

'At 7 pm sharp,' Albert continued with a roll of his eyes, 'the Englishman left the Tränenpalast pavilion and walked east up Friedrichstrasse towards the Weidendammer Bridge. Two of his three-man Stasi monitoring team are currently tailing him. The other team member is with me. He has a radio placing him in touch with his colleagues. But in the rush to make this call, I haven't had a chance to enquire as to the Englishman's current whereabouts.'

'And Elke Über?' Borkh whispered, his voice so faint that Albert struggled to hear him.

'No more than a minute after the Englishman left, Fräulein Über also exited the Tränenpalast crowd and walked west on Friedrichstrasse, that is in the opposite direction to the Englishman. On reaching Unter den Linden she turned left and proceeded directly to her apartment. I was well back but did catch her take a surreptitious glance down the street in the direction from where she had come. A certain back check in my estimation.'

'Are you confident she did not see you?' Borkh asked.

'Yes,' Albert said bluntly. The question was superfluous.

'Good,' Borkh said. The sound of Borkh's fingers drumming on his office desk were audible in Albert's telephone handset. 'The Englishman will either be at his hotel or eventually return there,' Borkh said after a time. 'Tell the Stasi fellow with you to join the other two Stasi and for the three of them to pick up the Englishman. You wait where you are. Depart from your present position only if our Bavarian lady friend leaves her apartment. I will join you shortly at which time you and I will pay her a surprise visit.'

'Understood,' Albert replied, preparing to ring off.

'Wait,' Borkh snapped urgently. He was not finished. 'You should instruct the Stasi who are to arrest the Englishman to take him to the special wing at Hohenschönhausen.' Hohenschönhausen was a Soviet-styled Stasi prison in East Berlin. Its special wing was a secret internal facility where the Stasi's most sensitive political prisoners endured interrogation followed, generally, by a grim and lonely death. 'And Albert,' Borkh said coldly.

'Yes.'

'Also tell the Stasi team that if they so much as breathe a word of the Englishman's detention to anyone, I Klaus Borkh will personally cut out their innards and feed them to the wolves in the Lusatia forest.'

CHAPTER 28

Earlier, after his clumsy contact with Elke Über on the Weidendammer Bridge, Daniel Lincoln had been obliged to return to the Frund Hotel. The strain of speaking to Elke had turned his stomach to molten lava. Making the lavatory in his room just in time, Daniel's bowels moved with confronting force. After which he washed his sickly grey face with cold water, dismayed that in the space of an hour his nervous condition should have deteriorated so violently. Shaken, Daniel thought of the techniques he relied on to restore his equilibrium, all the while wanting to believe the Stasi would not review the tapes currently recording him until late the next morning when, all going well, he would be back in West Berlin.

Kicking off his shoes and shrugging his suit coat onto the floor, Daniel extracted Kristiina Ahnger's photograph from his suitcase and placed it on the small writing desk in his room. Next, with his hands resting on the back of the desk chair, he ran frantically up and down on the spot until sweat formed on his forehead and trickled down his back staining his shirt, never taking his eyes off Kristiina's image. A quick glance at his watch told him he had to go. 'Just hold it together for a few hours more,' he told himself as he raced out. 'By nine tomorrow morning you will be safe in West Berlin.'

Light-headed and clammy in the heat of the August evening, Daniel did his best to look nonchalant as he hastened towards

Friedrichstrasse station. He sucked in deep breaths as he went, trying to stave off the sensation he might throw up at any moment. But the closer Daniel got to his destination the more his pulse pounded and the worse he felt.

Daniel had not seen the Tränenpalast pavilion before, given it was built only in 1962. The sight, therefore, of the structure – its lime green rendered walls, high flat roof and tall glass windows above the entrance vestibule – gave him a fleeting sense of achievement, for among many other things he had become fearful he might not be able to find the place. People were swarming everywhere as Daniel pushed through the crowd, tripping over luggage while feverishly searching for Elke.

Elke turned as if informed by a sixth sense. Bearing down on her through the mass of humanity was the living manifestation of Dougal frozen in time, in 1938 shortly before Dougal bolted for Liverpool distraught at having surrendered to his carnal desires. Daniel and Elke's eyes met; hers dark, clear and shining in anticipation, his wild and bloodshot as a torrent of tears flowed down his face.

'My God,' Elke exclaimed, her hands gripping Daniel's forearms.

Daniel looked uncomprehendingly at Elke, as if now not recognising her. All the while Elke gazed deep into his swollen blue-green eyes, those so revealing of his West Riding of Yorkshire heritage and, by virtue of his tearful vulnerability, reminiscent of Dougal. It was an extraordinary scene by any measure, a bizarre coming together of spy courier and field agent, one virtually unparalleled throughout the annals of British espionage for its monumental inappropriateness.

But it was also destiny. In selecting the Palace of Tears as the location for Daniel to hand Elke his letter, Sir Roger Holbrook's operation Spot had picked the one place in East Berlin where such an otherwise calamitous happening could be played out without a single person in the near vicinity taking a blade of notice.

And somewhere in the middle of this bewildering moment Daniel Lincoln felt a sudden impulse to tell Elke everything, every last detail. For over a year he had kept the most dreadful secrets bottled up inside. But now it seemed as if by some preordained miracle the woman called Elke Über had been sent to ease his burden.

Elke relaxed her hold and Daniel stepped back a pace. 'I have a letter for you,' he whispered, wanting first to get the business of the day out of the way.

'Where is it?' Elke asked calmly.

'In my jacket; inside pocket.'

Elke drew Daniel to her. 'You're from the West Riding of Yorkshire, aren't you?' she said, slipping her hand inside Daniel's jacket and wrapping her arm around his back. When Daniel didn't answer, Elke began to stroke his ribcage, the exercise culminating in a dextrous flick of her wrist and the transfer of the envelope inside Daniel's jacket into the bodice of her dress.

All the while, Daniel's mind continued to whirl. 'I am,' he said in belated answer to Elke's question as to his origin. 'But I'm not well,' he added in a seamless rush, anxious to confide before his illness reduced him to an incoherent mess. 'I am riddled with shame and massive guilt. I need to tell you about my fears.'

'I once knew a boy called Dougal whose eyes were identical to yours,' Elke said with a sad smile. 'He was also damaged.' Elke smiled again, this time exuding warmth. 'You can trust me with your problems,' she said. 'Confiding in me will mark the beginning of your recovery, and mine too.'

Daniel gulped, knowing he had limited time to tell his story and prepared to let Elke's mention of a Dougal pass unexplained. With that, he set about breaking every rule in the book.

'The letter,' he began, 'is to do with your defection.' Daniel scratched his head. 'I'm not entirely sure why, but it's a big secret my employer MI6 is keeping from the Americans. The CIA knows nothing of my cover name of Frank Middlemiss or of my visit here to East Berlin.' Daniel paused, panting for breath in his haste to get the words out. 'I'm to return to West Berlin tomorrow morning,' he said. Having not read Sir Roger Holbrook's sealed letter, he assumed Elke's defection was planned for the near term. 'When you are in England we can talk at greater length.'

Elke nodded. 'We will,' she said, rubbing a hand on Daniel's upper arm, encouraging him to continue. 'For now, just concentrate on what you want to tell me.'

Daniel filled his lungs with air. 'My real name is Daniel Lincoln,' he said. 'Last year, in July, I completed a three-year posting to Washington DC with MI6.' Daniel vigorously rubbed his forehead with the butt of his hand. He wanted to tell Elke everything but had not grasped just how difficult it was to say the words out loud. 'Earlier in the year I fell in love with a woman who unbeknown to me was an Israeli spy. In May she tricked me into providing Mossad with a highly sensitive document shared with us in trust by the CIA.'

Daniel swallowed. 'Were MI6 to find out I would face years in prison, particularly given my betrayal of the Americans. The shame of it would kill the person in this world I love and admire the most – my father. Falling into the Mossad trap has had a chronic physiological effect on me. It's caused me to suffer a mental breakdown, with debilitating physical side effects. I hide my condition from MI6 by avoiding the company of others as best I can, while using techniques that briefly strengthen me when I have to engage with colleagues.'

'What happened after the Mossad compromise?' Elke said, gently steering Daniel back to his story.

'The next morning, I very nearly got caught returning the document to its rightful place.'

'But you didn't get caught, I take it?'

'No. I managed to frame my boss in the Washington station so that he got blamed for it going missing.' Daniel sighed. 'His name was Ray Solter. He was not a good person. But blackening his reputation and ruining his life cuts across the grain of everything my father ever taught me about what is right and what is wrong. The whole thing – the Mossad deception and my conduct in respect of Ray Solter – has haunted me ever since.'

'Go on.'

Daniel waved his arms in the air in unspoken frustration. 'I've lost all confidence and self-esteem and am continually beset by panic attacks and feelings of inadequacy. The mental strain is making me physically ill.' He shook his head. 'They picked me to come here and give you the letter because I speak German and know Berlin. I accepted because I couldn't very well tell MI6 I was ill and explain why. I thought if I could successfully complete the task it might help me repair. But it hasn't. It's actually made things worse.'

Elke briefly hugged Daniel to her before releasing him with a touch of his cheek, much as she would with Dougal. 'We're out of time, Daniel,' she whispered. 'You must go. Be patient. Before too long, I will join you and help you to become well.'

Daniel looked at Elke, suddenly uncertain if it had been a mistake to reveal so much. Elke smiled. 'Have faith, Daniel,' she said with stern composure. 'I intend for you to find peace on the Sandymount Strand in Dublin.' And for Elke that thought sealed the deal.

***

Daniel left in a blur. Elke's promise that he would find peace on the Sandymount Strand in Dublin whirled in his mind, triggering visions of Kristiina Ahnger. Just a year ago he had dared to hope, only to be horribly denied. It reminded Daniel that afterwards he had sworn never to hope again. But here he was already breaking his sacred rule, simply because Elke's pledge suggested she cared for him. 'Wait until she's defected and we're both in London,' Daniel counselled himself. 'For now concentrate solely on what you must do. It might be different this time... in London... surely.'

With that, Daniel forced himself to think about what next. He had handed Elke the DG's letter and operation Spot stipulated his next step was to eat dinner. Lengthening his stride, Daniel headed for the Am Zwinger cafeteria in Brecht-Platz. Daniel would not have been surprised to learn two Stasi officers were following him, that tailing had resumed now he was no longer hidden in the Stasi no-go zone in front of the Palace of Tears. But he would have been perturbed to know that the third member of the Stasi team was shortly to re-join his colleagues carrying orders from Klaus Borkh to arrest him.

'Get your things, Mr Middlemiss,' the Stasi team leader said. An hour had elapsed since Daniel finished dinner and the Stasi trio had just intercepted him in the Frund Hotel foyer. 'You are under arrest for espionage activities against the German Democratic Republic.' And with that all Daniel could do was think of Kristiina Ahnger.

***

'Roger,' Peter Parnell-Brown whispered urgently, jumping to his feet, 'a quick word if you don't mind.' Since 9:30 am, for over an hour now, the Deputy had been waiting outside Sir Roger Holbrook's office, having declined the offer of Sir Roger's personal assistant to return to his own office and be summoned by telephone when the Director General finally arrived.

It was Friday 28 August 1964 and Sir Roger had been attending a cabinet meeting. He wore a heavy pinstriped suit befitting the occasion. In the day's muggy warmth a bead of perspiration had formed on his top lip. But Sir Roger knew crisis when he saw it. Without removing his suit coat, he ushered Parnell-Brown into the same secure room where four months earlier they had discussed operation Leopard before turning their attention to Daniel Lincoln's role in operation Spot.

'Bad news, I take it?' the DG said soberly.

'Possibly,' Parnell-Brown replied. 'The wires out of East Berlin are now carrying low key reports, fifth or sixth item in the bulletin, of a fire early this morning at the Frund Hotel. Talk of minor injuries, smoke inhalation that sort of thing, but caveated with mention of the fire people still searching the building.' Parnell-Brown paused. 'And,' he added ominously, 'our boy is not yet back across the wire.'

The DG frowned. Like the Deputy he was deeply suspicious of coincidences. 'OK, Peter give me a stocktake,' he ordered. 'Both operations, the whole box and dice.'

Parnell-Brown lightly rubbed his nose with a forefinger. There was not an awful lot of good news. 'Decoy phase of Leopard,' he began. 'Josef Sterck appeared on East German television on 26 August and did as required. But unaccountably the Sterck go-between, Ronald Hunt, stayed on and has since been arrested. The Foreign Secretary has called for Swiss diplomats to be allowed to provide consular assistance. This has been ignored. Separately, a private approach was made through the East German–Sweden Association, which was also rebuffed. The East German response was that consular rights do not apply to persons engaged in espionage. Hunt's whereabouts are currently unknown.' Parnell-Brown grimaced. 'There's every chance,' he said ruefully, 'that my personal choice for the operation Leopard decoy is in Hohenschönhausen.'

'Dear me,' Sir Roger muttered. 'Go on.'

'As per our contingency plans,' Parnell-Brown continued, 'we're playing innocent on Hunt. Know nothing, seen nothing is the word if the Labour opposition arcs up. Hunt's just an unfortunate who, for reasons best known to him, has ended up as a consular case in East Berlin. Our press line if asked is that he's the Foreign Office's responsibility and nothing to do with us.'

'Messy, isn't it?' the DG said with a slow shake of his head.

'Active phase of Leopard,' Parnell-Brown resumed after briefly nodding his agreement. 'Michael Anjelico reports the Cuban courier Paian Diaz carrying the Swiss banking records intended for Konrad Voite left Havana as scheduled on a charter flight. But owing to a mechanical problem with the plane en route Diaz's arrival in East Berlin was delayed, although presumably he is there by now. The charter returns to Havana on 6 September and until Diaz is debriefed, the CIA is unable to say what happened to the bank statements.'

Parnell-Brown ran his hand through his hair. 'I gave Anjelico a decent flea in the ear over this courier business. It remains to be seen if Diaz eventually mailed the papers to Voite and, if so, if he got them. All that said, Diaz's debrief is rendered largely immaterial by the fact that the SED conference will now be underway. We should know by this afternoon if Voite received the documents. Let's hope he did and that he manages to tip one very big bucket on the East German leadership.'

'Meanwhile Daniel Lincoln is MIA,' the DG cut in, 'leaving us with no clue if he executed Spot and delivered my letter to Elke.'

'Missing in action, he is,' Parnell-Brown confirmed with a sigh. 'But maybe the fire's held him up. Maybe he'll turn up presently.'

The DG suddenly looked very old. Peter Parnell-Brown assumed it was the strain of all the bad news. It was in fact Sir

Roger sensing that his last big career gamble had failed, his private quest to restore Britain's strategic clout to days of yore when Britain, and not the crass Americans, led the Anglo–US alliance. 'Sadly, Peter,' the DG said quietly, 'my water is telling me that we won't be seeing Daniel Lincoln any time soon.'

CHAPTER 29

In something of a rare occurrence, Daniel Lincoln was the second of two Englishmen transferred to the special wing at Hohenschönhausen prison on the night of 27 August 1964. Ronald Hunt, of course, had been picked up at Checkpoint Charlie in the early afternoon of 26 August as he tried to make it back to West Berlin in the aftermath of Josef Sterck's appearance on the *Aktuelle Kamera* television program.

MI6's Peter Parnell-Brown was later astonished to learn that neither Michael Anjelico nor any CIA other indoctrinated for operation Leopard had briefed Ronald on what he should say or do if detained by the East Germans. All Ronald had been told was to seek out Sterck on the morning of 24 August, hand over evidence of the East German leadership's minor corruption and demand the German go on television on 26 August and make a fuss about this, all on pain of the CIA green-lighting publication of a diary by Sterck's illegitimate daughter revealing Sterck's Nazi abuse of Friedrich Reinhold's sister-in-law.

After that, in accordance with the terms of his one-day visa, Ronald was to return to West Berlin later on 24 August whereupon, subject to Sterck doing as required on 26 August, he would be allowed to go free. In this, Parnell-Brown was more forgiving on discovering that the Americans had not anticipated Sterck tricking Ronald into remaining in East Berlin until the 26 August television appearance, supposedly as a guarantee of the

CIA's good intention. After all, Sterck had already fooled Ronald into carrying most of the burden for the murder of Staff Sergeant Horace Neitz in Munich in November 1946. And, as the saying goes, once bitten, twice shy.

But Ronald Hunt was a special sort of fool and Peter Parnell-Brown understood this better than most. The Deputy, therefore, was later unsurprised to learn that Ronald had swallowed Sterck's bogus assurance holus bolus: that East Germany's improving relations with the UK guaranteed Ronald's breach of East German immigration law would incur nothing more than a talking-to and a token fine before being sent on his way.

***

Against this background, and of course Josef Sterck's extraordinary outburst on television, Ronald Hunt made an unconvincing attempt to tell the Stasi who earlier intercepted him at the border how he had come to East Berlin to discuss possible business opportunities with Sterck. Yes, he'd come unannounced. But he and Sterck went back a long way, and up until the fatal shooting of Horace Neitz in November 1946 they had collaborated successfully on an admittedly illegal business venture.

'And the receipts pertaining to comrades Ulbricht and Honecker's visit to Bouzov Castle in Czechoslovakia, Mr Hunt?' the lead interrogator asked.

'Never seen them before in my life,' Ronald replied. Despite the years locked up at Fort Leavenworth in Kansas, Ronald had lost none of his ability to look people in the eye and blatantly lie. Only on this occasion it made him seem like a well-schooled spy. 'I think he was just looking for an opening to use the documents,' Ronald fabricated. 'When I turned up, I was the perfect patsy.'

'Are you a CIA spy, Mr Hunt?'

'No way, mate, sorry. No. I'm just an ex-con trying to make a living. Thinking over my future, I thought Josef Sterck might be a chance. Sorry about the visa overstay and all that. But being a British passport holder, Sterck assured me it was small beer at the end of the day.' Ronald winked at his interrogators. 'Got a handful of Westmarks on me, you know. You boys are welcome to them if you fancy a drink.'

***

Klaus Borkh couldn't explain why, not even to himself. But something in Ronald's ham-fisted attempt to bribe the Stasi officers caught his eye when reviewing the transcript of interview during the early evening of 27 August. For that reason, just minutes after ordering the arrest of the so-called Frank Middlemiss, Borkh also directed Stasi head office to remove Ronald to the special wing at Hohenschönhausen. The man was a spy and East Germany was quite entitled to ignore the British Foreign Office requests for access. He could remain locked up indefinitely, Borkh calculated, until it was clear why so weighty a level of intrigue seemed to attach to the bald Englishman. But the long game envisaged by Borkh was destined never to eventuate, not after his hand was forced just hours later.

Indeed, Ronald Hunt had a premonition in the early evening of 27 August 1964 when they took him from the Stasi cells in Berlin-Lichtenberg. It revolved around a Sunday in September 1942 in the flat in Streatham in London he shared with his then wife Janice, the day he suffocated their infant daughter, Carmel, while Janice was visiting her parents. The thing most disturbing Ronald was that only rarely did he think about his infanticide, and even then it was usually to gloat about how he'd gotten clean away with murder. Yet in the back of the car taking him the short distance to Hohenschönhausen prison and later when lying on the thin mattress in his cell, visions of Carmel kept flooding his mind, particularly of her squirming as he pressed the pillow into her face. All of which, Ronald feared, portended bad news.

For this reason, Ronald wasn't especially surprised when some hours later they came for him – scared witless, yes; but caught off guard, no. It was actually 3 am on 28 August, although Ronald had no way of knowing. Klaus Borkh's helper Albert and one other Stasi had bundled him barefoot out of the cell and into an unmarked Lada before placing a blindfold over his eyes.

The trip culminated in material of some sort being forced into Ronald's mouth. Next, with one man supporting each arm, Ronald was frogmarched up a structure he took to be an external fire escape. Certainly, the stairway was of metal construction because it dug into his bare feet and scuffed them as they went. Finally Ronald's bloodied toes detected carpet, followed shortly after by a door opening and closing and a hushed conversation in German between two men. The last sensation Ronald Hunt ever felt was a sharp prick in his right arm; and his last thought before the blackness of death claimed him was of Carmel and her innocent eyes gazing at him in terrified bewilderment as he snuffed the life out of her.

***

Elke Über had to read the letter twice, thinking that what with hearing Daniel Lincoln's tortured confession at the Tränenpalast pavilion barely an hour ago she was missing something. But no, there it was in Sir Roger Holbrook's beautiful copperplate handwriting: the agreement to her defection, but only after three years.

The DG's stipulation caused Elke to reflect on the Swiss banking records that had fallen into her lap, those proving systemic corruption by Walter Ulbricht and Erich Honecker. No question the documents were intended to pave the way for Konrad Voite's installation as East German prime minister. Did it follow, Elke wondered, that Holbrook wanted her to stay in place to support Voite? And if so, what type of support was she supposed to provide?

It was never likely to occur to Elke that Sir Roger had confided in his Deputy the intention to chase an unrivalled assessment both of Konrad Voite's capacity to kick-start German reunification and his appetite for such a fight in the face of ferocious Soviet opposition. Nor could Elke know Sir Roger had carefully omitted to tell Peter Parnell-Brown of his ambition for her assessments to restore Britain's strategic superiority over the Americans.

A brisk rap on the door made Elke jump. Although it was not late, a little after 8 pm, she seldom had night-time callers. And furthermore, the rat-a-tat had a policeman's authority. Elke slipped the DG's letter into the drawer of her desk before padding softly towards the door intent on peering through the fisheye peephole. Klaus Borkh was waiting on the other side one hand holding an optical reverser to the lens, the result of which was to cancel the fisheye effect and permit him to see into the apartment's entrance. Borkh waved his free hand directing Albert to speak.

'State security service,' Albert bellowed. 'Under the law of the state of East Germany, I am permitted to force entry should you not open the door immediately.'

Elke froze, thinking of the letter in her desk drawer and knowing the Stasi would burst in before she could find a better hiding place for it. She released the latch bolt, hoping fervently the intrusion would not involve a full-scale search of her apartment.

'You,' Elke exclaimed.

'Yes, me,' Borkh said with a thin-lipped smile. 'Aren't you going to invite us in?'

Elke stood arms crossed on the threshold. 'Your position affords you no authority to enter my home,' she retorted.

'Quite correct,' Borkh replied as if taking Elke's objection seriously. 'But my friend here is a Stasi officer and I don't need to tell you he has the power to do virtually as he pleases.' Borkh smiled smugly. 'I am here only in the capacity of a neutral observer, in order to ensure your citizen's rights are fully protected.' With that, Borkh pushed past Elke and walked into her sitting room.

Albert found the letter within a matter of minutes. The desk drawer was an obvious place to look. For her part, Elke sat on her sofa saying nothing, watching Albert go about his work. Borkh meanwhile roamed about the apartment inspecting art works and peering inside the occasional cupboard. The interlude was brief, but it did give Elke time to think.

'So Fräulein Über,' Borkh said gloatingly, 'what have we here?' He was holding up the DG's letter having just read it. 'A house on the Sandymount Strand in Dublin, what an intriguing asking price for your treachery.' Borkh glared at Elke. 'No doubt you took possession of this letter when you met the MI6 agent calling himself Frank Middlemiss at the Tränenpalast pavilion earlier this evening.' Borkh smiled, trying to unsettle Elke. 'Middlemiss has been arrested. The Stasi are taking him to the special wing at Hohenschönhausen prison. He will be kept there until such time as I have gathered all the information I need.'

'Why don't you send your Stasi lapdog home, Klaus?' Elke said. 'There's nothing more to find here and we need to talk.'

Borkh searched Elke's face, looking for signs of trickery. He saw none, but equally didn't want to risk his personal secrets being disclosed to Albert. He motioned for the Stasi officer to leave.

Once alone, neither spoke for a time, each weighing the other. Borkh cracked first. 'Well, come on,' he snapped, annoyed that Elke had outwaited him. 'Let's hear what you have to say.'

Elke smiled coldly at Borkh. 'On the face of it, Klaus,' she said softly, 'we are at a stalemate. You now know of my contact with the British MI6 and I, of course, know about your secret backer.' Elke was harking back to the Stasi briefing she and Borkh attended that morning, when Elke had deduced the existence of a secret, if unidentified, Borkh benefactor. And moreover Elke's delving had been nothing if not subtle – artful enquiries that caused the paranoid Borkh to fear she somehow knew about his liaison in Warsaw in February 1963, with the Polish general who later persuaded Erich Honecker to appoint Borkh as the leadership's minder.

'But,' Borkh said, waving the letter about, 'I have written proof and you are relying on rumour.' Borkh's gaze briefly flickered. 'In any event, the Pole is lying. He and I had a drink, that's all.'

Borkh was an accomplished opportunist. But in his rush to denial he had foolishly neglected to definitively confirm that Elke knew he was hiding an affair with a Polish man. Now Elke understood. Borkh's appointment took effect in May 1963. In February of that year he had attended a Poland–East Germany security summit in Warsaw. She joined the dots. 'My friends in Warsaw tell me quite another story,' Elke said levelly. 'I understand the gentleman in question is prepared to reveal everything if matters turn sour. Better a humiliating personal embarrassment than a cold jail cell, that sort of thing.'

Borkh's nerve failed him. He winced, not wanting to hear the details of his secret spill from Elke's mouth. 'OK,' he said changing tack. 'So, we're stalemated. What's there to talk about?'

'Well, Klaus, it turns out we're not completely stalemated. It has recently come to my attention that a serious threat to your masters exists, about which you know nothing.' Elke pursed her lips. 'It is my considered judgement that in view of tomorrow's party conference this oversight would likely result in your execution given it represents a gross failing on your part.'

'What?' Borkh exploded. 'We've checked everything. The party conference is scripted watertight. You're bluffing, you witch.'

Elke laughed. 'While you've been busy making much ado about nothing with Josef Sterck and his lackey Ronald Hunt, certain documents have surfaced.' Elke laughed again. 'You, Klaus, were too dim-witted to understand that Sterck's claim of leadership fraud based on trivial hotel receipts was a feint to preoccupy you while evidence of the most vulgar corruption by Ulbricht and Honecker made its way into other hands.'

Elke held up a hand as Borkh tried to speak. 'And don't bother racing off to beat the daylights out of Sterck – he knows nothing.' Elke sighed. 'I'm not entirely sure why he went on television and said the things he said. He was duped by Hunt, I expect, something to do with his Nazi past.' Elke took a deep breath. 'Conversely, I can help you with the incriminating documents, principally because I have them. But I will need something in return; something substantial, very substantial.'

'Like what?' Borkh croaked.

'Return to your office,' Elke spat. 'I will meet you there in an hour.' She paused. 'And no more games, Klaus, no more following me or other tricks. Do you understand?'

'Yes,' Borkh whispered.

'Good. Now get out of my home.'

CHAPTER 30

Elke Über had long made it a habit of erring on the side of caution. This meant trusting nobody, not even her loyal assistant. That's why Elke was not about to keep the Swiss banking documents in her office safe, not when the combination was recorded in a central registry. Her ingenious solution was to hide the records in plain sight. Placing the six pages delivered by Paian Diaz in standard SED stationery, Elke wrote *Ministry of Cultural Harmony Strategic Plan 1960-65* on the envelope before burying it under other papers gathering dust on a shelf in her assistant's office. If Walter Ulbricht and Erich Honecker's sidelining of Konrad Voite into the Cultural Harmony portfolio had taught Elke anything it was that most East German bureaucrats avoided cultural harmony like the plague.

Elke wore a scarf on the trolley bus up Friedrichstrasse heading for her office. East Berlin was a safe place, no different to other totalitarian cities where police power is absolute. But the last thing Elke wanted was to be recognised. So, she dressed down for anonymity. Even then, she rode the bus for a block more than necessary before wending her way back through the deserted streets, something which made the job of following her virtually impossible.

Satisfied the coast was clear, Elke made her way up to her office. Locking the door behind her, she retrieved the Swiss banking records from their hiding place. The first page she would take to Borkh while from the summary sixth page totalling the amounts syphoned off by Walter Ulbricht and Erich Honecker she copied the figures onto a blank piece of paper. Restoring the remaining five pages to their hidey-hole, Elke left, her destination Klaus Borkh's office across the river in the old Reichsbank building.

It was when passing the Tränenpalast pavilion on the rattling trolley bus heading down Friedrichstrasse that Elke put her earlier encounter with Daniel Lincoln into perspective. Yes, Daniel's eyes and his trauma did revive powerful memories of Dougal. But years had passed. To her, Dougal would always be twenty-two, like a soldier who had gone to war never to return. At forty-two, though, she was now old enough to be his mother.

Suddenly Elke sat bolt upright. It had just dawned on her that she was not in pursuit of a past long gone. Rather, it was her realisation that whereas Dougal was suspended in time, she had continued to evolve. She was now a different person, still caring deeply for Dougal to be sure, but nonetheless relating differently to him. So this is it, Elke thought. She was not drawn to Daniel Lincoln because of her past but because of her present, because of his embodiment as her troubled son. It was motherhood, she saw, maternal instincts so profound as to imbue her with the courage to commit to the perilous course of action on which she had embarked.

Elke laughed softly, her chuckle reverberating around the empty bus. 'So be warned, Herr Borkh,' she said out loud, 'it is my duty to protect Daniel. And in that I will do whatever it takes at whatever cost to ensure his safe passage out of here, so I can join him on the Sandymount Strand and help him heal in peace.'

***

Klaus Borkh almost choked. 'How do I know this Swiss bank document is not a forgery?' he asked, his hand trembling.

Elke sighed from the other side of Borkh's desk. 'Look at its watermark, Klaus,' she said. 'Even you would have to agree the record is genuine.' Elke smiled. 'And I think you also know that it and the other papers I am holding are enough to have you shot. Imagine if Ulbricht and Honecker became aware of your negligence. They could never trust you again.'

'What do you propose?' Borkh whispered.

Elke sat forward her dark eyes set in steel. 'Were it not for the banking records, we would be stalemated. I am prepared to allow a return to that situation, where your knowledge of my contact with MI6 is counter-balanced by my knowledge of your tryst in Warsaw and how your Polish male lover fooled Erich Honecker into appointing you as head of the office of the council of ministers.'

'And in return?'

'I have an extensive list of demands as regards Frank Middlemiss, who is currently in your custody. Once those demands are met I will give you the remaining banking records.'

Borkh scoffed. 'If I carry out your wishes, what guarantee do I have you will hand over all the records? And in any event, what's so important about this Frank Middlemiss character?'

Elke had anticipated both questions. 'My entire working life, Klaus, has been shaped by a certain philosophy.' She smiled. 'Ask Josef Sterck; he knows of it. That is, I have always operated on the principle that keeping things on a business footing achieves the best outcomes. Only if one of the parties departs from agreed terms are things likely to go sour.' Elke pursed her lips. 'This was a lesson Sterck learned the hard way in November 1946, after earlier fiddling with the deal he had struck with the American Horace Neitz.'

Elke was renowned in East Berlin bureaucratic circles for her word being her bond. Chances were, Borkh calculated, she would surrender the banking records if her demands were met.

In Elke's world to not do so would be to tempt fate. Borkh nodded, accepting the response. 'And the importance of Frank Middlemiss?'

'The Middlemiss consideration is beyond your comprehension, Klaus,' Elke said simply. 'It goes to compassion and other decencies of which you know nothing. But let us not waste time discussing this. All you need to know is that, once he is gone, Middlemiss will have no future impact on you.' Elke took a deep breath. 'Now if I may proceed.' With that, she began to set out her terms, Borkh's eyes widening with each stated requirement.

***

Friday night 28 August 1964 was a sombre affair on the top floor of MI6 headquarters in Century House on Westminster Bridge Road in south London. The SED conference in East Berlin had proceeded to form without so much as a hint of controversy. It concluded with a ringing endorsement of Walter Ulbricht and Erich Honecker and a standing ovation when the leadership duo was afforded a further five-year term at the party's helm.

At 6 pm London time, with Sir Roger Holbrook seated at his desk listening on speaker, Peter Parnell-Brown called the CIA's Michael Anjelico in West Berlin. It was 7 pm in divided Berlin and apart from a dinner, more backslapping and a good deal of alcohol consumption, the SED plenary conference was over.

Parnell-Brown was not in the mood to pull his punches and nor was the DG of a mind to temper him. 'You compromised Leopard from the outset with the Cuban courier arrangement, Michael,' Parnell-Brown said, bellowing down the secure line. 'We warned you it was dicey, but no you lot at Langley knew better.'

'I'd suggest you watch your potty mouth, buddy,' Anjelico spat back. 'How do you know Voite didn't receive the papers and declined to act on them? Before you start accusing me and the Agency of anything you'd best take care to establish all the facts.'

Parnell-Brown was unfazed by Anjelico's counter-aggression. He glanced at the DG who remained hunched, elbows on his desk with clenched fists supporting his chin and eyes half closed. The whole thing – Leopard and Spot both – was a disaster to be sure. But the dual failures seemed to have hit Sir Roger especially hard.

'You still don't get it, Michael, do you?' Parnell-Brown boomed. 'Can't you understand that without a correcting mechanism monitoring Diaz to see if he got the documents off to Voite, there was no way to stabilise or alternatively abort Leopard when it started to wobble? We were always going to be flying blind.'

Parnell-Brown exhaled exasperatedly. 'Who knows where the Swiss banking records are currently? Maybe Paian Diaz decided at the last minute he couldn't be bothered. Maybe the papers are now dumped in an East Berlin garbage bin waiting for a dustman to find them and give them to Ulbricht and Honecker. Once the leadership sees Konrad Voite's name on the envelope they'll execute him in a minute, all because the CIA didn't think it fit to put some form of control in place.'

'Why don't you go fuck yourself,' Anjelico said before slamming down the receiver.

Anjelico's next act was to take a long pull from the glass of whisky in front of him, after which he rang the CIA Director in Langley, Virginia. 'Something funny going on here, Chief,' he said. 'I expected MI6 to be pissed. But the reaction has been north of that. Like I floated when we talked on that Saturday in New York back in May, it seems the Limeys had a little side game attached to Leopard. And now that Paian Diaz appears to have fucked up, the home run they were hoping for has turned into a foul ball.'

Meanwhile in the DG's office in London, Sir Roger Holbrook looked at Peter Parnell-Brown with pained eyes. 'It's odds on that Daniel Lincoln is lost,' the DG said speaking slowly. 'I may have to resign now instead of finishing next January. It all depends on when the Americans learn of Spot, because they will and then move heaven and earth to make my position politically untenable.'

Sir Roger dejectedly shook his head, unaware he would make it through to his official retirement date of 31 January 1965. But only just. January 1965 was when the CIA, acting on information gleaned by the NYPD's Patrick Doherty and Lucy Rodriguez, began probing MI6 about Daniel Lincoln. The DG looked intensely at Parnell-Brown. 'You're still a young man in the prime of your career, Peter,' he said. 'Take care not to be part of the collateral damage.'

Parnell-Brown grimaced. Like Michael Anjelico 700 miles away in West Berlin, he was beginning to smell a rat. For the first time Parnell-Brown contemplated that Sir Roger might have more at stake in operation Spot than he was letting on. But the Deputy respected the DG too much to press. 'Perhaps I could put out some feelers through the neutrals,' he said instead, 'to try and ascertain what's happened to Daniel?'

'Better to have the company in Cardiff contact the Foreign Office,' Sir Roger said absently. 'Employee goes to East Berlin, disappears, and so on. Keeps it on a level footing and at arm's length from us, provided the Cardiff people are willing and able to play a straight bat.'

Parnell-Brown smiled to himself. Sir Roger's capacity to sum up the situation and make the right call, even from the depths of despair, underlined why he had made it to be the MI6 Director General. 'I'll get over to Cardiff tomorrow and have a word,' Parnell-Brown said. 'The private sector,' he added wryly, 'still has to work on Saturdays in this country.'

***

Eleven days after Michael Anjelico's heated row on the telephone with Peter Parnell-Brown, an *Exclusive for Anjelico* telegram was received in CIA headquarters. The American had been back in Langley for a week now. 'Jesus H. Christ,' Anjelico thundered on reading the message dated 8 September 1964 sent flash from Mexico City just an hour ago. Its CIA originator had dispatched the report the instant he returned from Havana. The day before the operative had debriefed Paian Diaz upon Diaz's arrival back from East Berlin. 'Get this,' Anjelico roared, 'the Cuban nincompoop we entrusted with the Konrad Voite banking material says that when he asked for directions to the SED headquarters in the old Reichsbank building, he was sent to the administrative centre on Schumannstrasse.'

Anjelico exhaled in frustration. 'And fuck-me-rone, rather than hightailing it over to the other side of the river once he savvied to being in the wrong place, if Diaz didn't leave the documents with some nice broad whose name he never got who said she would take care of them.' The American cracked his knuckles like the street fighter he was. 'He told our guy he thought she was going to give them to Voite. *Thought*, that's what he said.'

Anjelico continue to fume, railing volubly in incoherent, apoplectic bursts. 'OK,' he said finally, addressing the underling sitting opposite who was acting as his baffle. 'Let's get this over with. Call the Director's office and see if we can get in today.'

'I think we should sit on this for a while,' the CIA Director said calmly. Anjelico had secured a meeting with the CIA head within an hour of requesting it. 'What's done is done and there's no immediate need to update the British.'

'I agree, sir,' Anjelico said. He did not volunteer that regardless of his superior's directive he had no intention of alerting MI6 to the Paian Diaz debacle, not given the extent of the fiasco. In the current climate that was a hill Michael Anjelico would die on.

***

Later on, in January 1965, Peter Parnell-Brown came clean on MI6's secret operation Spot and what he truthfully believed to be the reason for it. The confession came at Sir Roger Holbrook's direction once it was clear the CIA knew the name of the New York City jumper was not Frank Middlemiss but rather MI6's Daniel Lincoln.

The ensuing talks were terse, brief and recriminatory at first but did eventually result in the CIA–MI6 rapprochement. Afterwards, Michael Anjelico would smile wryly when recalling his prospective insubordination towards the CIA Director on the day when Paian Diaz's debrief landed in Langley. Fortunately, the Director was like-minded and the need for disobedience did not arise. Even so, Anjelico knew his Latin temperament had dangerously bettered him at the time, inflamed as it was by Diaz's chronic ineptitude and stoked by the background tension with Peter Parnell-Brown over operation Leopard's failure.

But of course Michael Anjelico did not know the half of it on that 8 September 1964 day when he risked derailing his career. It can only be a matter of speculation, therefore, how Anjelico's fragile self-control would have coped had he become aware concurrent with the Paian Diaz disappointment that two days earlier Daniel Lincoln had travelled from East Berlin to Havana on the same charter flight as his underperforming Cuban asset.

CHAPTER 31

'Impossible,' Klaus Borkh shouted. 'That's just madness. Think of the attention it would attract.' It was midnight on 27 August 1964 and Elke Über was in Borkh's office in the old Reichsbank building. She had just revealed one of six pages of Swiss banking records sure to destroy Borkh, promising to hand over the whole cache subject to Borkh carrying out her special demand. And now Elke had spelled out her terms in full.

'The Soviets,' Elke said patiently in response to Borkh's heated objection, 'have spent a lot of time training the Stasi in the art of inserting agents into Western countries. My proposal fits neatly into that arrangement. Provided his extraction is restricted to a small group of Stasi sworn to secrecy no others need be involved.' Elke grimaced. 'Commandeering an LSK aircraft to fly him to Cuba, for example,' she said, referring to the East German airforce, 'would go outside that proposed small circle and be untenable. But fortunately there is a tourist charter flight leaving here for Havana on 6 September. It is this fact that makes my plan feasible given all other of its elements can be managed within a Stasi compartment headed by your friend, Albert.'

'And the fire at the Frund Hotel you want later tonight?'

'For centuries,' Elke replied coldly, 'spies have been setting fires to cover their tracks. Albert and those Stasi whom he enlists to help him will know what to do.' Elke turned the palms of her hands upright. 'It's actually a very simple undertaking when you think about it. Public safety standards are poor in this country. A hotel fire will not surprise anybody.'

Borkh shook his head. 'There's just so much of this I don't understand,' he said. 'On one hand you want to create the impression that Frank Middlemiss died in the fire. Yet on the other you're planning to send him to Cuba on the 6 September charter flight where our Stasi station in Havana is to put him on a plane to Mexico City from where he will fly to New York. And in advance of that Albert is to arrange for the Havana station to procure a false United States permanent residence card for Middlemiss from its Mexican drug cartel contractor.'

Borkh pinched his nose and stared at Elke, questioning her. 'I would bet my right arm that Middlemiss is an assumed name,' he said once it was clear Elke did not intend to reply. 'But surely American and British intelligence are collaborating on his East Berlin visit. How can you be confident the Americans won't have the Middlemiss name on a watch list of some sort and pick him up at his entry point into the US? You can hardly justify such a risk.'

Elke smiled at Borkh's confusion. She was not about to explain how Daniel had confided the British were keeping his East Berlin visit a close-hold secret from the Americans. Nor was she going to say how this made the United States the logical place to send Daniel, simply because MI6 would not initially raise the missing Frank Middlemiss with the Americans. But it might shortly after. That is why it was vital for the British to believe the so-called Middlemiss died in the Frund Hotel fire. Elke shuddered. The effectiveness of her plan to restore Daniel to full health in the sanctuary of the Sandymount Strand turned on this requirement. Here on display were Elke's all-powerful maternal instincts. Nonetheless, she did harbour qualms. *But it helps to know*, Elke thought, *that Ronald Hunt is nothing more than a common criminal.*

'Klaus,' Elke said. 'There is no time to debate the merits of my proposal. Suffice to reiterate that what I want is no different to the Stasi inserting a clandestine agent into North America, as it has done before. So, let's get to it. The Frund Hotel fire must be set within the next five hours. After that there are just ten days in which to make the necessary arrangements to get Frank Middlemiss into the United States as a supposedly returning permanent resident. Once I have proof he is safely ensconced in the New York City safe house, I will release all the Swiss banking records to you.'

Elke watched Borkh as he considered his position. She knew he would try to double-cross her at the first opportunity. But provided she remained alert to this, she would prevail. She had to. Daniel had betrayed the sacrosanct trust placed in him by MI6 such that his mental illness would afford no mitigation. He could not return to England until every shred of MI6's guaranteed outrage was washed away. And nor was this a simple matter of offering every last titbit she held on East German affairs in return for Daniel's immunity. In abusing the faith placed in the British by the Americans, Daniel had crossed into a dark, rarely visited and relentlessly vengeful MI6 netherworld. But she had a plan for securing British forgiveness. And for Daniel's sake, she had to be as hard and as brutal as necessary to execute it. Otherwise, he would face a lonely and painful death in a jail cell.

***

'So, no major complications, then?' Klaus Borkh said in summary.

'No,' Albert confirmed wearily. It was not yet 9 am on Friday 28 August and the Stasi man was functioning on barely two hours sleep. 'The fire investigation people will find the body in the room occupied by this Frank Middlemiss.' Albert smiled. 'We set the fire only after sprinkling the whole area with accelerant.

His remains will be burned beyond any possible physical identification. And beforehand we applied a blowtorch to the substitute's mouth, immediately after he died from the injection. The heat was intense enough to decalcify most of his teeth. Without calcium protection his dental formation will have largely disintegrated in the fire, making dental identification impossible.'

'Good,' Borkh said levelly. 'The rest of this charade will be more straightforward.' The two men sat in contemplative silence. Never one to offer praise, Borkh was privately pleased with the outcome. It had panned out exactly as Elke Über wanted, bodily remains that could be represented as belonging to Frank Middlemiss with virtually no likelihood of conflicting evidence later emerging. All the uninformed players would know, people like hotel staff and firemen, was the remains were found in Middlemiss's room. And pleasing Borkh most was the thought that having now effected Elke's wish to fake Middlemiss's death he was one step closer to getting his hands on the deadly Swiss banking records.

Borkh's thoughts turned to Ronald Hunt and his grisly demise. The Josef Sterck accomplice meant nothing to him. The man was as dispensable as a gnat, and in no sense a political irritant. Governments East and West both understood that clandestine agents were inserted without rights to mother country support if caught, even if those doing the sending usually engaged in some consular window-dressing as part of the standard denial process.

For all that, Borkh was intrigued why his nemesis had been willing to sacrifice one English spy in order to save another. By any measure, Elke Über's coming down on the side of Frank Middlemiss was a hard-headed calculation. Indeed it was, but unbeknown to Klaus Borkh Elke had little choice.

The fact was that besides needing to fake Daniel Lincoln's death, Ronald Hunt's remains were the vehicle by which Elke planned to get to West Berlin. There she would propose a deal to the Americans, with two specific conditions. In return for all she knew – not least her point of difference with the Americans relative to the British: Sir Roger Holbrook's hiding his defection offer from his alliance partner – she would ask the CIA to pardon Daniel, while also seeking its undertaking to compel MI6 to do likewise.

***

'May I ask a question?' Albert said, interrupting Borkh's pondering.

'If you must.'

'Why are we going to such lengths to assist Fräulein Über when we both know she's a traitor?' Albert coughed into his hand. Asking so pointed a question had made him nervous. 'I mean what's the endgame we're looking at here?'

Borkh smiled briefly. 'You know the rules, Albert. But I do appreciate you are apprehensive about appearing to assist an enemy of the state.' Borkh paused to collect his thoughts. 'The game we are playing, as you put it, is one in which Elke Über currently holds all the aces. So, until advised differently, we go along with her. But trust me when the wheel turns and we are in the ascendency, I will come down so hard on our Bavarian beauty as to make her wish she had never been born.'

Albert flinched. He was a senior Stasi officer and had seen a lot of hard men. But nobody he knew could generate the pathological bitterness of which Klaus Borkh was capable. Right now, Albert decided, the safest thing to do was to keep his head down and follow Borkh's orders to the letter.

'Fine,' Albert said, quickly moving on. 'I will cable shortly to instruct the Stasi station head in Havana to take personal care of Middlemiss's transit on 6 September. In the meantime, I will send him Middlemiss's passport in the diplomatic pouch. He will be directed to take it to the cartel in Mexico in time enough for a US permanent resident card to be forged using the passport details. Middlemiss will be handed back the passport on arrival in Havana while at the same time be issued with the false residence card. And before it leaves here his passport will be stamped to reflect he departed East Germany on 6 September, to avoid immigration authorities asking questions on his entry into Mexico City.'

Albert paused before continuing. 'The cartel charges excessively for it services. But it counterfeits American immigration documents most days of the week and has the means to place bogus background papers on relevant US government files. It will be a substantial and unauthorised expense I'll have the Havana station meet from its off-account slush fund.' Albert did not mention that the Stasi station's relationship with the Mexican criminals also involved it sending plentiful quantities of narcotics around the world under East German diplomatic auspices.

'And the New York City safe house?' Borkh asked.

'She wants the place at 388 Vesey Street, correct?'

Borkh eyed Albert. 'Yes, why do you ask?'

Albert laughed. 'It's because I'm betting it's the only one of our two safe places in the US she knows about.' Borkh's raised eyebrows prompted Albert to expand. 'Apartment 18E at 388 Vesey Street,' Albert explained, 'was the first bought by the Stasi foreign intelligence directorate. We did so with the assistance of the Mexican cartel, which made the purchase through a dummy company in El Paso, Texas. But we soon realised this involved moving large sums of money in view of too many people, including Fräulein Über it appears. The later purchase was arranged through the Soviets, which was cheaper and offered better security.'

Borkh nodded. 'How will Middlemiss access the place?'

Albert shrugged. 'We have keys. The Vesey Street apartment was purchased because many people have residences there for use on visits to New York. Apart from the on-site building superintendent, few of the occupants will know Middlemiss has moved in. I've blocked out the place for three months as you requested.'

'As Elke Über requested, actually,' Borkh broke in archly.

'As Elke Über requested,' Albert said, correcting himself. 'We'll tell him to leave the key inside the apartment when he departs on 30 November.'

'OK,' Borkh said. 'Anything else?'

Albert hesitated before finally deciding his conversation with Borkh had gone smoothly enough to take the chance to satisfy his curiosity. 'How will this Frank Middlemiss survive in New York? I mean does he have any means of support?'

Borkh placed his hands behind his head and gazed through his office window. 'I have discussed this with our lady friend,' he said as if talking to the Kupfergraben canal. 'She is a bureaucrat and understands such things.' Borkh turned back to Albert and clasped his hands together on his desk. 'Long ago,' he said earnestly, 'before the Wall went up, she and Josef Sterck had business interests, the exact nature of which are unclear to me since I was not here in East Berlin at the time. But I know their business was successful because Sterck spent a lot of convertible Westmarks during the 1950s in furtherance of his political career.'

Borkh did not add that now Elke had put the screws on him, he would dearly love to investigate her financial relationship with Josef Sterck. But this would have to wait for now. 'I understand that Fräulein Über still holds a pool of Westmarks from those days.' Borkh smiled coldly. 'Mr Middlemiss, I am advised, will carry her remaining West German currency with him to exchange for US dollars on arrival into New York City.'

CHAPTER 32

Around lunchtime on Saturday 29 August 1964 Peter Parnell-Brown met with the young Mr Jenkins, managing director of A.H. Jenkins and Sons of Cardiff. Shortly after the same Mr Jenkins rang the police to advise that a Jenkins employee named Frank Middlemiss was overdue from a visit to East Berlin. The police helpfully contacted the Foreign Office duty officer, since it was Saturday and the FO was closed. Early Saturday evening Mr Jenkins received confirmation that Middlemiss had not returned to England. The British embassy in West Germany was making enquiries, the Foreign Office added, and on Monday the FO's London consular section would contact the East German government.

True to its word, the Foreign Office got a letter off to the East Germans first thing on Monday via the good offices of KfA Ltd in London. With MI6 watching on from a distance, all involved were blissfully unaware, save for the admirable Mr Jenkins who played along in the name of doing his country a good if unspecified service.

The wheels turned slowly. Not until 7 September did the East German Foreign Ministry volunteer that an Englishman had been killed in a fierce fire at the Frund Hotel in the early hours of 28 August. Every item in the man's room was burned to a cinder and all that had been recovered were blackened skeletal remains.

'Perhaps you might have earlier seen fit to consult the hotel register and advise us that the deceased was most likely a British citizen,' came the Foreign Office's pithy reply.

The East German diplomats were miffed. They had done exactly that and would have alerted the Foreign Office before the end of August were it not for some thug from the Stasi foreign intelligence directorate storming into the building and instructing the diplomats to do nothing until otherwise notified. And as soon as the Stasi gave the go-ahead on 7 September the Foreign Ministry had acted promptly. But now, goaded by the British sarcasm, the ministry decided it would no longer tolerate being thought of as a bunch of lazy *Dummkopfs*.

'The remains will be returned to the current British presence in the temporarily separated region of Berlin as soon as possible,' the ministry replied, its formal response to the FO's dressing-down deigning neither to recognise West Germany's claim to statehood nor Britain's endorsement of this by virtue of its embassy there. 'But please be aware that certain important sanitary protocols apply to the repatriation of human remains,' the ministry's note went on. 'In this regard, we kindly request the United Kingdom respectfully observes the legal requirements of the East German state.' Translated, the Foreign Ministry had just told its UK counterpart to get stuffed and that the British could jolly well wait until it suited the East Germans to return the charred corpse.

***

Meanwhile in London and Washington those indoctrinated for operation Leopard were behaving like feuding lovers. Not a word had passed between Langley and Century House since Peter Parnell-Brown and Michael Anjelico's spat on the telephone on the evening of 28 August, after Leopard's failure had become obvious. As a result, Anjelico was growing increasingly steadfast about not updating MI6 when finally the CIA got to debrief Paian Diaz, assuming Diaz wasn't in an East German jail cell, that is.

But of course, thanks to Elke Über, Paian Diaz was a free man. His tour group had departed East Berlin for Havana on 6 September as scheduled. All were happy to be going home after enduring a gruelling eleven days of East Berlin's dubious hospitality. To the last person, the tourists were now grateful to have been spared a further forty-eight hours of suffering thanks to the party's old Russian aircraft breaking down in the Mauritanian capital Nouakchott on the way over and delaying its arrival.

For his part, Paian Diaz was something of a first among equals when it came to happiness. He had lived in fear of being arrested ever since handing the accursed package meant for Konrad Voite to the woman at the SED administrative centre on Schumannstrasse. But to his great surprise there had not been a hint of trouble in the days after she shooed him away. Nonetheless, Diaz had remained on edge, which explained why once they were in the air his relief quickly became unmitigated joy. The only minor factor tempering Diaz's elation was the pasty-looking fellow who had joined the charter flight in the company of another just before take-off. The pale man was clearly not German, unlike his companion whose hard face and square jaw would have been right at home in the turret of a Panzer tank not that long ago.

But the two interlopers, Diaz self-consoled, were seated at the front of the plane and well apart from the touring party, telling him there was unlikely to be any contact with the pair. It was an accurate assessment; certainly neither Daniel Lincoln nor the Stasi officer sent along to accompany him had any intention of interacting with the other passengers.

The Americans, of course, had someone waiting in Havana for Paian Diaz to arrive, the same man of Mexican extraction who gave Diaz the Swiss banking records in the first place. The debriefing interview took place in a park less than twenty-four hours after Diaz's return. With that, the CIA man promptly beat retreat to Mexico City where at the American embassy on 8 September 1964 he dispatched a detailed cable to CIA headquarters in Langley, Virginia, the same report that so upset Michael Anjelico.

***

Daniel Lincoln had been in a bad way when eventually they threw him into the bleak concrete cell in the special wing at Hohenschönhausen prison on the evening of 27 August 1964. For a time after leaving Elke Über at the Palace of Tears, his hope had run unchecked; that she was for real and could help rectify the terrible mess his life was in. But when arrested on his return to the Frund Hotel later that night, Daniel had gone into a despondent dream state while packing his suitcase, before the Stasi drove him deep into the East Berlin suburbs. And as mounting fear replaced his numbness, Daniel began to wonder if his concern was about dying or the possibility they might let him live.

Soon enough Daniel lost track of all time. At various intervals the slot in his cell door would open and a sparse meal appear on the retractable shelf. And twice since arriving, perhaps it was three times, unspeaking jailers had dragged him down a cold and barren corridor to an ablutions block where under their steely gaze he was told to shave and shower. Then one day, unannounced, he had a visitor.

'Arrangements have been made for your transfer, Mr Middlemiss,' Klaus Borkh said. 'I trust you have enjoyed your week's stay with us.'

Daniel was clinically depressed and highly disorientated. 'What?' he gasped.

'Two days from now, on 6 September, you will leave East Berlin on a flight bound for Cuba. After overnighting in secure accommodation in Havana you will travel to Mexico City on 7 September. From there, using a permanent resident identity card you will be issued, you will take a flight to New York City. From John F. Kennedy airport you will take a taxi to an apartment in Lower Manhattan. On the morning after your arrival, that is the morning of 8 September, you will receive a telephone call from Fräulein Elke Über, who of course is known to you. The call will be brief and its purpose is to allow you to confirm to Fräulein Über that you have safely reached the New York address.'

Daniel stared at Borkh, his face contorted with bewilderment. It was at this point that Borkh decided it was pointless continuing with the instructions. He would be courting disaster were he to dispense with Stasi assistance once this Frank Middlemiss character was on his way to Havana. The man was a blubbering wreck who would be lost in no time. An escort taking him every step of the way from East Berlin to New York was required. Albert, Borkh knew, would complain of mission creep. But the fact was that Elke Über's turning over all the incriminating Swiss banking records depended on her hearing Frank Middlemiss confirm he was in New York.

'Take this brain-dead fool back to his cell,' Borkh snapped to the guard he'd summoned. 'We'll be back to pick him up first thing on 6 September, when an escort will take charge of him and ensure he gets to where it's intended. Until then, treat him well but be sure not to let anybody speak to him.'

Albert did object, vociferously, despite Borkh's hold over him. 'Look,' he said to Borkh, counting off a mental list starting with his index finger, 'placing Middlemiss on the charter flight to Havana is no problem. Enlisting the support of the Stasi station there to put him on a plane to Mexico City without a record of him having entered Cuba is only slightly more difficult. And being senior in the foreign intelligence directorate I was able to block out the New York City safe house until 30 November without needing to offer an explanation.'

Albert took a deep breath. 'But the cost to the Havana station of the false US permanent resident card,' he said, 'is substantial, slush fund or no slush fund.' Beads of sweat formed on Albert's brow. 'And this expense becomes doubly difficult to manage when you add in the cost of organising a Stasi escort to take him every inch of the way from East Berlin to the apartment in New York City. The escort needs a false passport, Swiss or Swedish commonly, documents the cartel does not deal in that Stasi headquarters will have to provide. Then there's airfares and accommodation and the simple matter of the escort's unexplained absence from the office…' Albert allowed his voice to trail off.

Borkh smiled coldly at Albert for a good ten seconds, reeking of menace. 'Albert,' Borkh said finally, 'I would not be asking for an escort if it wasn't absolutely necessary.' Next thing Albert knew Borkh was on him, literally having leapt across his desk to clasp both hands around the Stasi man's throat. 'Just arrange it, Albert,' Borkh hissed in Albert's ear. 'Or else we're both dead. Dead, understand that.'

Many things raced through Albert's mind, but uppermost was the thought that his life now hung by a thread. How he wished he had never become tied up with this Borkh madman. 'There is the training budget,' he whispered. 'Somehow I'll find someone suitable already holding a forged passport. There will be massive fallout but I'll deal with that after the event.'

Borkh relaxed his hold. 'Good man,' he said affably. 'I won't forget your cooperation when the day comes and I am in a position of political power.'

CHAPTER 33

Elke Über was known to the officer in charge of the Hohenschönhausen prison guard detachment and had a reputation that preceded her. For this reason the commander did not point-blank deny her access to the cellblock when on 5 September, without prior notice, Elke arrived carrying a heavy, navy blue herringbone jacket replete with black leather elbow patches and requested to be allowed to give it personally to the English prisoner.

The officer was in a bind. Klaus Borkh's departing instruction the day before, to treat Frank Middlemiss well, came with the strict rider to allow the Englishman no visitors. But, on the other hand, the conventional wisdom was you didn't mess with Fräulein Über. He sought to walk a diplomatic tightrope.

'I wonder if there has been a misunderstanding,' the commander said courteously. 'Herr Borkh spoke to the prisoner yesterday. We were instructed to treat the Englishman well until he is removed tomorrow and handed to an escort who will accompany him to his intended destination. But pending that comrade Borkh did order us not to let any other person speak to him.'

'As head of the SED secretariat,' Elke snapped assertively, 'I am hardly an ordinary person. And,' she added, holding the jacket aloft, 'where he's going, he will need this.'

The officer nodded. Providing the prisoner with a jacket that could be inspected beforehand did not represent a problem.

Indeed it fitted comfortably within the realm of treating the prisoner well. But Elke's next request did pose a headache.

'I also need to speak privately with him, in the exercise yard. Just for a few minutes.'

The guard inwardly fretted. 'Fräulein Über,' he said with strained formality, 'a jacket is one thing. To have an untaped conversation with the prisoner, however, is quite another. It's highly irregular even were I to accept you are not beholden to comrade Borkh's no visitors instruction.'

Elke had made her demand knowing nothing of Klaus Borkh's edict. But she was well aware that special wing cells were wired with microphones. She had anticipated opposition to her request.

'Tell me, captain,' she said levelly, 'how many special wing prisoners leave here other than in a casket?' Elke stared hard at the man's blank face. 'That's right, none. And also ask yourself how many come in here and are left to vegetate without undergoing interrogation. None again, correct?' Elke paused for emphasis. 'So what does that tell you? Does it not make you think there is something very different about this prisoner?'

Elke held up her hand as the guard tried to speak. 'The fact is,' she continued, now conciliatory, 'the prisoner Middlemiss is part of an extremely complex and sensitive undertaking for which Herr Borkh and I have joint carriage. As you say that exempts me from Borkh's rulings. And on your general regulations, I know it is irregular for me to speak to a prisoner alone. But this whole thing is unorthodox and far too vital to be bound by inflexible procedures.'

The officer grimaced. He was no match for Elke's unrelenting logic and now prepared to think an agent exchange of some sort was in train for which the prisoner was to be given further secret instructions. 'Five minutes, not a second more,' he said tersely.

'And I'm going to make an entry in the log recording that you ordered me to allow you time alone with the prisoner.'

***

Elke was shocked at Daniel's appearance when they ushered her out of the rear door of his cell and into the tiny exercise yard. But his pallid face did brighten on seeing her, a hint of light coming to his eyes. Elke resisted the urge to hug him; she needed to treat this as a professional meeting.

'They're sending you to New York, with an escort,' Elke said softly. 'Take this,' she added, offering Daniel the herringbone jacket. 'It's made in Austria. It will be getting cold when you arrive.'

'Someone came yesterday to tell me about New York,' Daniel whispered, much like a child in awe. 'I just don't understand.'

'Daniel, listen to me,' Elke said, speaking sternly as if his mother, which to all intents and purposes in her mind she was. 'Explanations can wait. You must go along with this and follow the escort's guide. When you get to New York I will call to confirm you are there, addressing you as Frank Middlemiss. But say nothing on the telephone beyond the bare necessity because people will be listening. After the call you will have to be patient. But we have the apartment until 30 November and I will be there by no later than then. In the meantime you will have money to live on. I have a plan to fix everything, so you can go back to England without fear of repercussion and eventually achieve a full recovery.' Elke looked pleadingly at Daniel. 'Promise me you will do exactly as I ask.'

Daniel stared deep into Elke's dark eyes, his confused senses slowly processing what she had said. He got most of it; all except the timing, thinking Elke had said she would be there *on* 30 November and not *by* 30 November. Daniel shrugged. Only Elke cared for him and this gave him hope. It was she or nothing. 'I promise,' he said solemnly.

Elke's wish for Daniel to regain his health on the Sandymount Strand in Dublin would never be realised; indeed, thanks to an unwitting Klaus Borkh and Daniel's timing error, she would never see him again. For now, however, Elke slapped Daniel's upper arm in a comradely gesture – controller to field agent-style – before pushing past the guard standing arms crossed in the cell doorway, willing herself not to cry.

***

Thereafter for a time things seemed to go smoothly in the strange world of Klaus Borkh and Elke Über. Daniel's passage to New York via Havana and Mexico City was largely uneventful. The escort was taciturn but efficient. He had seen Daniel into the Vesey Street apartment late on 7 September, whereupon without a word he disappeared into the New York night to begin his long trek back to East Berlin. Now alone Daniel turned to unpacking his suitcase: the clothing he brought with him to East Berlin; the small framed photograph of Kristiina Ahnger; his copy of Ernest Hemingway's *For Whom the Bell Tolls*; Elke's expensive, Austrian-made navy blue herringbone jacket; and finally his Frank Middlemiss passport.

By now Daniel was exhausted. For the first time in a long time he actually slept, fitfully though with strange dreams flittering in and out of his consciousness. The ring of the apartment's telephone early the next morning shook him from his slumber. 'Hello,' he breathed into the mouthpiece.

It was Elke as promised, causing Daniel's spirits to soar. 'Please tell me where you are, Mr Middlemiss,' she said stiffly.

'New York City,' Daniel croaked excitedly. 'I got here last night. I'm in apartment number 18E, in a place somewhere on Lower Manhattan.' With that, the line went dead.

Daniel thumped the receiver and tried to dial the operator, hoping to achieve what he wasn't sure. But the burr of the dial tone could not be broken, causing Daniel to realise the telephone was configured to receive only incoming calls. Two days later the line went completely dead.

'So, Fräulein Über,' Klaus Borkh said, taking the handset from Elke and replacing it in the cradle. 'Are you satisfied?' It was early afternoon 8 September in East Berlin and the pair was in Borkh's office. 'By the way,' Borkh added without waiting for Elke's response, 'I will now have a message sent to our Mexican friends to disconnect the apartment's telephone. Just in case you get the bright idea of ringing your dear Mr Middlemiss on the sly.'

Elke ignored Borkh's taunt. Daniel's safe arrival in New York City was the only thing that mattered to her. Within weeks she would join him and, armed with his pardon, take him home. Her dealings with Borkh could now thankfully cease. It was back to the position of stalemate, until the time came to activate her plan to get out of East Germany. 'I will return with the banking records in an hour,' Elke said coldly.

***

Elke Über did not go back to her office after dropping the envelope on Borkh's desk, watching as he ripped it open but leaving before the greedily panting Borkh had the chance to say anything. It was towards the end of the business day when she reached the Foreign Ministry, having taken a circuitous route while checking for tails.

'We are quite upset with the British at the moment,' the senior diplomat said. Elke had gone to his office unannounced, knowing that more likely than not he would be there late in the day. She had just asked the diplomat about timing for the return of the remains of the Englishman killed in the Frund

Hotel fire. 'For reasons unclear,' the diplomat said, 'State security had us delay the repatriation. The British were very pompous towards us as a result.' The man smiled. 'So, where the Foreign Office is concerned, we are on a go-slow.'

Elke laughed heartily. 'I understand,' she said. 'They can be so arrogant.' She took a deep breath. 'The SED hierarchy, however, is keen to avoid friction with the United Kingdom given it is currently exhibiting signs of warming to the idea of diplomatic relations with East Germany. But obviously our leaders don't want to be seen as fawning. The thinking from on high is that were I, the head of the party secretariat, to go to West Berlin with your officials returning the remains it would send a calibrated signal demonstrating East Germany's political commitment to closer ties with Britain is as steadfast as ever.'

'I see,' the diplomat said thoughtfully.

'Yes,' Elke said brightly. 'Although of course the leadership wouldn't want news of this gesture to be broadcast from the rooftops.' Elke smiled warmly. 'I think the best approach when seeking West Berlin entry permits would be quietly to include my name in the returning party, making no fuss about this.'

'I see,' the diplomat repeated vaguely for a second time, leaving Elke to wonder if he had grasped she was playing him.

'Now to the related issue,' Elke continued briskly, trying to bluff her way through, 'which is timing.' She looked at the man, searching his eyes. On detecting no hint of objection she pressed on. 'I personally have a good deal of sympathy for your ministry over the criticism it has received when the blame for the delay in returning the remains rests with others. But our political masters will be upset if the friendship with the British is stretched for too long. Today is 8 September. Can I suggest the British be advised that the repatriation will take place on Friday week, 18 September?'

The diplomat briefly bristled. 'We rebuked Whitehall only yesterday,' he said, his forced restraint not escaping Elke. 'To ensure the message is heard loud and clear, we had envisaged not making the return until at least early October.'

Elke made a show of considering this, all the while thinking she would lose this fellow were she to muddle about. 'Franz,' she said, 'may I be direct?' Franz nodded. 'Honecker personally asked me to drop by and have a chat with you. You would be foolish not to listen to me.' Elke sighed. 'Politics,' she said, knowing she had taken a supreme risk in fabricating high-level political backing.

Franz's face slightly reddened. 'Yes, politics,' he said bitterly.

Elke recognised Franz's back down. But equally she needed him to save face to keep him onside. 'Might I propose, then,' Elke said, 'you advise the British on Tuesday 22 September that the repatriation will take place on Friday 25 September.'

The suggestion caused Franz's diplomatic training to kick in. As he saw it, Elke was making a concession on timing so that the ministry might avoid accusations of caving in to British pressure. He also took it for granted that the leadership would be unimpressed by the further delay, and Franz valued Elke's willingness to run this gauntlet for the sake of the ministry's reputation. It was in fact a gamble on Elke's part, one that to her imperceptible relief had paid off. 'We have a deal, Fräulein Über,' Franz said, extending his hand.

'And Franz,' Elke said, reaching across the desk to grip the damp fingers on offer, 'remember this conversation never happened, particularly that Honecker wishes for me to be included in the team taking the Englishman's remains to West Berlin.'

Elke's had been a masterful manipulation rich in charm, negotiating skill and courage. But ultimately it was a pyrrhic victory – for the cost of pushing back the repatriation until 25 September was Daniel Lincoln's life.

CHAPTER 34

The town of Sopot in northern Poland sits on the Baltic Sea. It is a spa town some dub the *Polish Riviera* thanks to its expanse of sandy beach and vibrant nightlife. To be sure, to visit there in September risks lower temperatures than during the height of summer. But provided one arrives before the fall officially commences on 23 September, balmy days and lovely cool nights can be confidently predicted. Sopot, therefore, is a place offering much respite from the pressures of business, especially for those working in the capital Warsaw and especially for those who happen to be generals in the WSW, the Polish military's counter-intelligence service charged with protecting Poland from domestic security threats.

A key feature of Sopot is its quaint jetty extending some fifty metres into the sea where it terminates at an exclusive use marina. It was here that General Lukasz Pinkert kept his small sailing boat moored. General Pinkert had a wife, seldom seen, and an adult son who rumour had it was estranged from his father. Whatever, the general had carved out an impressive career, most recently as head of the WSW directorate responsible for coordination with other Warsaw Pact countries. It was he who in February 1963, in the margins of a Poland–East Germany security summit, had recommended to Erich Honecker that Klaus Borkh be made responsible for the reputational integrity of the East German leadership.

Borkh and General Pinkert had spent the previous night together. Borkh in fact was essentially asexual, with the tiniest nod to heterosexuality, a by-product of his chronic self-absorption. But as a Stasi officer just senior enough to be included in the East German delegation attending the Warsaw talks, he had seen how General Pinkert and Erich Honecker enjoyed reminiscing about the old days, when apparently the two were in some sort of working relationship.

Never one to miss a chance to curry favour, Borkh was quick to respond upon receiving a wide smile from Pinkert at the dinner held on the first night to welcome the visiting delegation to town. And when on the second night he felt the general's hand briefly brush his buttocks, Borkh knew he had a decision to make. It didn't take long, not after witnessing another display of good fellowship between Honecker and Pinkert during the third and final day of talks. There followed Borkh's suggestion during the afternoon tea break that he and the general catch up later in the evening, perhaps for a nightcap in the general's hotel suite?

Nineteen months later, on Sunday 20 September 1964, there was much confusion in Sopot how an experienced sailor like Lukasz Pinkert had ended up in the sea without wearing a life vest. The mystery deepened when late on the same Sunday Pinkert's small sailboat was spotted drifting off Sopot, the ensuing inspection failing to reveal damage to the vessel's hull, mast or rudder – or any other possible reason for the drowning.

The tributes that followed were largely positive, save for a few less than fulsome obituaries. Monday morning and the Polish authorities issued a statement of regret, the government press office disseminating the release to those domestic and international media outlets represented in Warsaw. But in the great scheme of things Pinkert's death was no big deal outside of Poland. Hence it was only on Tuesday 22 September, on page four of *Neues Deutschland*, that Klaus Borkh was to learn the general had died in a boating accident.

On the very same day, in an unrelated development, the East German Foreign Ministry had sent a note to the British Foreign Office. The message advised that the remains believed to belong to Frank Middlemiss, the English citizen killed in the Frund Hotel fire in the early hours of 28 August, would be repatriated to West Berlin on Friday 25 September.

Klaus Borkh could barely believe his eyes. He read the newspaper report at least a half-dozen times, recalling as he did how the pillow talk secrets he had eked out of General Pinkert in February 1963 came slowly at first. The thought made Borkh smile, remembering how he initiated the disclosures by telling the general that his career as a Stasi officer had stalled, simply because he came from faraway Pomerania and did not have the connections of those fortunate enough to have gone to school in Berlin with others who in adult life also joined the Stasi.

Even so, it took another bout of passion to get the general talking, of how his desire for young men seemed to increase with age rather than diminish and what a problem this caused him in the hyper-masculine world of Polish military intelligence. It was then the general had Borkh swear never to tell a soul about their assignation, in return for which he, Pinkert, would have a word with his old friend Honecker about getting Borkh a decent job.

Borkh smiled again, this time even more broadly. He hadn't bothered to try and read between the lines of the newspaper report. It was irrelevant whether General Pinkert had died accidentally or by his own hand. Rather, Borkh was thinking how the general was a professional, an old school intelligence officer who knew the importance of keeping his mouth shut. The Pole would have died before telling anybody about the February 1963 liaison. Borkh giggled like an excited schoolboy. *And what a gift you've left me, Lukasz,* he thought. *You have just delivered me Elke Über's head on a platter.*

***

Elke was in her office at the SED administrative centre when a four-man Stasi team led by Klaus Borkh's functionary, Albert, arrived later on Tuesday afternoon. It was just sixty hours before Elke was due to visit West Berlin with the Foreign Ministry repatriation detail.

'Leave everything, Fräulein Über,' Albert said formally. 'State security earlier today came into possession of a letter that proves you have made an offer of defection to the British Secret Intelligence Service, to its Director General no less. You will of course receive a fair trial but be mindful of the fact that the penalty for such egregious treason is death.'

Elke did a quick mental calculation. It was clear that the homosexual benefactor issue Klaus Borkh was anxious to keep hidden from the East German leadership had resolved itself. All she could do now that Borkh had the upper hand was to make use of the scant leverage remaining at her disposal. 'Why are you bothering to spout such nonsense?' she scoffed at Albert. 'You and Borkh are both well aware that I know you two have had the letter in your possession for weeks. Wait until I tell the court about this.'

'I have no idea what you're talking about. The letter was revealed to state security only today.' For an hour preceding Elke's arrest, Albert had been in Klaus Borkh's office discussing the way forward. 'The letter,' Albert continued, 'was handed in by a Frund Hotel employee who some time ago found it in the room of Mr Frank Middlemiss, a now deceased MI6 officer who posing as a businessman had been sent to pass it to you.'

Elke's mind flashed back to Daniel Lincoln's awkward intervention on the Weidendammer Bridge on the evening of 27 August, when he told her to wait for him at the front of the Palace of Tears. 'Someone stole the padlock,' Daniel had first blurted. Elke grasped that since Daniel's arrest the Stasi had interviewed the Frund Hotel staff, with one owning up to thieving the padlock from his room. It was a logical extension to invent a story of the same hotel employee also taking the letter Daniel subsequently gave to her, the one that in fact Albert found in the drawer of her apartment's writing desk.

Albert and one other led Elke away, apprehension flooding her mind. With Klaus Borkh now in complete control it was Daniel, safe but not safe in New York, that most concerned her. While she and Borkh were stalemated he wouldn't dare touch Daniel for fear of repercussions. But the scales had tilted disastrously, paving the way for Borkh to arrange Daniel's execution, out of spite if for no other reason. *Think*, Elke demanded of herself as she was bundled into an unmarked van. Then it hit her. Klaus Borkh's deep and abiding hatred of her was her one last hope. But the trick was to convince Borkh there existed a punishment worse than putting her to death. Only then would Daniel have a fighting chance.

CHAPTER 35

Klaus Borkh's Stasi man, Albert, was feeling positive for the first time in a fortnight. He received a fierce rebuke from his bosses on 9 September when they learned he had ordered the Stasi station in Havana to make an expensive and unauthorised purchase of a forged US permanent resident card. But this paled into insignificance with the tirade soon after when the Stasi command discovered that, heaped on top of his earlier indiscipline, Albert had diverted a Stasi officer holding a forged Norwegian passport from preparation for insertion into Denmark and sent him to New York and back again, all in the space of forty-eight hours. Eventually, every last detail was prised out of Albert, to the point where he feared a lengthy prison sentence, or worse.

'It was all very political and secret,' the desperate Albert invented, prepared in the circumstances to tell his Stasi masters anything. 'Klaus Borkh, the head of the office of the council of ministers, orchestrated it on behalf of the leadership.' Having dipped his toe in that pond Albert had nothing left to lose. 'I understand that Erich Honecker was taking a close personal interest in the matter,' he assured his gobsmacked supervisors. It was a wonderful lie, not unlike Elke's to Franz the Foreign Ministry diplomat, a falsehood with a lengthy half-life in paranoid East Berlin. With that, the nervous Stasi bosses decided to discontinue their investigation, as if the strange matter of New

York, Cuba and Frank Middlemiss had never occurred. Thereafter, Albert was ordered to return to his duties with the metaphor-rich parting warning to keep his nose clean because right now he was skating on very thin ice.

But just two weeks later and Albert was happier. Bringing in Elke Über with incontrovertible evidence of her treachery meant he would win back some of the ground lost in doing as Klaus Borkh had bid. For this reason Albert was indignant when Elke piped up from the back of the van taking her to Stasi headquarters that day of Tuesday 22 September 1964 to ask if she could first be taken to Klaus Borkh's office.

'My relationship with comrade Borkh has come to an end,' Albert said with a firmness that didn't escape Elke. 'I will be handing you to the Stasi counter-intelligence division, which will have responsibility for your prosecution. Once I make a final report I will have no further say in your fate.'

Elke laughed. 'You seem to forget, Albert, I can establish I was involved in your recent activities. The log at Hohenschönhausen, for example, will show that on 5 September I visited Middlemiss, whom you had arrested on Borkh's orders without telling your superiors. I can also tell from your relief to be done with Borkh that currently your supervisors are mightily upset with you. Were I to make up some things, I suspect they would be in a frame of mind to believe me.' Elke paused. Having softened up Albert, she was readying to appeal to his common sense. 'You know as well as me,' she said calmly, 'that I am in a lot of trouble. What have I got to lose in making your life a misery, just when you are thinking you can get back in the good books?'

Albert cursed under his breath. 'Old Reichsbank building,' he snapped at the driver before turning to Elke. 'I'll give you fifteen minutes. But I don't want to know about it. I will wait in the outside anteroom while you speak with Borkh. After that, I'm taking you in as per procedure.'

***

'Fräulein Über,' Klaus Borkh said, feigning surprise. He was lounging in his chair with his feet resting on the top of his desk. 'You could have knocked me over with a feather when they called to say you were here to see me.'

'I've come to burst your bubble, Klaus,' Elke said soberly. She was beyond fear but not without aim.

'Really?' Borkh said, continuing his relaxed pretence.

'Yes. Before I'm put to death I wanted you to know that all the trouble you went to with Frank Middlemiss was unnecessary.' Elke smiled coldly. She had declined to sit and was standing in front of Borkh's desk. 'I still have no clue as to the identity of the Polish man with whom you were involved. All I know is that the threat he posed to you has suddenly gone away.'

Klaus Borkh removed his feet from his desk and glared at Elke, his blue eyes cold with hate. He had been feeling smug, thinking that although the Swiss banking records obliged him to go along with Elke Über, the reward for his patience was a stunning piece of luck in the form of General Pinkert's death. But now the fiendish woman was telling him the indignity endured while waiting for a chance to turn the tables was unwarranted. 'Damn Frank Middlemiss,' the voice in Borkh's head roared, 'and Elke Über's preoccupation with him.'

Vindictiveness rose in Borkh's throat and his senses ran wild. He stared at Elke desperate to thrust an emotional dagger into her heart. His thoughts turned to Frank Middlemiss, how much it would hurt Elke were he to be killed and the fact that he knew the Englishman's current whereabouts. Borkh's mind was made up. To be sure, he could no longer call on Stasi assets to execute Middlemiss. But the Mexican drug cartel was a viable alternative, even if it meant going personally to Mexico City to mobilise it. The assassination, though, would have to take place before 30

November, when Middlemiss was scheduled to leave the 388 Vesey Street apartment.

Elke, of course, understood that now he held sway Borkh would decide sooner or later to kill Daniel. It was this fact that had brought her to Borkh's office. It was also why she could not go meekly to her death while the man she regarded as her son was in grave danger. So long as she was alive until 30 November she could protect Daniel, and this was her driving ambition. 'I have some more bad news for you, Klaus,' Elke said, breaking a silence that had turned toxic.

'Is that so?' Borkh said, raising his eyebrows. He had recovered his swagger. 'What might that be?'

Elke's face was stone cold. 'Has it ever occurred to you the political leadership won't want it publicly known that the head of the SED secretariat sought to defect?' The blank look on Borkh's face answered Elke's question. 'No, I didn't think so.' Elke took a deep breath. Her assertion on the leadership's wish to avoid publicity was validly made; it also paved the way for her deliberate falsehood to come. 'The upshot is,' Elke said matter-of-factly, 'I will be secretly tried and executed within a week.'

Borkh was suddenly exasperated. 'What's the point you're trying to make, Fräulein Über?' he said angrily. 'Spell it out.'

'My point is twofold,' Elke said. 'One is that you will be tasked by our leaders to explain my sudden absence.' Elke paused to study Borkh, steeling herself to make the crucial pitch. 'And the other is that my virtually overnight elimination will deny you the demented pleasure you crave to see me suffer before I die.'

Borkh's body language said it all. He sat stock-still, stunned into disbelief by his sudden realisation. But Elke wasn't finished. She now had to feed Borkh his solution, one that would require political approval before he could implement it. 'And I am not your only headache,' she continued, as if not noticing Borkh's shocked reaction. 'Ulbricht and Honecker know it is not feasible to keep a party elder like Josef Sterck under indefinite house arrest in a guarded hotel. The leadership will look to you to make suitably punitive arrangements in amends for his outrageous public behaviour last month. But, for reasons of public consumption, it will want this disguised as an appropriately measured sanction.'

Elke shuddered as convincingly as she could, the exaggerated movement of her shoulders designed to capture Borkh's total attention. 'Better you than me,' she said grimly. 'Josef Sterck,' she added for subject confirmation now that Borkh's eyes were upon her. 'The appalling man has always made my flesh crawl, and these days he's little more than a deranged alcoholic.'

***

A sharp-eyed lad in MI6's Eastern bloc media monitoring section picked up the snippet in the East German press. He was unaware of operation Spot and its players but nonetheless had been told to bring any mention of the name *Elke Über* to the immediate attention of Peter Parnell-Brown. So, the lad dutifully trudged upstairs to the Deputy's office, taking with him an English-language translation of the offending article dated 3 October 1964.

Parnell-Brown's first move on absorbing the news was to go to Sir Roger Holbrook. Twenty days had now elapsed since 25 September when the British received the remains recovered from the Frund Hotel fire. 'Let's assume,' the Director General said after reading the transcript of the scarcely believable East German report, 'that for whatever reason Daniel Lincoln did not deliver my letter to Elke on the night of 27 August, and subsequently the letter was destroyed in the fire that killed Daniel early on 28 August. In which case Elke would have continued on as normal, still waiting for us to make contact.'

Parnell-Brown had read the DG's mind and raced ahead of him. 'But judging by Josef Sterck's bizarre television performance,' he said, 'he's an over the hill boozer. Not to mention the fact that in January this year Elke wrote to you asking to defect. And take a look at the photograph. They both seem to be sucking on lemons. The article just doesn't ring true.'

The DG shrugged. 'Maybe she'd given up on us,' he said, playing the devil's advocate. 'January to October is nine months and people do change their minds. And Elke and Sterck worked in tandem for years. It's not unheard-of for couples thrown together for long periods to one day wake up and find they're in love. As for the television appearance, well Ronald Hunt did go there under operation Leopard's aegis and demand that Sterck make a commotion.' Sir Roger pursed his lips. 'But I do agree their smiles are rather strained.' He glanced at Parnell-Brown. 'By the way, what news of Hunt these days?'

Parnell-Brown sighed. His nominating Ronald Hunt to be the operation Leopard decoy still rankled. 'I understand the Foreign Office makes the occasional representation. But from what I can gather, the Ossis have thrown away the key. My best guess is he's currently in Hohenschönhausen and will be there for the long haul unless a swap of some sort is eventually arranged.' Parnell-Brown shook his head. 'But at least Hunt's situation makes more sense to me than Elke Über supposedly marrying Josef Sterck and the anything but happy couple being sent to faraway Guben where Sterck is to open an outpost of the Ministry of Cultural Harmony.'

CHAPTER 36

Guben is a small town centrally located on the former East Germany's border with Poland, one that in September 1964 was gloomily blighted by a decomposing chemical plant. Klaus Borkh had thought of Guben early the morning of the day after Elke Über called in to chide him while on her way to the cells at Stasi headquarters. Borkh, in fact, had swallowed Elke's provocation whole. But not until 3 am did it permeate that to force Elke to marry Josef Sterck would be to inflict an insufferable hardship on her. At the same time the solution provided a sound reason why she was no longer walking East Berlin's corridors of power. And being sent to atrophy in Guben was also an ideal punishment for the egregious Sterck, a measure able to be presented such that the public would appreciate the compassion it extended to a wayward party elder.

Borkh had called on Erich Honecker's principal adviser later in the day. Now that his plan contained elements necessitating media exposure he needed political cover – just as Elke Über had foreseen when linking her survival to Borkh's retribution against Josef Sterck.

The adviser had readily endorsed the Josef Sterck outcome. But on the associated other he had one key stipulation. 'She must be kept alive until the New Year. After that do as you please.' Honecker's aide had just erred on the side of caution and ordered Borkh not to move against Elke until the end of the year.

'That way,' the adviser said, 'we can be sure people will have forgotten she existed.'

***

Elke's impassiveness surprised Klaus Borkh when he informed her on Thursday 24 September 1964 that nine days later, on Saturday 3 October, she was to marry Josef Sterck. Immediately thereafter she and Sterck would be sent to Guben for the foreseeable future. 'Have you nothing to say, Fräulein Über? I thought you might have been pleased to hear your trial has been postponed to the early New Year for reasons of political convenience.'

Elke smiled wanly. She was dressed in prison fatigues and felt like she had nits in her hair. 'You're a fool, Klaus,' Elke said softly. 'I was never going to be executed within a week. Yet you were so blinded by the thought you might not see me suffer that you allowed yourself to be manipulated into consulting Honecker's office. It was always going to be conservative on timing, on how long it would take for people here in the capital to adjust to my absence before I could be eliminated without need for a difficult political explanation. And now as you cannot touch me before 30 November, Klaus, you vengeful little psychopath, this means you have a problem.'

Elke beaded Borkh, her eyes bright with fire. 'What I mean is if you kill Frank Middlemiss while he is in the safe house, your Stasi man Albert will be among the first to know. He is done with you, Klaus, utterly, and whatever hold you have over him. It would suit Albert nicely to see you dead. And although circumstances prevent him from doing this himself, there is nothing to stop Albert providing me, for example, with a copy of a local Lower Manhattan newspaper reporting Middlemiss's death. Then, Klaus, you are a rabbit in the open and I am an eagle coming for you, all the way from Guben.'

Klaus Borkh could take it no more. Hands clasped over his ears and shaking his head, he bellowed for the guard to take Elke away. Afterwards Borkh sat in his office trying to control his trembling. Slowly he stabilised, his mind settling on Elke's suggestion that a newspaper article could conceivably report Middlemiss's death. Suddenly Borkh brightened. It was the thought of the Englishman's fragile emotional state he had witnessed at Hohenschönhausen prison on 4 September, that and Middlemiss's evident delight in hearing Elke's voice in her brief telephone call just days later.

Here was Borkh's evil laid bare. He might no longer be able to kill Frank Middlemiss before Middlemiss left the Vesey Street apartment on 30 November. But not to be denied some measure of perverse pleasure, he could still taunt the unstable man with news of Elke's betrothal. With that, Borkh picked up the telephone, leaving instructions for the press earmarked to attend the 3 October wedding to be told to take a wide variety of photographs.

Borkh sat back in his chair considering next steps, hands linked behind his head. His first move would be to have a suitable press article taken to West Berlin and posted to Frank Middlemiss in the New York apartment. But on timing he was less sure. No doubt the troubled Middlemiss would be perplexed on learning of Elke's marriage whenever news of it reached him. But would not the report have maximum impact if he received it just as he was about to leave the apartment for somewhere new? *That's it,* Borkh thought excitedly. He would order the article's dispatch so that it reached the Vesey Street apartment in the last week of November.

***

Klaus Borkh had miscalculated. Perhaps he gave the West German postal system more credit than it deserved. Whatever, the article sent in anticipation of reaching Daniel early in the week commencing 23 November arrived in New York City only on Friday 27 November. In consequence, the US Post Office delivered the letter to the building superintendent's office at 388 Vesey Street in its Monday morning 30 November round, after which the super did the neighbourly thing and took it up to apartment 18E.

The unintended timing was perfect from Borkh's warped perspective, even though he had no knowledge of it nor expectation the article would do other than aggravate Middlemiss's existing anxiety. But timing, as they say, is everything. During Daniel's twelve emotionally uncertain weeks in New York, Elke Über had dominated his every thought, eclipsing all functionality to the point where he existed only on the muscle memory of previously living in the United States. But now, or so Daniel believed, 30 November had arrived when Elke would finally knock on his door and he could leave behind his crippling fear and loneliness.

This, of course, was not what Elke had said. But a thick, soup-like fog had clouded Daniel's thinking and he held child-like to the conviction gained in Hohenschönhausen prison that Elke would arrive *on* 30 November. The truth was Elke had told the befuddled Daniel she would be there by *no later than* 30 November.

Daniel was dismayed, therefore, to fling open the apartment door shortly before noon and find not Elke standing there but the building superintendent. Were it any day other than the deadline of 30 November, Daniel would have no expectation of Elke arriving and assuredly have seen the newspaper clipping for the fraud it was. But now on 30 November the shredding of his resolute faith in Elke coming to New York had poisoned his addled mind. Daniel stared at the photograph, dark thoughts of repudiation washing over him. Like Kristiina Ahnger before her, Elke had lit the pathway ahead. Now, however, without so much as a word of regret she had abandoned him to get married.

A malign rush overpowered Daniel's last vestige of reason, and him with it. Slumped to his knees, head in hands, he began to weep, distraught to know he would never reach the sanctuary of the Sandymount Strand where Elke Über had promised he would be safe. He had dared to hope because Elke gave him cause. But in his wistfulness he had ignored the bitter lesson of Kristiina – that hope is the most dangerous thing of all. And now it was time to pay the piper, for all was lost and there was no coming back from here.

***

The wind that day was blowing from the west, sweeping in across the Hudson River until dispersed by the Manhattan skyline, sending an air current south to the Financial District. The offshoot, as ever, carried the sound of the striking clock on the Howard Watch and Clock Company building a half-mile away at 346 Broadway: a gust those in Lower Manhattan called *The Wind From New Jersey*.

Daniel, of course, was a literature scholar. And the Howard clock, in beginning to chime noon, had roused memories of John Donne's *No Man Is an Island*. Daniel took his father's gift from his bedside table, Hemingway's *For Whom the Bell Tolls*, and briefly studied Donne's poem inscribed inside. With that, he stood stock-still listening intently to the pealing bells as if they contained an important message, which in a way they did.

Only when the last of the twelve gongs had sounded did Daniel return the book to the bedside table and place the letter from West Berlin in the chest of drawers in the bedroom, alongside the framed photograph of Kristiina, his Frank

Middlemiss passport and what remained of his US dollars. After which he washed his face, combed his hair and, with solemn ceremony, donned the herringbone jacket given to him by Elke Über. Then he made for the building rooftop.

Daniel stood hands resting on the safety rampart thinking of Donne's poem and its celebration of human companionship, that epigraphically immortalised by Hemingway and so loved by his father, yet to Daniel always seeming in its last stanza to speak of lost hope: *And therefore never send to know for whom the bell tolls; It tolls for thee.* He mounted the parapet and looked down on New York City. 'No more,' Daniel Lincoln whispered, foreshadowing the imminent topple into the void that would end his pain forever.

EPILOGUE

For years after Peter Parnell-Brown would often ponder operation Leopard, its secret companion operation Spot and the ill-fated players involved. It was clear, he had long concluded, that each operation in its own way was far too ambitious. For this reason it troubled him to think how the then MI6 Director General, the usually sage and cautious Sir Roger Holbrook, had gone so hard on both undertakings.

Moreover, even allowing for the unlikely eventuality of Leopard and Spot fulfilling their lofty goals, Sir Roger's all-in commitment was still ultimately contingent on Konrad Voite grasping the chance to lead East Germany. And for Parnell-Brown this posed a confounding puzzle: How could Sir Roger have so seriously entertained that Voite, had he achieved the leadership, would commit to German reunification? And further, accepting the thesis that Voite would have, what if Elke Über *had* come out after three years only to tell MI6 he was not up to it?

These two questions had lived in a special compartment in Parnell-Brown's mind for the dozen years gone by since Daniel Lincoln's death, remaining there even after the rapprochement with the Americans cleared the air. He'd always meant to ask the old man but for some reason would constantly find an excuse not to, suspecting it was his deep respect for Sir Roger garnered in the days when the DG was firing on all eight cylinders. The years slipped by and there suddenly was Sir Roger wrestling with dementia, until it was too late. Sir Roger had died, a Service kind heart rang to advise, sad but peaceful, and a good age and all that.

'I won't stay long,' Parnell-Brown told Sir Roger's daughter in the drawing room of her Folkestone home. 'I'm travelling back up to London tonight.' Sir Roger had spent his last years in a nursing facility in Kent to be closer to his only daughter, a vivacious woman called Gretel who was hosting his wake.

'Well, have a cup of tea at least,' Gretel said. 'I'll get you some of Dad's old photographs to have a look at while you drink it.' She giggled. 'You'll probably recognise some of the faces,' she said, which was as close as Gretel ever came to conceding that her father was as spy.

Parnell-Brown took the cardboard box on offer and began to rummage through its contents. By this stage it had been five years since he finished with MI6, or more like vice versa once the politicians got around to apportioning blame for Daniel's suicide. Nonetheless, as Gretel had promised, there were a few shots of people he remembered from times long ago and now viewed, it must be said, in a combination of good memories and bad.

Working methodically through the photographs, Parnell-Brown came across an ancient sepia image, the bottom half of which was wrapped in a piece of blue note paper. Lifting the photograph from the box, the paper fell away leaving Parnell-Brown gazing at a very young Sir Roger standing in what appeared to be a pub with another man of a similar age. Both wore the tweedy clothes of the pre-war era and the unidentified man smoked a pipe, as was the upper crust's wont in those times. Parnell-Brown smiled. Even at this early stage, the pair was clearly well down the path to becoming foppish dons.

But it was not the studied intellectualism that had caught Parnell-Brown's eye. It was in fact that the other male had his hand on Sir Roger's shoulder in an apparent show of solidarity, the two standing ramrod straight and staring at the camera with an intensity that conveyed shared purpose.

'Oh yes,' Gretel said, flitting by to offer Parnell-Brown a sandwich on the run. 'That was dad's twenty-first birthday in 1926, when he was up at Oxford.'

Still examining the photograph, Parnell-Brown absently picked up the blue note paper with his free hand. It was while unfolding the paper when preparing to replace it around the image that he noticed the nine handwritten lines of German. Parnell-Brown was not prying; indeed, it was not a time to pry. But his tradecraft was deeply imbued and instinctively his eyes strayed to the foot of the page and the words inscribed in English beneath the German text.

Now, at long last, Parnell-Brown understood. Sir Roger knew Elke Über was never going to question Konrad Voite's calibre; and his plan that Elke stay in place for three years was not as claimed to assess Voite's commitment and capacity to achieve German reunification. Rather, the only sensible conclusion to be reached was that Sir Roger wanted to give Elke unassailable credibility in the eyes of the Americans. In his last lap as MI6 Director General, Peter Parnell-Brown realised, Sir Roger Holbrook had been intent on clawing back the strategic heft forfeited across the Atlantic by the UK in the years after the Second World War. The words in English on the blue note paper made this abundantly clear: *Until Berlin, when I am Chancellor of Germany and the West's bulwark against the Bolsheviks, eternally Konrad Voite.*

Printed in Great Britain
by Amazon

43245005R00165